# How to Date a Rockstar

**Arabella Quinn**

Copyright © 2023 by Arabella Quinn

All rights reserved.

No part of this publication may be reproduced, distributed, or transmitted in any form or by any means, including photocopying, recording, or other electronic or mechanical methods, without the prior written permission of the publisher, except as permitted by U.S. copyright law.

If you purchased a copy of this eBook, thank you. Also, thank you for not sharing your copy of this book. This purchase allows you one legal copy for your own personal computer or device. You do not have the rights to resell, distribute, print, or transfer this book, in whole or in part, in any format, via methods either currently known or yet to be invented, or upload to a file sharing peer-to-peer program. It may not be re-sold or given away to other people. Such action is illegal and in violation of the U.S. Copyright Law. If you would like to share this book with another person, please purchase an additional copy for each recipient. If you're reading this book and did not purchase it, or it was not purchased for your use only, then please purchase your own copy. Thank you for respecting the hard work of this author.

The story, all names, characters, and incidents portrayed in this production are fictitious. No identification with actual persons (living or deceased), places, buildings, and products is intended or should be inferred.

# Dedication

---

In loving memory of my dear mother,
The one who championed my writing journey,
These books stand as a testament to your never-ending belief in me.
As my biggest fan, your encouragement was unwavering throughout
the years I spent writing this book series. Though you're not here to
see the culmination of my efforts, I know you are watching over me,
cheering me on from a place where love transcends all boundaries.
Your absence is deeply felt, but I carry your love and support within
me, inspiring me and giving me the courage to chase my dreams.
You are forever in my heart.

# Contents

---

| | |
|---|---:|
| Prologue | 1 |
| Chapter 1 | 6 |
| Chapter 2 | 16 |
| Chapter 3 | 22 |
| Chapter 4 | 35 |
| Chapter 5 | 46 |
| Chapter 6 | 54 |
| Chapter 7 | 62 |
| Chapter 8 | 71 |
| Chapter 9 | 81 |
| Chapter 10 | 93 |
| Chapter 11 | 100 |
| Chapter 12 | 107 |
| Chapter 13 | 117 |

| | |
|---|---|
| Chapter 14 | 127 |
| Chapter 15 | 138 |
| Chapter 16 | 148 |
| Chapter 17 | 156 |
| Chapter 18 | 162 |
| Chapter 19 | 174 |
| Chapter 20 | 180 |
| Chapter 21 | 186 |
| Chapter 22 | 194 |
| Chapter 23 | 203 |
| Chapter 24 | 219 |
| Chapter 25 | 227 |
| Chapter 26 | 240 |
| Chapter 27 | 250 |
| Chapter 28 | 259 |
| Chapter 29 | 266 |
| Chapter 30 | 277 |
| Chapter 31 | 289 |
| Epilogue | 296 |
| Next in Series | 307 |
| Arabella Quinn Newsletter | 310 |
| Bad Boys of Rock Series | 311 |
| Also By Arabella Quinn | 314 |
| Other Novels by Arabella Quinn | 316 |

| | |
|---|---|
| About the Author | 319 |
| Excerpt | 320 |

# Prologue

*One year ago...*

## Summer

A LITTLE SWOOSH SOUNDED on my phone. Disappointment flooded me as I stared at the text I'd just received.

> **JACK HARTMAN:** I can't make our lunch meeting. Something's come up. Reschedule?

I wanted to be angry with him. Complain to him. Whine a bit, maybe. Stalk by his office to see what was up. But I'd do none of those things because I was a professional and he was my boss. I hissed out a breath and typed out a reply.

**Me:** Sure

Meek. Compliant. Doormat.

No, I was strong. Confident. In total control of my emotions. Mature. Yeah.

It was well past noon and the office lunch crew had already left. I could probably text Jana and find out where they went, but I wasn't in the mood for that exuberant crowd today. I could hit the cafeteria, but that didn't appeal either.

So fast food it was. There was nothing like a greasy burger to lift a bad mood. I pulled my raincoat off the hook in my cubicle and grabbed my umbrella before I headed out the door.

I walked as briskly as I could manage in my high heels through the wet parking lot with my umbrella held over my head, thankfully blocking most of the rain. I passed by Jack's metallic gray Range Rover parked in its usual spot. Every time I went in and out of the building, I couldn't help but look for it.

Thirty minutes later, I was sitting in my car finishing up my super-value meal. It had cheered me a little, but my mind was still on Jack. I wanted to see him. Hell, I needed to see him. That's when the plan started to take shape in my head.

After cleaning my fingers with some hand wipes I kept in the glove box, I drove out of the parking lot and onto the highway. I passed by the Days Inn on my left, the one that charged $88 per night. Less than a mile down was a small strip mall that contained a liquor store. I picked out a bottle of champagne and bought two novelty glasses that had been on display near the register. I headed back to work and waited.

The day went on forever. I tried my best to concentrate on work, but I was constantly daydreaming about my plan. I was so distracted. At 5 o'clock, most people were packing up to head home for the night. A few had left even earlier. As was usual, by 6 o'clock the place was deserted.

I plucked my jacket — a beige trench coat that tightened at the waist with a wide belt and fell to mid-thigh — from its hook and strolled casually to the ladies' room, scanning the cubicles along the way. To my relief, no one was working late.

Inside the bathroom stall, I took off all my clothes until I was standing naked in my black stilettos. I slipped into the trench coat and tied it closed with the belt, forgoing the buttons. When I stepped back in front of the bathroom mirror, I felt uncomfortably exposed when I saw my bare legs sticking out from the coat, but realistically, anyone would assume I was wearing clothes, maybe a short skirt. I assessed my appearance critically to make sure no one could guess that I was naked underneath.

I freshened up my hair and makeup and then wrapped my clothing into a tight ball. I took a deep breath, trying to tame the butterfly riot in my stomach, and then headed back to my cubicle. All was quiet. I dropped my clothes onto my office chair and then slid the chair completely under my desk. That way, no one would see the small pile of clothes if they happened to walk by.

This next part was tricky. I didn't want to be seen carrying a bottle of champagne to Jack's office. How would I explain that? I decided to do a quick reconnaissance stroll without the champagne first. Jack's office was a corner office, down the end of a short hallway. Everything was quiet as I headed toward the hall. The only other office in Jack's hall, Ben Miller's, was empty. Across the hall, the conference room was dark. The coast was clear.

A few more steps let me see that the door to Jack's office was shut.

That meant he was still there. Jack was always the last to leave. He was the boss, after all. Thank God. I would have felt stupid getting naked under this coat if he had already left for the day.

My body surged with giddy anticipation as I hurried back to my cubicle and pulled the champagne bottle and glasses out from under my desk. I suppressed a giggle as I imagined Jack's face when I opened my trench coat and let it drop to the floor in a puddle around my feet.

My strides were quick, and I could feel the heat of arousal between my legs as I went. I stopped in front of his door to take a calming breath. I wanted to look sexy, not desperate. None of the office doors had locks, and I knew I could just barge in and surprise him, but I didn't want to do that. We had a special knock that I used whenever we'd had an after-work rendezvous — knock, knock, pause, knock-knock.

My hand trembled as I raised it to the door and rapped lightly. A muffled sound came from within his office and I assumed he'd said something like 'enter'. I'd probably surprised him; he wasn't expecting me today. Emboldened, I opened his door, strutted inside with an extra swizzle in my hips, and then struck a sexy pose.

When I saw the look of horror on his face, I knew something was wrong, but I didn't quite know what it was. He was standing behind his sleek, modern office desk facing me, his arms spread wide and braced on the desk with his shirtsleeves rolled up and his tie askew. Two computer monitors on his desk blocked most of his body from my view, but I could clearly see the panic that sparked in his eyes.

I stood rooted to the spot for a moment. My brain was still trying to process something important here. What?

I heard something. Wet and sloppy. Slapping? No, sucking sounds.

My insides grew ice cold. No! This couldn't be happening.

The overhead lights were off, but there was still enough ambient light streaming through the windows that I could see some slight movement beneath his desk. I angled my head and bent down slightly, just enough to see the worn soles of a pair of red high-heeled shoes. Shoes that I knew belonged to Missy Peterson, two cubicles down from me — shoes that were attached to a naked body on hands and knees, wiggling ass jutting out toward me as she sucked off my boss. It was the exact position I had assumed several times in this very same office for the very same boss, who only a few weeks ago had told me that he loved me at the Days Inn.

The champagne bottle slipped from my hand. It exploded like an improvised bomb all over the floor. Small shards of glass flew everywhere like shrapnel and a puddle of champagne began expanding across the floor. The noise of the crash must have startled Missy. I heard her head crack loudly against the top of the desk, followed by a grunt of pain from Jack. Hopefully, she bit his dick off.

Adrenaline surged through me. *Fight or flight.* I stumbled a few steps backward toward the door, utterly shell-shocked. *Fight or flight.* I didn't even glance at Jack again. I had only one thing on my mind.

*Flight.*

# Chapter 1

---

**Knox**

IT WASN'T SO UNUSUAL for me to wake up with a woman in my arms. What was unusual — extremely unusual — was that we were both fully dressed. I popped open an eye to get my bearings. I was crammed on a couch, my neck jammed against the armrest at an ungodly angle, in some unknown flat with a petite brunette on top of me.

My head was fuzzy, but thankfully, not pounding. The night before slowly came back to me. I'd been flirting with this girl — Sharon or was it Karen? — with sensational breasts that were almost too big for her slight frame. She'd heard my accent, the one that always became more prominent the drunker I got, and clung to me like glue for the rest of the night. For her benefit, I might have called her a 'bonnie lass' and thrown in a few extra 'ayes' and 'wees' into the conversation. My Scottish accent never failed to leave a girl's panties soaked. At least that had been my experience here in America.

At the end of the night, we'd ended up together. We were going at it hot and heavy on the couch, practically sucking each other's tonsils out, when she'd passed out with her hand down my pants. I never would have fooled around with her if I'd known she was that drunk. Since the party was over, I'd removed her hand from my raging hard-on like a gentleman and fell asleep with a case of blue balls. Not my most successful of nights.

It appeared to be mid-morning, but no one was up yet. I tried again to think back to how I'd gotten here or whose flat I was at, but I couldn't remember. I'd started the night out partying with Ghost, but he'd disappeared before I'd left the weird nightclub with Sharon.

Ghost was the frontman for our band, Ghost Parker, and I was the lead guitarist. Besides me, he was the only one left who still partied regularly; the others had all fallen over the last 18 months or so. Ryder was married and just had a brand new baby girl with his wife Talia. Sid, our bassist, had just gotten engaged to his girlfriend, Kaylie. Her brother, Bash, our drummer, lived out in the suburbs with his son, Kody. Two years ago, Kody had been abandoned on Bash's doorstep with a note claiming he was the baby's father. Bloody hell. If that wasn't close to a guy's worst nightmare, I didn't know what was.

So much had changed, but the guys in Ghost Parker were still my best mates here in America. I'd been living in the U.S. for almost six years already and had been playing with Ghost Parker for nearly five of them. We'd been on the road touring for the last year and a half, and then I had to travel back to Scotland to get my work visa extended. Now, we were all enjoying a much-needed break, while our record label was already making noises for us to get back into the studio.

We'd made a ton of money, mostly thanks to the hit single Sid wrote, so now was the time to enjoy it, but I didn't know how to do that. Buying a fancy house like two of my bandmates had, or even a penthouse apartment like Sid's didn't interest me. I was content in the same flat I'd lived in for years. A luxury getaway sounded appealing, but the band had just spent months traveling all over the world. They wanted to stay in L.A. so they could spend time with their families. Who would I even go with?

We hadn't been home long, and already I was feeling restless. I needed to be moving. Playing guitar. Keeping busy.

What I really needed was to get out of this flat and away from this girl before she woke up. It was a Saturday morning, but I had no plans. There was no practice with the band today; I had no commitments. Hours of nothing lay ahead of me.

I didn't enjoy sitting still. It gave me too much time to think.

Last Saturday, I'd spent it with my band family at Bash's house to celebrate Kody's second birthday. It was a crazy day, but surprisingly fun. It was great catching up with Ghost Parker's extended family. Even Josie, the nanny, was there. After Sid found out that he wasn't Kody's father — long story — Josie continued to watch Kody until Bash moved into the suburbs.

I'd been surprised to see Josie there, especially on such good terms with Bash. Back when Bash was living on my couch, he used to complain about her all the time. He had some kind of hate-hate relationship going on with her. According to Bash, she was some kind of militant grandma that had taken an instant dislike to him. Now they seemed like good friends.

A surprising feeling of nostalgia washed over me. I thought about the months before we left on tour. At the time, I wanted nothing more than to have my space back to myself, but now it seemed so empty. Before Bash had been living on my couch, Ryder had camped out there for about a month after he sold his house to pay off a loan shark, but he hadn't been partying every night like an animal. I'm pretty sure Bash had been fucking chicks on my couch and that was just...no.

That should be the first thing on my list of things to do: buy a new couch. Eighteen months had gone by and I hadn't spent much time in my flat during them. It didn't feel like much of a home anymore. I shook off my glum thoughts, telling myself that I just needed some more time to get used to being off tour again.

The tour schedule was brutal, but it had kept me busy. The longer I spent aimlessly floating around without focus, the more I felt like the walls were closing in on me. I had to keep moving — then maybe next time I could outrun whatever shite life wanted to fling at me.

Speaking of moving, it was time to split. I slowly maneuvered myself out from underneath the snoring girl on top of me. It wouldn't be too awkward if she woke up; it wasn't like we'd done anything, but I didn't feel like sharing a cab or making small talk with her. She sleepily resettled on the couch while I stretched my aching muscles.

I patted down my pockets, making sure I still had my keys and wallet, found my shoes and baseball cap, and then headed toward the door. I'd let my hair grow longer since the last round of promo photos were taken and I hadn't shaved since I'd gotten back from Scotland. That and a ball cap were my disguise.

We'd all gotten used to living with mobs of fans always wanting a piece of us, and we'd learned the hard way to follow our security team's rules while we were on tour. Now at home, we were all having to readjust to new rules. I'd been able to get around without security with various levels of success, depending on where I was and who I was with. Ghost wasn't having any luck. He stood out like a sore thumb.

I hit the sunny streets outside the apartment building feeling restless as I started my walk of shame. First off, I hadn't gotten any action last night, so that was pretty shameful. Second, I probably looked as shitty as I felt. I was rocking rumpled clothing, severe bed head (or was it couch head?), lots of itchy hair on my face, and a nasty drool ring on my T-shirt that circled my left nipple, compliments of Sharon. Looking like this, I didn't think I'd have to worry about anyone recognizing me.

My first order of business was to get some food; I was starving. A cup of coffee would help clear my head. Then I'd figure out where the fuck I was and get the hell home so I could play some guitar. I began scanning the shops, looking for sustenance as I walked down the sidewalk.

I walked about a block when I noticed a line of people spilling out the door of a shop across the street. The sign read Underground Coffee Bar. Good enough for me. I crossed the street and got onto the back of the line.

I vaguely noticed the girl in front of me only because she was so bundled up. It was sunny out with almost no breeze; it must have been close to sixty degrees Fahrenheit. Hell, in Scotland we only got this kind of beautiful weather at the very height of summer.

Her outfit was classy. Immediately, I thought she was rich. I didn't know much about fashion — she had on one of those really long sweater-type jackets over some skinny pants and was wearing high-heeled short boots. But this girl looked ridiculous because she was wearing a knit hat and scarf with her getup like she'd been exploring the polar ice caps. I couldn't see her face, because her back was to me, but the long blonde tresses that spilled out of her knit cap looked pretty.

Because I was bored, I watched her, hoping she'd turn around and show me her face.

Five minutes later, I don't think the line moved an inch.

"What's the hold up here?" I spoke out loud.

I snickered to myself when I heard the thick Scottish accent that came out of my mouth. Yeah, after living in the States for six years, I could imitate an American accent pretty spot-on when I wanted to. My natural accent had definitely softened a bit according to my family back home when I recently visited, so this heavy accent that slipped from my lips was for show. I guess I needed a wee bit of attention.

She turned around, probably wondering who I was talking to. I wished she wasn't wearing sunglasses because I couldn't see her eyes, but I'd confirmed she was definitely pretty.

She gave a small shrug. "This place is always slow."

I had a feeling she was looking me up and down from behind those sunglasses. It only took seconds, but I must have come up lacking. She turned back around and returned her attention to her phone.

Well, shite.

I chuckled softly. "Is there a blizzard in today's forecast that I didn't hear about?"

She whipped around and pulled off her sunglasses. This time she eyed me up and down very obviously; unfortunately, zeroing in on my left nipple—or rather, the drool stain on my wrinkled T-shirt—and the words that read 'BLINK if you want me' across my chest.

Her eyes narrowed with disdain. "I'm not blinking."

Ouch.

The line moved, so we both took a step forward.

This girl was feisty, and I was bored. Yeah, I was going to mess with her a bit.

Something about her seemed familiar. Her eyes pulled me in; they were the bluest blue. Maybe she had colored contact lenses because I'd never seen eyes so bright blue. The hair poking out of her hat was long and blonde, her teeth were straight and super white, and her nose was just adorable. Not one blemish marred her skin and her lips were glossy pink with a pronounced cupid's bow on the top lip. Those lips ... yeah, my cock twitched.

Then it hit me. She was one of the 'beautiful' people. The people I'd watched on television growing up in Scotland. I used to watch this show about some high school kids in America. The kids were all impossibly beautiful and rich with endless amounts of designer clothing, fancy cars, and impossibly white teeth. And the weather in America was always sunny and warm. It looked like paradise.

It was no wonder when I had to get out of Scotland that I ran to the U.S. It had always seemed like a fantastical wonderland to me. Reality had tamed that notion over the years. I'd toured through most of the states with Ghost Parker and had met an incredibly wide variety of people and experienced an amazing variety of weather and landscapes. America was fucking huge and not all the people were beautiful looking.

But this lass? She was the embodiment of the perfect American girl from that show I used to watch. They were a dime a dozen here in southern California, but a lot of them had shitty personalities to go along with their beauty. Entitled. Bitchy. Fake.

"Is the coffee good here? Is it worth this wait?" I muttered.

She didn't even glance my way when she answered. "There's another coffee shop a couple of blocks down. Maybe you should go there?"

I rocked back on my heels. "Well, aren't you just a wee ray of sunshine?"

She looked like she was ready to unleash an unholy torrent of curses upon me, but then she took a deep breath and shrugged casually before turning her back on me as if I didn't matter.

I wasn't going to let her ignore me. It was too much fun messing with her. "Such a sensitive lassie."

That did it. I heard her sharp inhale and then an actual gasp of outrage as she whipped around to confront me. "Did you just call me a dog?"

I wanted to laugh out loud, but I kept my smile lazy. "You're a lassie, aye? You don't look like a lad to me."

Her eyes narrowed. "Isn't there some leprechaun meeting somewhere you should be running off to?"

Fuck me. This girl thought I was Irish. This time, I couldn't hold back my chuckle. "Sorry to disappoint you, but that meeting was last night. But, I heard the Barbie club was meeting today. It should be right up your alley."

Her face turned bright red. She was so mad; she actually spluttered. I braced myself for what she was about to let loose when her phone rang. She paused, eyeing me for a long moment before answering her phone.

"Hey, Mom."

She turned away from me, her back toward the street. The line moved forward another step as she listened to whatever her mother was saying.

"No, I'm not at my apartment right now. I just stepped out to get a coffee."

I was blatantly eavesdropping but didn't feel the slightest bit bad about it.

"Yes. He took me out to dinner. It was lovely."

Was she talking about a boyfriend? Shite. Now, that was oddly disappointing.

"Mom! Don't be so nosy."

She glanced over her shoulder and our eyes met for a brief second before she looked away. She looked flustered.

"I told you, I don't want to jinx anything. Maybe you can meet him if we make it to the six-month mark."

She kicked at the pavement with her boot. "Has it been six months already? Are you sure? Wow, time flies, I guess."

I heard her sigh at least once as her mother launched into a long diatribe in response.

Finally, she replied, "Well, we'll see Mom. You know, his schedule is always so busy. There's no way he'd be able to take enough time off to fly out to Kentucky right now. Maybe this summer would be better?"

Her body language was tense as she listened to her mother again.

She sounded like she cut her mom off. "No. No, he's really good to me. He makes plenty of time for me, Mom. He's so sweet."

She lowered her voice so I could barely hear what she said next. "Yes, he's right here with me now. We're getting coffee."

I looked around. I hadn't seen her with anyone this whole time.

"Just down the street from my apartment."

Hmmm. Was she telling tall tales to her mother?

"No, I told you; he's just shy about taking pictures."

She stole a quick peek at me again. Sorry, lassie, this was good. I was listening.

"Argh. Yes, he's tall. About six foot two."

Another big sigh escaped from her pretty lips.

"Well, let's see. Light brown hair — a little on the longish side. Brown eyes."

Shite, so far, she could practically be describing me.

"Yes, he's fit and muscly."

Now I knew she must be describing me.

Her nervous giggle was so feminine. "Yes, Mom. You'd definitely consider him 'eye candy'."

Her eyes flicked back to mine again briefly before skittering away. I couldn't help the smug smile that spread across my face.

She was so engrossed in her phone conversation that she didn't see the woman barreling down the sidewalk, making a beeline straight for her. I'd felt the woman's eyes latch onto me from afar as she approached. The woman was blatantly looking me over while she spoke on the cell phone that was clutched against her ear. At first, I thought she might have recognized me from the band, but as she approached, it dawned on me that she was an older version of the feisty lass standing right next to me. The wee lassie was in for a big surprise.

I had a feeling that this was going to be highly entertaining.

# Chapter 2

## Summer

I CRINGED AS I described my fake boyfriend to my mother. Dammit, I was shit under pressure and I might have just described the annoyingly sexy guy behind me in line at the coffee shop. I didn't mean to, but I took a quick peek at him. Yep. I'd described him to a T, including his delicious muscular physique. If I had met this guy in my sorority days, I'd have been thinking about dropping my panties for him; however, these were my 'I hate men' days, so sex was the last thing on my mind.

Who was I kidding? The guy was insanely hot. Sizzling. He oozed sex appeal. And if sex wasn't on my mind, why were my panties so wet right now?

I sighed. He was just the kind of guy I didn't need in my life. Didn't need and most definitely didn't want. My mom was still babbling on the phone with me about how much she wanted to meet my fake boyfriend. It was getting harder and harder to put it off. My lies were getting more preposterous every time I talked to her. *He's really shy about getting his picture taken.* Yes, I knew it was time to break up with my pretend boyfriend. He'd been a great buffer from my over-eager mom while it lasted.

My eyes swept over to the Irish guy in line behind me. Did I mention that he had an absolutely panty-meltingly sensual Irish accent? If I could just ignore the dumb stuff that came out of his mouth — he'd called me Lassie the dog, for God's sake — I'd be in heaven just listening to him talk. Now, if he'd only whispered some dirty things in my ear...

My brows narrowed in confusion. What was going on? He had a smirk of epic proportions on his face. His arms were crossed. Smug. Satisfied. Like maybe he thought he'd won our little sparring battle? As if. No, that wasn't quite right. It was like he was about to witness the greatest show on earth. Or maybe it was that he was about to witness my downfall. Like I was about to get steamrolled. What. The. Fuck?

Then the steamroller hit.

Mother.

She was here. On the phone with me, but also right in front of me. In the flesh.

What. The. Absolute. Fuck!

"Mom?" My mouth hung open in shock.

"Baby!" She squeezed me in her arms in one of those warm, swaying hugs. "I'm so happy to see you. I've missed you so much."

"Mom, I've missed you, too. What are you doing here in California? Is Dad here?" I whipped my head around, searching for my dad.

My mom waved her hand. "He's busy hauling all our suitcases up to your apartment, but I couldn't wait, so I came down here to find the coffee shop and surprise you."

"Oh, wow." I bit my lip. "This is such a great surprise."

I had been vaguely aware of the sexy Irish guy watching our little reunion with interest. I really didn't want him to bear witness to the shitshow when my mom discovered my fake-boyfriend fib. The line had moved up so that we were almost in the door now. If I wanted to retain any shred of pride, I needed to get my mother out of there now.

But, of course, my mother was always two steps ahead of me. Before I could make a move, she turned to the hot Irish stranger and beamed at him. "You must be…"

I blushed. I winced. I opened my mouth to say … what? How could I stop this disaster in the making? Think, Summer. Quick!

"Scotty." He offered his hand to my mother.

"Scotty!" My mother was a hugger. Scotty didn't stand a chance. She enveloped him in a big embrace. "My daughter has told me so much about you!"

I snorted. I purposefully had only told her about three things in total about my fake boyfriend.

My mother took a step back from him and looked him over critically. "And she wasn't kidding!"

His smile lit his eyes. He was clearly amused. And he had two dimples, which were like my kryptonite.

Oh, My God. Shoot me now.

"It's nice to meet you, Mrs.…" his voice trailed off.

"Oooh. You can call me Lara." She turned to me and squeezed my arm. "You forgot to mention that Scotty has such a lovely accent, sweetie."

Suddenly, Scotty was at my side. His arm wrapped possessively around me, and he pulled me flush against his hard body. "Sweetie, you didn't tell your mum where I'm from?"

How was I supposed to stop this nonsense? It was like a slow-motion train wreck. I swallowed. "Right. I can't believe I forgot to mention it. Scotty is from Ireland."

Scotty sniggered. "Oh, my wee bumpkin. How many times have I told you?" He actually kissed the top of my head. "I'm from Scotland."

My mother frowned. "Bumpkin?"

Scotty didn't hesitate. "It's a term of endearment in Scotland. She actually prefers to be called Lassie as a pet name, but I like to call her my wee bumpkin ... My Bouncy Bumpkin. Because she's so ... bouncy."

Bouncy Bumpkin? I was ready to knee him in the balls. "And I call him..." I could never think quickly on my feet. "Limpie Pie."

Mom scrunched her nose. "Limpie Pie?"

I held up my pointer finger and then slowly cricked it until it drooped. "It's an inside joke."

"Oh, I see." Mom gave Scotty the side-eye.

When he squeezed my side in warning, I flashed a pretty smile at him. His eyes narrowed into little slits and his teeth clenched. I guess I hit the target with that one.

Scotty turned on the charm. "That's just a joke, Lara. Don't worry. There's no problem there, I assure you."

Mom twittered like a bird. "Oh, well, that's a relief."

Yuck. This was kind of gross. Time to ditch this guy. "Well, Scotty, I wasn't expecting to see my parents today — what a surprise! So, I'll have to take a rain check on our plans. I'll, uh, call you later."

"Nonsense!" my mom exclaimed. "Your father would love to meet Scotty, too. I told him I'd pick us both up a coffee while I came to see you — our flight was so early. We can bring the coffee back to your apartment so your father and I can get to know Scotty better."

The hundredth lie of the day flowed from my tongue quite easily. "Oh, that would be nice, but Scotty has an important meeting this morning with his club. It's a heritage thing, you know, leprechauns and man-skirts and stuff. He can't miss it." I patted his biceps. "Isn't that right, Limpie Pie?"

The muscle in his jaw clenched. "I would like to get my coffee first, if that's okay with you, Bouncy Bumpkin?" He held the door open as we entered the shop. We'd finally made it inside.

The coffee shop was fairly chaotic inside. I asked my mom a million questions, generally trying to keep her busy and away from Scotty. I had no idea why he'd gone along with my crazy deception, and I didn't really care. As soon as I could, I'd whisk my mom away from here and never see him again. If I played everything right, my parents would never find out that Scotty was a fake. If they planned on staying more than a few days, an unexpected breakup with my fake boyfriend was in the cards.

Scotty stood behind my mother and me as if he was the next customer in line, which was exactly what he really was. He wasn't really paying that much attention to us anymore. For some insane reason, that disappointed me. I liked our crazy conversation and silly insults, and I certainly didn't mind getting attention from a sexy guy. But I knew I couldn't trust myself around men like him. And this one unquestionably looked like trouble.

While I was paying for the four drinks I ordered (I figured I owed Scotty a coffee for his trouble), I noticed my mom had cornered Scotty and was talking animatedly with him. I felt a moment of panic when I couldn't get over to them to run interference. What was she saying? What was he saying? I couldn't hear anything over the din of the crowd.

As soon as I could, I stepped over to my mom and locked arms with her, drawing her away toward the counter to wait for our order. When it was up, I handed Scotty's coffee to him and spoke to him pointedly. "I know you need to get off to your meeting before you're late."

He had a naughty glint in his eye. "Can't keep the leprechauns waiting. Thanks for the coffee."

"No problem."

My mother gave him a big hug. "I look forward to getting to know you better, Scotty."

He nodded to my mother and then flashed me a mischievous smile. Before I could take my next breath, we were kissing. He caught me by surprise, so I didn't have time to turn my head to reject him. He captured my lips thoroughly with his and lingered a few seconds longer than a chaste goodbye kiss should last. Both my hands were filled with coffee, so I couldn't even shove him away.

Sweet holy hell! The kiss left me breathless. Buzzing and fluttery. Aching in a place that felt long dormant. I couldn't even move.

His answering smirk was all-knowing. "Later, my wee bouncy bumpkin."

I was too gobsmacked to put him in place with a sarcastic retort, and then suddenly he was gone. He flitted in and then out of my life like some kind of sexy apparition. What the hell?

My fingers traced my lips. The simple kiss couldn't have been that good. I was just so sexually repressed right now from swearing off men like a nun. And that 'no man' plan had worked out well. Life was orderly. Even. Successful. In a few days, I'd forget all about the drop-dead gorgeous stranger who'd pretended to be my boyfriend for a hot five minutes. And I'd forget about that kiss — the no-tongue five-second lip contact that had my lady bits clenching with need.

# Chapter 3

## Knox

I HAD THE WHOLE day to myself, so why was I just wandering aimlessly around the city? During my haphazard exploration, I found a furniture store and bought a new sofa. The place didn't look particularly high-end, but I wasn't picky. I found a dark brown leather sofa for $5,000 that could be delivered to my flat the next day. The salesman couldn't hide the glee in his eyes when I'd said I'd take it. I guess I was supposed to haggle with him about the price, but I didn't really give a damn. I had no idea how much furniture cost, let alone if it was quality or not.

After that, I stopped at a tavern with outdoor seating that was serving lunch. I sat in the back corner of the patio with my hat on and no one bothered me. I was relaxing my guard a bit. Last night, when I was out with Ghost, things were a lot different. We'd been approached dozens of times and bombarded twice to the point where security had to step in. It'd been impossible to have any fun until we'd gone to this obscure club where no one had recognized us.

I pulled down my ball cap and crossed the busy intersection when the traffic light changed. What the hell was I going to do with the rest of the day? I was itching to play some guitar, but I didn't want to go back to my flat and hang out alone. For the past two years, I'd spent almost every waking second of the day with my bandmates, and now one was busy raising a kid by himself, one was married with a newborn, and one just got engaged. Naturally, Ghost and I, the last two standing, had grown closer.

I texted Ghost, asking him what he was up to. A reply came right away. He texted, *come check out my new place* and left an address. I hailed a yellow cab and gave the driver Ghost's new address.

Ten minutes later, I was dropped off downtown in front of one of those mirrored glass skyscrapers. It was a far cry from his old place. He just moved out of the upstairs apartment in a house owned by two little old ladies. The house was old and quirky and Ghost had lived there ever since I'd known him. This modern monstrosity seemed nothing like him.

The security team the band used, Vector Security, had been pressuring Ghost to move from the moment our mega-hit single, *Okay Babe*, was released. His old place was too hard to secure. At some point, after our tour ended, fans had learned his home address. Once they descended on the house and harassed the landladies who lived downstairs, he relented and agreed to move. I had a better inkling why he'd chosen this place after it took an arm and a leg for me to get through security. Finally, I was heading up the elevators to his new apartment.

He left his door cracked open, so I knocked on it a few times and stepped inside. The place was spacious, clean, and modern with an open floor plan, pure white walls, dark hardwood floors, lots of lighting, and large windows that looked out over the city.

"Ghost?" My voice echoed through the empty space.

He appeared somewhere from the back, where I assumed the bedrooms were located. "My new place. What do you think?"

I scanned the spacious living room and then over to the kitchen, which looked brand new. "Really nice. When are you moving in all your stuff?"

He shrugged. "This is it. My old place came furnished, so all that crap belonged to the ladies. I didn't have a bed, so I bought a mattress that could be delivered the next day. It was crazy; it came in a little box and expanded when I opened it, but my sheets from the old bed don't quite fit on it. They keep slipping off the edges."

I gestured around the sterile space. "You need rugs and furniture and stuff on the walls, mate. You need to hire someone professional or it'll look like you're slumming in here if you do it yourself."

He frowned slightly. "Yeah, I'll think about it. Maybe to help me take care of the basics. I only signed a 6-month lease, so I don't want to go crazy. I don't want to go through all the trouble of decorating the entire place if I end up leaving."

"Why would you want to leave? This place seems okay."

I followed him into the kitchen. "Who the fuck knows? Maybe I'll want to live in a penthouse like Sid. I don't know. I didn't put much thought into it. Vector gave me a list of suggested places to look at and I picked the first one. I paid out the remaining months on my old lease and moved out right away. I didn't want Edith and Rosie dealing with all my shit."

The kitchen was amazing. Loads of cabinets, many with glass front doors, open shelving on one wall, top-of-the-line appliances, and a giant island with seating — all expertly finished with high-end materials.

Ghost opened the refrigerator to grab a couple of beers. Besides the beer, a few takeout containers were the only things inside the fridge. I imagined his kitchen cabinets were just as empty.

I took the beer he offered me. "Sid's penthouse is pretty sweet."

"Yeah. I just didn't need all that space. I didn't even need two bedrooms, but this unit was available right away. A few one-bedroom units are becoming available at the end of the month if you're looking. We could be neighbors, bro. This place has some sweet amenities."

I rubbed the back of my neck. "It's a lot nicer than my place. How much is it per month?"

"Twenty thousand."

I rocked back on my heels and whistled. "Fuck, mate! You're paying twenty grand a month? I pay four grand right now for a one-bedroom and I thought that was expensive."

Ghost chuckled. "The penthouse in this building is three times what I pay."

My eyes widened with shock. "Sixty thousand dollars. Per month? That's fucking insane! Sid's going to wind up in the poor house if he's paying anything like that."

We headed back into the main room and Ghost gestured for me to take the bean bag chair that was parked in the center of the room in front of the large-screen TV mounted on the wall. Those were the only two items in the room. Ghost went into a closet near the entrance door and dragged out a fold-up canvas chair. "Have you checked your bank account lately?"

I sank into the bean bag chair that had seen better days. "Not really. I'm using a financial planner that Donovan recommended. The planner told me not to let the money collect in the bank, so he's been investing it. I've got an accountant who reviews it quarterly and says it's performing well."

Ghost unfolded the black director's chair and sat down, stretching out his long legs. "You should still monitor how it's doing yourself. You haven't touched any of it yet?"

I took a big swig of the cold beer. "I bought a guitar I've had my eye on. $65,000. I've got nothing else to spend it on."

Ghost rubbed the scruff on his chin. "You need a chick to spend your money."

I grunted with disgust. "That's the last thing I need. It was bad enough in the early days when the groupies were only out for a good fuck that they could brag about on social media. Now that we've hit the big time, we're attracting nothing but gold diggers and fame whores. I can barely get my dick up anymore for those women."

Ghost tipped his beer bottle to me in a mock toast. "Welcome to the top, brother."

We both took a drink and then sat silently for a few minutes before Ghost cut into my sour thoughts. "You're wearing the same clothes as last night. Were you able to get your dick up for that short chick with the nice rack?"

I sighed. "Yeah, but then she passed out with her hand down my pants. Maybe that's why I'm in such a shite mood today."

"You waited too long to close the deal."

Probably. I'd been trying to talk to her. Get to know her a little better, but we hadn't been clicking. "That club was fucking weird last night. No one had any clue who we were. I liked it, but there was a weird vibe going on."

Weird was an understatement. The club was decorated with clowns, ugly dolls, and taxidermy galore, and had obscure genres of punk music pumping through the speakers all night. I stood out among the crowd for looking so normal.

"This guy Huxley told me about it. Said I could probably remain incognito there. He said that no one there listened to Top 40 music." Ghost scoffed. "Christ, that fucking song changed everything. Ghost Parker is now Top 40 music."

He was more joking than bitter, but I still wanted to lighten things up. "Yeah, but we're set for life. If you ever get too sick of it all, you can leave the band. Do something else. The sky's the limit, mate."

Ghost shook his head. "I'll be with Ghost Parker till the end, even if Vicious writes bubblegum pop and BVR turns us into the newest boy band. Ride or die, man."

My arse had finally sunk completely through the beans in the chair and settled onto the hard floor, so I readjusted my position. "So, what happened to you last night? I never saw you take off from the club."

Ghost stared unfocused into the distance for a moment. "Fuck, last night was a trip. Thank God for Bishop. He came through when things were looking sketchy and got me out of there."

My ears perked up. "What happened?"

Ghost shifted in his seat. "I was hanging out with this girl and her friends. They were creative types — into art and literature without being pretentious about it. They seemed harmless, just out for a good time, and she told me she was a professional masseuse, so yeah, that intrigued me."

I remembered him talking to a girl wearing black lipstick who was loaded up with piercings and tattoos. She was most likely the masseuse. Raising a brow, I asked, "Did you get your happy ending?"

Ghost grunted in reply and then took a big pull of his beer. "One guy, supposedly some well-known sculptor, suggested we take the party back to his uncle's house. The group was pretty enthusiastic about it, so I just went along with them."

He gulped down the rest of his beer and then put the empty bottle on the floor by his foot. "I got reamed out by Bishop for that. I guess we weren't supposed to split up last night? Anyway, he said he had a gut instinct to follow me, but that left you unprotected. My bad, man, but I'm glad Bishop listened to his gut."

I waved away his concern. "Nobody was paying any attention to me once we got to that club, mate. I was fine."

Ghost winced. "Yeah, but after Bishop reamed me out, he told me that each one of us is getting our own assigned guy when we go out together."

I shrugged. The guys at Vector were experts at blending into the background. So far, I hadn't felt hampered in any way, but I knew Ghost was chafing at being constantly monitored.

"So, I hopped into a car with Aura—"

"Aura?" I chuckled. "That should have been your first red flag."

His mouth twitched with a faint smile. "My friends call me Ghost, so I'm not about to judge."

"True," I agreed.

"We smoked some weed during the car ride, but by the time we pulled up to the uncle's house, I was feeling a little off." He ran a hand through his hair.

I sat up as much as I could in a bean bag chair and frowned. "Off? Like how?"

Ghost idly played with a hole in his jeans while he answered. "Like it was more than just weed I was smoking, but it was really subtle at first. I watched them pass around the bowl and everyone smoked from it, so I wasn't overly concerned. I didn't have too much time to worry about it because the house we'd pulled up to turned out to be a fucking funeral home."

"A funeral home?" My mouth dropped open. "Shite, there's the second red flag."

Ghost continued, "Ivan, the sculptor dude, told us not to wander around. We had to stick to the back of the house, which was a residence. Apparently, there'd been a wake or a viewing earlier and there was a funeral planned for today. There was a dead body lying in a casket in the next room and no one blinked an eye. Ivan said there were probably several bodies in the house and in the embalming room, so we shouldn't go exploring."

I shook my head. "You were partying in a house full of dead bodies? That's pretty messed up."

"Yeah, it was a first for me, but no one else seemed to care. I mean, somebody lived there — his uncle, I guess. Life goes on. Parties happen and the dead bodies didn't seem to mind."

I raised an eyebrow. This was a weird conversation, but it was Ghost I was talking to. I should be used to it by now. "Okay. So what happened? Why did Bishop have to rescue you?"

Ghost's leg started bouncing with unleashed energy. He swiped a hand down his face. "Yeah, so I was feeling strange. Drunker than I should have been for what I drank. High, but in a bad way. Definitely paranoid. I was pretty sure they mixed something else in with the pot, but it didn't feel like anything I'd done before. Not X or acid. My mind was racing. I sat back and pretended to be resting, but I was watching the group like a hawk. Fuck, I'm not positive, but I swear, man ... I think they were swapping out the bowl they were passing around."

I didn't like where this story was going. "You think someone was slipping you some drugs to fuck you up?"

Ghost nodded slowly. "I'm not sure. As soon as I was suspicious, I started faking that I was taking a hit every time the bowl came around to me and kept a close eye on what was going down, but the shit I already smoked was kicking in hard. I had a hunch that they were all in on it, but my mind was already fucked up, so who knows?"

I swallowed down the rest of my beer and then studied his face. "So, then you called Bishop and got the fuck out of there?"

Ghost chuckled. "Well, then it gets hazy. The next thing I remember, those fuckers were trying to get me to climb inside a casket. Naked. They were egging me on to do all kinds of weird shit."

"Fuck, mate." An uneasy pit formed in my stomach. "That's not good."

He wiped his brow as if just thinking about it was making him sweat. "When I saw some guy taking video of me with his phone, I sent out an SOS to Bishop. I had about one working cell left in my brain and thank God I used it. After that, I don't remember much."

I jumped to my feet. My arse was killing me from the stupid bean bag chair, and I was too restless to sit any longer. "You dodged a bullet, Ghost. That could have gone sideways to absolute shite really quick."

Ghost stood too and headed into the kitchen for new bottles of beer. "I could barely stand when Bishop finally got to me. He had to kick open the door because no one was answering it. They weren't 'cooperating' — his words — so he lied and told them that cops were on the way. It gave him enough cover to pull me out of there."

I followed him into the kitchen. "How are you feeling today?"

"Dizzy as fuck this morning, so I drank a gallon of water and then went back to sleep. I woke up five hours later and took a shower right before I got your text. Now, I'm feeling back to normal." He grinned slyly, like he knew he was one lucky bastard. "Ready to party."

I shook my head in disbelief while I leaned up against his kitchen island. "You're lucky you caught on to whatever was going on and didn't smoke anymore. Who knows what would have happened?"

He shrugged like it was of little concern now. "Maybe they knew who I was all along and just wanted to sell some insane photos to the media?"

I took a deep breath. "That's the best-case scenario, mate. They could have been some weird cult that was going to lock you inside a coffin for some ritual, or maybe even something worse. Who knows? You've got to be more careful who you party with."

Ghost scoffed. "You sound like Bishop. He called a group of guys from Vector into an emergency 'off-the-record' meeting this morning to analyze the situation. Bishop said they're going to do some surveillance missions or some shit in their free time. He thinks there's something more significant going on with them. Crazy fuckers, that kind of shit gets those ex-military dudes off better than porn."

I'd opened my phone while he was talking and scanned social media. Luckily, nothing about Ghost or our band was trending. "Did you give the social media team a heads-up?"

"Nah." He frowned. "The only photos or videos they got of me maybe showed I was a little wasted. I never got naked or went near the dead bodies."

"Fuck. You're going to be more careful, yeah? Maybe stick to hanging with the groupies?"

Ghost groaned. "My therapist complains that I already have too many trust issues, Knox. Don't make it worse by getting all worked up about nothing."

I let it drop but vowed to myself to keep a better eye on Ghost when we were out. "So, what's going on tonight? Maybe you should lie low for a few days?"

"Fuck no." Ghost began telling me about a girl he'd hooked up with a few weeks ago that turned out to be a B-list actress. She invited him to some celebrity bash tonight. She was probably using him for publicity to boost her career, but I kept my mouth shut.

I was pulling up a picture of this celebrity lass on the internet when I received a text message from an unknown number.

> **Unknown:** Hi Scotty! This is Lara. I know your rash is acting up again and you have another heritage meeting this evening, but it would mean so much to Jim and me if you could rearrange your schedule and come out to dinner with us. We won't be in town for long and we'd love to get to know you better.

I had to hold back a burst of laughter. My rash? Well played, my wee bouncy bumpkin.

Ghost shot me a look. "What's so funny?"

"This girl's parents just asked me out to dinner, so they could get to know me better." I shook my head in disbelief.

"What girl?" he asked.

"Some hot babe I kissed at the coffee shop this morning. I don't even know her name, but her mother got my phone number."

"Wait, what?" Ghost furrowed his brow in confusion. He knew that I never gave out my number. "You gave her mother your phone number?"

"Yeah, I did." I chuckled to myself in disbelief.

"So let me get this straight." He counted off with his fingers as he spoke. "You kissed her at the coffee shop, you don't know her name, and yet you're going out to dinner with her parents? You work quickly, my man."

"I'm not going to dinner with them," I clarified. "I only kissed her because she was so bonnie. She was one of those all-American girls that my teenage dick used to get hard for. She had fucking gorgeous blonde hair and bright blue eyes with blindingly white teeth. She was the poster girl for what my wet-dream fantasy girl looked like."

"So, what's the problem?" Ghost raised an eyebrow in question.

"Go to dinner, show her the rock star charm, and you'll get your fantasy fuck afterward."

It was a good thing I was standing behind the kitchen island because I felt my dick growing hard just thinking about her. I had to adjust my stance to relieve some of the pressure.

"The lass looks like an absolute angel, but she spent the entire 15 minutes of our acquaintance insulting me. She's a real sassy lass and I could tell by her clothing that she was rich and probably snobby. She was busy busting my balls and then her mum showed up and she lied to her for some inexplicable reason and told her mum that I was her boyfriend. I don't know, mate, she's probably a complete psycho."

Ghost raised his eyebrows. "Fuck yeah, but she's probably a great lay."

I agreed. "She's definitely a spitfire, that one."

He tapped his fingers on the counter. "So go to dinner. I haven't seen you this interested in a chick in forever. Go have a bit of fun. Do you have better plans for tonight?"

I grimaced. "Nah. Then I'd have to get security involved. She doesn't even know who I am, even though that's kind of refreshing after having all those fans throwing themselves at me for the past year. Sometimes that gets old."

Ghost nodded. "Tell Vector you don't want any interference. You'll handle any fans unless there's an absolute safety issue. They know how to be discreet. If you don't want to tell the girl you're in a hugely popular rock band, she doesn't have to know."

I shifted back and forth on my feet. Was I even considering this? "I don't know, mate. Wouldn't it be kind of weird just showing up? I don't even know her name."

His eyes danced with mischief. "You were invited. Just go and do a little ball-busting yourself. Make her beg for your cock." He laughed.

"It sounds like fun. I wish I could be a fly in your soup and watch how it all goes down."

I hesitated. "I don't know."

"Give me your phone. I want to see what the mom texted."

I slid my phone across the kitchen island to him. Big mistake. He started typing in a reply.

"Fuck. What are you doing? Give that back to me."

His smirk deepened while he ignored me and continued to respond to the text.

"Fuck," I muttered.

Finally, Ghost tossed my phone back to me. "You're welcome."

I looked down at the text he'd made on my behalf.

> **Me:** I would love that, Lara! My rash is much better now. Send me the time and place and I'll be there. Don't tell my girl I'm coming. I want to surprise her!

"Fuck. Did you have to use exclamation marks?" I grumbled.

My phone binged with a new text.

> **Unknown:** Perfect!!! Thank you so much! 7 p.m. at The Rusty Anchor.

I groaned and turned off my phone without replying. "I'm not going."

Ghost just laughed.

# Chapter 4

## Summer

WHY DID I ANSWER the phone?

Lindsay, a friend that attended the same private high school in Kentucky that I'd graduated from, was droning on endlessly. She'd just gotten engaged. Ugh. Cheers to another expensive bridesmaid's dress hanging in my closet that, no, I'll never have altered to wear again. I successfully faked the appropriate level of enthusiasm for the future nuptials, but then started tuning out when the discussion turned to upcoming bridal party Zoom meetings, my responsibility to post comments on the Lindsay & Grant Forever wedding website, the bridal party diet pact, and of course, hints as to where she wanted the bachelorette party weekend to take place.

Even my mom was getting bored with the conversation that was broadcast throughout my apartment on speakerphone. My apartment was small, so she couldn't help but listen while my dad sat in front of the TV watching sports.

A few muttered replies were all I needed to uphold my end of the conversation while I looked around the small space I'd made a home, seeing it through my mother's eyes.

I lived on the third floor of a walk-up apartment building in a cramped one-bedroom unit. It was hard to disguise the shabbiness of the place even though I'd attempted to make it more pleasant and homier over the past year I'd lived here. The appliances were old and worn, the floors scratched and scarred, and the walls in desperate need of a fresh coat of paint. The bathroom, however, was the most disturbing. No matter how much I scrubbed, it never looked clean. Mustard-colored ceramic tile with brownish-gray grout, that at one time must have been white, covered the walls and reddish-brown splotches stained the chipped porcelain sink and the tub. The inside of the toilet bowl was a permanent disaster no amount of elbow grease could fix.

I missed my cute apartment in Kentucky. It was much newer, twice as big, and had a light and airy feel to it, but I'd never be able to afford anything close to that in Los Angeles. When my one-year lease renewal approached, I'd searched long and hard for someplace better that was still in my budget. I finally realized it wasn't going to happen, so I begrudgingly renewed my lease.

My eyes crossed when Lindsay began listing out and gushing over what items she'd registered for as wedding gifts. My mother was no longer paying the conversation any attention. She had a gigantic smile on her face as she texted back and forth with someone on her phone — at least one of us was in a good mood. Maybe dinner out with my parents would cheer me up.

I missed my mom. We were always very close as I grew up. I told her everything. Even after college, when I moved into my own apartment in Kentucky, we remained close. Then last year, from her perspective, I suddenly quit my job and moved halfway across the country with no explanation.

I'd made an epic mistake and instead of dealing with the consequences like an adult, I ran. Since my love life consisted of one disaster after another, I couldn't admit my latest blunder. I needed a fresh start where nobody knew me. And a new job where I didn't know what my boss's dick looked like.

I hadn't been having any luck finding a new job locally, so when the recruiter called with a promising job opening in L.A., I interviewed on a whim. A few weeks later, I was moving away from Kentucky, escaping the humiliation of another bad mistake.

A male voice in the background interrupted Lindsay as she described the china pattern she'd chosen. "Ooh. Summer, I've got to run. Grant just got home."

Thank God.

"Okay, Linz. I'll talk to you later. Congratulations again!"

I hung up the phone.

"Another one of your friends is getting married?" My mom's question sounded innocent enough, but I felt the sting just the same.

"Yeah. You remember Lindsay? The one who had the botched nose job sophomore year?"

"Oh, right." Mom nodded. "But she looked lovely when it all got fixed in the end."

"Yeah," I agreed. Her parents had flown her to some world-renowned plastic surgeon to fix the horrible first surgery. Her nose looked fine in the end, but no one in our high school had forgotten the first outcome. She endured countless 'nose' jokes throughout high school. It should have made her more compassionate and sensitive to others, but she was still an entitled, snobby bitch. We'd been friends only because it was far easier to stay on her good side.

Mom put down her phone and looked up with a smile. "Sweetie, I'm going to take a shower. I've made dinner reservations for 7 o'clock at the Rusty Anchor. Have you ever been there before?"

"No. I've never heard of it."

"The Henderson's recommended it. Why don't you wear that emerald green dress that I like so much?"

My brow crinkled. "I wasn't planning on dressing up that much. It's just dinner."

My mom dismissed my words with a headshake. "I'm wearing my blue Oscar de la Renta. Ooh, I know. How about you wear that black off-the-shoulder dress? It's not as formal and it looks so lovely on you."

An argument formed on my tongue, but I bit it back. It was better to pick my battles with her, and this wasn't one I needed to win.

Honestly, it surprised me she wasn't asking more about Scotty, my fake boyfriend. She'd peppered me with a million questions about him when we got back from the coffee shop, but I'd done my best to give her the run-around. That she'd given up so easily was suspicious, but I'd take the reprieve. I had a feeling she was gearing up to give me the third degree over dinner, so I needed to get my story straight in my head.

How could I juggle this lie that had grown so dramatically in the past few hours? Unless I came clean, the only answer was to lie some more, which didn't sit well with me. Her meeting a real person as my boyfriend and having a name and face to go along with the idea of him was like adding kindling to the fire of her curiosity. I was toast.

Needing a way out of this mess, I racked my brain. I could tell her we were having troubles, and that I was ready to break up with him. Then I would tell her that I didn't want to ruin her visit by talking about him, but I knew that wouldn't shake her. She'd step into the counselor role to console me and ask me a million more questions about our relationship.

My brain grappled with the problem for the rest of the afternoon while Mom remained suspiciously silent about Scotty when normally she'd be relentless. It was making me super nervous.

While I got ready for dinner, I came up with a million scenarios in my head about my supposed boyfriend, each more preposterous than the next. Even though I was desperate to come up with a reasonable story to tell my mom and time was running out, my mind kept drifting. I was daydreaming about Scotty. Underneath his sloppy clothes, I could tell that the man was built. And he was so damn attractive. He dressed like a bum but had a level of arrogance to him that was insanely appealing. He was just the kind of loser I usually fell for.

I stared into the mirror and realized I went a little heavier on the makeup than I wanted to. I wasn't about to wash it off and start all over, so I just sighed. Mom would love that I was getting all dolled up. Besides, if I was going to wear the black dress that Mom wanted, I might as well complete the look. Instead of tossing my hair into a sleek, long ponytail as I'd planned, I pulled out the curling iron, added soft wavy curls to my hair, and let it cascade down my back.

Glancing at the clock, I realized it was almost time to leave for the restaurant and I still hadn't come up with a solid plan.

Frankly, I was wondering if it would be better overall if I just came out and admitted the truth. She'd be so disappointed that I'd lied to her all these months, but what else could I do? Everything had become too complicated. I'd only lied in the first place to get some breathing room from all her questions and to stop her from worrying about me in a new city. I'd just needed a reprieve from her kind-hearted meddling in my love life.

Mentally exhausted, I rubbed at my temples. I didn't enjoy lying to my mom. Keeping up the pretense of having a boyfriend was draining my energy. Now that Mom had met him, she wasn't going to let this go. Her eyes had sparkled with glee when she'd first clapped eyes on him. She was deliriously happy that I'd found Scotty.

Inwardly, I rolled my eyes. I was even starting to think of Scotty as my real fake boyfriend when he was just a fake, fake-boyfriend. How did I ever let things get this far?

♫♪♩♩

My mom looked gorgeous. Her dress hugged her curves, her makeup hid the tiny signs of aging that I'd just started noticing, and her blonde hair looked elegant in a French twist. It wasn't the first time that I'd noticed how much we looked alike, nor was it the first time I said a silent prayer that I'd age just as beautifully.

The biggest difference in our looks was that she was about 20 pounds heavier than me. Mom enjoyed eating and thoroughly despised working out. I hardly ever ate out and so far my metabolism kept my weight in check naturally. I'd cross the diet/workout bridge when I came to it.

Mom and I posed together while my dad snapped several photos of us with Mom's cell phone. When my mom was satisfied with the pictures, we left my apartment and headed out to the waiting taxi.

On the car ride to the restaurant, my parents discussed an issue my dad was having with one of his employees. I tuned out their conversation as I stared out the window.

I'd made my decision. If Mom started asking about Scotty, as painful as it would be, I was going to come clean about the whole thing. The fake boyfriend had started with a small fib over the phone.

Now, it had tangled into something much more complicated and my conscience was balking. I'd explain to Mom how I was doing the "no man" plan and that I was happy with it. I wouldn't tell her what happened with my boss, but I'd let her know that another breakup had me hightailing it out of Kentucky for a fresh start.

My mom slipped her arm through mine as we stepped into the restaurant. "I hope we didn't bore you with all the shop talk, sweetie. I think we got it all out of our system."

My parents always talked about Dad's work. Mom had always been a good sounding board for him, and she understood the nuts and bolts of Dad's business better than most of his employees did.

"I don't mind. I'm just glad that business is doing so well."

We stood behind my dad as he gave the maitre d' the information about our reservation. I was smoothing the fabric of my dress as we waited for the maitre d' to consult the reservation book, but then I felt his eyes on me. He was appraising me with a quizzical expression but glanced back at his book when I caught him. The second time he did it, I knew I wasn't imagining it.

He marked something in his book and then looked up with a smile. "Please follow me."

He led us through the restaurant, winding us past several empty tables. Just when I suspected he was going to lead us straight out the back door, he guided us to a fairly isolated table way in the back corner. My brow creased as I surveyed the multitude of empty tables he could have placed us at.

No one else seemed to find the table placement lacking. My father was already pulling out a chair to seat my mom while the maitre d' ushered me to the chair directly across from her.

I hesitated to sit. "I feel like we're being put in time-out in the corner."

My mother disagreed, "No, this is perfect! It's cozy back here."

Reluctantly, I sat down facing the dark back corner, my back to the entire restaurant. I could only see my parents and one other couple if I turned my head to the right, but I guess it didn't matter. Privacy was better for the confession I needed to make.

I was engrossed in the menu when our waiter came to take our drink order. I didn't have a very sophisticated knowledge of wine, so we ended up ordering a bottle of the red wine my mom preferred.

My dad was questioning me about my job, but my mother didn't seem very interested in my answers when normally she would. She kept glancing over my shoulder. I had to fight the urge to turn around in my chair and see what kept grabbing her attention.

When my mom's eyes lit up with unbridled excitement, I couldn't resist any longer. I turned around in my seat and saw the haughty maitre d' lead a man right up to our table and then nod his head rather obsequiously to him.

As soon as my gaze shifted to the man standing behind the empty chair right next to me, I gasped. For one brief moment, I thought that by some freaky cosmic joke that he was our waiter, but then my mother sprang up from her seat and circled the table so that she could hug him in greeting. Was it possible I'd conjured him up by thinking about him so much today?

What was going on here?

My mouth dropped open as I stared at the too-sexy-to-be-fair man hugging my mom. If I had any doubts that my memory was wrong about his level of attractiveness, they were over. He was drop-dead gorgeous and my lady parts were screaming out their absolute approval.

He was dressed in navy blue slacks and a white button-down dress shirt that showed off his muscular build so perfectly — the clothes looked tailor-made. His thick hair, which fell almost to his shoulders, was a light shade of brown that had an auburn tinge to it when it caught in a certain light. Instead of rumpled and messy, this time, the mop of wavy hair was styled with product, but the effect was just as devastating. He looked like he'd just stepped out of a GQ magazine shoot.

My mom finally released him from her grasp. She was looking up at him, smiling. "Scotty, I'm so glad you could make it!"

My father had also risen and was now shaking Scotty's hand as they exchanged names.

"It's nice to meet you, Mr. Meadows."

I only caught snippets of the conversation as I vaguely watched the scene unfold because my thoughts were furiously spinning. And I was a bit distracted, because the moment I'd clapped eyes on Scotty, my whole body had reacted. My heart rate had sped up, a heated flush washed over my skin, and butterflies went on a rampage in my stomach.

I tried to blame this extreme reaction to him as an adrenaline rush from nerves. My fake boyfriend had just shown up at dinner with my parents. It was completely unexpected, and I already felt guilty about perpetuating this crazy lie to my parents. Of course, that would cause a massive case of the butterflies.

I may have tried to latch onto that excuse, but in truth, my crazy response felt a lot like lust. What else explained that throbby feeling centered right between my legs? Hot. Achy. Swollen. Wet with want. Heat surged through my body as I felt a tingling sensation between my thighs. I squirmed in my seat, desperately trying to relieve the tension that had built up inside of me.

I'd experienced lust at first sight before. A few times, but never this intense. Not to where it overpowered all reason.

I may have had a few sexy daydreams about Scotty this afternoon when I thought it was harmless — when I thought I'd never see him again. But he was here again, in the flesh, invading my mind. Making me think about those full lips — preferably relieving the ache now blossoming between my thighs.

He was still talking to my dad when he glanced over at me and smiled knowingly. I inhaled sharply. Did he know what he did to me? His smile wasn't a pretty boy smirk. It was a smile of pure confidence. He oozed alpha male, and my body responded accordingly. I had to grit my teeth and clench my thighs together.

Quickly, I looked away, needing to compose myself. I took a sip of ice water with shaking hands. What was I going to do? My thoughts were scattered. I couldn't think straight around him. I was way too flustered.

Think Summer!

He was dressed to kill and looked devastatingly sexy. So, he wasn't homeless after all. Still, he was some kind of psycho. A stalker. What the hell was he doing here, anyway? I had to get rid of him.

I smoothed my sweaty palms on the skirt of my dress. If my damp panties were any indication, I was shooting off pheromones like mad. If I was going to survive this dinner, I needed my wits about me and had to shake off the lust. I'd met plenty of hot guys before — even dated and slept with my fair share. And if there was one thing I'd learned, the hotter the guy, the bigger the inevitable disappointment. Guys who knew they were hot were generally assholes looking for insecure girls to stroke their oversized egos. No thanks. Been there, done that.

My breathing had almost returned to normal when my mom returned to her chair. She was looking at me with a gigantic smile on her face.

Scotty slid into the chair next to me. His movements were graceful. Fluid. He moved like an athlete.

He leaned in and kissed my cheek. His lips against my skin sent my heart pounding inside my chest again. His mouth lingered a few seconds too long and then drifted over to my ear. A shiver ran down my spine as I felt a soft puff of air tickle the shell of my ear when he spoke against it. "Sorry, I'm late."

My head turned to look at him. He was so close. He was even better looking up close. His expressive brown eyes held a glint of mischief that had me narrowing my eyes even as his obscenely long eyelashes and chiseled jawline had turned my insides to a liquified pool of mush. He was clean-shaven, but I kind of missed the masculine scruff. I could imagine the delicious feeling as it scraped against my inner thigh.

I blinked away the naughty image even as my cheeks heated. Was I panting? God, I had to get ahold of myself.

He was so close. Right next to me. I felt the heat emanating from his muscled thigh, teasing my own. I could smell the faint notes of his cologne mixed with his natural scent, and I liked it. It was a potent aphrodisiac. I wanted to bury my face in his neck and breathe him in.

I licked my lips, preparing to say something, but my mind went blank. I was struck mute. Dazed.

He crooked an eyebrow, waiting for me to speak.

"What are you doing here?" I choked out at last.

His lazy smile was devious. Cocky. It should have pissed me off.

But he had dimples. They were my utter undoing. I just stared at his beautiful face while he answered. But I had no idea what he said because I was too busy drowning in him.

# Chapter 5

**Knox**

What was I doing here?

I'd let Ghost talk me into this bloody dumb idea because I had nothing better to do. I'd been restless and bored ever since the tour ended, and attending some starlet's Hollywood party with him sounded like everything I'd been avoiding. Besides the sex and drugs, those parties boiled down to mindless exchanges hoping to upgrade status and social standing and weird networking rituals designed to increase publicity by pretending to know the right people. Getting laid would have been a sure thing, but I'd rather do that with a fan than some shallow Hollywood princess, only to have the lurid details and photos of us splashed all over the entertainment media.

It was ironic that I was thinking of the emptiness of that scene as I walked into a restaurant to meet up with my fake girlfriend and her parents. Why did everything in my life seem fake? As much as

I moaned about two of my bandmates finding their 'forever girls', the relationships they had were something I secretly envied when I admitted it to myself.

I craved a deeper connection with someone. I hardly ever saw my family in Scotland and I never got close to any women. Except for the guys in my band, I was floating around untethered.

It hadn't always been that way. Once, I'd thought I'd had everything figured out. I had the girl. I had Aila, and I thought we were content with the life we had. We were surrounded by extended family and friendly neighbors. I'd gotten a job straight out of school; it was easy to find work in our industrial town if you weren't afraid of long hours and working with your hands. My wages would be enough to afford us a small plot of land to raise a passel of kids on.

It would have been a simple life. One that I wanted with Aila. One that I thought she wanted as well. When I lost her, everything withered and died within me. It had taken me over five years and dozens upon dozens of meaningless hookups to work that betrayal and guilt out of my system.

I stopped walking for a moment as the revelation hit me. Was I really ready to move on? Bloody hell! Was I finally over it all? It had been brewing for a while, but it took this lass with the feisty mouth that looked like the American fantasy girl of my youth to realize that the simple life I imagined living with Aila was never my destiny. It wouldn't have lasted even if she hadn't died a few days before our wedding.

As the maitre d' led me to the table, I spotted Hudson from Vector Security. The guy was massive but did a surprisingly good job of blending in with restaurant patrons.

Hudson had arranged everything. If he thought it was weird that I was eating dinner with a girl and her parents whose names I didn't know, he kept it to himself. He'd given the maitre d' my description of my bouncy bumpkin and her mother and had promised to take care of all my security needs discreetly. Tonight of all nights, I did not want to be hassled by fans. That's probably why the maitre d' was leading me to the worst table in the house, intimately shoehorned into the back corner next to a door marked 'private'.

Lara greeted me vivaciously and Jim Meadows was quite cordial, but I couldn't help but notice that my wee bumpkin was less than pleased to see me.

Meadows. At least I had a last name now. Of course, it was possible that Meadows wasn't her last name. Jim could be a stepfather, but the physical resemblance was there. If only one of them would call her by her name, I'd be set.

After the introductions with her parents were finished, I sat down in the chair beside her. She was avoiding my gaze, but that just gave me time to soak her in. Once again, she took my breath away with how excruciatingly beautiful she was.

She was even more beautiful than memory had painted her. Her eyes were a vivid blue color with a darker blue ring around the edge of her iris and fringed with thick lashes. Her eyes were so mesmerizing that I had to force myself to take in the rest of her pretty face. Even the slight frown on her pouty lips couldn't detract from her raw beauty.

I sat down next to her and leaned in to give her a peck on the cheek as an actual boyfriend would in greeting. My lips drifted toward her ear and whispered some apology about being late when actually I was busy inhaling her intoxicating scent. It wasn't a floral or fruity scent that so many women wore, but something more sensual and rich.

Bloody hell, I wanted to bury my nose in her skin and trail my lips down the elegant column of her neck until I reached the creamy smooth skin at the top of her shoulders. The rounded swell of her breast was just visible above the fabric of her dress, and that was where my lips ached to wander. It was a good thing I was sitting down because just the thought of doing those things had my cock hardening visibly in my dress pants.

But instead of mauling her in front of her parents, I retreated to a respectable distance and flashed a smile. "You look beautiful."

She didn't answer or even acknowledge I had spoken. Her eyes were wide with shock, and her chest was heaving with shaky breaths. She was still processing the surprise of me showing up here, but I knew her feisty side could still reveal itself. At any moment, she could make a huge public scene and expose this whole charade.

Then her father started asking me about Scotland and the opportune moment for her to tell the truth passed. The conversation flowed easily between me and her parents as I attempted to charm them with stories about my homeland. Never once did my lass enter the conversation. I expected her to make clever or biting quips about bagpipes or man skirts, as she called them, but she remained quiet. Wanting to see that fiery spark in her eyes again, I tried to draw her into the conversation. But she remained silent, only reaching to refill her wineglass several times.

After we all ordered our meals, Jim turned to me and asked, "What do you do here in America?"

I'd been expecting a question along those lines, and since I didn't want to outright lie, I answered as truthfully as I could while giving nothing away. "I work in music production."

"Oh." Jim rubbed his jawline. "You work in a music studio?"

"Sometimes," I answered vaguely.

He picked up his beer bottle and seemed to contemplate it for a beat. "Is it lucrative?"

"Jim…" Lara warned, but I didn't mind.

"The band I work with is pretty good, so it can be lucrative. I travel with them when they do, so that's a perk. I love what I do. Music is my passion."

I glanced over at my lass, but she didn't seem to be listening to anything I was saying. She was distracted; her teeth chewed at her bottom lip when she wasn't sipping her wine. Her lack of interaction was making me uncomfortable. This dinner wasn't turning out at all like I'd imagined it would.

After a natural lull in our conversation when our server was handing out our meals, Lara smiled warmly at me. "We were so happy to meet you, Scotty. I was so worried. When my daughter ran off to Los Angeles with no warning, I was worried, but I'm so glad she has you here looking out for her."

Not sure how to respond, I smiled weakly at Lara. My fake girlfriend — the one whose name I still didn't know — was suddenly shooting daggers at me with her eyes.

Lara took a sip of wine and then grimaced, "She has a terrible track record with men—"

"Mom!"

Lara waved her protest off and continued undaunted. "I was worried when she wouldn't let us meet you. I thought you must be another poor choice. But I am so relieved and happy to know that she's in excellent hands." She paused for a moment and then added, "She is in good hands, right?"

"Yes, ma'am." What else could I say?

Lara laughed. "You're not married, right? No other women?"

I heard a groan of embarrassment next to me. "No, and no."

Lara cocked an eyebrow and threw another question at me. "You won't steal her credit cards and drain her bank account before skipping town?"

My lass gasped beside me. "Mother, stop!"

Jim put a hand on his wife's arm. "Honey, I don't think we need to get into all that."

Lara glanced at her daughter. "I'm sorry, sweetie. But you know how much I worry about you all alone in a big city. Knowing you have Scotty and finally meeting him has set my mind at ease. I'm so happy for you, darling."

My lass put down her fork. "I don't need a man, Mom. I'm perfectly fine on my own."

Lara frowned. "After Jake ... I just worry about you. It's a mom thing."

We finished our meal, making small talk while my lass silently stewed. Her mother had irritated her and it was more than obvious that she didn't want me there. It was painfully uncomfortable tiptoeing around her bad mood. I'd wanted the dinner to be fun and flirty, but somehow I'd screwed up the whole thing.

After our plates were cleared, Lara insisted that everyone order dessert. This seemed to be the last straw for my lass. She looked like she was ready to explode.

She stood up suddenly. "I'm going to the ladies' room. Excuse me."

After a few minutes, I was getting fidgety, waiting for her to return. She was taking a long time. I wondered if she'd gotten so mad that she just ditched us all.

I excused myself from the table. "I'll just go check on her."

As I crossed the restaurant to get to the restrooms, I noticed a few people watching me. Shite, the last thing I needed right now was for my cover to be blown. Hudson stood from his spot, ready to intercept anyone who headed my way.

I didn't slow down until I got to the narrow hall that led to the restrooms. My stomach twisted when I saw her. My lass stood alone against the wall, her arms crossed tightly across her chest and a scowl darkening her features. "What's wrong?" As if I didn't know.

Her head whipped my way. "Why did you come here tonight?"

I stopped just in front of her. "Because your mum invited me. She's very persuasive."

She inhaled deeply before lashing out. "You've made this all a thousand times worse. They really like you. Especially my mom. I don't enjoy lying to them."

I raised an eyebrow in disbelief. "You've been lying to them for months, apparently. Suddenly you don't like it?"

Her eyes flashed with fire and my dick got instantly hard. This was the second time tonight. The black dress she wore hugged every curve of her body, and my hands itched to slide all over every single one of them. This girl was breathtakingly gorgeous.

"You're an asshole," she ground out between clenched teeth.

I couldn't help it; I took a step closer to her and growled in warning, "Easy, lass."

Her eyes narrowed. "Don't call me that."

I was staring into those angry blue eyes, trying to restrain myself from kissing her. "Bouncy bumpkin, then?"

"No!" She crossed her arms under her chest, only making her tits look more spectacular. I had no willpower to stop my eyes from sweeping over them. My cock throbbed in appreciation at the sight. I may have licked my lips.

"What should I call you then?"

Her eyes widened, and her forehead creased as she studied me. Emotions crawled over her expressive face. Her blue irises flickered with confusion, then her lips parted slightly in pure disbelief. Finally, the corners of her mouth turned down into an expression of disgust.

Her lip pursed with disdain. "You don't even know what my name is, do you?"

I fidgeted back and forth on my feet, trying to come up with a quick answer, but I couldn't.

She blinked her eyes closed for a second. "God, you're ridiculous."

My hand lifted to cup her cheek, but then I caught myself. I rested it on the wall behind her. "I'm sorry. You never told me it."

She swallowed. "You should just leave. I'm going to go back to the table and tell my parents the truth. I can't keep lying to them."

This had been a big mistake. It would be far easier to just bail right now, as she suggested, but I didn't want to be the asshole she'd accused me of being. I'd do my penance and pay the bill for the dinner and hope to bloody hell this fiasco didn't end up as the lead story on Hollywood Expose.

My voice was soft and filled with regret. "I'm sorry. I didn't intend to upset you tonight. Listen, I'll go back to the table with you. We'll eat our dessert and you can tell them. I'll pick up the bill for all your trouble. It's the least I can do."

# Chapter 6

## Summer

It was a complete clusterfuck. I rarely used vulgar language, not even in my head; needless to say, that word was the perfect encapsulation of my current situation.

Scotty had shown up to dinner and charmed both of my parents so thoroughly, to where they were fawning over him. And I didn't stop it. I had the chance, but I'd been too tongue-tied by a mixture of shock and lust.

Scotty was insanely hot. I'd known that this morning at the coffee shop, but tonight my traitorous body had gone absolutely haywire over him. I couldn't stop imagining him doing wicked things to me. The way he looked at me made me burn.

But I wasn't looking for a boyfriend. Or a quick fling. And even if I was, Scotty wasn't who I'd pick. I'd been listening carefully to him as he talked to my parents. I was fairly certain that he'd lied to them. Or had been very evasive. His tell was whenever his leg started bouncing. He claimed to be a 'music producer' that went on tour with bands, and all the while his leg was bouncing away under the table. Please! It was obvious that he was a roadie. He'd looked just like one this morning when I met him.

Why he had even bothered to get all spiffed up and come to dinner was a mystery. He didn't even know my name, and yet he still came. Why? I still couldn't figure it out, and it scared me. It made me suspicious. I had a bad track record with men, as my mother so eloquently put it, so I didn't trust myself to understand their true motives.

I'd been burned too many times to count. First, my high school boyfriend talked about us getting married and then dumped me the day he left for college. Then there was my college boyfriend of two years who accepted a job offer across the country. He'd abruptly left me behind and then ghosted me. Then came my rebellious phase with Jake, the bad boy my dad hated who rode a motorcycle. He was the one who moved in with me, stole my credit card numbers, and emptied my bank account before taking off. Next was the online dating stage with all the horrible men that were only interested in sex. My mom set me up with the next guy, Grant. We dated for eight months before I found him in bed with another man. Finally, there was the failed affair with my boss. He was more mature — ten years older than me. I thought for sure that things were different that time. It took him more than a year to romance me until I gave in and slept with him. What I was so deluded into thinking was true love turned out to be the same old story.

God, I was hopeless with men. This year, swearing them off had been soothing to my soul. So, when a guy like Scotty pinged my radar, I needed to run the other way as fast as I could.

I felt Scotty following behind me as we headed back to the table. I noticed people in the restaurant staring at him as we walked by. If I had any doubt that he was an exceptionally gorgeous male specimen, the women and men that were checking him out dispelled that. He definitely had charisma — I'd felt it in spades.

Scotty held the chair for me when we got back to the table. My parents were drinking their coffee, but the desserts hadn't arrived yet. Part of me wished I had insisted that Scotty leave — this confession was going to be so humiliating, but part of me was glad that he stayed. It had absolutely nothing to do with my attraction to him, I swear. I just thought he might act as a buffer from my parent's disappointment in me.

Fessing up was going to suck. I sat down and took a deep breath. It was time. "Mom—"

"Sweetie," she interrupted me, holding up a hand for me to stop. "Before you yell at me, let me apologize for making you uncomfortable before. You know I love you to pieces and I worry about you, but I realize I overstepped. My only excuse is that I miss you so much. And you're still my little girl. I'll always worry about you."

Guilt pooled in my stomach as I watched my mom wring her hands apologetically. "I know, Mom. You don't have to worry about me so much. I'm perfectly fine."

She smiled. "It helps that I see with my own two eyes that you're doing fine." She flashed a big smile at Scotty. "I promise I'll let up on the phone calls and all the worrying now that I know you're really okay."

I had to bite my tongue. Was it any wonder I'd faked a boyfriend in the first place? She was only relieved because I had a man looking out for me, and I was about to dispel her of that notion quite unceremoniously.

I didn't need a man. In fact, I was proving it every single day that I spent making it out here in L.A. on my own. That I didn't need a man didn't mean I didn't desire one. All my disastrous relationships were evidence that, deep down, I still wanted a man in my life. Just not the losers that I seemed to perpetually attract, but that was a discussion I'd had with my mom over and over that never seemed to stick. My parents were high-school sweethearts. I'm sure my mother couldn't even imagine living without my dad's support and vice versa.

Regardless of what my mom believed I needed, it was time to rip off the Band-aid and confess the truth — I didn't have a boyfriend. I glanced over at Scotty and he nodded reassuringly to me.

"Mom, there's something I have to..."

My voice trailed off because just then the server arrived at our table with our desserts. Even after our waitress left, my mom was too busy exclaiming over her tasty masterpiece, chocolate mousse topped with raspberries, to hear my confession. I pushed the slice of carrot cake around my plate; the slight reprieve had only made me more nervous.

God, I couldn't believe I got myself into this situation!

"Sweetie," — Mom's gaze was overflowing with happiness — "I have a surprise for you!"

"What kind of surprise?" I asked a bit warily.

She glanced at Dad like they'd been sharing a secret before she answered. "I know your birthday is not until next month, and I know this is last minute, but I booked the four of us for a long weekend getaway at the Crystal Cascadia Spa and Wellness Center in Idaho. It's going to be so much fun!"

Wait. What? "A spa trip?"

"Yes!" She was bursting with excitement. "When you told me you had leftover vacation days from last year that you had to use or lose, I booked it. Your flight leaves from LAX to Boise at 10 a.m. on Thursday. There will be a shuttle waiting at the airport to bring you to the resort, which is about 2 hours north of Boise. Dad and I will fly in from Kentucky, so we'll be several hours behind you."

I sucked in a breath. "Wait, you mean this Thursday? I don't even know if I can take the time off work. And you said the four of us? You want Scotty to go with us? This is crazy!"

My mom laughed, a sweet tinkling sound. "I knew this might be a bit too spontaneous for your liking, but you've been working so hard. I just want to spend some time with my daughter and celebrate your upcoming birthday."

"Mom, I don't know. This is too much. I can't just drop everything and go on vacation."

The smile dropped from her face. "Please say you'll go. It's very important to me."

I felt my dad's intense gaze on me. It was like he was willing me to say yes without speaking any words.

"It's just so last minute. Maybe we can book a trip later? When I can plan for it better."

Her voice was almost a whisper. "I can't wait till later."

The disappointed look in my mom's eyes was making me squirm. "I just don't think I can get away right now."

Her devastation was palpable. Her eyes had gone glassy; I was pretty sure they were filling up with tears. What the hell kind of guilt trip was this?

Scotty's hand found mine and squeezed it under the table. How could the man that didn't even know my name understand how riotously my emotions were swirling, mainly with confusion? His instinct was to comfort me. He sat solidly beside me, a wall of support, and suddenly, I wished he really was my boyfriend. I knew I should remove my hand from his, but I liked the feeling it evoked too much.

I watched while Dad laid his hand on my mom's shoulder in a

calming gesture. He leaned in and spoke quietly to her, soothing her like she was a toddler about to burst into a tantrum. He was treating her like a piece of fragile glass.

My confusion turned to anger. I didn't like being manipulated. All these antics because I couldn't go on a surprise trip my mom foisted on me at the last minute? It seemed so over the top, even for my mom. The more I watched my dad whispering to her, the more I felt like I was about to erupt.

I opened my mouth, about to spout off, when Scotty squeezed my hand in warning. My head turned to him and he shook his head, mouthing the word 'no'. He was telling me to cool it — to stop whatever dumb stuff was about to come out of my mouth.

I bit my tongue, keeping myself from exploding like a recalcitrant child. Scotty was right; the middle of a crowded restaurant was not the place to get into a fight with my parents.

Dad was still rubbing her arm. "You have to tell her, Lara. It's time."

My ears pricked up at the words. "Tell me what?" I demanded.

My mother looked horrified while my dad watched her sympathetically. Something else was going on here and I had no clue what it was, but the reluctance mixed with dread in my mother's eyes had me terrified. I clung to Scotty's hand, waiting for the shoe to drop.

My mother wiped away a single tear that had escaped her eye. "Sweetie, I have breast cancer. I'm going in for surgery and treatment right after the trip. I was hoping we could have one last time together before I was too sick to enjoy it."

Her words hit me like a ton of bricks.

"Mom?" I choked out. The pit of my stomach twisted in a terrible knot. My vision swam and my throat felt like it was closing in on itself.

My mother's lips were trembling. She was struggling to speak so my dad stepped in for her. "After the experimental trial didn't work, her last checkup showed the cancer had spread to some lymph nodes. The doctors felt there was no time left to try anything else. They want to act aggressively. Mom will have the mastectomy and radiation and then chemotherapy, starting about a month after the surgery."

My voice came out shaky. "You said experimental trial? Mom, how long have you known you've had this?"

She took a deep breath before answering. "About six months."

My hand flew to my mouth.

Six months!

I thought about all the time I'd wasted that I could have been spending with my mom. Helping her through this. Comforting her. Instead, I was ignoring her calls. Telling her I was too busy to come home to visit.

"It will be a really tough time for me, but the doctors are optimistic that I have a chance to make it through all this." She sounded more composed now, even as I was falling apart.

"We have every reason to be optimistic." My dad smiled at her like she was the bravest woman alive, and then he turned to me. "After the last results, the oncologist wanted Mom to go into surgery immediately, but Mom insisted on seeing you first. It would mean a lot to her if we could all go on this trip together, Jellybean."

Mom pleaded with her eyes. "I want to spend some time with my baby girl before I go through all that ... misery."

I was crying now. Tears were running down my cheeks, one after the other. I could barely grasp this was happening. Scotty wrapped his arm around me and now he was the one soothing me.

"I'm sorry. I didn't want to tell you." My mom dabbed at her eyes with a napkin. "I didn't want you to worry about me. I'm going to be okay, sweetie."

I sniffled in a very unladylike manner, and Scotty handed me a cocktail napkin. "Mom, I can move back home and help you after the surgery—"

She cut me off before I got much further. "That's exactly what I don't want. You're not going to give up your job and your life here in L.A. to run back home to nurse me. Dad will take care of me and we'll hire help if we need it."

I blew my nose on the napkin and wiped the tears from my face with the back of my hand. "I just want to help you."

Mom smiled lovingly at me. "What would help me the most — what would make me the happiest — is if you two would go on the spa retreat with Dad and me."

I nodded as I wiped away a few stray tears that had fallen. "Of course, we'll go."

# Chapter 7

---

**Knox**

MY NIGHT HAD GONE downhill so fast that my head was still spinning. I'd gone to dinner, goaded by Ghost, on a lark, thinking I'd amuse myself trading barbs with an American princess whose beauty made my cock twitch. Instead, I'd ended up embroiled in the middle of a weighty and depressing conversation.

Her mum had cancer. Fuck. Suddenly, acting as the fake boyfriend and playing around with everyone's emotions seemed anything but harmless. When the conversation turned personal, downright uncomfortable, I'd wanted to bolt. I shouldn't have witnessed all that. I was an arsehole of the highest order.

After her parents had dropped that bomb, Lara decided she needed her rest. She insisted we go out and enjoy the night without them. My lass wasn't about to argue with her mum anymore; she'd shut down. I could see panic reflected on her face: that along with guilt, fear, and worry were all vying for the top spot with her.

Sure, I wanted to bolt, but I couldn't abandon her now; she needed some time to process the news. To decompress. But I wasn't sure where we should go. It was too cold to spend any time outside, and she was wearing heels way too high for any significant amount of walking. Where could we go indoors where no one would recognize me?

I sent a quick text to Hudson, who was still sitting twenty feet away, watching over me. Jim and Lara had already left and my lass was in the ladies' room fixing herself after crying, while I settled the bill that I had remained firm upon paying despite Jim's protests.

I rejected Hudson's first suggestion, a coffee/dessert cafe, but then okayed his suggestion of a jazz club. At least the lights would be low and I could listen to some good music. He texted me the address and said he'd make all the necessary arrangements.

When she returned from the restroom, I couldn't even tell that she'd just been weeping with sorrow. Her stunning beauty struck me all over again. If the perfect woman had been molded precisely to meet my every specification, she'd look just like her. No wonder I was caught knee-deep in this mess.

She looked at me and frowned. "I should just go home. You don't want to hang out with me; I'd be terrible company anyway..." Her voice trailed off.

I felt bad for her. She'd had a rough night. In fact, she'd been utterly knocked down on her arse. She certainly wasn't the feisty lass I'd sparred with this morning.

I stepped close to her and gently touched her elbow. Even though we were still practically strangers, I felt the strong urge to comfort her. "I know a place we can sit and get a drink. We don't even have to talk if you don't want."

She nodded with relief. "I don't want to go home and face my parents just yet. I don't want to face reality."

My phone pinged, and I glanced down at the text from Hudson — a car was waiting out front.

Just then, a high-pitched shriek emanated from someone to the left of me. "Oh, my God! Knox!"

It was time to leave. Out of the periphery of my vision, I saw Hudson rising to intercept the teenaged shrieker who was making a beeline straight for me. Thankfully, my lass seemed to be lost in thought as I hastily guided her out of the restaurant and into the waiting cab.

She didn't speak during the short drive to the jazz club, just stared forlornly out the window. When we arrived, the club was already fairly full, so the hostess seated us at a table near the back of the room.

The atmosphere was perfect. The crowd was relaxed, mesmerized by the elegant female vocalist in the spotlight, who was crooning into the microphone with her sultry voice. Behind her, the band played popular cover songs with a Bossa Nova flair. I focused on the guitar, but the seamless blend of music from the guitar, piano, bass, and drums accompanied by the saxophone and perfected with the various percussion shakers soon enthralled me as a whole.

We were sitting on the same side of the tiny table so that we could both watch the band. Blue and purple lighting enveloped the club, creating a cozy and romantic atmosphere, but my lass was still shell-shocked. She wasn't paying attention to the music. When our drinks arrived, I scooted my chair closer to hers, so that I could drape my arm over the back of her chair. She didn't object or flinch away from me, so we both sat in silence while the band played song after song.

I had almost finished my second beer when she finally turned to me and said, "I'm sorry."

I kept my voice low even though we were near the back of the club and wouldn't be disturbing anyone by talking. "What for?"

She chewed on her bottom lip. "I'm sure this isn't what you had in mind when you showed up tonight."

I couldn't keep my eyes off her lush lips. God, I wanted to kiss her. "This is perfect."

"You like this band?" she asked.

"I love it. I love all types of music."

She leaned a little closer to me. "That's right. You're a ... what did you call it? A music producer?"

So, she had been listening when I was talking to her dad. I hadn't been sure. I thought she had been too busy stewing in her anger at me for showing up.

When I didn't answer right away, she continued, "And you said you travel — you go on tours with bands. With popular bands? Like actual rock bands?"

"Yeah." I squirmed a bit. I should come clean. Let her know I was the guitarist for a hugely popular band. But every single girl I'd met in the past five years had wanted to be with me only because I was in a rock band. They didn't give a shit about me. I was interchangeable with my four other bandmates for all they cared. Mostly, it didn't bother me, but it was certainly refreshing talking to someone who didn't know. She wasn't trying to get into my pants solely to boast about it on social media. Unfortunately, she wasn't trying to get into my pants at all.

She laughed, amusement lighting up her entire face. "So, basically, you're a roadie."

I lifted an eyebrow at her dig. "It's more complicated than that."

"Uh-huh."

My fingers were tracing little circles on her shoulder. "And what do you do, Jellybean?"

"Ugh, don't call me that!" she protested. "That's what my dad calls me, even though I'm not ten years old anymore." She rolled her eyes but then answered my question. "I'm a marketing associate for an international cosmetics company."

My lips tipped upward. "Ahh. So you play with makeup all day?"

Her mouth fell open in shock, but then she giggled. "Touché." It was the first look of genuine happiness to flit across her face since I'd met her, and I wanted to make it happen over and over again. Christ, she was achingly beautiful.

The waitress came by and asked if we wanted another drink. I looked over, deferring to her, but she shook her head. "No, I should get back home soon."

I had to hide my disappointment. I didn't want to let her go just yet. The night was young, and I hadn't spent nearly enough time with her. There was something about her that intrigued me beyond reason.

She took a sip of the cocktail she'd been neglecting. "I don't know how I'm going to tell my parents the truth. It was supposed to be a harmless little fib, but what I did seems extra cruel now."

It made little sense to me. A girl like her would have no trouble getting a boyfriend. "Why did you make up a fake boyfriend tale to your mum?"

"I did it to get her off my back." She huffed out an exasperated breath of air. "My mother was always so worried about me living out here in L.A. She was constantly pestering me, asking me if I'd met anyone. She didn't believe that I could be happy on my own. So, instead of dealing with all her nagging, I made up a fake boyfriend, and voilà, she stopped hounding me so much. It sounds so pathetic, I know. Especially now that I know that she's been going through so much the whole time."

It was momentarily too loud to speak as the band ended a song and the audience clapped their approval. After the next song began, I leaned closer to her, subtly inhaling her feminine scent, and asked, "How long have you had this imaginary boyfriend?"

She cringed with embarrassment. "About six months. For as long as she's had cancer, apparently. I feel awful. I was ignoring her calls when she began asking so many questions about you. Well, not about you. About the fake boyfriend. Not that you're the real boyfriend. Ugh. I'm not even drunk and I sound so dumb."

I laughed at her babbling uncertainty. It was so different from her sarcastic, sassy side. Still, I could see that she was worried, but her mum seemed like a kind-hearted soul. "You think she'll be upset about all this?"

She bit her lip and nodded. "Yeah, I think she will be, unfortunately. She was so excited to meet you finally, and she really likes you. Did you see how disappointed she was when I pushed back on the spa trip? If I had known about her cancer, I would never have done any of this. Now it's going to be unbearable to confess. I'm so selfish. God, I'm such a terrible daughter."

Her eyes were welling up with tears by the time she finished. The look of sadness on her face gutted me. I just wanted to make her smile again. "Don't beat yourself up over it. It was a wee white lie, and you never meant to hurt her. And she didn't tell you about the cancer either. I think she'll understand when you explain it to her."

She swiped angrily at a tear that spilled from her eye and ran down her cheek. "She's just dealing with so much right now and I don't want to upset her before her surgery. In fact, I may not tell her the truth until after it's over. I'll just tell her you have a work obligation at the last minute and can't go on the spa trip. Then I'll tell her the real story after she's recovered from the surgery."

"I'll go on the spa trip with you," I blurted out.

It slipped from my lips without much thought. It was either the best idea or the worst idea I'd ever had. Most likely the worst, but there was something about this lass. I didn't want to let her go just yet.

Her lips pinched tightly together. "What? You would do that?"

She hadn't outright rejected the idea, so that was good.

"Aye. I'm not doing anything much right now and I was just thinking earlier today that I could use a vacation." Holding my breath, I waited for her answer. I was suddenly aware of how badly I wanted this. Of how badly I wanted her.

It was a preposterous suggestion, but she seemed to waver back and forth as she contemplated it. "We barely know each other. A spa weekend together seems a bit extreme."

I leaned back in my chair, affecting an air of casualness I didn't feel. "I've never been to a spa before. Do they have manly stuff to do there? Things besides manicures and seaweed wraps?"

"Don't knock seaweed wraps until you've tried them." She arched a brow and then leaned forward, resting her elbow on the table and propping her head on her hand as she studied me. "Wouldn't we just be prolonging the lie if you came?"

I didn't even realize that I was rubbing a lock of her silky hair in between my fingers. "I would go if it would keep your mum stress-free and happy. Besides, I'm kind of curious about the spa. I think it would be fun." I flashed her a devilish smile. "And we're friends now, right? So, you wouldn't be lying to her anymore — technically. I'm a boy and I'm your friend. I really am your boy-friend, Miss Meadows."

Her eyes narrowed. "What a great boyfriend you are! You still don't even know my name."

I leaned in close to her. "Are you ever going to tell me it, lass?"

Her eyes closed briefly, and she muttered. "I can't believe I'm even considering doing this whole thing."

"Why won't you tell me your name? It must be really hideous, I bet," I teased with a smirk on my face.

I waited for an answer, but she kept stubbornly quiet.

Tapping a finger to my lips, I pretended I was thinking hard. "Is it Brunhilda?"

That got a little laugh. "No."

"Eunice?"

"Oh God, no. My name's not hideous. It's just a little cheesy."

"Cheesy?" My brows furrowed. What kind of name was cheesy? "Is it Brie?"

She chuckled but shook her head.

"Feta? Gouda?"

This time, a burst of laughter escaped her lips. She fake slapped at my arm and her hand remained on my biceps. "No! It's Summer."

Summer.

It was a beautiful name. Perfect for her.

"It suits you." I stared into her eyes and felt like I was getting lost there. "It's not cheesy."

She frowned. "Summer Meadows? My parents must have been in a hippy stage when they named me."

Summer Meadows. Shite. Even her name turned me on. "Ah, I get it now, but I think it's very pretty."

She sized me up and then shrugged. "I guess it's no worse than Scotty from Scotland."

I froze. Now was my chance to come clean and tell her that Scotty was a nickname my mates called me. And, to tell her about the band and our success, but I hesitated a few seconds too long, and then the opportunity was forgotten.

"Okay, let's do this!" Her eyes were sparkling. "Let's go on the spa trip together. For my mom."

A smile spread across my face. "Really?"

"Yeah, but don't think we're going to sleep together. There will be no sex or anything remotely like it. Just so you know."

I sure as hell wasn't going to force her into anything, but I think we both knew that it was going to happen. There was too much smoldering chemistry between us. I wanted her more than I'd wanted any other woman in a long time. Maybe in forever.

I nodded. "So, we're going as friends. Got it."

She bit into her bottom lip. "I'm going to regret this. I just know it."

There was no way I was going to let her back out now. "What's there to regret? It'll be a low-key weekend of pampering and massages. Pure zen relaxation. It's exactly what you and your mum need. Don't worry, you won't even know I'm there."

She rolled her eyes at my last statement. "Somehow I doubt that."

I'd take the win and move on before she changed her mind. A prickle of unease stirred in my gut over how much I wanted to do this, but I shook it off. Why the hell not go? I wasn't doing a damn thing next weekend, and I wanted to be around this girl that made me feel something.

Before we parted for the night, we exchanged information so that we could coordinate the details of the trip. Then, I'd tucked Summer into a taxi before heading home myself.

I inhaled the cool night air. I felt settled. Less antsy. Maybe it was because I had something to look forward to.

Summer Meadows.

# Chapter 8

---

**Summer**

WITH EACH ANNOUNCEMENT, I grew more anxious. First, they called the customers with special needs, then the first-class ticket holders, families with young children and strollers, and military members to board. Next came the long list of frequent fliers, premium members, and award cardholders. Ten minutes later, general boarding began with the back of the plane. By the time the front section was called, the waiting area at the gate was empty.

The lady behind the desk lifted the microphone to her mouth and looked directly at me, one hand on her hip as she challenged me with a raised eyebrow. "All remaining passengers on flight 252 to Boise may now board."

I reluctantly grabbed the backpack that was leaning against my foot and stood. It was a good thing my backpack was small enough to stow under my seat because I'd never find room in the overhead bins at this point. The flight was packed. Why the hell were so many people going to Boise, Idaho, on a random Thursday morning?

I couldn't deny the disappointment I felt as I headed down the jetway toward the plane. He didn't show.

It wasn't surprising. Even though he'd been slightly flirty over text when I'd initially sent him the information for today's flight, he hadn't reached out to me in the three days since. Worried that I hadn't heard from him, I'd sent him a text this morning — see you at the airport. I waited for an answer with bated breath, but nothing.

I didn't blame him for not wanting to come on this trip. After all, it was a spa weekend accompanied by my parents, hardly a guy's fantasy vacation. Plus, we barely knew each other, and he certainly didn't owe me or my parents anything.

Rationally, I understood it — I even thought it was for the best. Never mind that I'd been fantasizing about him all week. Why did he have to be so hot? There was this running fantasy that looped over and over in my head. We'd show up at the spa hotel and discover that my mother only booked one hotel room for us. Oh, my gosh! And there were no more rooms available — the hotel was booked solid. Oh no! Now what? We'd have to share a room. Gasp. Of course, there was only one bed in the room. Heavens! But I wasn't a cruel person, and we were both adults. We could share the bed as long as no one crossed the giant pillow barrier I'd erect down the center of the bed. Quite sensible! Of course, I would be too irresistible for him to withstand and during the night...

The fantasy always ended the same way with crazy-hot sex replete with mind-blowing orgasms. Plural. Too bad I only knew about multiple orgasms from raunchy novels. In reality, they were as fantastical to me as unicorns.

Thinking about orgasms and unicorns, I headed down the aisle of the plane until I reached row 12. A woman with close-cropped gray hair whose nose was buried deep in a paperback novel occupied the window seat. She didn't acknowledge my presence; she was giving off 'don't talk to me' vibes, which was fine with me.

I dropped my backpack into the empty middle seat and plopped down onto the aisle seat in a huff. My ticket was for the middle seat, but since I knew no one would be showing up for it, I gladly took the aisle. The empty seat next to me was just a bitter reminder that Scotty didn't show.

He should have texted me that he couldn't make it. He was so rude. Even if his excuse was lame, or an obviously fake one, it would have been better. But he didn't even bother. He ghosted me. I was ghosted by my fake boyfriend.

While I kept trying to deny my disappointment, I knew I was. I almost felt ... crushed.

Ugh, I gave myself a mental shake.

Snap out of it. You've only known the guy for about a day. Altogether, only a handful of hours. And there was something darn suspicious about a man who didn't have a visible or easily findable social media presence.

Okay, so I'd spent some time stalking Scotty online. Or at least attempting to stalk him. It was a matter of safety, really. A girl's got to know what she's dealing with. He could be a serial killer. Not that I thought he'd list that on his profile, but...

Anyway, a lot could be inferred about guys from the photos they posted — what kind of friends they had, what type of activities they were into, and what places they visited all painted a picture. Any photos that contained women could give good insight. My intricate method of discernment boiled down to this: pictures with mom — good, pictures with strippers — bad.

This method of judging a man was not foolproof (hence the history of bad decisions my mother had mentioned), but that didn't stop my overwhelming need to find pictures of my fake boyfriend to drool over.

This wasn't my first social media stalking rodeo; I knew to begin with Instagram. There were so many Scottys or Scott Stewarts that I couldn't believe it. I'd even looked up Scotland Stewarts, just in case. Jeezus, there were so many. Just when I thought I got to the bottom of the list after scrolling for pages, a whole new set of Scottys appeared. It took over an hour to check out all the accounts that I couldn't discard right away based on the profile picture.

I was reasonably sure Scotty wasn't on Instagram. Next up was Facebook. Everyone had a Facebook account to keep in touch with their parents and older relatives, right? Well, hundreds of Scotty Stewarts did, that's for sure.

I couldn't find any accounts with a profile picture of my Scotty McHottie to verify it was him, but I found way too many of their accounts with the default featureless gray blob or profile pictures of dogs or such that I couldn't rule out. It took hours of my time going down that rabbit hole trying to hit pay dirt without any luck.

When I was surfing LinkedIn, I knew I was getting desperate. I wasn't sure if rock band roadies had LinkedIn profiles, but I checked. After hours of fruitless searching, I gave up in defeat. Either he wasn't on social media or he was super low-key about it, and either option was suspect. He must have something to hide.

So, it was just as well that he didn't show up. I would be just fine on this trip without him. Better even.

There was no doubt about it: Scotty was a bad idea. I'm not even sure why I agreed to let him come in the first place. Yet another bad decision. I did it for Mom, but let's face it, if Scotty wasn't a hottie, I would have kicked him to the curb. I was deeply mired in a self-imposed dry spell and Scotty was just the type of guy that could push me over the edge and make me break the promise I made to myself. I'd be making the same mistakes I always made — falling into the pattern. He was trouble. My kind of trouble. Which made it worse.

The flight attendants were walking down the aisles and closing all the overhead bins. I grabbed my backpack and yanked open the zipper of the front pocket. I dug through the random assortment of junk stuffed inside until I found a stick of gum and my AirPods.

This was a three-hour flight. I still didn't want to confess my sins to my mother right before her surgery, so that was plenty of time to think of an excuse to tell my parents why I was solo this weekend.

My head was buried between my legs, trying to stuff my bloated backpack under my seat, when I heard his voice.

His rich baritone dripping with that sexy accent sounded like pure silky seduction. "Excuse me, lass. But I believe you're in my seat."

I whipped my head up so fast that I was momentarily dizzy. I blame that for the way his name slipped from my lips, all breathless and throaty.

The sight of him had my brain cells scrambling and my heart racing. He looked so good. His clothes weren't a designer label or even a discernable brand, but they fit so perfectly on him, showcasing the incredibly fit body beneath. He wore a plain gray henley long-sleeved shirt that highlighted his broad chest, the muscles in his arms, and the outline of his defined pecs. He was dressed more casually today, more like when I'd met him on the sidewalk, in jeans with a baseball cap on his head and scruff on his face. My eyes were mere inches from his crotch and my mouth was watering, imagining his body without any clothes obstructing my perusal.

The faint smirk on his face told me he knew exactly where my mind was going, but I didn't have time to set him straight — even though he was right.

A beautiful flight attendant, with perfect porcelain skin, bright red lips, and her hair pulled up in a professional yet saucy-looking chignon, approached from behind him.

She placed a hand on his biceps. "I'm so sorry. I'll take care of this for you." The smile dropped from her face when she glanced at me. "Ma'am, I need to see your boarding pass."

Ma'am? Did she just ma'am me?

Scotty's eyes lit with mischief as he watched my face turn sour. He chuckled low in his throat. "No, it's fine. I don't want to cause any trouble. I don't mind sitting in the center seat."

"It's absolutely no trouble at all," she spoke seductively, practically licking his ear. Then she looked down at me with a frown.

Really? It was my parents who paid for these tickets. Why didn't Scotty stick up for me? Or, at least, tell her we were together.

The flight attendant held out her hand for my boarding pass. Fine! I made an audible huff and then stood up so that I could slide into the center seat.

She still had her hand resting possessively on his arm. "Can I store your bag for you?"

"Thank you." He flashed her a dimpled smile.

"It's my pleasure," she purred. She oozed sexuality.

I gagged, as I could almost smell the pheromones she was shooting his way.

She bent slightly to take the handle of his bag, giving him a nice view of her cleavage. "My name's Cynthia. Just give me a shout if you need anything. Anything at all."

I bet Scotty never worried about overhead bin space like the rest of us, with all the Cynthias running around feeling him up and purring in his ear. It felt like forever, but finally, she was walking away, rolling his bag, and he was sitting down next to me.

His amused smile made my heart stutter in my chest. "Hi, Sunshine."

My heart was still beating irregularly. I'd thought he wasn't going to show up and then he'd just sauntered in at the very last minute like it was no big deal.

"You're late." It was the only thing I could think of to say; I was still so flustered by his sudden appearance.

"I made it." He shrugged, a smile tugging on his lips. "It was close. They held the cabin door for me."

The lady next to me, who couldn't spare me a glance when I arrived, was making eyes at Scotty. Jeez, did every female swoon over this man? He was entirely attractive enough to dampen panties by looks alone, but it had to be that sinful accent in his deep, velvety voice that pushed women over the edge. I vowed not to be so obvious like the lady sitting next to me. Or the fawning Cynthia. He seemed to have a big enough ego as it was.

"Of course, Cynthia held the door for you." Her name came out in a jealous sneer. Oops. "She was busy spraying her sex pheromones all over you like a skunk."

Laughter danced in his eyes. "Why Summer, are you jealous that she slipped me her number?"

My mouth dropped open in surprise. "She did not!"

"Well, she put something in here." He reached into his back pocket and pulled out a small piece of paper. He glanced at it and smiled before handing it to me.

Handwritten on the paper was a phone number, followed by 'Call me tonight' and her name, Cyndie, the letter 'i' dotted with a heart.

"That skank!"

Cynthia was slowly heading down the aisle towards them, performing the final check of the cabin. Between asking passengers to stow their carry-ons, close their tray tables, and buckle up, she kept glancing directly at Scotty with a sultry stare. She'd even wetted her red lips with the tip of her tongue a few times. She looked like a starving barracuda heading our way.

I wanted to gouge her eyes out. How dare she? I was sitting right here. He was my boyfriend. My hackles were not only raised, they were rocketing out of the earth's orbit. My blood was boiling.

I couldn't control my overpowering emotions. I placed my hand on Scotty's cheek, intent on making him look away from her. That was my intent, but somehow I'd twisted my body towards his and pulled his face to mine so that I could kiss him. And it wasn't an innocent peck on the lips.

My goodness, I was making out with him with lots of tongue and breathy moans. All that intense emotion I'd felt had suddenly channeled into pure unbridled lust.

I forgot about everything. There was no Cynthia. No airplane full of passengers. Not even my overwhelming urge to stake my claim, because his kiss was sending fire scorching through my veins.

He had quickly taken control of my overly eager kiss; his lips were masterful in teasing a response, but his tongue sliding against mine would be my undoing. A jolt of pure need sizzled down my spine. Desire rocked through me, throbbing hot and wicked between my thighs. Each thrust of his tongue pushed that desire higher until I was moaning for relief.

Just when I thought I might explode from sheer pleasure, he slowed our kiss to a sensual dance, a deep and toe-curlingly thorough exploration of sliding tongues that was even more intimate than before.

Ecstasy pulsed through every nerve ending in my body. The hot throbbing between my legs morphed into a clawing ache of pure need. The kiss had stoked an unquenchable thirst in me. I needed all of him. Touching me. Kissing me. Filling me.

He pulled his lips off me with a stifled groan. I only realized his hand had been anchoring my head to his lips when he disentangled it from my hair and pulled back. I was still dazed, even as the plane came slowly back into focus. His drugging kiss had made me forget everything.

Hadn't I been the one to initiate the kiss? Yes. Because of Cynthia. I quickly looked around for her. She was nowhere in sight. Ha! I sat back in my seat again. She may have thrown down the gauntlet, but I had won the battle. The momentary cocky feeling quickly washed away.

I had gotten completely carried away with that kiss. I'd only meant to stake my claim — a claim I didn't really have — and put Cynthia in her place. That's what I'd meant, but who knew what Scotty thought of the whole thing? My face burned red. I was so embarrassed by what I'd done.

Before Scotty could say anything, I quickly put in my earbuds and pretended to listen to the music. We didn't talk as the plane took off. I was lost in thought.

That kiss was too good. There was no denying that I wanted Scotty, and that was dangerous. I'd completely lost myself in that crazy kiss. It was earth-shattering. Soul changing. The best kiss I'd ever had. I couldn't even imagine how good sex with him would be.

The little devil on my shoulder was whispering into my ear. Why not? Why not have sex with him? Use him to satisfy that itch. You don't have to fall for him.

It was a terrible idea. A big mistake. One that I'd made many times before. I wasn't looking for mindless sex or frenzied, meaningless lust. I was looking for a partner. Someone that loved me and wanted to be with me long term.

And Scotty didn't fit that bill. He was probably the king of one-night stands. He followed bands around for a living, and I wasn't naïve about that lifestyle. I'm sure he slept with a different girl in each new city as he traveled with the musicians. He was hot, so he probably had twenty girls a night lining up to give him blowjobs or more, all for the favor of meeting the band members. He was the polar opposite of what I was looking for.

I was a confident woman. I was secure in my looks. I was confident that men wanted me. Sexually, at least. It was after that when it all fell apart. I didn't have what it took to keep a man. Whatever the hell that evasive 'thing' was. I'd learned that lesson over and over until my self-worth was bound to take a hit. My confidence and pride had ended up in the gutter, but over the past year, I'd been slowly building them back up by avoiding the mistakes of my past. Avoiding men. Especially men like Scotty.

A tap on my arm from Scotty's fingers broke into my thoughts and had my pulse spiking again. I took out my earbuds and turned to him expectantly, my heartbeat thundering in my ear.

"Summer..."

Just the way he said my name sent shivers skittering down my spine.

When he didn't say anything, I blurted out, "We need to talk."

# Chapter 9

---

**Knox**

*D*OMAIN, *K*INGDOM, *P*HYLUM, *C*LASS, *O-something*, *Family, Genus, Species.*

Dear King Phillip came over for good soup.

What the hell did the 'O' stand for? Ocean? Octopus? Orbits? I'd been grappling with it for at least five minutes, but I couldn't remember it for the life of me. I'd been forced to memorize that list years ago in biology class, never to be used again in my life. Well, except now, to tamp down my raging boner. I guess it turned out to be useful knowledge after all.

Christ, my balls were still aching after that scorching kiss. I'd been totally thrown for a loop when she put her lips on mine, but it only took me a second or two to get over my shock and kiss her back, no holds barred.

Everything about that kiss had been perfection — her soft lips, the way her tongue tangled with mine, her sweet taste. Every second we kissed I was pulled farther under her spell. It was intoxicating. I think I was hopelessly addicted after just one hit.

That kiss had spun up a torrent of need that utterly consumed me like a raging inferno. I'd wanted to fuck her right there on the plane. Push my dick right between those lush lips. Trail my lips all over her body until I buried my head between her thighs.

I had been so ridiculously close to losing all control; it was a miracle I'd been able to pull away before I did something stupid in front of a planeload of people. I'd been fighting my crazy response ever since, breathless and close to bursting, while she looked composed and unaffected. In fact, she'd even looked around to make sure that the man-eating flight attendant had gotten the message.

I was absolutely positive I saw fire blazing in her gaze before she kissed me and I swore I heard her making little mewling sounds and moaning into my mouth while our tongues tangled. But, she acted like the kiss meant nothing. My cock was still hard as a rock and throbbing while she'd casually popped in her earbuds as if nothing had just happened.

I couldn't remember ever losing control like that and never from a kiss. I'd kissed plenty of women, but I didn't spend a lot of time kissing them — on the mouth, at least — because it never really turned me on that much. I was usually quick to move sex along to the good part. But, Summer? I could kiss her all day. I couldn't wait to do it again.

I'd finally gotten my dick back under control, but I was still mulling over that intense physical reaction to her and that kiss. I couldn't have gotten any harder if her lips had been wrapped around my cock instead. I wanted her so badly; I physically ached to bury myself deep inside her.

Fuck.

I had to stop thinking about that kiss because my dick was coming back to life.

*Domain, Kingdom, Phylum, Class, O-something, Family, Genus, Species.*

The plane was halfway to Idaho before I composed myself enough to face her. I craved her attention and she'd been studiously ignoring me, so I tapped lightly on her arm. She pulled out her earbuds and looked at me expectantly.

"Summer…" I'd never been at a loss for words when talking to a lass before. Shite. I didn't even know what to say to her.

Maybe she read some of the confusion whirling in my eyes because she blurted out, "We need to talk."

Words that no man ever wanted to hear.

I suppressed a groan and schooled my features. I pushed aside all the crazy notions that were going on inside my head, talking myself down. I was reading more into the lust that I felt because I hadn't had sex in a while. Not since before I went to Scotland. Not since the end of the tour. And, it was starting to get to me. There was no doubt how much I wanted Summer. I'd wanted her from the moment I first laid eyes on her. There was nothing more to it than that.

"Okay," I leaned back in my seat, feigning a calmness I didn't feel.

She chewed on her bottom lip for a moment before declaring, "We need rules."

This didn't sound good. "Rules?" I grumbled. "What kind of rules?"

She looked me directly in the eye. "Actually, there's really only one rule." Heat bloomed on her cheeks. "There will be no sex," she declared primly.

It was cute how she still thought we weren't going to have sex. And her blush gave away just how much she'd been thinking about it.

"No sex. Us?" I pointed my finger back and forth between us.

She crossed her arms over her chest. "We are so not having sex. We will let my parents continue to think we are, but we will absolutely not do the deed. Get it out of your head. Don't even think about it."

I was internally rolling my eyes. "I didn't come for sex, Sunshine." I smiled lazily at her. "I came for pampering, seaweed wraps, and massages."

The lady sitting in the window seat shifted in her seat and subtly leaned toward us, and I realized that she was listening to our conversation. Shite. I had to be careful. If she recognized me and was recording this little exchange, our entire conversation could end up as the top story on Hollywood Expose and go viral.

Part of the reason I was late for the flight was to lessen the chance of Summer finding out who I was. I didn't want to be at an airport with Summer where someone was bound to recognize me. People were always on the lookout for celebrities at LAX.

As it was, I ended up taking some pictures for a few fans and signed some autographs, and that started to attract even more people, but Summer wasn't around to witness any of it. I was sure the pictures were already posted to social media, but Summer wasn't likely to see them without knowing my real name. I wasn't too worried about being recognized once we got to Idaho. I was confident that it'd be much easier to remain incognito at a spa in Idaho than in Los Angeles. At least that's what I'd told Vector Security when I convinced them not to follow me on this trip.

The other reason I was late was that I'd purchased a first-class ticket — the only seat still available — under my real name and I didn't want Summer to know. I was worried they wouldn't let me board the plane when the name on my ID didn't match my boarding pass. In the end, they barely glanced at my ID.

I'd gone to a bit of trouble to mislead Summer about my real identity and I couldn't deny that I felt a stab of guilt now. There was something about her thinking I was an ordinary bloke that made me feel good. I wanted her to want me, not a member of Ghost Parker. I didn't want her to fuck me for some vanity points on her social media. I didn't want to be her one shot to fuck a rockstar. Somehow, none of that shit had bothered me too much before. I'd had too many meaningless fucks on and off tour to keep count, but Summer felt different.

Still, I was lying to her. The guilt took me by surprise. I had rationalized going on this weekend trip as something that would be fun. It would give me something to do, and sure, I couldn't deny that I'd spent the week fantasizing about this dream girl who managed to invade my every thought and thoroughly intrigue me. I told myself that she'd never have to know about Ghost Parker. And if she someday did find out who I was, I'd be long gone.

That kiss had me rethinking things. I'd never felt anything like it. Not with any of the girls on tour. Not even with Aila. There was something about that kiss and my response to it that shook me to my core. And it scared the shite out of me.

Summer was frowning at me with narrowed eyes. "Not only are we not having sex, but there will be no sex with anyone this weekend. Got it? No skanky flight attendants, no handsy masseuses. No happy endings. This will be a weekend of abstinence."

I leaned closer to her and kept my voice low so only she could hear me. "And that goes for you too?"

She paused for a second then nodded.

I flashed her a sly grin. "Hmmm. We'll see."

The crazy lust this lass stirred in me might have turned my brain to mush and might have me confused about all sorts of strange feelings she'd awakened in me, but there was one thing I was sure of and that was my ability to seduce her. She'd be begging me for sex by the end of the weekend.

She ignored my comment and tucked a lock of hair behind her ear. "So, now that that's settled, we need to get to know a little more about each other. Just so my parents don't get suspicious."

I held my hands out palms up like I was an open book. "What do you want to know? Ask away."

She thought for a moment. "How long have you been in the States?"

I did a quick calculation in my head. "About 6 years."

"Why did you come here?"

"I wanted to get out of Scotland. Explore the world a bit." It was mostly true.

She tapped a finger on the armrest between us. "Do you have family here? In America?"

"No. They're all in Scotland."

"Where do you live currently?"

I shifted in my seat. "I have an apartment in L.A."

"Do you live alone?"

"Yes."

"Your parents are in Scotland?" Her questions were coming in rapid fire.

"Yes."

"Any siblings?"

I nodded. "Two younger brothers."

"You miss them?"

I paused a moment before answering. "I just saw them. I was in Scotland two weeks ago."

She raised an eyebrow. "Do you go back there often?"

Fuck no. I avoided it like the plague. That was only the second time I'd been back in six years and I'd only gone because I had to in order to renew my visa. I'd counted down every torturous day until I got out of there.

I knew my mum missed me and that made me feel bad about staying away. My father was a silent, stoic bastard, so who knew if he cared? I'd drifted apart from my brothers so visiting with them had felt strained and awkward.

Just being back in Scotland had been even more horrible this time than the last which was saying something. No one in Scotland had heard of Ghost Parker the first time, but after *Okay Babe* had put us on the map worldwide, my local celebrity status had grown exponentially. Once it got out that I was back in town, I was hounded non-stop and the local press had a field day picking up the story about when my fiancee died. All the old shit was drudged up again.

I hated being there. It had stirred up bad memories. Things I wasn't ready to deal with. Even my old recurring nightmares had started up again. I'd felt trapped back home in Scotland and I didn't have my music to keep me grounded or my bandmates to keep me sane.

I had been sucked right back into the past. Drenched in guilt and crushing anger. Reliving the pain and heartbreak. Drowning in a swirl of confusion mixed in with sorrow and a hefty dose of anxiety.

After being in Scotland for a week, I'd tried to sneak into the local pub to avoid the fans and local press and drown my sorrows, but peace eluded me even there. I'd run into an old mate. I hadn't seen him in six years. He tried to talk to me, but I blew him off and walked right back out the door. He was once my best mate, but now the sight of him made me physically sick.

When I finally returned to L.A., I was still mired down by my past. I couldn't shake it. I was untethered. Restless and bored. I had too much time on my hands while Ghost Parker was on break. And then I ran into Summer. She'd lit up something inside me. I was no longer stewing in the past.

Summer was waiting for my response, so I shook off my thoughts of Scotland and forced myself to recall what she'd asked: Do you go back there often?

"I don't get the chance to go back that much." That sounded reasonable. "Is this third degree finished yet?"

"I've got one more." She looked like she had about a hundred more questions, but I guess she could see that I was finished. "Do you play the bagpipes?"

The sassy lass was mocking me and she looked quite proud of herself. A mischievous smile slowly lit her face even while she fought to contain it. Lord, she was beautiful. She was like a burst of sunshine on a cloudy day. She was goodness, happiness, and joy all rolled up into one feisty little package.

What the hell was wrong with me? I felt like a fool reciting poetry in my head to her beauty. At any moment, I might break into a song with lyrics as equally stupid as *Okay Babe*, but hell, maybe we'd have another mega-hit on our hands.

I smiled slyly at her cheeky bagpipe question. "I have, but I don't. I'm more of a guitar man."

"Guitar, hmmm. Bagpipes are so much sexier." The corner of her lips twitched upward. "So, what do you want to know about me?"

Right now, I wanted to know what she looked like naked, but I kept that to myself. Beyond that, I couldn't think of anything off the top of my head to ask her. I was stumped.

I'd studiously avoided getting to know any woman for years. I hadn't gone on a date with a woman — no dinners, no movies, no solo time together unless we were naked — since I was in school. For what I wanted from a woman, no-strings raunchy sex, I didn't have to talk to them. Or care about them.

And no lass had asked any questions about me that didn't have to do with the band. After years of not caring, I'd simply forgotten how to converse with a lass like a normal person.

The silence, while I scrambled to think of what to ask, was getting uncomfortable, so I quickly decided a variation on the same questions she asked me would have to do. "Where did you grow up? Your mum mentioned Kentucky, I think?"

"That's right. I was born and raised in southern Kentucky. My parents still live there in the same house I grew up in. I went to the University of Kentucky for college where I was a Business, Management, and Marketing major and graduated cum laude. I was president of Theta Kappa Delta sorority senior year and won Sorority Woman of the Year..."

Her answer was nowhere near as succinct as mine. In fact, she was still listing all the philanthropic organizations, women's clubs, and historic preservation societies she had been a member of in Kentucky. I was listening to every word she spoke. There was something about the sexy southern drawl that was starting to blend naturally into her speech that had me mesmerized. I wondered what she'd think if she knew her innocent and prim answer in that smooth-as-honey, lilting accent had my dick as hard as steel once again imagining doing sexy things with her.

"...treasurer of the Jewels of Southern Central Kentucky."

I shifted in my seat, trying to adjust myself discreetly, as I asked the next question. "What made you leave for L.A.?"

She smiled widely, but it didn't reach her eyes. "A fantastic job opportunity came up." Her smile was as fake as her answer.

"At the makeup factory, was it?"

The lines around her mouth tightened. "At an international cosmetics company, yes."

I waited, but she didn't add any more details. It was curious that she didn't expound on her job as she had about everything back home in Kentucky.

"Where do you live now?"

Her shoulders relaxed. "I live in an apartment. Near the coffee shop."

"Alone? Or with flatmates?" I figured it was safe to ask since she'd asked me.

"Alone."

She blushed, but I had no idea why.

"Do you have any siblings?"

She shook her head. "No. I'm an only child. Hence, my very over-protective parents."

"Did you just say hence?"

Her eyes narrowed for a moment, but then she laughed. "What's wrong with hence?"

"Nothing." My lips twitched trying to suppress a smile. "Your mum said you had a bad track record with men? What's that all about?"

"She was just exaggerating." She swallowed nervously, looking down at her hands. "Are we done with the inquisition yet? I've told you everything important."

"Just one more question." I tried to think up something funny, similar to her bagpipes question, but instead, I asked her something I really wanted to know. "Why did you really leave Kentucky and move to L.A.?"

She gave me a canned response, sticking to her career opportunity answer. It was a polished answer as if she was on a job interview, but it was all bullshit. She couldn't even meet my eyes when she responded.

I guess that was fair. I hadn't exactly been honest with her. The completely crazy part was that I even cared to know the answer, but I'd find out eventually. I was pretty persuasive when I wanted to be.

We were silent as the plane began its descent. I couldn't wait to be in a hotel room alone with this lass. Normally, I'd be running fast and far away from a girl like her. She was a snobby sorority girl. Her job interview answer that listed off all the high society functions she was involved with should have turned me on as much as a bucket of ice-cold water dumped over my head. Instead, I was itching to tell her the truth about who I was. I wanted to impress her. I wanted to be worthy of her.

I would give up my secret just to have her, but I bit my tongue. Even more important than getting inside her pants, I wanted her to accept me without all the celebrity trappings. I wasn't sure why that meant so much to me with this particular lass, but it did.

After we deplaned, I jokingly gave her some grief as we headed for baggage claim to get the huge suitcase that she'd packed for a weekend trip. According to Summer, winter clothes were bulky.

We found our shuttle and after stopping and dropping off passengers at two ski resorts on the way, we finally made it to the spa about three hours later. The sprawling resort was tucked a few miles off the highway, down a twisting lane that wound up a graduated incline through a dense forest of evergreen trees. The air was crisp and cold with the occasional biting gust of winter wind blowing and a few inches of snow covered the ground. Neither of us was dressed for cold weather, so we grabbed our bags and hurried into the warm lobby.

As we headed to the reception desk to check in, a surge of excitement stirred in my veins. I was looking forward to this weekend more than I knew possible. The anticipation had my cock twitching. Damn, I really did have a one-track mind.

Summer. Naked.

*Domain, Kingdom, Phylum, Class, O-something, Family, Genus, Species.*

# Chapter 10

## Summer

AFTER TURNING OFF THE highway and following a twisty, bumpy back road for miles, the spa resort finally came into sight. It was tucked into a huge forest of evergreen trees in the middle of nowhere. The snow covering the ground seemed deeper here than it did even outside the Boise airport.

When the van stopped, the driver helped us collect our bags. With Scotty trailing silently behind, I quickly pulled my heavy suitcase through the automatic sliding doors of the main building eager to get out of the biting cold. The lobby was enormous.

I paused for a moment searching for the check-in desk. Clusters of furniture with groupings of sofas and chairs upholstered in earthy sage greens and beiges took up the center of the space. A contemporary steel fireplace crackled with flames across the room on my right.

Straight back, I spotted the giant reception desk with the live-wood edge and geometric metal design inlaid along the front surface of it. I headed toward it, walking past the gurgling full-wall water feature lit with changing colored lights from behind. Sprinkled throughout the lobby were oversized cement planters containing tall leafy plants mixed with green bamboo chutes.

The overall ambiance of the lobby was very relaxed; the decor was neutral and zen-like. The muted lighting and soft instrumental music tinkling in the background promoted an atmosphere of peace and harmony. I'm sure even the Feng Shui was on point, but my stomach was churning with nerves.

I was chewing on the inside of my cheek like it was my business. All because I was here with Scotty. I barely knew him and I was about to check into a hotel with him. I was pretty sure my mother would have only booked one room for us, considering she thought he was my boyfriend for the last half a year. And to make matters worse, that stupid daydream where I had no choice but to share a bed with Scotty was running through my head with all the subtlety of a flashing neon sign.

I approached the lone man standing behind the enormous desk and waited while he finished clicking away at what I assumed was a computer keyboard tucked beneath an overhang where it was completely out of view to customers. My fingernails tapped on the desk's surface, not with impatience, but with nerves. Should I act surprised when we were given only one room? Insist on a separate room? Or play it cool?

The man finally looked up. "How can I help you?"

Instantly, I recognized that he was very good-looking. The name tag pinned to his white polo shirt read 'Dewey', and I wondered if that was his first name or last name. He was slightly younger than me, perhaps in his mid-20s. His dark hair was swept back in a trendy pompadour hairstyle and his strong jawline was covered with immaculately trimmed facial hair. He had piercing blue eyes, trendy glasses that made him look smart, and a tiny stud in each ear. Put together, the whole package presented an exceedingly handsome man. I smiled warmly at him, but his gaze flicked right past me and lasered in straight on Scotty. A sharp inhale of breath had his nostrils flaring slightly as he stared at my man.

Jeez, this hot guy was eye-fucking my fake boyfriend? I really couldn't win.

"Reservation under Meadows," I answered with a clipped voice. "First name is Summer."

I didn't like putting my first and last names together out loud. Summer Meadows. I was self-conscious about it, but hardly anyone ever commented. Or probably cared.

"One moment." Dewey managed to drag his eyes away from Scotty and began tapping at the hidden keyboard.

"I was wondering," I casually leaned against the counter and lowered my voice slightly, "if you had any rooms that had two separate beds? Two queens or two kings?"

"We do." He didn't look up or even stop typing, but his lips twisted into a knowing smirk. Bastard. "I can check to see if we have any currently available in one moment."

I risked a glance over at Scotty. He stood at my side with his hands tucked into the pockets of his jeans. He raised an eyebrow at me, looking faintly amused about the whole thing.

When Dewey stopped typing, he stared at the computer screen for several long seconds. "So," — he finally looked up — "you have reservations for the yurt."

I blinked. I wasn't even sure what he just said. "The what?"

"The yurt." He glanced over at Scotty and laughed under his breath.

What the hell?

My eyes dashed to Scotty as my brain quickly flipped through a mental index file of spa jargon. Reservations for a yurt? Was that a type of new-age treatment? Some crazy new form of massage?

"There's a note attached to your reservation. It's from a Lara Meadows. It seems she was the one who booked and paid for the reservation?"

I nodded. "That's my mother."

He glanced down at his screen and read off it in a flat voice. "The note says, 'Surprise! I booked you and Scotty into the yurt for the weekend. I know how much Scotty enjoys the outdoors. The pictures online were absolutely gorgeous; I couldn't resist. Happy Birthday, Summer. Dinner reservations at the Crystal Restaurant tonight at 7. See you then!"

He finished reading, then looked up at me. No one spoke a word while I fidgeted with a strap on my backpack. I had that uncomfortable feeling of being the only one who didn't understand the punchline of a joke. That usually only happened to me when it was a really dirty joke.

"Um, I'm not sure what you mean by a yurt?"

Scotty rubbed his mouth, almost like he was suppressing a laugh. "It's like a round tent."

My eyes rounded in horror. "A tent? We're staying at this luxurious spa and my mother booked us into a tent?"

Dewey grimaced slightly. "To be fair, the yurt is hardly a tent. It's very nice. Think of it more like glamping than camping. It's very romantic. Honeymooners love to stay there. It has its own hot tub and it's very, very private." He raised his brows suggestively.

"But, but..." I stuttered.

Scotty took a step toward me smiling sympathetically. Or psychotically. I couldn't tell. "Sunshine, this weekend is about your mum. This was a surprise she planned for you. We should at least check it out."

I spun to face him. "She didn't do this for me! I don't enjoy sleeping in tents! You're the one she did this for." I stabbed a finger at his chest as I accused him. "You're the one who loves the great outdoors!"

Scotty folded his arms across his chest. "I don't particularly love the great outdoors, Summer."

I frowned as realization dawned. Oh yeah, that was just one of the many little lies I told my mom — that my boyfriend was an avid outdoorsman.

Scotty laughed at the deflated look of defeat on my face. "Oh, what a tangled web we weave…"

I blew out a puff of air. I was trapped in another lie, he was spouting literary quotes, and the reservation clerk was practically drooling as he stared dreamily at Scotty. I guess he had a thing for well-read men. The more he ogled my boyfriend — I mean my fake boyfriend — the less attractive Dewey was looking to me.

"Fine," I pouted. "We'll stay in the yurt thingee."

Dewey's lips twitched but, for the most part, he maintained a poker face. "We don't get a lot of people staying in the yurt this time of year. Let me double-check that it's all ready for you. One moment, please."

This time of year. My cheeks puckered as if I'd just sucked on a lemon. It was winter. There was no way I was staying in a tent in this cold weather.

Dewey lifted a phone to his ear, waited a few seconds, and then spoke, "Gary, is the yurt ready for guests?"

He glanced up at me and then spoke again. "Yeah, the yurt." He listened for a moment and then lowered his voice to almost a whisper. "And how long will that take?"

My eyes narrowed and my lips thinned as I glanced over at Scotty.

How did he look so calm?

He took one look at the expression on my face and let out a chuckle. Sliding up next to me, he rested a hand on my shoulder and leaned in so he could whisper in my ear. "Take it easy, my wee bouncy bumpkin."

I growled in reply and I could tell he was suppressing an even bigger laugh at my expense.

Dewey hung up the phone and lifted a finger indicating that we should wait a moment before he strode across the space behind the desk and disappeared behind a door.

I blew out a frustrated breath and muttered, "What the hell?"

Scotty's eyes danced with amusement. "This should be bloody interesting."

Before I could question Scotty, Dewey returned with a lady following him. She wore a black pinstripe skirt suit with a bold fuchsia blouse underneath, and she had a mop of curly hair that was barely contained in a hair clip.

She stepped around the desk to greet us with a big smile. "Hi, I'm Macie, the spa manager. Dewey told me that you're staying in the yurt. Is it your honeymoon?"

"No." I quickly dashed the sparkling hope I saw in her eyes. She was grinning so eagerly, it almost seemed fake.

She looked back and forth between Scotty and me. "Unfortunately, the yurt isn't quite ready for guests yet, but to make it up to you — while you wait — we'd like to treat you to a complimentary couples massage."

My suspicious nature started to kick in. "What do you mean? The yurt isn't ready?"

"There's a wood-burning stove that keeps it nice and toasty. We have to fire it up." She must have seen the skepticism in my eyes because she continued, "Don't worry, it's not a camping tent. There's electricity, a real bed, a bathroom, and a hot tub on the deck a few steps outside. It's a permanent structure."

It didn't sound so bad. Maybe I was overreacting. "Sorry, it was a surprise from my mom. I wasn't expecting it, but it sounds lovely."

She smiled warmly at me. "You'll love it. It's a great place to snuggle up in. Room service is available, but not overnight — they will tell you the hours. Gary will give you golf cart service since the ground is snowy. I hope you brought some snow boots."

I looked down at my feet and frowned. "I'm sure I'll be fine."

Macie gestured toward the hall. "You can leave your bags with Dewey and I'll get you set up with your spa technicians."

# Chapter 11

**Knox**

I F I WAS GOING to get a massage, I might as well make it count. When she'd asked, I told my therapist to spend some time concentrating on my right shoulder and that my goal was to relax. She was asking other questions about hot stones and the like, but I wasn't paying too much attention to how I answered. I was too busy watching Summer.

My fake girlfriend couldn't keep her eyes off me. She wasn't thrilled with this entire fake dating situation, but she wasn't as immune to my charm as she pretended to be. As soon as she realized that we'd be lying naked within feet of each other, she started to balk at the idea and tried to back out of it. I quickly swung my arm around her shoulder and told her she could really use the relaxation — that she seemed so tense. Without making a big scene in front of Macie, she couldn't back out.

Now, she was eyeing my massage therapist, Daisy, like she'd like to tackle her. It was amusing that my therapist was a young and fairly attractive woman while hers was older and more robust looking. The size of Maria's hands had me jealous; it seemed more likely Summer would get the better massage.

After we had answered their questions, we followed our therapists down a hallway filled with a soft, calming light, and then stepped into a dimly lit room. The walls were painted a soothing shade of blue, and the smell of lavender and eucalyptus wafted through the air. Two massage tables had been set up side by side. I felt my heart pounding in quiet anticipation as Daisy instructed us to disrobe down to where we felt comfortable and lie on the table, strategically covered by a white fluffy towel, before the two therapists left us alone in the room.

Summer put her hands on her hips. "I am not getting naked in front of you."

"Suit yourself." I pulled off my shirt.

Her cheeks colored with a light blush. She averted her gaze, but not before I caught her checking out my bare chest.

Staying fit and in shape was a part of my job. Besides our PR rep from our label drilling it into our heads that our image as a band was half of the money-making equation, we needed incredible stamina to maintain our high-energy performance for an entire concert.

So, I had no doubt that Summer liked what she saw. And I didn't have a shy bone in my body when it came to flaunting it. I unbuttoned my jeans. The energy ricocheting between us was ratcheting up.

I chuckled as she stood motionless. Was the stubborn lass really going to leave all her clothes on for a massage? I yanked my pants off but left my boxer briefs on. Maybe they'd be able to contain anything that popped up, considering I was already semi-hard thinking about seeing a naked Summer.

I could feel her hesitation from across the room. She huffed out an exasperated breath and then turned her back to me. She kicked off her shoes and began unbuttoning her blouse.

The corner of my lips turned up. I pretended to be a gentleman and not watch her, but I wasn't able to resist sneaking a peek.

She slipped off her shirt and then quickly glanced my way. Playing it off well, I made some haphazard motions of folding my wadded-up clothes. I felt a buzz of anticipation as she began working her pants down her legs. She had to bend at the waist to remove them and that just enhanced the curves of her gorgeous heart-shaped ass. She left her bra and panties on and then quickly wrapped a plush white towel around herself. Sadly, the show was over.

I tossed my jumble of clothes onto a chair and then climbed onto the massage table, not bothering with the towel. I rested my arm under my head and turned to face her empty table. She was hovering just out of view.

She was ignoring me and I didn't like it, so I decided to mess with her a bit. "I'm really looking forward to this. I need to release some ... tension."

She made a disgusted, scoffing noise in the back of her throat, but didn't fall for the bait.

I heard a rustle of activity, so I lifted my head to see what she was up to. Through a feat of sheer determination, she managed to wrestle her bra off without removing the towel. She placed it on top of her neatly folded stack of clothes, which were sitting in a cubby hole shelf. I guess that was where I was supposed to store my clothes. Oh well.

I put my head back down on my arm and waited for her to get onto the adjacent table. I had to bite down on my knuckle not to laugh when she awkwardly rolled herself onto the table, like a stiff slab of meat, making sure the towel kept all her secrets tucked safely out of sight.

"Looks like you could use a little stress relief, too." I kept my voice low.

"Me? Nah." She turned her head to glare at me. "What's there to be stressed about? Just that my mother has cancer, that I've been telling her lies for the past six months, and that I'm currently lying naked next to some guy that I barely know and I'm staying in a yurt with him. I've never even heard of a yurt."

I rubbed my chin like I was deep in thought. "That's a lot to deal with. Maybe Maria can give you a happy ending?"

Her eyes flashed with fire. "You're a disgusting pig!"

She was so pissed off that she jolted up, pulling her upper body off the table and leaning on her elbows in order to confront me, but only succeeded in showing off her amazing tits. A charge of lust shot straight to my groin, as heat raced through my veins. I wanted her badly, no matter how much we bickered.

She squeaked with rage as she saw my eyes feasting on her tits, but in my defense, there was no way I could not look at them. They were spectacular. I couldn't wait to get my hands on them. And my mouth. Maybe my...

My hard cock pressed uncomfortably against the table, but I wasn't going to turn over. Hell, the head of my cock was poking out of the top of my boxer briefs as it was. No need for Daisy to be confronted with my monster of a cock. See, I was a gentleman!

Summer fixed her towel and then repositioned herself so that her head was turned to face the wall. I was trying to figure out something else to say to rile her up — maybe I'd get another glimpse of those luscious tits — when our massage therapists came back into the room.

Neither of them said a word; they went right to work. My eyes fluttered shut as Daisy began kneading the muscles in my back. She started off gentle but then started to use more pressure, digging into the tight knots that had been building up over the past few weeks. I let out a contented sigh, reveling in the feeling of her hands massaging away my aches and pains.

With each movement she made, I felt my body relax further and further into the table. I could feel my heart rate slow down and my breathing deepen. All the stress of our travels seemed to disappear with each stroke of the therapist's fingertips across my back.

Then, I heard it. A soft, breathy moan coming from Summer. It sounded sinful. Like pure sex. It was a sound of uninhibited feminine pleasure that sent a bolt of sheer lust straight to my cock and turned it to steel. All I could think about was sinking into her, getting lost between her creamy thighs.

My eyes drifted open. I couldn't resist looking at Summer. Her towel had been moved, now only covering her ass, so Maria had access to her back as she worked. Her long blonde hair was swept to the side, so I could see the swell of her breasts as they pressed against the table. I could just see the flare of her hip before the towel blocked my view, but then my eyes tracked down to sweep over her long, toned legs. Her body was perfection and watching Maria's hands running all over it made me crazy. Fuck, I wanted her like the burn of a thousand suns.

Her head turned my way, and she caught me staring. She glanced at Daisy's hands massaging my lower back for a brief second and then our eyes locked. Tension filled the air between us. Summer's lips parted slightly and her eyes clouded with desire. Her cheeks flushed a rosy pink, and she bit down lightly on her lower lip.

My breathing became more ragged. Time seemed to stand still as we just stared at each other. Every cell in my body screamed for me to get up and go to her.

She must have seen the intense need burning in my eyes because she slammed her eyes closed and kept them closed for the remainder of our massage.

Daisy moved to my side work on my shoulder and blocked my view of Summer. I willed my body to relax and to stop thinking about Summer. After a few minutes, my overheated reaction to Summer had cooled down some. Daisy had me flip over and continued to concentrate on my shoulder. She finished up by working through the rest of my muscles, from my pecs down to my calves.

Daisy stepped back from the table. "I hope that was satisfactory, Mr. Stewart. Your shoulder might be a bit sore later, but it should feel much better tomorrow. Your circulation should be improved. Make sure to drink plenty of water to help flush out the toxins that were released."

I attempted to lift my head, but it was too much effort. "Thank you, Daisy. That was great."

Maria's thumbs were rubbing spirals into Summer's calves. "Is there anything else I can do for you, Ms. Meadows?"

Summer's eyes finally opened again. She caught me staring and looked away immediately. "No, that was perfect. Thanks."

Maria opened up the folded towel that was covering Summer's ass and spread it out over her torso, just as it had been when she'd started the massage. "We'll leave you to get dressed. Take your time."

Maria followed Daisy out the door before shutting it with a quiet click.

I swung my legs over the table so I could sit up. "For a lass with such little hands, Daisy worked my shoulder pretty good. How was Maria? You looked like you were enjoying it."

She ignored my question. "Would you just get dressed and then turn around so I can?"

I'd never seen a girl with such an amazing body be so modest about exposing it. Granted, what I thought was normal for girls was skewed because I was around groupies who flaunted their bodies, spectacular or not, in front of me, without a hint of shyness. Hell, I saw more skin at meet and greets from both the underage girls and the mothers that brought them.

I'd seen it all, but Summer being so modest was kind of refreshing. It was one of the reasons I was glad that Summer didn't know who I was. Would her behavior change if she did? Would she just want to fuck me like all the others to get her 15 minutes of fame? Summer was fighting her attraction to me and it had nothing to do with me being a rock star. That made me want her even more.

I hopped off the table and grabbed my jeans. "After I get dressed, I'll give you some privacy. I want to find the ladies and give them a tip, so I'll meet you back in the lobby."

She didn't move while I dressed and then checked inside my wallet before heading out the door. So far, this weekend getaway was starting off nicely.

# Chapter 12

---

## Summer

"THE GOLF CART IS right outside." Gary gestured toward the automatic sliding doors. The smell of pine and the outdoors wafted inside with him.

He was an older man, in his 60s, slightly overweight with thin, white hair and wearing a navy blue parka with Crystal Cascadia Spa and Wellness Center embroidered on it. We followed him out the lobby doors into the frigid air. I wrapped my arms around myself; it was cold. "How far away is this yurt?"

Gary led us to the golf cart. "It's not too far, about half a mile. I'll get us there in about three minutes."

My teeth clenched against the biting cold, but I could handle three minutes. As if to mock me, a sharp gust of wind rustled down from the trees and pummeled us, lifting my long hair off my shoulders and forcing ice-cold air to funnel down my neck.

"Hop on." Gary slid into the driver's seat.

Scotty led me to the back of the cart, where there was a bench seat that faced backward. "I'll sit back here with you and see if I can keep you warm. You packed a winter coat, didn't you?"

I didn't object to sitting next to him. My teeth were already chattering. "No. I didn't bring a coat."

Scotty slid onto the seat and then wrapped his arm around me. He pulled me tight against him when I sat down and I didn't argue. I needed every bit of warmth I could get.

"I hope like hell you have some warm clothes in that giant suitcase you brought." He rubbed my arms, trying to warm me.

Trying to hide from the wind, I pressed my face into his chest. I mumbled into the soft fabric of his henley, which smelled deliciously of his scent. "How was I supposed to know that we'd be traipsing through the snow in the great outdoors? I packed for a five-star spa weekend."

Gary started up the golf cart, and we lurched forward. "The yurt will be nice and toasty by now. You'll be there in no time."

I clung to Scotty, partly to keep warm, partly to avoid being buffeted by the stiff wind, and partly because he felt so amazing. I'd gotten an eyeful of his exquisite body during the massage and it was enough to make my mouth water.

How would I survive the weekend with this temptation? He was like a walking billboard for sex and dirty fantasies, and I hadn't slept with a man in over a year. My pact to stay away from men was doomed. I was already concocting rationalizations of how sleeping with Scotty would be different. I would do it and keep any emotions out of it. I'd just scratch an itch; it didn't have to be anything more. My resolve to stay away from men, especially ones who were trouble, was crumbling with every passing second.

The golf cart finally stopped. Scotty hopped off and offered me a hand to help me down. I already missed the warmth of his body. My thin canvas sneakers sunk into the snow as I stepped down. I turned around and saw the yurt.

It was fairly ugly from the outside. It was much larger than a camping tent but similar in that the walls were made out of beige tent-like material. This monstrosity was round and had two small windows and two wooden steps out front that led up to a real wood front door.

Gary was leading us inside. I jogged forward to get inside as fast as I could. Warm air hit me as soon as I stepped inside.

I looked around with relief. The inside was much cozier than would appear from the outside. It was very small but rustic and charming, with a wood-burning stove blazing on one side of the yurt.

It was sparsely furnished, so the king-sized bed, piled high with quilts and blankets, seemed to fill up most of the interior. I swallowed nervously. I was going to be sleeping with Scotty in that bed. Dragging my eyes away from the bed, I let my gaze wander around the room, focusing on the details of our temporary home. A lattice frame held up the heavy canvas material of the ivory walls. Area rugs were scattered throughout the space, covering most of the wooden floor. The roof came to a low peak that was anchored by a plastic dome which let in a small amount of light.

Gary was giving Scotty instructions on how to use the wood stove, so I decided to poke around. There wasn't much to see beyond the bed. Our suitcases had been placed next to a chest of drawers that stood to the right of the bed. On the other side of the space was a small table, a mini refrigerator, and a farmhouse hutch with a coffeemaker sitting on the shelf.

Toward the back, there was an interior wall that blocked off a tiny room. I walked a few steps to check it out and pulled back the privacy curtain. I had discovered the bathroom. It was rather luxurious for a tent with its real toilet, sink, and claw-foot tub that had a curtain surround for showering, but all I could think about was how the heck was I going to do my business in there with only a flimsy curtain for privacy.

I backed out of the bathroom to find that Gary had left. My breath caught in my throat as I saw Scotty standing in the corner, his eyes watching me. He was tall and handsome, his hair falling in soft waves around his face. I felt a sudden heat course through my veins, and I quickly turned away, my heart pounding in my chest.

"So, this is the yurt," he said, his voice low and deep.

I nodded, my gaze focused on the bed. I was struggling to keep my composure, to not give away the fact that I was incredibly attracted to him, despite my attempts to remain indifferent.

Scotty was surveying the room. "Gary is going to stay late tonight to drive us to the restaurant at 7 o'clock, but then he's going home. We'll have to walk back here. He said the restaurant is fancy, but you should skip wearing a dress and high heels and bundle up as warmly as you can."

I frowned, trying to figure out if anything I'd packed would work for trekking half a mile through snow. "What was my mother thinking? At least she could have warned me to pack appropriately."

"Maybe we can find a clothing store tomorrow? We can buy you a warm coat and boots." His eyes pinged from me to my suitcase. "You must have something warm in that giant suitcase of yours? It's February, for fuck's sake."

I bristled at his tone. "Huh, is it February? I must have forgotten. I only packed bikinis and lingerie. Do you think that would work for dinner?"

My sarcastic tone didn't stop Scotty from reacting to my words. His lips curled into a mischievous smirk and his eyes smoldered. Intensity radiated from his piercing gaze.

His voice was low and raspy, like a growl, sending a shiver of pleasure through my body. "No, but that will work just fine for after dinner."

My mouth went dry and my stomach fluttered at the intense heat in his eyes. I had to look away.

Needing some space, I retreated to my suitcase and began loading its contents into the drawers of the dresser, constantly aware of Scotty's presence.

He began checking out the yurt. "It's only three o'clock. What are we going to do until dinner?"

What, indeed? There was no television to watch. I could read, but a quick check of my phone made me realize that I didn't have cell service. "Darn. I don't even have cell service. Do you?"

"No." He answered while he wandered around the yurt, peeking in all the nooks and crannies.

I finished unpacking and then sat on the bed. I didn't feel like walking up to the main resort or calling Gary again when he was already staying late to drive us to our dinner later.

Scotty shuffled through some papers sitting by the landline phone. "We could order room service. I could use a snack."

"Go ahead and order something. I think I'm just going to take a nap." I pulled off my shoes and laid down on the bed on top of the covers, but pulled a blanket over me.

I listened to hear if he would order food, but he never did. A few minutes later, I felt the bed sink down as he lay down on the other side. Willing my eyes to stay closed, I succeeded for about ten minutes, but then I couldn't take it any longer. I opened my eyes. He was watching me.

He spoke first. "I can't sleep. I don't usually take naps."

"This is pretty boring, huh?" I pulled my hand out from under my cheek and turned toward him.

I blinked as I studied his face. He was devastatingly handsome up close. His light brown hair was on the longish side and cut in a purposefully messy style that begged for my fingers to be run through it.

I could get lost in his eyes, which were wide and expressive with a rich brown color, ingrained with flecks of gold, and framed with sinfully long eyelashes. He had a strong jawline, well-defined eyebrows, a straight nose, and full lips. The total effect had my insides burning with desire.

"Yep." He smiled, setting those dimples loose on me. "What could we do to spice it up a bit?"

I narrowed my eyes at him. "We could talk."

He shifted to get more comfortable. "So, your birthday is next month? How old are you?"

I studied him, suspicious and maybe a little disappointed that he'd given up so easily. "I'm 26. I'll be 27 next month. How old are you?"

"Twenty-nine," he murmured.

I traced circles on my pillow with a finger. "What would you be doing right now if you were back in L.A.?"

"Probably playing my guitar or hanging out at my friend's place. Sometimes it gets boring when I'm not out on the road."

"Touring with a band?" I asked.

A smile crossed his lips. "Yeah."

I propped myself up on my elbow, looking into his eyes. "When will you be back on the road?"

He rolled onto his back and stared up at the ceiling of the yurt. "I don't know. I just kind of roll with it. We just got back from a long tour. It started in the U.S. then we did Europe. We were a solid

18 months on the road with only a few breaks. Then I had to go to Scotland for a couple of weeks. I should be relieved to be back home and settling down a bit."

He was finally home, but he'd immediately jumped at the chance to leave again. "What bands have you toured with?"

He paused for a long moment and then answered, "Cold Fusion. Have you heard of them?"

My eyes widened with surprise. "Oh, sure. That brings me back to my high school days."

He nodded. "I got to be friends with those guys. They're great."

I was impressed that he worked with such a well-known band. I had expected him to name some small obscure bands. "Isn't Tyler Matthews a celebrity judge on one of those TV talent shows?"

"Yep," he confirmed.

"That's pretty neat. Who else did you work with?"

He listed off a bunch of other bands that I'd only vaguely heard of: Burnt Crimson, The Raging Tide, and Marauders of the Temple.

"Is the rock and roll lifestyle as crazy as it seems?"

He shifted onto his side, turning to face me again. "It can be pretty crazy. Luckily, I'm surrounded by some pretty smart guys. We keep an eye out for each other. It keeps the excesses—with booze and drugs and partying—from taking over."

I crooked an eyebrow. "And women?"

He smiled coyly. "There are lots of women, but no time for attachments. All of it gets kind of stale after a while. Except for the music."

It was a hectic lifestyle that I didn't understand. "Do you ever dream of doing more than what you're doing?"

"No, I'm happy with where I'm at." He brushed a piece of hair from my face. "How about you?"

My heart leaped at his touch. A slight brush of his fingertips against my forehead had my blood pumping. It was pathetic but undeniable. But, as he'd all but just confirmed, I'd be only one among a long list of conquests. The question was, could I resist?

I huffed out a breath. "My dad owns several franchises back home. Donut shops, fast food, delis ... stuff like that. I know he wants me to go back to Kentucky and manage the empire for him and eventually take it over when he retires, but I'm not sure that's what I want to do. He's happy for now that I'm getting experience out in the real world, but now that my mom has cancer..."

"Your dad seems like a great guy, Sunshine." He searched my eyes. "I don't think he'd want you to do something that wasn't your dream. Have you talked to him about it?"

"No." I sighed softly. "I didn't want to disappoint him. And now? Forget it."

"Because of your mum?" he gently prodded.

My mother had cancer. It hit me all over again — panic and fear and a bit of denial, too. I'd spent all week researching breast cancer on the internet, but everything felt so out of my control.

My throat tightened with emotion, and my eyes instantly teared up.

Scotty sighed and tugged me close to his body so he could wrap me in his arms. I didn't resist; it felt too good. Comforting. And right.

"I'm a bit of a hypochondriac. If I get the sniffles, I run to the internet and suddenly I think I have some terrible autoimmune disease. Mom knows that, and I think that's part of the reason she kept it from me." I swiped angrily at my teary eyes. "I googled the shit out of breast cancer, but she wouldn't tell me what stage or type of cancer she had. She knows me too well. She says she has it all in hand, but it scares the crap out of me. I want to help her."

He was rubbing my arm soothingly. "Being there for her is helping her. That's what she wants. You're a good daughter, Summer."

Scoffing at his comment, I shook my head. "I'm a terrible daughter. I'm still lying to her."

"You're doing it with a good heart. Not maliciously," he reasoned.

"I lied because it was more convenient for me," I countered. "I didn't want to deal with her. With her worry for me and her not-so-subtle matchmaking. I was being selfish. And now I'm stuck. I don't want to upset her right before her surgery while she's dealing with all of this. And, she's so happy for me. It's really screwed up."

He was quiet for a minute. "What's your plan, then?"

I wasn't sure if he was worried that I was going to cling to him. Honestly, being in his arms felt so good that I was worried myself.

"After surgery, when she's recovered, I'll gently tell her that we're not working out. We've broken up. I'll tell her that we decided we'd make better friends than lovers."

He looked down at me. The fire in his eyes was so intense I thought I might be swallowed up by it. "Hmmm. That might be a lie."

My brain was busy short-circuiting, so I wasn't quite sure what he meant. "What?"

"Never mind," he said, his voice low and throaty. His lips were so close to mine that I could feel their heat.

Before I knew what was happening, Scotty's lips pressed passionately against mine. He cradled my face in his palms as his tongue explored my depths, igniting an inferno of desire within me. His touch was electric, each brush of his lips unleashing a wave of pleasure so strong I trembled in his arms. The kiss was like no other, so intense and erotic that my pulse quickened until all the air escaped my lungs. I was drowning in it.

He pulled away after a few moments, his breathing ragged and his eyes glazed with desire. I looked up at him with wide-eyed amazement, feeling my cheeks flush with embarrassment and arousal.

"Scotty..." I managed to whisper, not sure what else to say. He just smiled as he stroked my face lightly with his thumb and fingers.

"That didn't feel like friends," he said softly.

I closed my eyes, still too nervous to speak and still stunned by the intensity of the kiss we had just shared.

"We both wanted that," he said, his voice a husky whisper.

I shivered in his arms. I was still trying to process what had happened. "No. I can't do this."

"Why not?" he asked.

I could barely breathe, my lungs aching for air. My chest felt too tight to think, and his arms wrapped around my body only added to my confusion. I pushed away from him, and when I looked up into his face, it was like looking at a storm-filled sky; the intensity of his gaze was almost tangible. He let me go without a word.

"I'm going to take a shower," he said quietly as he stood up and stepped away from me. I wanted to tell him not to go, that I wanted him to stay even though I knew it was a very bad idea; but instead, all I could do was watch as he slowly made his way toward the bathroom.

Just before he left, he turned around one last time and looked at me, a soft smile on his lips. "I'm a very patient man, Sunshine," he said before slipping into the bathroom.

# Chapter 13

---

**Knox**

SUMMER HADN'T DONE A great job of packing for this trip. Granted, we didn't know we'd be staying in a yurt, but she'd barely brought any cold weather clothing at all. Although we had about a ten-minute walk back to the yurt after dinner, she insisted on wearing a dressy outfit. She'd chosen a black skirt with a pretty blue blouse that looked amazing on her. The problem was that the thin material did nothing to block the cold, and her bare legs and high heels didn't help either.

I knew what a disaster this would be. The day I met her at the coffee shop, it was mild, beautiful, and sunny, and yet she was dressed up like an Eskimo. I insisted she bring a change of clothes and shoes for after dinner and that she wear one of my hoodies over her outfit for the golf cart ride to the restaurant. I also grabbed a blanket off the bed and wrapped her in it.

Now we were inside the entrance of the elegant and upscale restaurant, and she was frantically trying to remove the hoodie before anyone saw her. I chuckled when she managed to wrestle it off, because her hair looked crazy, standing on end with static electricity. She jammed my hoodie into the canvas tote we'd brought to carry her change of clothes and tried unsuccessfully to stuff the blanket in, too.

She spoke to the hostess, who was watching with interest. "Would you be able to hold on to my change of clothes while I have dinner? We're with the Meadows reservation."

The hostess took the bag and blanket which Summer had folded up. "No problem. Let me just set this down somewhere safe and then I'll lead you back to the rest of your party."

"You look like you've been rubbing a balloon through your hair," I teased Summer while we waited for the hostess to return.

Her hand shot up to her hair. "Oh my God, I told you I didn't need that dumb hoodie. Now my hair is ruined."

I began patting down some of the flyaways. "You won't be calling my hoodie dumb when we're walking back."

She pulled away from my hand. "I'm going to the restroom to see how bad it is. I'll be back in a second."

The hostess and I waited for her to return. My anxiety spiked for a moment when I noticed the hostess scrutinizing me, since she was younger — in her early 20s — but she didn't recognize me. So far, no one here had. I wasn't surprised people at the spa didn't recognize members of Ghost Parker, but I thought maybe a younger demographic here would. Then again, Idaho was like a whole different beast from L.A. There were no paparazzi here. People here didn't anticipate running into celebrities 24/7. The lifestyle was more laid back, which was nice. Still, I didn't want to let down my guard and wind up getting ambushed. I wasn't even sure how I'd explain my real identity to Summer at this point. She was lying about our relationship to her parents and I was lying about my real identity. What was the saying? Birds of a feather...

After a few minutes, Summer returned, her hair looking perfect once again. I took her hand in mine as the hostess led us to our table. Summer's parents were already seated. Jim stood up to hug Summer and to shake my hand, and I could feel Lara's eyes on me from head to toe. It was important to Summer that this dinner went well, so I didn't want to screw it up. Luckily, I had packed a dark suit and crisp white shirt for the occasion. It worked perfectly, and I could see Lara smile her approval just before Summer swooped in and gave her a hug in greeting.

I held out Summer's chair across from her mom, and then I sat down beside her. I smiled reassuringly at her as she spread the napkin over her lap. This dinner in front of her parents was the perfect time to show her affection that she wouldn't be able to scurry away from. I wanted her, and I knew she was attracted to me. That kiss we shared on the plane and the equally scorching kiss at the yurt were proof of that. I had no clue why she was fighting it so hard.

When the waiter came to take our drink order, I followed Jim's lead and ordered a glass of whiskey. Lara was not drinking alcohol, and Summer ordered a glass of wine.

As soon as the waiter left, Lara offered us a sly smile. "So how is the yurt? It looked so romantic online."

Summer's fingers plucked at her napkin. "Oh, it's lovely, Mom. What a surprise! It's out in the middle of nowhere, but it's so cozy."

Lara glanced expectantly at me, and I felt the need to chime in. "It's very romantic, Lara. Thank you for your generosity."

She beamed in reply. I breathed an inward sigh of relief; I'd answered correctly.

After we received our drinks and ordered our dinner, Summer and her mother began gossiping about people they both knew from Kentucky. I asked Jim about the franchises that he owned, and that was enough to keep our conversation flowing until the waiter brought out our food.

Summer relaxed more as the evening went on. I kept checking on her to make sure she was okay. I refilled her wine, stole some touches, and even leaned over to give her a soft kiss a few times. We were having such an enjoyable time, that I forgot that it was just an act.

Our discussion about Scotland had morphed into traveling in Europe. I didn't travel much as a child, but I'd been all over Europe with the band. Summer's parents liked to vacation abroad, and they'd taken her to several places when she was younger, but she expressed an interest in seeing more sights. Italy and Greece were on her bucket list.

When dessert arrived, Lara switched topics. "I booked you two into a spa session for tomorrow at 10 o'clock. It's a hydrotherapy circuit. It looks really neat."

Summer's forehead creased. "Why don't you and I do it instead, Mom?"

Lara exchanged a knowing look with Jim. "I'm already signed up to take some classes tomorrow and do a reiki body cleanse. I prefer to do those with your father. But I'd love to steal you away Saturday afternoon. We could get some spa treatments and some pampering in while the boys entertain themselves."

Summer glanced over at me, worry etched on her face.

I knew she was nervous about me being alone with her dad, but she needed to spend time with her mom. "Don't worry about me, Sunshine. I'm sure I can find plenty of things to occupy my time."

Jim cleared his throat. "We have a rental car and there are a few breweries that aren't too far away. I thought we could have lunch in town and then go on a brewery tour. Afterward, we could find a sports bar and relax for the afternoon. Do you follow any sports, Scotty?"

I was going to miss out on spending the afternoon with Summer, but relaxing with a pint of beer sounded enjoyable. "That sounds like the perfect plan, Jim. I've followed the Celtic Football Club since I was a wee lad. That's uh, er, soccer. I played soccer until I came to the U.S. But, I enjoy watching American football, too. And hockey and college basketball."

Jim's eyes were shining. I was guessing by the look on his face that he was a rabid sports fan. "I'm sure we could catch the Kentucky game. The Wildcats are playing Tennessee."

I nodded. "That should be a good game."

Lara put down her water glass. "Then it's all settled. I'll go ahead and schedule our appointments for Saturday, Summer. I'm booked solid tomorrow, so we'll just plan to meet up for dinner tomorrow night. Is 7 o'clock good for you?"

"Sure," Summer answered.

We said our goodnights and then Summer headed off to change into different clothes for our trek back to the yurt. I sat back and smiled. I had Summer all to myself for the next 24 hours and I planned to use every one of them.

She met me at the entrance of the restaurant when she was done changing. She was now wearing jeans and a sweater, and she was out of the heels and into more practical socks and sneakers for the walk back.

I handed her my hoodie. "It's going to be cold. The weather app says it is 22° outside."

She didn't argue. She bundled into my hoodie and even put up the hood this time. I took the bag of clothes from her and handed her the blanket. We stepped outside and damn, it was cold. Summer wrapped the blanket around herself and we began following the path through the trees back to the yurt.

"Well, that was interesting." As she spoke, I could see the condensation of her breath as it puffed out into the cold air.

I shortened my stride to match hers. "I thought it went well."

A gust of biting wind whipped through the trees and she pulled the blanket tighter around her. "Yeah, you really charmed them."

"It comes naturally," I answered with a smile of pride.

"Can you not act so perfect?" she griped. "My parents are really starting to like you."

"Maybe I'm not acting." I felt the huge grin on my face. I was certainly far from perfect.

"Oh, please," she scoffed. "Do you always suck up to parents so much?"

I couldn't even remember the last time I'd had to impress the parents of a girl I was with. It was probably Aila's parents years ago. "I'm not sucking up. They're good people. I don't mind hanging out with your dad."

The sliver of moon that had been barely lighting up our pathway through the trees disappeared behind a cloud. I pulled out my phone and turned on the flashlight app.

She stopped for a moment to adjust her blanket and then kept walking. "I hope you really do like college basketball because if there's a Wildcat game on Saturday, that's what you'll be doing with him."

"I do like watching sports, so I'll be fine. And you'll get to spend some time with your mom."

She was quiet for several minutes after that, probably thinking about her mom's situation.

She sighed. "It sounds like we're doing a hydrotherapy session tomorrow. I'm not sure what that is. Do you know?"

It didn't matter to me what it was. If I got to see Summer in a bikini, it was going to be fun. "Maybe it's water aerobics or something? She did say it looked neat."

"That's what she said about the yurt," Summer responded sardonically.

"The yurt is neat."

"It would be neater if I didn't have to traipse through the snow in the bitter cold," she grumbled.

I watched her from the side of my eyes. "It's very romantic, though."

"True," she agreed. "Are you a romantic guy?"

I thought about it. My knee-jerk answer was 'no'. There wasn't much romance in my life. Sex was just a transaction to me. It occurred backstage, in hotel rooms, on the tour bus, in our dressing rooms, and sometimes it was even less glamorous places — in restrooms or dark corners of parties or nightclubs. Occasionally, I went back to a girl's apartment, but I always left as soon as possible. Sex had been limited to one-night stands and most of the time those encounters lasted much shorter than a night. They were more like one-hour stands. And not one of them had even a lick of romance involved. Maybe I was missing out?

"I have a romantic side." I was being flirtatious, but it didn't feel misleading. If romance was what it took to get Summer to have sex with me, I'd happily go for it.

She grew quiet, and I wondered if she was thinking about us spending the night together in the yurt like I was. Would she sleep with me? I wanted to, but she had to want me. I wouldn't push her into it. Persuade her, sure.

The chill was seeping into my bones and I estimated we were only about halfway to the yurt. I rubbed my hands together, trying to keep them warm.

Summer offered me some of the blanket. "You must be freezing."

Without speaking, I took her up on her offer. Sliding next to her, I pulled the blanket around the both of us. I expected it to be difficult to walk together because of our differences in sizes, but she fit perfectly tucked in under my arm. Within minutes, I was feeling much warmer. Warmer ... and hornier.

The path bent to the right, and then the yurt came into view.

"Thank God," she muttered.

We both picked up the pace and finally, we were inside, huddled around the stove that was giving off a lot of heat until we'd warmed up. Summer folded up the blanket and dropped it onto the bed and then peeled off my hoodie.

"What are we going to do now?" She looked at me quizzically.

Her question was innocent, but as the seconds ticked by, the dirtiest of thoughts were running through my head and I was pretty sure hers, too, as evidenced by the blush on her cheeks.

She looked away quickly. "I'm going to take a shower."

She gathered up her things and then escaped to the tiny bathroom nook that was separated from the main room by a flimsy hanging curtain.

The water started running. I needed a distraction, but there was really nothing to do in here. Without my guitar, cell service, or even something to read, I was lost. I sat down on the edge of the bed.

Less than ten feet separated me from a naked Summer. I could hear the water tempo change as she moved around in the shower. My hands fisted in the blanket.

The scent of sweet, tropical florals with a hint of citrus wafted from the tiny nook and hit me like a punch to the gut. My hands squeezed into fists as I imagined the soapy water running all over her curvy body. By the time the water stopped, I was as hard as a rock.

Ten minutes later, she came out of the bathroom dressed in modest pajamas with a freshly scrubbed face and her hair combed but still damp. God, she was adorable.

"There's no blow dryer," was all she said.

I watched as she fluttered around nervously, putting away her toiletries. "We can pick one up at the hotel tomorrow if you need it."

She nodded and then looked around the room. She seemed indecisive, but then she climbed onto the bed and pulled the covers over her.

"You're going to bed now?" I asked incredulously. "It's not even 9:30."

She rolled to her side so she could see me. "What else am I going to do?"

I could think of plenty of options, but she seemed determined not to go there with me.

Her eyes narrowed. "And don't even say whatever you're thinking that's put that smile on your face. It's not going to happen."

Fuck, the lass was stubborn. "Fine. I guess I'll take a shower then."

After gathering what I needed, I went into the bathroom nook. I strategically left the privacy curtain half open. If she chose to, I knew she could easily look through and see me from where she was on the bed.

I'd give her a show. I stripped off my clothes slowly and then turned on the water. The thought of her eyes on me had my cock throbbing. The water was already warm, so I stepped right under the spray. I'd showered earlier, so now I just wanted the warm water to help relieve some tension. Wrapping my fingers around my cock, I gave myself a few strokes.

I'd love to have Summer watching me, but I couldn't leave the shower curtain open without getting water all over the floor. My hand slowly slid up and down along the length of my cock, searching for relief. I'd never spent so much time around such a beautiful girl without getting any action; blue balls were a very real thing. Vaguely wondering if she could hear the faint slapping noises, I began working hard and fast, with my entire focus on finding release as soon as possible.

I was almost there when the hot water started running out. There was no stopping now, so I finished up under a stream of ice-cold water.

"Damn," I cursed. That had been the most unsatisfactory climax from wanking I'd ever experienced. Quickly shutting off the water, I hopped out and searched for a towel. I found a clean one under the vanity and dried myself off. Then, I slipped on a new pair of briefs and ran my hands through my hair where only the ends had gotten wet.

The stove did a great job of keeping the yurt toasty warm and the bed was piled high with blankets. As I left the bathroom, I glanced over at Summer. Her eyes were closed tight. I didn't think she was actually sleeping, but she certainly was pretending to be. I shut off a lamp near the 'kitchen' area and then climbed into bed.

"Goodnight, Sunshine." I reached over and turned off the lamp on the small nightstand. The yurt was dark except for a faint glow from the stove.

Summer didn't answer. Fine. She was going to play her games, but she wasn't going to win. She somewhat correctly thought I was a male slut, and for some reason, I was determined to prove her wrong. I'd act like a boy scout tonight, but I was slowly running out of time to convince her how much she wanted me. Why did I even care what she thought of me? I was the one doing her the favor this weekend. Wasn't I? She really confused the hell out of me.

# Chapter 14

**Summer**

I WAS SO NOT a morning person. So after the first few groggy moments of pulling myself from a deep sleep wore off, I was surprised at how happy and relaxed I was sleeping in Scotty's arms. I felt warm and secure, my body melting into his as if I belonged there. His warmth enveloped me and kept me cozy despite the frigid air I could feel on my face.

Oh shit!

Sometime in the night, I'd managed to seek him out, and I was so completely entwined in all his gorgeous male flesh that I couldn't escape without waking him. I was trapped in bliss, but I didn't want to get caught enjoying it.

I willed my breathing to remain even while I tried to figure out a way out of this. Should I take the slow, inch-by-inch method and risk him waking up while I was in flagrante delicto, or should I just yank out of his arms all at once and hope he was too sound asleep to register what was happening?

Or should I just lay in his arms and enjoy every second of his hard body pressed up to mine and imagine an entirely different ending to my morning? Because that's what I wanted to do. He was damn near naked. With his ripped body and handsome face, he was as handsome as sin. He was also supremely confident, almost cocky, yet he was also kind and generous. He was going along with this ridiculous charade, for my mother's sake, when he didn't have to. The more I thought about it, the more I wondered why the hell I was resisting him so hard, anyway?

The first lie that I'd told myself and tried to cling to fiercely was that I didn't want to be with a man. Any man. Well, I did. I wanted to have sex with Scotty something fierce. What would be the harm in indulging if I kept it to this weekend? After all, these were pretty unusual circumstances.

Was I going to go without sex forever? No. I'd just gotten a bit wary of men after picking up a lot of duds over the years. And I'd gotten way too invested in them way too fast. But, if I were honest with myself, holding out on sex hadn't really worked either. I held my old boss off for almost a year and still, he turned out to be an unfaithful jerk.

Maybe I just hadn't picked the right man. Scotty wasn't offering me a lifetime of commitment. This was just fun. If I kept that in mind — took the fun without expecting anything else — maybe I'd be okay? Even though every single time I'd tried that in the past, I'd ended up getting burned.

I needed to escape his arms. They were making me crazy. Just because he was hot, didn't mean I had to give into my base desire. I'd proved for the last year that I'd evolved beyond that; I'd grown up. I'd learned my lesson and knew to stay away from trouble. No matter how much I wanted to.

All my life, the good Summer always struggled with the bad Summer. Bad Summer was the one who'd never turn down a dare. She was the one who cheated on her 5<sup>th</sup> grade math test. She's the one who hopped on the back of Jake's motorcycle despite having some niggling misgivings. Good Summer was the one that tried to talk me out of doing that. She was the one who usually lost that argument and ended up regretting the bad choices.

Bad Summer was not evil. She was just more daring and reckless. She took chances. The most fun stuff I'd done in my life was all at her behest. I even looked back and laughed at all the fun and mischief that she got me into. But she wasn't the one who should be directing serious life choices.

I needed an intervention from Good Summer before I did something stupid. It was up to me to be the adult, responsible person in the room. Good Summer needed to decide if Scotty was a bad life choice or just a fun distraction that I could put aside when it was over.

"Morning, Sunshine," Scotty mumbled into my ear as he grabbed me tighter.

I hadn't moved a muscle since I'd woken up, but the instant I heard his words, I froze. Maybe I just stopped breathing.

He chuckled. "I know you're awake."

I exhaled. My first instinct with Scotty was always to give him sass. "What are you doing? Let me go."

"Let you go?" He feigned outrage. "You're the one pinning me down to the mattress."

Crap, I was pretty much on top of him, but in my defense, he was holding me there. I tried to wiggle free of his grasp but ended up grinding on him instead. Oops.

My legs were still entangled with his, but I managed to push my upper body off his chest. The blankets slid down my back and I was immediately assaulted by ice-cold air.

Letting out a little squeak of surprise, I dove back under the covers with him.

I wanted to wipe the smug grin from his face, but his dimples were so distracting I could only stare. I wanted to lick him up.

He raised an eyebrow. "Back so soon?"

"It's freezing out there," I huffed. "Like, see-your-breath freezing."

He frowned and then sat up. "Fucking hell, I should have fed more wood to the stove last night."

I burrowed under the covers while he stood up and began rustling through his luggage for clothing. I peeked out from under the covers to get a last glimpse of his glorious body before he covered it up. Damn, I'd been cuddled up to all that male perfection and had squandered my opportunity. That was when I made up my mind that I wouldn't leave this weekend behind with regrets.

♫♫♪♪

Our spa technician, Janelle, led me to the women's changing room. I didn't know what to expect for this ten-step hydrotherapy session, so I tried to get Janelle to give me an idea.

"Oh, you'll love them all. A lot of the clients balk at the polar plunge, but afterward, they rave at how invigorating it is."

She left me in the changing room with instructions to meet her back at the blue door with the 'hydrotherapy' sign on it which we had passed.

I changed into my bikini and surveyed myself in the mirror. I'd worn this bikini in public many times, to pool parties or to the beach, and

I'd never felt so obscenely exposed before. Why did it suddenly feel so scandalously skimpy? I needed to shake off my self-consciousness. I had a great body; there was no need to try to hide it from Scotty.

I turned away from the mirror and slipped into the plush, white spa robe, tightening the belt at my waist. My feet slid into my flip-flops, and then I was ready. I stuffed my clothes and shoes into a locker and slammed it shut. I took a deep, cleansing breath and then headed back to where the technician told me to meet.

Scotty had already finished changing and was waiting at the door. He was wearing a pair of black swim trunks and he looked hot. I'd have plenty of time to check out his delicious body and I didn't want to ogle in an obvious manner, so I kept my eyes locked above his shoulders. He was chatting with Janelle, who had her hand resting on his arm. She pulled her hand off and took a step back as I approached.

"Looks like we're all ready! There's a light near the exit door at each station. When the light turns green, you may proceed to the next step on the circuit. None of the steps will last longer than ten minutes, and some of the steps are quite short." Her voice took on the fake enthusiasm of someone who'd repeated the same spiel over and over.

Scotty put his arm around my waist and pulled me close. "Janelle, you mentioned that this was a private session. Does that mean we won't run into any other guests?"

"That's right." Her eyes sparkled with mischief. "The sessions are staggered, so even if you didn't vacate one of the steps, it would take two cycles for the next session to catch up to you. And if you do decide to remove your swimsuits, you'd want to cover up again before you finish step 10."

Scotty squeezed my waist. "Oh, that's very interesting."

Janelle used a key card to open the heavy door. "I wish you both a refreshing and invigorating journey."

Arrows were painted on the floor, directing us which way to go. I followed Scotty down a narrow walkway, my heart racing with anticipation. The air was thick with the scent of lavender, as we followed the arrows to the first step. The sign on the door read, STEP 1 AROMATHERAPY STEAM ROOM.

We stepped inside the hot room and closed the door. I took my robe off and hung it on a hook near the door, feeling Scotty's eyes on me the whole time. The mineral-enriched water felt like a balm on my skin. A eucalyptus scent filled the room and I felt my body relax. The room was small, and the seating was tight. I sat down on the wooden bench next to Scotty, pretending that his nearly naked body, so close to mine, didn't affect me. I relaxed the tension in my shoulders and I could feel my worries begin to melt away.

"This is heaven." I closed my eyes. "I hope all the steps are this nice, but Janelle said something about a polar plunge."

"She also said something about getting naked."

I teased him playfully. "You're going to take off your swimsuit and do the polar plunge? Isn't shrinkage a thing with guys?"

He chuckled. "You have a point. That might not be so impressive. That's why I've got to impress you now."

"Keep your pants on," I said dryly. "I'm trying to relax."

I could feel him moving around on the bench next to me. "What if you took off your top? That would be relaxing, no?"

I popped one eye open. "You have a one-track mind."

He shifted his body, leaning closer to me. "Let's make a bet. If you win, I'll take off my trunks. If I win, then you take off your top."

I pushed him away with a hand. Was I flirting with him? "It sounds like a win-win for you."

He grinned and shrugged nonchalantly. "A win-win would be both of us getting naked."

I eyed him warily as I cautiously replied, "And what is this bet?"

A look of triumph — like he'd already won — gleamed in his eye. "I bet that I can make you laugh in the next five minutes."

I felt a bead of sweat drip down my neck. "Please, you are so going to lose. I never laugh at jokes. You could tell the funniest joke in all of history and I won't even crack a smile."

"I guess we're on then." He held out his hand for me to shake.

"Okay." I shook his hand. "But how are we going to know when five minutes is up without a timer?"

He pushed away my concerns as if they didn't matter. "We'll have to estimate it. I'll leave it up to you to decide when the time is up."

I narrowed my eyes at him suspiciously. He'd better have something up his sleeve, or this was going to be a cakewalk. "Fine. You have the next five minutes to make me laugh. Let the games begin."

He patted his thigh. "Come sit on my lap."

"What?" I scoffed. "You think that's going to make your jokes funnier? Spoiler alert: it's not."

He didn't even crack a smile. "Then come over here. I dare you."

He dared me? What was this insanity? And why was I standing up and stepping toward him?

Ever since waking up curled around him this morning, I'd wanted to touch him again. Here we were, all hot and sweaty, with lots of skin showing. No wonder I couldn't stop myself.

I crossed over to him and sat daintily on his lap, but he anchored his hands on my hips and pulled my back snugly against him. My head fell back against his chest when his lips touched my neck. He was kissing me, and then his tongue was following a drop of moisture as it ran down my neck into the hollow of my shoulder.

I gasped. "What are you doing?"

"I'm trying to make you laugh," he grumbled against my skin.

Desire crashed through me. "That's ... that's not going to work."

He chuckled, low and deep, the sound vibrating against my skin. "Maybe not, but I bet I can make you do something else."

I shivered at the promise in his words. This dare had taken a turn I hadn't anticipated. But why did it feel so right?

He nipped at my shoulder, his teeth grazing over the sensitive skin. I moaned, a sound that surprised me as much as it seemed to surprise him.

"You like that," he said, his voice thick with arousal.

I tried to deny it, but my body was betraying me. I shifted on his lap, trying to find some relief from the throbbing ache between my legs. I couldn't focus on anything else but him and the way he was touching me.

"Stop," I said weakly, even as I arched my back to give him better access. "We shouldn't be doing this."

He nipped at my earlobe, making me gasp. "Who says we can't have a little fun?" he whispered hotly in my ear before trailing kisses down my neck and collarbone.

I couldn't find the words to argue, not when every touch from him was making me feel so alive. I found myself grinding against him, wanting more of the pleasure he was giving me.

Just as I was about to reach my peak, the light on the sauna wall suddenly came on. We were supposed to move from this room to the next.

Reluctantly, I broke apart from him. I hauled in a shaky breath. My body burned for more of his touch, and I looked away, belatedly embarrassed by my wanton behavior. "That's our cue to leave."

"Janelle said we could stay longer," he murmured.

I stood up and grabbed my robe from the hook. "Let's go. We've got nine more stations to get through."

He stood up and wiped the sweat from his brow before he fanned his face and blew out a long breath. He adjusted the noticeable bulge in his swim trunks with such a look of pure concentration on his face that it was comical. "Is it just me, or was it getting really hot in here?"

His entire demeanor was so absurd that a chirp of nervous laughter escaped my throat.

He stopped mid-motion and stared at me.

"That wasn't a laugh!" I insisted.

He pinned me with cunning scrutiny. "Yes, it was."

I turned away and scurried to the door. It was time to escape to the next station. I left the sweltering heat box and followed the arrows to the second station, aware that Scotty was following me.

Step 2 was Spa Shower with Massaging Body Jets. The instructions said that the shower was pre-programmed, so we should 'just press start and relax'.

Scotty followed me as we stepped into the enclosure. Dual showerheads were mounted overhead and the tile walls were covered with an array of jets pointing in every direction and from every angle.

"Ready?" Scotty asked.

I nodded and watched him press the button.

It was exactly how I imagined the ice bucket challenge. Torture. I squealed with alarm as a stream of ice-cold water fell from above, drenching us. Seconds later, as I was reaching for the door to escape, it stopped and was replaced by warm water pulsing from the jets in the walls.

There was no discernable pattern to the water assault. The water stayed mostly at a warm, comfortable temperature, but occasionally a hotter stream cycled through. Random blasts of cold water had me trying to escape their paths as I cursed the spa gods. Sometimes the streams of water were gentle, but sometimes they were powerful enough to sting, especially if they were too close and aimed at a tender body part. I was trying to hide behind Scotty from a particularly rough jet that was determined to pummel my boobs with a powerful blast of cold water every so often.

What was probably only a few minutes felt like an eternity. Finally, the light went on, signaling us to move stations and I was happy to leave. We shut down the shower and stepped out. My heart was thumping and my skin was tingling. If nothing else, it had been invigorating.

I wrung out my hair. "Wow, that was crazy. I feel like I went a few rounds with a boxer."

Scotty agreed. "That's not what I consider relaxing. I wonder what's next."

The next room was STEP 3: DETOXIFY IN OUR MAGNETIC CLAY BATHS. Hesitantly, I stepped inside the next room. Two tubs sat side by side in the middle of the small room. They were already filled with a grayish-brown liquid. I dipped a finger into the clay water and sighed with relief to feel the hot water.

"This, I can deal with." I stepped gingerly into the tub and, in seconds, I had sunk into the soothing water up to my shoulders.

Scotty eyed his tub for a moment and then followed suit.

Under the murky water, I began unfastening my bikini top. "Well," I said wryly, "I'm pretty sure that five minutes is up."

He shook his head. "I'm pretty sure I heard you laugh."

"Fair is fair, and I'm not a cheater." I pulled the bikini top from my chest and tossed it on the floor in between our two tubs.

The clay began to work its magic as I laid my head against the back of the tub. I could almost feel the toxins being pulled from my body as I relaxed.

I snuck a peek at Scotty and this time I really did have to suppress a laugh. He looked like he was about to swallow his tongue as he tried to peer through the dark water into my tub.

# Chapter 15

## Knox

AS A MEMBER OF a rock band, I'd seen thousands of breasts. We got flashed tits pretty much wherever we went in public. On stage, we were probably flashed at least five times a show. I'd actually signed my autograph across too many chests to count. And after a show? They were offered up to me on a platter — big tits, little tits, enhanced tits, and once even seventy-year-old tits. I'd grown immune to it all. Somewhere along the line, seeing a girl's tits had lost its excitement.

So why was my dick acting like I'd never seen a pair of tits before? Summer was relaxing in the tub next to me and I was tense as fuck. This lass was twisting me up in knots. As a test, I lifted my arm out of the clay water to make sure no gunk was sticking to my skin. It wasn't, so when the light eventually turned on and indicated it was time to go to the next station, I was going to feast my eyes. I stared at the light, waiting impatiently. I felt like a horny lad.

The room was so silent I could hear my own ragged breathing. The wait was excruciating. This felt much longer than ten minutes. I opened up a water bottle that was placed on a small table just within reach.

"Do you want some water? Janelle said it was important to keep hydrated, especially during the detox steps."

She didn't open her eyes but held out her hand and answered, "Sure."

I handed a new bottle to her and guzzled down most of my own. C'mon light, turn on.

She took a sip. "This is so relaxing. I could stay in here all day." When the light finally flashed on, my eyes swung to her. "The light's on. It's time to hit the next station."

She didn't move a muscle, but her lips curved into a cunning smile. I stood up, hoping to move this along faster. My eyes remained fixed on her as I didn't want to miss a thing. I was prepared for her to scramble for her robe or her bikini top to cover up and I wanted to look my fill while I could.

I waited with bated breath until finally, she rose gracefully out of the tub. She didn't try to hide herself. Her beauty and confidence made her look like a goddess rising from the sea. Her perfect feminine curves and pert breasts glistened in the light as tiny droplets of water ran down her skin. Her breasts were round and full, with nipples that matched the color of her lips, a dark, dusty pink. I wanted to reach out and touch her, to feel the warmth of her skin and run my fingers over her every curve.

Her beauty mesmerized me. "Your, uh, breasts are... really nice."

She cupped both of them in her hands, bit her lip, and then swiped her thumbs over her nipples. Bloody hell, my cock was throbbing.

She arched a brow. "Why, thank you. But what were you really going to say? Before you censored yourself?"

I blinked at her. She was right; I hadn't wanted to sound like a crude arsehole. "Uh, your chebs are braw."

"Is that a compliment?" She picked up her bikini top from the floor.

"It is, Sunshine. I wish I were more poetic, but trust me, lass, your tits are magnificent."

To my dismay, she covered them up with the robe. "Let's see what's next."

I followed her out the door and to the next station, STEP 4: THE RAIN SHOWER. Summer disrobed before stepping into the small enclosure and this time I was within reaching distance of her phenomenal body. Christ, it was torture.

The air was heavy with moisture and thick with a floral smell I couldn't identify. Summer pressed the start button on the electronic pad and a gentle and warm stream of water fell from two showerheads in the ceiling. Sounds of a tropical jungle, calling birds and buzzing insects mixed with the sound of wind shaking the branches of trees, were piped in from somewhere.

Summer was rinsing her hair and scrubbing a few clay clusters that were still stuck to her skin in the water. She wasn't even paying attention to the fact that I was standing right beside her. When she was satisfied, she reached for her discarded bikini top and began rinsing it under the water.

"Make sure you get all the clay off you," she advised.

I half-heartedly used my hands to rub at my chest and arms. "I'd rather help you. Are you sure you've got everything clean?"

She turned to me. I had to suck in a breath — her nipples were practically touching my chest. "How about you make sure?"

"Can I touch you?" my voice sounded hoarse.

Water streamed down her face as she looked up at me. "Yes."

I hesitantly reached out and ran my fingers over her shoulders. She made a noise of encouragement, a feminine mewl that turned my cock to stone. I traced a path down her arms and then looked into her eyes. The look on my face must have been one of lust because she shuddered slightly in response. I held my breath as I let my palms slide over her tight nipples. Her breathing was shallow as I circled them with my thumbs until she trembled and moaned softly. A thundering need tore through me.

Suddenly, the water turned off. I groaned as she stepped away from my hands. She scurried out of the room, clutching her robe and her bikini top to her chest.

I trailed behind her. The next room was called the CRYSTAL MEDITATION AND COLOR THERAPY ROOM. The room contained cushions and pillows scattered across the floor and had a large crystal in each corner that sat on a pillar. Lining the edges of the room were trays laden with crystals and glass orbs. Overhead, a series of track lighting shined different colors that reflected off the crystals and bounced different colors all over the entire room. The effect was a mix somewhere between New Age spiritualism and hippie psychedelic, but as I sat next to a topless Summer, calm meditation was not on my mind. There was a lot of energy in the room; I could feel it radiating between us, but it wasn't from the crystals. It was pure sexual desire.

I brushed a strand of wet hair away from her face and leaned in to kiss her. She welcomed me with open lips and soon, our tongues were playing together. I cupped the back of her head with my hand, deepening the kiss further. I wanted to feel every inch of her body, to get lost in it.

Feeling my rock-hard erection, she made a sound in the back of her throat and shifted, wrapping her legs around my torso so that I could feel her heat through my swim trunks. I growled as I reached down to cup her ass. She shivered at my touch and began to move against me slowly.

Her breathing quickened as she brought her mouth close to mine again, our lips barely touching as we explored each other's mouths with our tongues. She tasted like strawberries, sweet and intoxicating.

I ran my hands up and down her body, exploring every curve, feeling every inch of her skin against mine. My fingers traced lazy circles on her curves and dips, eliciting moans from both of us. Her passionate response only increased my need for more; I wanted to explore further but was afraid of going too far too fast.

Summer seemed to sense this and took the lead by reaching down between us and tugging at the waistband of my trunks. Not needing any more encouragement, I pulled Summer's bikini bottom to the side and stroked her clit until she was rocking against my hand. I sunk my fingers inside her and her moans turned into desperate pleas for more.

I laid her back against the pillows and quickly removed her bikini bottom. Pushing open her knees, I looked my fill as her flesh was painted in multi-colored lights from the lights flashing above. I didn't have a condom, so as much as I wanted to sink inside her, I couldn't. Instead, I planned to give her the orgasm of her life using my fingers and mouth.

Not wasting another second, I buried my face between her legs. "Oh God, Scotty." She moaned and braced her hands against my head. "Don't stop."

I'd been waiting for this for so long.

I teased her clit with my tongue over and over again until she was arching off the floor in pleasure. As she moaned and writhed beneath me, I inserted a finger into her tight heat. Her wetness glistened against my finger, proof of how turned on I made her.

I increased the speed and pressure as I circled her clit, while at the same time thrusting faster with my fingers. She gasped and her breaths came out in short, choppy bursts. Her pink nipples had tightened into stiff peaks and I couldn't help but lean down to take one in my mouth.

Summer's head thrashed from side to side as she begged for more, and I obliged by pushing an extra finger inside her. She clenched around my fingers, screaming out my name as an orgasm crashed through her body like waves against a beach.

I gave her a few moments to collect her wits while I tried to rein in my straining cock. I decided right then and there that tonight, when I had a condom, I was going to fuck her so spectacularly that she'd never have sex again without thinking of me.

Summer's breathing had finally steadied, and her eyes opened, a dazed expression on her face. She looked up at me and sighed. "Tell me I'm not going to regret this."

"You won't." I leaned down and captured her lips with mine for a gentle, sensuous kiss.

She must have felt my hard cock pressing against her thigh. "What about this? Do you want me to..."

Yes, I'd wanted her lips around my cock since the first time I'd seen her standing in line at the coffee shop. But this tit-for-tat didn't seem right. It seemed off. I wanted something more meaningful from her than the faceless, nameless transactions that I got from fans.

Just then, the light clicked on in the room, signaling that our time was up at this station. That was good. I didn't have to explain what I didn't even understand myself.

"We've got to go." I stood up and handed the white spa robe to her.

To my dismay, she quickly pulled her bikini back on and then put on the robe. Within seconds, we were out the door and following the arrows to the next room, which turned out to be the Ice Room.

Electric blue light suffused the room and a strong smell of peppermint lingered in the air. Layers of ice crystals that almost looked like snow covered parts of the walls, floor, and ceiling.

Any arousal I felt was instantly frozen. My private parts were in full retreat. "I'm literally going to have blue balls."

Summer laughed, forming a puff of condensation from her mouth. "Oh my God, this is like a meat locker. It's freezing. This doesn't seem very therapeutic."

I wrapped my arms around my chest, trying to keep warm. "It said it was supposed to increase your circulation and make you feel refreshed and revived."

"We're going to have to be revived after this." She muttered. "This is crazy! We're wet, too."

The light finally turned on, and we both bolted for the door. We were probably only in there for two minutes, but it felt like forever.

The HIMALAYAN SALT SAUNA was next. Neither of us spoke. We sat on the bench and let the dry heat warm up our bodies and relax our muscles.

"Ahh, this is much better." Summer sighed as she leaned her head against the wall.

I nodded in agreement and soon enough the lights clicked on and we were heading to our next station — THE RAIN TUNNEL AND THREE POOLS. I had no idea what to expect, but when we walked in, it was like walking into a tropical jungle. A huge wall framed by bamboo entwined with orchids and other leafy plants overlooked the three small pools that were filled with milky-blue water.

The air was thick with humidity and the sound of a waterfall cascaded from somewhere deep in the room. The walls were lined with different kinds of rain showers, from a light mist to a heavy downpour. I looked at Summer and she smiled, stepping forward through the tunnel and towards the first pool.

We slowly made our way across the damp floor and into the water of the first pool, gasping as we felt the warm caress of the liquid. The sensation was unlike anything I'd ever experienced before. As I stepped into the salty, warm water, a wave of serenity enveloped me. I felt like I was wrapped in a comfortable embrace.

Summer's cheeks were flushed, and she had a soft smile on her lips as we made our way past one of the rain showers and to the center pool. The water in this pool was cold and clear. I followed as Summer waded across to the other side fairly quickly.

When we came to the third pool, Summer dipped a toe into the water. "It's ice cold. This must be the polar plunge."

I grabbed her hand. "C'mon, we'll do it together. We'll jump in and then get right out."

She tried to pull her hand out of mine. "I'm not a fan of cold water."

"You'll be in for less than a minute. It'll be worth it."

I thought about pulling her in with me, but I thought better and let go of her hand before jumping into the pool. Icy-cold water enveloped my body and for a moment, all my senses were in shock. I popped up above the surface and laughed.

"Get in here. Don't be a big chicken."

She held her nose, jumped in the water, and came up sputtering. "Shit! I hate cold water."

She scrambled the ten feet or so to the far edge of the small pool and pulled herself out in record time. I was right behind her.

This time, she didn't even wait for the light to turn on. She pushed through to the next station, which was called the BUBBLING WHIRLPOOL. Basically, it was a hot tub with jets.

We relaxed in the hot tub until the light turned on and then reluctantly pulled ourselves out. The arrows led us to the PEBBLED

Walkway Foot Massage, which was a shallow trench filled with water and lined with smooth pebbles that twisted and turned in a maze-like pattern. Warm jets were incorporated to massage the foot and ankles as you walked in the warm salt water.

At the end of the path, there was a sign that read:

This is the last stop on your hydrotherapy journey. Please make sure you have all your possessions with you. A technician will meet you as you exit the door. Come visit us again.

Two fresh robes hung on hooks by the door. I pulled them down, handed one to Summer, and then put the larger-sized one on.

Janelle was waiting for us on the other side of the door. "How was it? Did you enjoy the circuit?"

Summer laughed. "Let's just say it left me hot and cold. Literally."

Janelle turned to me. "And you? Did you like it?"

"Yes." I winked at Summer and she blushed. "I especially enjoyed the crystal room."

Janelle agreed, "Oh yes. That room is very soothing."

She waved us over to a small sitting area. There were several tables set up, but Janelle led us to a little alcove that had a built-in leather bench seat in front of a window. A small teapot and two cups with saucers sat on the table in front of it.

"Relax and enjoy some tea. When you are finished, you can head back to the locker rooms to get changed. Head right through this doorway and down the hall and you'll see them."

Janelle departed and Summer poured some tea into our cups. The tea had a pungent aftertaste and tasted a bit like dirt, to be honest. I didn't even finish a full cup.

Summer had no problem drinking it, though. She sipped her cup and said, "That was so unexpected. I do feel kind of invigorated after that."

After she finished her tea, we made our way back to the locker rooms. I felt refreshed, recharged, and rejuvenated after my hour completing the strange therapy, but the best therapy of all was seeing Summer naked and making her come.

# Chapter 16

**Summer**

"I WANT TO FUCK you when we get back to the yurt." Scotty leaned in close to my ear and growled the sexy words at me.

A sudden rush of intense heat coursed through my veins, making my body go rigid from the sheer force of it. It felt like a million sparks were igniting inside of me, moving and twisting through my veins, traveling to my fingertips and the tips of my toes. My heart raced, pounding in my chest like a drum as a deep blush rose into my cheeks. The effect those words set off inside me was akin to an atomic bomb going off. Judging by the cocky smile on Scotty's face, he knew it, too.

My parents were sitting across the table, only a few feet away, but thankfully, they were totally oblivious. I squirmed in my seat, thinking about Scotty's words. Did I want to have sex with him? Of course, I did. That wasn't the right question, though. The question was if it was a good idea to have sex with Scotty. My head said no, but I was almost certain I was going to ignore it. That orgasm had been too good.

After lunch, we'd started the afternoon being painfully polite with each other, but before long, we relaxed into having a fun time together. We borrowed my parents' rental car, shopped for a winter jacket for me, and then spent a couple of hours at an indoor ice rink we'd found online. Next door to the rink was an escape room. Since we still had a few hours to spare, we decided to try it. We had a blast working together to solve puzzles and figure out clues in order to escape from Alcatraz.

Now, dinner was winding down. Once again, Scotty had effortlessly charmed my parents. I was barely following the conversation; I was busy thinking about what would follow dinner.

Soon enough, though, we were saying our goodbyes and getting ready to head back to the yurt. As if sensing my thoughts, Scotty took my hand and gave me a devilish smile. He said nothing else, but the message was clear; he wanted me as much as I wanted him.

Our playful banter from the afternoon was gone on the walk back.

Scotty squeezed my hand. "Are you okay? You're so quiet."

The air was brisk, but there wasn't any wind tonight and the winter jacket was doing its job and keeping me warm.

"You made me nervous," I admitted.

He stopped in his tracks. "About tonight?" He ran a hand through his hair. "I thought you wanted it, too."

I tugged on his hand so we could resume walking. "I do. I just don't think it's a smart idea."

"Why not?" He fell into stride beside me.

I kept my focus on the dimly lit path ahead. "We're not a real couple. This is just pretend."

"So what? It's something we both want. Why can't you just enjoy yourself?" He didn't sound angry, just perplexed.

I tried to explain it to him. "I only have sex with men I think love me. Guys that I could have a future with."

"And where are all these men now?" he asked sardonically.

I winced. He'd hit the nail on the head. "You heard my mom. I have a terrible track record when it comes to picking men."

"Maybe you're just doing it wrong. You don't need a marriage proposal to have sex. Or even be in love. I have sex with women that I'm attracted to or who interest me. It doesn't have to be a huge thing. You can have a fucking amazing time together. Then, when you each go your separate ways, it's not a huge fucking deal. There are no feelings involved, so there's never any heartbreak."

"That sounds sad, actually." Even though he couldn't see my face in the dark, my lips pressed together into thin lines of contempt. "Is that what you do when you're traveling with a rock band? Fuck all the rejects the rock stars didn't want and call it fun?"

Instead of being offended, he laughed. "That's not how I would describe it, but essentially. Listen, I'm attracted to you. Bloody attracted. And I have fun being with you even when we're just hanging out. I know more about you than 99% of all the girls I've fucked."

"Should I be honored or something?" I scoffed. "That's pretty pathetic."

He threw up his hands. "I don't understand you. I know you're attracted to me. And you want to have sex with me. Why don't you just let yourself enjoy it? What's the bloody big deal?"

I didn't want to get hurt.

Somehow I already knew that Scotty had the power to hurt me, but I didn't answer. This night was already going downhill. It had started with heady anticipation, and now all of that was crashing down around me.

We got back to the yurt, and Scotty busied himself filling up the wood-burning stove. I had my fears, and I believed they were justified, but I couldn't bear for this night to end without having sex with Scotty.

So, I made a decision right then and there. I was going to put my fears aside and just let myself experience what Scotty was offering me — 'no strings' sex.

We were two consenting adults with nothing but my fears in the way, and I was done overthinking it.

I hung up my jacket and kicked off my boots. Before I could talk myself out of it, I walked up behind Scotty and wrapped my arms around his waist. "Let's just do this," I whispered in his ear, my breath tickling his neck.

He spun around, a look of surprise etched across his handsome features. "Are you sure?"

I nodded, my heart racing as I stepped into his embrace.

"You have no idea how much I've been wanting this," he said, his hands snaking around my waist and pulling me close to him.

Our lips met, a gentle brush of skin that generated an invisible spark of energy igniting between us. His kiss was tender and full of longing, his tongue tracing paths of fire on my own as if committing my taste to memory. I felt myself melting into him as his arms pulled me closer. His muscular arms enveloped me in a cocoon of warmth and security, heat radiating off his body and filling my own with a sense that we belonged together.

He broke away from our kiss and made a primitive growling noise in the back of his throat. Without warning, he scooped me up in his arms and carried me to the bed. He tossed me down on the thick blankets and then crawled on top of me like a predator trapping its prey.

He reached behind my neck and slowly pulled down the zipper on the back of my dress. Reverently, he peeled the material off my shoulders and let it slide down my body, trailing his fingers behind. His lips found every inch of skin he uncovered, sending me into a whirlwind of desire until every inch of me was aflame with urgent need.

Desperate to see him, I began fumbling with the buttons on his shirt. He hauled himself up and then quickly tore off his shirt as if he resented the interruption that separated us for a few seconds. When his shirt was gone, he made quick work of removing my bra.

My hands slid across the smooth skin of his toned chest, feeling the contours of his muscles and brushing over his nipple, but then buried in his thick hair when his lips found my breast. As his teeth grazed my hard, tender nipple with a gentle bite, I gasped in pleasure. His fingers lightly tugged on my other nipple, sending shockwaves of arousal through me. My fingers scraped along his scalp to urge him on. When he sucked the peak of my breast into his mouth, I panted as licks of desire radiated from the sensitive spot between my legs. His mouth on my body had me melting into pure bliss.

Scotty moved downward, his lips trailing down my stomach, making me crazy with arousal. His tongue darted out to lightly trace a path of desire across my skin and his hands continued to explore my body, massaging the ache that had built in me since the day I first saw him.

His mouth slid lower until it reached my panties. It didn't break contact with my skin while he slowly worked the panties down my legs. My body trembled as I laid exposed before him. His breath was heavy and ragged with desire, his passion evident in the burning intensity of his gaze. He moved closer, wrapped a hand around my thigh, and parted my legs wide. His eyes smoldered hungrily as he took in the sight of me.

He ran his fingers over my trembling skin and groaned, "You're so beautiful, I can't wait to taste you."

My breath caught as he lowered his head between my thighs and inhaled. "Fuck, you smell as good as you look."

His tongue ran over my sensitive core, and I cried out in pleasure. He swirled his tongue and licked me until his lips were coated in my essence and my legs trembled in ecstasy.

"Scotty," — I writhed beneath his mouth — "I'm so close."

"Not yet, sweetness," he rasped, spreading my legs even wider. "I'm not nearly done with you yet. I want to fuck you with my mouth."

He buried his head between my thighs and sucked my clit into his mouth, applying just the right amount of pressure. I clawed at the sheets as he thrust two fingers inside me, pushing in and out while his tongue moved in slow circles. My body arched off the bed as the intensity built to a level so impossible I thought I might implode.

"Scotty," I whimpered his name, "Oh God. I'm going to come so hard. Please."

I squirmed beneath him, thrusting my hips upwards to meet his mouth, begging him to send me over the edge. Instead, he pulled back. "No, not yet, Sunshine. We're not done yet."

He rubbed his hand up my thigh and hip, lightly skimming across my stomach to my breasts. His thumb stroked across my nipple, teasing and toying with me. At the same time, his other fingers began stroking the secret spot inside me.

I screamed out as I came undone around him. My muscles tensed and tightened, spiraling and coiling until I thought I would burst. A blazing sensation rippled through me as my orgasm surged and pulsed, jolting up from the base of my spine, every nerve ending in my body alive with pleasure.

"Fuck, Summer," he groaned into my pussy.

I was too wrung out to be embarrassed that I had just come all over his face and fingers. In a daze, I watched him scramble to remove his pants and then fumble in his wallet for a condom. His cock was just as beautiful as the rest of his body. It was long and thick and its head was swollen and glistening with precum. It throbbed as if it was on the verge of bursting with raw energy.

The need was clear on his face, a mix of desire and urgency. "Are you ready for me, Sunshine?"

My body shook with the aftershock of an intense orgasm, but watching him as he rolled a condom onto his cock had me licking my lips. "I'm ready."

"Good." He nodded his approval and then positioned his knees between my legs, opening me up to him. "Because I'm going to fuck another orgasm out of you."

Reaching down between us, he placed his cock at my entrance and slowly pushed inside. A hot flush of desire swept over me as I opened for him. I moaned as he planted a trail of kisses along my collarbone and down my neck. Tilting my hips up, I began to grind against him, demanding more.

He sucked in a breath as he slid further into me until he was completely buried inside of me. The feeling was so intense, so exquisite, that it was almost overwhelming, but I didn't want him to stop. I needed more.

"Please," I whimpered, my body beginning to shake as he started to move inside of me.

"You feel so good, Summer." He clenched his jaw, thrusting his hips to meet mine. I felt my body begin to tighten again as he continued to pump into me, faster and faster, until we were both panting and moaning.

"Oh, God," I murmured, feeling his teeth nipping my neck as he reached between our bodies and strummed his thumb against my clit.

"Come for me," he demanded, and I could feel him pulsing.

I detonated. My orgasm tore through me like a violent storm, tossing me about as I clung to Scotty. I cried out, my muscles twitching as I clenched around him. He groaned as he came, thrusting one final time as he spilled himself inside of me.

"That was amazing," he said, rolling onto his side and pulling me with him so that I was lying next to him on the pillows. I smiled and wrapped my arms around his body, resting my head on his chest.

He kissed the tip of my nose. "Let me go take care of this condom. Do you need anything?"

"No." I was still caught in a hazy, dream-like state. Why had I deprived myself of this for so long? Then again, no other man had ever made me feel as if thunderstruck.

Scotty returned and then held the covers so that we could both climb inside. He pulled me close, and I rested my face against his chest so that I could hear his heartbeat. His fingertips lazily traced circles on my arms. My eyes fluttered closed.

# Chapter 17

## Knox

I WOKE UP IN the morning with Summer tucked against me. Her leg was draped over mine, her hand was resting on my chest, and her chin was nestled in the crook of my neck. She was so close that I could feel each soft exhale on my skin. Deep satisfaction settled into my bones. I felt like a caveman, feeling a swell of possession at having my woman in my arms. She wasn't quite my woman, but she was the closest thing I'd had to a girlfriend in a long time.

Last night, I'd wanted to go for another round. Or more. But Summer had fallen asleep right away, and after our incredibly exhausting day, I didn't want to wake her.

I'd woken horny as fuck, but I was afraid of how she was going to feel about having had sex with me when she woke up. Would she regret it? I wasn't sure. But, I didn't have any. Sex with her had been mind-blowing.

When I first laid eyes on her, I thought she looked like my fantasy girl. She was a blonde-haired, blue-eyed, delicate beauty with perfect skin, hair, and teeth. On top of that, she was stylish and confident, sassy and funny. Not only was beautiful, but she had a terrific personality. She was the whole package.

And that was before I'd seen her with her clothes off. Now that I had, I was powerless to resist her. She wasn't just my fantasy girl; she was my dream centerfold. Her gorgeous figure with luscious curves and velvety soft skin was womanly and decadent, and the taste of her was just as intoxicating. I had to stop thinking about it because now my hard dick was poking into her stomach.

I took a deep breath and just allowed myself to enjoy having her in my arms. It was a rare feeling to wake up with a warm body next to me and not panic. I didn't feel the immediate urge to flee. I wasn't worried that a picture of my cock and a review of my sexual performance had made it to some fan site on the internet.

Summer wasn't a celebrity chaser or a groupie who'd had sex with most of my friends. She chose to be with me, not the fame or rock star. And I'd gotten to know her. I'd spent time with and I actually enjoyed talking to her, teasing her, and just spending the day with her.

Based on her appearance, I'd initially thought that she was a bitch. Then, she'd been so sassy with me. In reality, she was a sweet girl. She genuinely cared about others. Behind the sass, she was shy, but once she got past her hang-ups, she didn't hold back in the bedroom. She'd actually shattered in my hands, fallen apart under my tongue, and looked at me like I was a god. She was looking at me, not the rock star.

A twinge of guilt prodded me. She'd gotten hurt by men before and it had made her wary. Was I being selfish to fuck her? Would I end up another bloke on her list of arseholes who'd used her? What would happen when she found out that I'd hidden my real identity from her?

Every time she called out my nickname, Scotty, while my face was buried between her legs, I'd felt a stab of guilt. I wanted her to be screaming out my real name as I brought her to a state of bliss.

I'd gotten what I was after — to fuck her — maybe it was time to reveal the truth? How badly would she react? What would her parents think of me? After this weekend, we wouldn't be together, so what did it matter, anyway?

I rubbed at my chest as I felt a weird, foreign sensation. Was it regret? Guilt? Or was it the fact that we wouldn't see each other again bothering me? I really like her. Why did I have to walk away from that? What the bloody hell was going on with me?

Summer stirred in my arms. Her blue eyes popped open, and she gazed at me.

I grinned at her sleep-confused face. "Good morning, Sunshine."

She tried to slide her leg out from mine, but I squeezed it, trapping it in place.

I arched an eyebrow. "You're not going anywhere, sweetness."

Her eyes darted around in panic. "I have to take a shower. I'm supposed to meet with my mom today. And you're going out with my dad! Oh my God!"

I sighed. She was in full panic mode, so I let her leg go. Within seconds, she was pulling all that soft, warm flesh from me.

I watched her scramble out of bed. "Relax, we have plenty of time. I can order us some breakfast. We can eat in bed."

She scampered behind the bathroom curtain. "Um, okay. Breakfast would be fine. Get me an omelet and some orange juice, please."

She came out of the bathroom nook wrapped in a towel, hiding her delectable body. She dug through the dresser drawers, searching for clothes.

I sat up in bed. "Summer, are you okay?"

"Yeah, sure," she answered off-handedly. "All good. I'm just going to jump in the shower before breakfast gets here."

A few seconds later, she disappeared into the bathroom nook. I guess we weren't going to eat in bed. Too bad, because I had an appetite and it wasn't just for food.

I got up and put on a pair of sweatpants, ordered breakfast, and then tended to the wood-burning stove. I knew she couldn't stay in the bathroom forever. The hot water didn't last that long. Briefly, I thought about attempting to join her in the shower, but that probably wasn't a good idea. She was too busy freaking out.

I needed to put her mind at ease and smooth over the awkward morning after. I wanted to dispel her fears, but I wasn't sure how to, without leading her on.

The shower stopped. I kept expecting her to emerge, but time ticked on. What the hell was she doing in there? When she finally came out of the bathroom, she was fully dressed in gray leggings, a pink zip-up hoodie, and thick wool socks. She had no makeup on and her hair was pulled up in a bun. She looked adorable.

"Breakfast should be here in about 15 minutes," I told her.

She walked straight up to me and placed her hands on my chest. Fuck, her hands on me felt good.

"That should be enough time," she said cryptically.

"Enough time for what?"

Her hands swept across my pecs and then lowered onto my abs. I sucked in a breath as they traced even lower, catching the waistband of my sweatpants with her fingers. My cock thickened with arousal. What was she doing?

Slowly, she lowered my pants until they were around my ankles. My cock stood at attention. I hissed when she wrapped her fist around it.

"Sunshine?" The word came out raspy and hoarse with the lust squeezing my throat. She had sunk to her knees, her mouth only inches from my straining dick. She looked up at me with her big blue eyes and traced her tongue over her lip seductively.

Ignoring my question, she went right to work.

"Oh, fuck!" I moaned.

Her mouth felt as heavenly as I thought it would. She flicked her tongue across the head of my dick, swirling it around my slit. She traced a line up and down my length while paying special attention to the sensitive spots. Her fist encircled the base of my cock, and then her mouth engulfed me as she sucked me in deep, her lips making a tight seal around my hard length. When her head began bobbing up and down my dick, a raging passion ignited inside me that spread like wildfire. I closed my eyes and moaned out in pure, unadulterated bliss.

She wasn't letting up. I buried my hands in her hair, trying to slow her down, but only ending up spurring her on. It was too much. My balls tightened and lust blazed through my veins. Pressure flooded my cock as an aching burst of need licked down my spine.

My release roared through me with the fury of a tsunami. It was so intense that I thrust even deeper inside her mouth, even as I was coming in jolt after jolt of spurting convulsions until I could barely see straight.

She pulled off my cock and then wiped the corner of her mouth with a sly smile on her face. I stood rooted to the spot, not trusting my legs to move.

She sat back on her knees and then bent her head as if listening to something. "That sounds like the golf cart. Breakfast must be here."

I stared down at her, still too dazed to even attempt speech. She grabbed my sweatpants and worked them back up my legs and over my hips. She gave my ass a playful pat and then walked to the door. I heard the door open and then she was gone.

I needed to shake off this stupor, but I was in shock. Out of nowhere, my fantasy girl had dropped to her knees in front of me and given me the best head of my life. I'd had plenty of blowjobs before and not one had ever come close to that. It astonished me and confused me at the same time.

I shook my head to clear it as Summer came back inside the yurt with a tray of food.

She breezed through the room and placed the tray on the table. "Gary is going to give me a ride up to the hotel with the golf cart so I can meet my mom. I'll have breakfast with her. You're probably getting sick of me and this will give you some time alone to enjoy your breakfast. I'll have my dad text you what time he wants to meet you in the lobby."

My mouth dropped open. "What just happened?"

"The blowjob?" She shrugged nonchalantly. "It's no big deal. We're adults. I was just having fun."

I couldn't believe it. "You're leaving?"

She grabbed her winter jacket off the hook near the door. "I'll see you at dinner. Have a good time at the brewery with my father."

Before I could say anything more, she walked out the door. She said something to Gary and giggled, and then moments later, the golf cart was pulling away.

I didn't want to eat breakfast alone; I wanted to eat with her. The weight of her absence pressed down on me as I stared into empty space, trying to comprehend why she had left.

How could she give me the blowjob of my life and then just drop the mic and walk away like it was nothing?

# Chapter 18

## Summer

I SPENT THE DAY focused on my mother. She took pampering to an extreme by signing us up for every conceivable service. In the morning, we both got manicures and pedicures, followed by facials. I got a deep cleansing facial, and she got an anti-aging facial treatment.

After a light lunch, we spent some time in the hot tub relaxing, and then came the non-stop treatments: body exfoliations, waxing, body wraps, deep hair conditioning treatments, and make-up consultations. My mother did some of those with me and some different ones of her own.

It had been over a year since I'd spent such quality time with her, and I enjoyed our time reconnecting. We talked, gossiped, and generally had a good time. As she requested, we didn't talk about her cancer, even though it was front and center in my mind. I could tell that not talking about it made a much more relaxing day for my mother, but after this weekend was finished, I was going to demand more information.

What wasn't off-limits was talking about Scotty. My mother gushed about him continuously and always found a way to bring his name into the conversation. Constantly deflecting her was getting tiresome, so I kept things about him on a superficial level. I didn't want to think too deeply about him for my own self-preservation.

As usual, I felt myself having deeper feelings for a man when I shouldn't. This time, however, the potential heartbreak was ten times worse. Not only was I physically attracted to Scotty, but our sexual chemistry was off the charts. He knew exactly how to work my body and he wasn't half-hearted in his efforts. I'd never had such uninhibited and satisfying sex in my life.

The difference had been eye-opening. My experience of sex with other men was akin to waving a sparkler, which fizzled out after 30 seconds. In comparison, sex with Scotty felt like the grand finale at the world's biggest fireworks show. His good looks, personality, and prowess between the sheets were a lethal combination, and I fully understood just how at risk I was for falling for him and having my foolish heart get trampled. I had to take a step back before I got burned.

It was late afternoon when my mother finally shooed me out of her hotel room. I didn't have much to do to get ready for dinner. At the spa, my hair had been blown out and curled into waves and my makeup had been applied by an expert, giving me a blue-gray smokey eye. It was heavier and sexier than my normal look, but it was suitable for a fancy dinner. Beyond the hair and makeup, my skin was as soft as a baby's behind and glowed, unwanted body hairs had been removed, and my nails were mini works of art and ready to be shown off.

All I needed to do was slip on a fancy outfit, spritz on some perfume, and adorn myself with some sparkly jewelry, but Mom had ordered me to get back to the yurt and 'spend some time with my man'.

That was the last thing I should be doing. All day, I'd been doing my best to keep him off my mind. He'd texted me throughout the day, asking me how it was going and giving me funny snippets of his day with my dad, but I refrained from answering, only texting back once with a brief 'It's going great'.

I was proud of myself. I wasn't going to turn down the fireworks tonight, but I was determined to think of it merely as a sex transaction. Just like Scotty did. That way, at the end of this, I could walk away unhurt. That was the goal.

There would be no emotional attachments. No getting close or learning about him as a person. And absolutely no cuddling afterward. Just because we were sleeping in the same bed didn't mean I had to cozy up to him all night. I would enjoy the sex without all the other intimacy.

Scotty was in the shower when I got back to the yurt. I used the time to finish getting ready for dinner. For our last night here, my parents made reservations at a restaurant in a nearby town. We were meeting them in the hotel lobby shortly so that my father could drive us all there.

By the time Scotty stepped out of the bathroom with a towel wrapped around his waist, I was ready to go. There was no mirror in the yurt, but I knew that I looked pretty glam compared to the last few days of no makeup, crazy air-dried hair, and yoga pants.

Scotty took one look at me and a giant smile, complete with gorgeous dimples, broke out on his face. "Wow." He let out a slow whistle. "You look hot."

I was pleased with his reaction, but I tamped it down. I would not let myself get sucked in because there was no future for Scotty and me. He'd told me as much.

"Thank you. I was thinking about going to... hmm, what was it? Oh yeah, my Barbie club meeting after dinner." My cutting wit and sharp tongue had kept men at bay for over a year now. It was time I got back to that.

He wasn't deterred. His eyes sparkled as he approached me, and then he wrapped his arms around me in a hug. "Everyone knows how hot Barbie is, Sunshine. And she's got nothing on you. Really, you look beautiful."

I stood stiffly in his arms. Where were his insults? Why was he complimenting me and being so sweet? We didn't have to fake anything when my parents weren't around.

Feeling his muscular arms around me was dangerous. I stepped back out of his embrace. "You're going to get me all wrinkled. You better get dressed. We have to leave soon."

I spun around, but not before I saw something flash across his face. It looked like confusion mixed with a little bit of hurt. I didn't want to be a bitch, but I had to protect myself. I wasn't built like him where I could live in the now and not worry about the future.

Scotty's motto was 'Love the one you're with'. That wasn't me. He wouldn't be the one suffering when the weekend was over and he walked away like it was nothing but an enjoyable romp in the sack.

"Did you and your mom have a good time at the spa?" He began pulling out clothes for dinner.

I didn't want to watch him get dressed, but there really was absolutely nothing to do in the yurt. I walked the few steps to the hutch in the kitchen area and began opening its drawers, not even sure what I could be pretending to look for.

"Yes, we had a nice time catching up."

"I'm glad. I had a great time with Jim." He began an excited appraisal of his day. "The brewery tour was nothing special, but they had this awesome beer-flavored pretzel with dips. And the samples were all really good."

"That's nice." I was only half listening.

He continued speaking as he got dressed. "Then we went to this Irish pub and watched the Kentucky game. Holy shite, Sunshine, your father is insane. He is such a crazy sports fan! Thank God Kentucky won or I don't know what he would have done. He is definitely not a boring guy."

I snuck a peek and breathed a sigh of relief to see that he had pants and a shirt on. Somehow, from that small rolling bag of his, he was able to produce another stylish outfit. For a guy who I had first thought was homeless, he sure had great taste in clothes when he dressed up. He was wearing gray dress pants and a light blue button-down shirt with a darker sport coat over it. Everything was proportioned perfectly to show off his fit physique.

Scotty looked up and caught me staring at him. Darn. I quickly looked away. "Are you almost ready to go? Gary should be here any minute."

"Almost." He looked at my feet. I was wearing a pair of my favorite black stilettos with fringe around the ankle straps. "Are you going to bring some shoes to change into for the walk home? We can leave stuff your stuff in the car this time."

"Good idea." I rounded up a bag and stuffed socks and sneakers into it.

Gary arrived shortly after that and brought us up to the lobby where my parents were already waiting. I didn't have to do much talking because my parents were fawning all over Scotty like he was the best thing ever and Scotty was eating it up.

I was quiet in the car's backseat next to Scotty while everyone chatted.

Scotty leaned next to me and slid his arm around my shoulder. He whispered in my ear, "Are you worried about your mum, lass?"

I nodded, and he kissed my temple, tightening his arm around me.

Of course, I was worried about my mother. And sad that this weekend was almost over. And, curse it all, I was worried that I was not going to react well to saying goodbye to Scotty and parting ways with him.

He was a good guy. I liked him. Why couldn't a guy like that be interested in me for more than sex, anyway? What was wrong with me that I wasn't a long-term prospect?

I felt a lump in my throat. Crap, I was already getting upset. The only thing I could do now was mitigate the damage. I'd broken my vow, acted foolishly, and had to pay the price. I needed to keep my distance, so it didn't hurt as much.

I leaned away from Scotty and studied the landscape as it rushed by my window.

Dinner wasn't enjoyable. The food was delicious, and everyone seemed happy, but I was miserable inside. The more I ignored Scotty, the more attentive he was to me. He seemed determined to draw me out, to talk to me, and to keep giving me little touches, all the while charming my parents. He was so affable that I had to work hard to make sure I wasn't appearing churlish to my parents.

I didn't want to ruin their dinner. I ate and smiled and put in just enough effort that they wouldn't catch on that something was wrong.

On the car ride home, the conversation morphed from talking about the Wildcats basketball game to the Kentucky Derby, which got my attention, especially when Mom was inviting Scotty to attend.

My mom had turned in her seat to talk to Scotty. "I should be fully recovered from the surgery by then. You really just have to experience it! Come stay with us, Scotty. It's a wonderful time."

My dad chimed in, "You don't even have to follow horse racing to enjoy it. It's something else."

My mom agreed. "It's a grand spectacle. There are parties all day, fancy outfits and crazy hats galore, mint juleps, and tons of after-parties, too. The entire city goes wild. Really, the Derby should be on everyone's bucket list."

Scotty grabbed my hand and held onto it. "It sounds like a good time."

Mom beamed at him. "Oh, it is. Derby Day is on the first Saturday in May, but Thursday and Friday are fun, too. You should come for a long weekend visit."

I tried to pull my hand away, but Scotty wouldn't let it go. "Mom, I told you that Scotty's job keeps him very busy. He doesn't get much time off. We're lucky we got him here this weekend."

My mother's face sank. "Oh, that's a shame."

"I'd love to experience it, Lara. I'll see what I can work out with my schedule," Scotty promised.

My eyes narrowed and my jaw tightened. I threw him a look of disbelief and frustration before he could get her too excited about the idea of him going. Even though he hadn't said it, we both knew there was no chance of him actually making it.

I tried to temper her expectations. "Mom, I'm not even sure I can go this year. Flights into Kentucky are crazy expensive that weekend."

Her mouth fell open. "But, you've never missed the Derby except for that one year you got sick. And all your friends will be there."

"I'd like to go, but I live in Los Angeles now. It's not as easy anymore.

I didn't miss the expression on her face before she turned around in her seat. She was upset.

The lively conversation in the car grew quiet. I'd thrown a damper on my mother's enthusiasm. The Kentucky Derby was an event she eagerly anticipated every year and now more than ever, she needed something to look forward to in the future. Angry at distressing her, I yanked my hand out of Scotty's and scowled.

When we pulled into the long road that led to the resort, I pulled out my bag and changed out of my heels and into my sneakers. We said goodnight to my parents in the parking lot because we had to walk back to the yurt, which was in the other direction from the hotel. We made arrangements to meet up with them for breakfast at the hotel because they were driving us to the airport since our departing flights were not too far apart.

I snuggled inside my new down parka and started hiking back to the yurt while Scotty was still saying goodbye.

He jogged to catch up with me. "What's wrong? You've been upset all evening."

"Nothing's wrong. I'm just ready for this weekend to be over." In a twisted way, it was the truth. You play with fire, you were going to get burned.

My harsh words had finally shut Scotty up for a moment so I could think. We trudged back in silence.

The yurt was still warm and cozy when we got back, but Scotty pulled off his sports coat and rolled up his sleeves before adding more wood to the stove. I sat down and removed my sneakers and socks that had gotten wet from the snow.

Scotty finished up with the stove and then turned around to watch me. "If you're upset about your mom being sick, it's understandable, Sunshine. Maybe talking about it will help?"

Right now, I was more upset about this whole situation I'd gotten myself into than my mother's cancer and that was completely fucked up.

He came and sat next to me at the small kitchen table. "Let's talk about it."

"Let's not." I got up and went over to the bed.

This stupid yurt was so small and there was absolutely nothing to do in it. It wasn't even ten o'clock and I might as well get ready for bed, because what else could I do?

"I hate this yurt," I grumbled.

Scotty stood up and ran a hand through his hair. "Is it me? Are you mad at me? Talk to me. I just want to make you feel better."

He sounded really sincere, and that just made me angrier at him.

I ripped off my blouse and threw it on the floor. Then, I began tugging on the zipper of my skirt. "You want to make me feel better? Then, just fuck me."

He stood still and watched as I pulled off my skirt. I was wearing a sexy bra and panty set, but he didn't even seem to notice. His eyes were pinned on my face.

"Is that what you want?" His voice held a dark edge as his jaw clenched tightly and his brow furrowed.

I jutted out my chin. "That's what I want."

He stalked over to me, a glint of fierce determination with a smidgeon of anger in his eyes.

As soon as he reached me, I grabbed his belt and began crudely unbuckling it. His restraint was broken. The air between us crackled with electricity as we feverishly started to undress each other. His hungry mouth devoured my neck and shoulders, scraping across my sensitive skin and sending quakes of pleasure coursing through my veins. Our clothes hit the floor as we explored each other's bodies with frenzied urgency, desperate to get closer.

Once we were both naked, he picked me up and tossed me onto the bed. I lifted up on my elbows to watch him but then scrambled backward when I saw the fire in his eyes. His eyes were wide, with an animalistic glint in them, and his pupils were dilated. He leaned forward, closing the gap between us, and all I could hear was his heavy, labored breathing. He grabbed my ankle and halted my retreat.

He was on top of me in a second. I panted, trapped beneath him, my body tight with a pulsing desire. I couldn't think straight. The only thing I could hear or feel was him. My whole body belonged to him. I was his. I wanted him to take me, to conquer me.

"Yes," I moaned as he kissed me, hard.

This was what I wanted. My heart thundered in my chest. He let go of my ankle and grabbed both of my wrists, holding them above my head. I was completely at his mercy. He could do anything he wanted to me, and I wouldn't stop him. My body was on fire.

When he bit my neck, his teeth grazing my skin, I arched my back, my body desperate for more of him. He growled and sucked on my skin hard, probably leaving a mark. I squirmed beneath him as a molten heat gathered between my legs. I was going to explode.

"Please," I begged. "I need your cock."

He released my wrists and slid down my body, his mouth trailing hot kisses down my abdomen until he reached my dripping-wet pussy. He dove in hungrily, his tongue plundering deep inside me. Then his mouth latched onto my clit and sent shivers down my spine with his hot, slow suction. When I thought I couldn't take anymore, he nipped my sensitive clit with his teeth, sending shockwaves of pleasure rippling through my body.

I yelled out as I buried my hands in his hair. My legs quivered as he thrust his fingers inside me. He sought out the sweetest spot inside me and sent me into a feverish frenzy. My hips moved frenetically to match each of his urgent thrusts until I rode higher and higher, building toward an explosive release.

With an agonized groan, I climaxed violently, shuddering and writhing beneath him. I felt like every nerve in my body was sparking and igniting. Scotty pulled away from me and stood by the bed. I watched, breathless, as he found a condom and then rolled it on his cock.

His nostrils flared, and his jaw tightened as he watched me with a predatory focus. "Turn over. On your hands and knees," he ordered.

I had barely gotten into position when he was already pushing inside me. I whimpered as I felt every inch of him. He pulled back and then thrust forward, his forceful entry making me shudder.

"You feel so fucking good," he moaned.

"Scotty, yes! Don't stop."

"Fuck, you're tight." He pulled back and then thrust into me again.

I pressed my ass back to meet his hips, reveling in the feel of him inside me. I was completely lost in the sensation and when I realized I was going to orgasm again, so soon, I was astonished. As if he knew how close I was, he reached around and found my clit, massaging me as he thrust in and out.

"Oh my God, Scotty! I'm going to come again!"

"Come on my cock, Summer. I want to feel you come on me," he growled as he worked me into another orgasm. I threw my head back and let out a long, low moan as I came, my whole body shuddering.

He pumped into me hard and fast until, finally, he found his own release. After a few shaky breaths, we both fell into an exhausted heap of entangled limbs.

Scotty got up to use the bathroom, and I took that time to put on a pair of pajamas. I switched off the lights and then crawled back into bed. I closed my eyes and willed my body to fall asleep. He crawled back into bed and slid behind me so that he was spooning me.

At one point, in the middle of the night, I awoke to find myself sleeping in his arms. It felt so wonderful, but I knew I needed to protect my heart. I gingerly slid over to my side of the bed and forced myself to go back to sleep.

Tomorrow, I would walk away from Scotty, and I wouldn't look back, with either regret or sorrow.

# Chapter 19

**Knox**

I opened my eyes, blinked away the sleep, and noticed that Summer had already left the bed. The sound of running water came from the shower and the sweet, floral scent of Summer's soap wafted through the air. I felt a pang of regret; today was our last day in the yurt and I wanted to wake up with her in my arms, smelling the sweet scent of her skin.

She had been upset last night, but I couldn't get her to tell me why. I guess it didn't matter since we were heading home today, and after today, we wouldn't have to pretend to be dating anymore. We could go our separate ways, but I was hoping we could remain friends. We both lived in the same city and she'd been fun to hang out with. It was time I expanded my circle of friends outside of the band.

She was unusually quiet when she got out of the shower. She began packing up her clothes while I showered and got ready for the day. By nine o'clock, we were ready to check out of the yurt.

We met her parents for breakfast at the hotel. We had a nice, leisurely breakfast and then loaded all our luggage into the rental car. Summer spent most of the car ride talking to her mom or playing on her phone. There wasn't much chance for us to talk.

Part of me felt like I was getting the cold shoulder, but I wasn't too worried. I'd have plenty of time to talk to her on the plane and figure out what was going on with her. I suspected that her mother's cancer and upcoming surgery were heavy on her mind and that was understandable, but I wanted to help instead of her shutting me out.

We parted ways with her parents at the airport. I got a big hug from Lara and then a backslap and a handshake from Jim before I stood back to give them some privacy and watched Summer say goodbye. Even Jim had a tear in his eye when Summer and Lara pulled apart from their long embrace.

Summer kissed them both and then pulled herself away, a few tears trickling down her face. I grabbed her hand as she neared and we walked toward our gate for a couple of minutes until I heard a stifled sob and saw the tears really spilling.

I pulled her into my arms and rubbed her back. She melted into me, accepting my comfort for several long moments, until she pulled away. She angrily wiped the tears from her eyes and then continued walking without speaking a word. I trailed after her, wishing I could soothe her anxiety and fear about her mom.

When we reached our gate, I sat down next to her. "Can I get you anything?"

"No, I'm fine." She distracted herself with her phone, and I decided to let her be for now.

Suddenly, I wanted my guitar. I couldn't even remember the last time I'd gone so long without playing. After Aila died, playing guitar had been my only solace. In a way, playing was an escape from reality. Bored out of my mind as I waited to get on the plane, with Summer all but ignoring me, I needed that escape.

I sighed with relief when the announcement came over the speakers that the plane was boarding. We gathered up our stuff and got in line to board.

A girl, in her early 20s, was sitting in the aisle seat of our row. She was watching us approach with wide, beseeching eyes, and her whole face lit up when we sat down next to her. Christ, did she recognize me? I suddenly wished I'd put on my baseball cap. We were on a plane back to L.A. and back to reality, where people might recognize me.

The last thing I needed was for Summer to find out who I was right now when she was in a horrible state of mind. I needed to tell her myself the next time I saw her. I'd set up a date with her and tell her in private. I'd find a way to make her understand why I did it.

The girl turned to me and I cringed, waiting for what was about to come out of her mouth.

"My boyfriend and I got separated. He's seated way up front. Would either of you mind switching seats with him?"

I blew out a breath of relief. I pointed between Summer and me. "We're together, too."

Summer looked at me funny. "We're not really together, so I wouldn't mind switching. Where is he sitting?"

A huge smile broke out on the girl's face, and she bounced in her seat. "Thank you so much! He's in the aisle seat in row 7. His name is John."

Summer picked up her backpack off the seat and hurled it over her shoulder. "I'll send him back."

I grabbed her arm before she could leave. "Wait, you're going?"

"Why not?" She shrugged. "She wants to sit with her boyfriend."

I dropped my arm, and she walked away without another word.

The flight was long and boring, and I was trapped with nothing but my thoughts. And they were in turmoil.

Summer and I had grown closer and the thought of her slipping away was like a stab in the chest. I knew she was scared and worried about her mom, but why was she pushing me away?

I wanted to help, but she shut me out. It felt like every time I tried to get closer to her, she'd just back away. I couldn't understand why she was acting like she had no feelings for me at all. We had amazing sex together, and we got along great. I liked her and yet it felt like she was brushing me off.

What the fuck! There was absolutely no way she was walking away from this without a backward glance.

When the plane landed at LAX, I dug my baseball cap out of my bag and put it on my head. Impatiently, I waited for the people in front of me to deplane. When I finally made it off the plane, I looked around for Summer. She was nowhere to be found.

Dammit. My blood boiled. What kind of game was she playing with me?

She'd checked her giant suitcase, so I knew I'd find her in the baggage claim area. I scanned the airport as I walked, keeping an eye out for her, and made my way to the baggage carousel for our flight.

I found her leaning up against a pillar, standing back from the crowd of hungry vultures waiting for their bags to spit out onto the conveyor belt.

"You didn't wait for me."

Summer turned around to face me, and my breath hitched at the sight of her. Today, she was wearing tight jeans with a frilly pink top that hugged every curve of her body, and her hair was pulled up in a ponytail. She looked wholesome and cute, but my cock was busy remembering last night.

"I didn't think you'd want me to." She crossed her arms over her chest, her eyes daring me to argue.

I stepped closer, our bodies almost touching. "Don't be ridiculous. Of course, I wanted you to. You were going to leave without saying goodbye?"

She looked away and shrugged, seemingly without concern. "What does it matter? We had a good time. Now we can go our separate ways."

I was speechless. Is that what she wanted? A million thoughts ran through my head, but nothing came out of my mouth. This lass was tying me up in knots.

Finally, I'd had enough. I couldn't take it anymore. I wanted to pull out my hair or break something, anything, to release my frustration. But instead of doing any of that, I did the only thing that made sense — I grabbed Summer by the shoulders and pulled her into a tight embrace.

She was stiff at first, but she didn't fight my embrace. She stood awkwardly in my arms, her body unwavering.

"I guess this is goodbye, then." The gruffness in my voice betrayed the tightness in my throat.

"Goodbye, Scotty. Thanks for the fun memories." She gave me a quick squeeze.

Fun memories? That's what she had reduced us to? The crowd surged around us as suitcases began dropping onto the carousel.

She stepped forward. "I better go get my bag."

"Wait, I'll help you." I guess I was a glutton for punishment.

She waved me off. "It's better if you don't, for both of us. Just leave now."

My hands dropped helplessly to my sides. "Can I call you? To see how your mother is doing?"

She shook her head, but her bottom lip was trembling. "That will just complicate things. You were right. It's better not to get emotionally involved. I'm just taking your advice. We had a great time, but now that it's over, I have to take care of myself."

I just stood there as she turned around and disappeared into the thick crowd surrounding the baggage carousel.

Everything about this felt wrong. I was as cold and empty inside as a marble statue.

I wanted to go after her, but the words she said were true. We had a good time together, and now it was time to move on. I'd never had a problem doing that before, but hearing her say it had cut through me, slicing open a wound that kept bleeding until I thought I'd bleed out.

The ache in my chest felt a lot like the exact thing I'd been avoiding ever since that awful fucking day when Aila broke my heart.

# Chapter 20

**Summer**

I didn't have time to think about Scotty. I was too busy worrying about my mother and finishing up a big project at work so I could go back to Kentucky and spend a few days with my mom helping her post-surgery.

Oh, who was I kidding? He was on my mind day in and day out. I had tried to keep my emotions in check. I'd iced him out. I did everything in my power not to allow myself to get too attached to him. Just because we fucked didn't mean I had to fall head over heels in love with him.

He should be nothing but a great memory seen in the rear-view mirror. But this anguish that dogged me? And this moping around? The second-guessing that I should have done something differently? With all the protections I'd put in place, it turned out that I was miserable, anyway.

If I had been just attracted to his looks, moving on would have been easy. His good looks combined with the fantastic sex made it much harder. His sexy accent was like icing on the hotness cake. But, after spending time with him, it turned out that I actually liked him. He had a great personality. I liked the respectful way he treated my parents; he was friendly with a great sense of humor, and he was kind while also being confident, intelligent, protective, and self-assured. What was there not to like about him except that he was a player?

Celia, my closest friend in L.A. was also a co-worker. During our lunch break, I'd described my crazy weekend at the spa with my fake boyfriend to her. Although she was the opposite of me when it came to men — she had a new boyfriend every week — I occasionally listened to her advice, if only to moderate my tendency toward the extreme.

Needless to say, Celia was team Scotty all the way. She oohed and ahhed when I described him to her, only stopping her over the top gushing to chastise me that I didn't have a picture of him or his social media account info so she could check him out.

When I'd gotten around to describing the airport scene, her mouth dropped open. In dramatic flair, she told me I was a complete idiot. I didn't trust her instincts very often, but her reaction left some doubts in me. Had I done the right thing? Did I walk away from something potentially amazing just to protect my heart from getting trampled on again?

When Scotty texted me to ask how my mom's surgery went, Celia told me to call him. I didn't. I texted back a polite reply. When he texted a few more times, she demanded I call him. I was on the fence, but I refrained.

When my mom was about a week post-op and had already started her first cycle of chemotherapy, I flew back home to help out since Dad was going back to work. She still needed to take it easy because of the surgery and she was dealing with some side effects from the chemo. I was going to spend some time with her and keep an eye on her so she didn't overdo it.

I walked in the door of my childhood home and the first thing I noticed, prominently displayed, was a gorgeous arrangement of fresh flowers. The Purple Prince tulips caught my eye because of their stunning color, a vibrant fuchsia on the outside of the petals with a darker royal purple on the inside. A mix of shorter hyacinths, my favorite spring flowers, surrounded the cluster of tulips in dark plums and pink shades. The mix of colors was divine, and the air was sweetly scented with the delicate blooms.

I walked right over to admire the arrangement. "Mom, these are gorgeous!"

"They are. They make me happy every time I see them." She smiled at me. "They were from Scotty. He's such a wonderful man."

I kept my face neutral, containing the avalanche of emotions I felt on the inside. One of my goals while I was home was to tell my parents that Scotty and I had parted ways and end the charade and parade of lies. He wasn't going to make it easy.

She picked up a piece of cardstock from the table and handed it to me. "This is the note he sent."

```
Lara,
It was wonderful getting to know
you and Jim at the spa this past
weekend. Thank you for inviting me.
I hope these flowers will bolster
your spirits while you are recov-
ering from your surgery. Wishing
you a speedy return to health and
```

```
please let me know if there is
anything I can do to help.
Scotty
```

I set the card down. "How lovely." I couldn't help the fluttering feeling in my stomach at the thought of him doing something so sweet.

I shook off my thoughts of Scotty and focused on my mom. "Can I fix you a little snack? Dad said your appetite hasn't been great."

She slumped back on the couch. After she expended even the smallest amount of energy, like getting up to go to the bathroom, she had to sit down and rest for a while. "It's the damn chemo. It's given me some painful sores in my mouth and it's making me nauseous." She laughed and tried to lighten the mood. "I don't have much of an appetite. At least it'll be great for losing weight."

My mouth twisted into a grimace. Her attempt at humor only served to make the atmosphere more tense. "Mom, don't even joke. I'm going to make sure you eat some small, nutrient-packed meals. You have to keep your energy and your health up to fight this."

She leaned her head back against the pillows and closed her eyes. "I know, honey. I'm just feeling sorry for myself. This morning, I noticed how my hair is already thinning. I'll be bald in the next couple of weeks. I just can't imagine."

When my mom told me she didn't want to go the wig route and that she'd just cover up her baldness with scarves, I went out and bought her about twenty of the most stylish headscarves that I could find. She'd been delighted with my gift, yet distraught at facing the reality of what was to come.

I couldn't imagine what she was going through. "It's not forever, Mom. Your hair will grow back."

"First, I lost my breasts. Now, I'm going to lose my beautiful hair." She sounded tired and weak. "I can't even imagine what your father thinks when he looks at me. I won't even feel like a woman anymore."

My stomach sunk with how despondent she sounded. My throat clogged up and tears threatened to fall, but I was determined not to let my mother see me upset. "Dad didn't fall in love with your hair or your breasts. None of that matters ... to either of us. He fell in love with you. If this is what you have to go through to stay with us for a very long time, then we'll help you every step of the way."

"I know that, honey." She rested her wrist across her forehead. "I'm just being a big baby. I'm just tired. Let me take a little nap and I'll be fine."

Later, after my dad came home, we all sat around the kitchen table to eat the meal I'd prepared. My mother had regained her spirits, or at least she was faking it for our benefit. I gently tried to coax her to eat more, but she mostly pushed the food around her plate, claiming she wasn't that hungry.

Dad and I were doing our best to hold up the conversation and keep it positive. Inevitably, the subject came around to Scotty and I knew it was time to announce our breakup.

It turned out that my dad was still texting with Scotty. I assumed that Scotty was just being nice and keeping up the charade. He must have realized that I hadn't told my parents yet. Even though I knew they'd both be disappointed, I had to tell them. Not the whole truth, but a convenient truth.

I took a deep breath and put down my fork. "Scotty and I broke up. We decided that things just weren't going to work out between us."

Both my parents looked shocked, but my mother was near tears at the news. "What? You two were perfect together. He's such a wonderful young man! Surely you can work it out?"

I shook my head. "A relationship just isn't in the cards for either of us right now. We both decided it was better if we just remained friends."

My father cleared his throat. "That's disappointing, Jellybean. I was hoping you'd finally found your someone special. But at least you're handling it maturely."

I forced a smile, trying to ignore the sinking feeling in my stomach that came with telling these little white lies.

My mother didn't take the news as well. She wiped her mouth with a napkin and then stood. "I need to lie down for a while."

I watched as my mother disappeared from the dining room, still wondering if I had made the right decision. Upsetting her right now was the last thing I wanted to do, but I couldn't keep stringing her along under the illusion that Scotty was my boyfriend when it was far from the truth.

# Chapter 21

**Knox**

Bash's house in the suburbs was nice. It was nowhere near as fancy as Ghost's luxury apartment or the penthouse Sid and Kaylie just moved into, but he and Kody had a lot more space and the neighborhood location was undoubtedly more kid-friendly. One of its cooler features was a kick-ass pool house.

I reclined on the leather sectional sofa as Bash handed me a cold beer from the refrigerator. The small kitchen had a pass-through window overlooking the backyard pool area. Outside, four barstools were pulled up to the counter below the window for a makeshift outdoor bar.

Inside, the space had become Bash's man cave. Besides the kitchen and lounge area in front, there was a full bathroom and a guest room, which he'd converted to a music space. He had a full drum kit permanently set up, with enough room for the rest of the band to practice.

The main room was equipped with a fireplace, a poker table, and a large screen television with theatre surround sound and a gaming console, all separated from the backyard swimming pool area by large sliding glass doors that could be opened to create an indoor/outdoor effect. A few of Kody's toys were lying around or tucked into corners, but overall, the space was very masculine and comfortable.

The band had gotten together to practice today and whenever we could; we liked to come here. It was a bit out of the way, but that was part of its appeal. Ghost and Sid had left together to head back to the city. I wasn't in a hurry, so I'd stay and hang out with Ryder and Bash for a while.

Ryder sunk down on the couch next to me. "None of the houses we've been looking at have pool houses like this. I kind of like the idea of having a place to escape."

I watched Bash pull out a few bags of snacks for us in the kitchen. "How's the house hunt going? Is Talia still dragging you up and down the coast, looking for the perfect place?"

"Yeah. She's trying to find some mythical bargain house, but we're going to have to pay a pretty penny if we want to live right on the beach. I think she's finally starting to figure that out."

Soon I was going to be the last one in the band left who hadn't traded up to better digs. Did I want to go somewhere bigger and better? Maybe if I had a family, a wife and kids, but for now, my small apartment was fine.

Ryder continued, "We're ready to pull the trigger as soon as we find the right house. The really nice ones don't even make it to the market before they're snatched up. It's insane."

Bash joined us with a few bowls of snacks. "Josie took Kody to the park, so I've got a couple of hours to kill. Call of Duty or Madden?"

I sat back against the cushions. "You guys go ahead. I'll watch. I just need to unwind for a bit."

Ryder gave me a shove. "You need to unwind? From what? Try buying a house while you're planning a wedding."

Bash piled on. "Try being a single dad and then you'll really need to de-stress."

"It's nothing. Just a lot of shite on my mind lately." I shrugged it off with what I hoped was an indifferent answer.

"Are you ever going to get out of that dump you're living in?" Ryder asked with a trace of amusement. "You're living like a pauper and that neighborhood isn't the greatest."

I replied with fake indignation, "It was just fine when you were slumming on my couch. Both of you, if I recall correctly."

Bash sunk into a recliner and swiveled to face us. "I thought you were going to get an apartment in the building Ghost is in?"

"Nah, it's too much work." I took a healthy gulp of my beer. "Besides, why should I pay all that money if we're going back out on tour? It'll just sit empty. It makes sense for you two. You have a kid and you're getting married soon. I have nothing." I cringed, hoping a didn't sound like a loser.

Bash pulled a handful of pretzels out of a bowl and began munching on them. "There's nothing tying you down. I miss that. I wouldn't trade having Kody for anything in this world, but going on tour with him in tow wasn't easy." He shook his head. "Man, I struggle to try to make sure I'm always doing the right thing for him."

"You're doing a pretty good job of it, mate," I reassured him, and Ryder agreed.

Bash turned to him. "What about you? Do you miss the single life? We had some wild times."

Ryder shook his head, laughing. "We did, but I don't miss it. After a while, fucking random groupies got old. Somewhere along the way, it lost its appeal for me and just became a habit. Then Talia showed up and I could never go back to that. It's hard to explain to two assholes like you, but having sex with a woman you love is a thousand times better than fucking a random groupie."

Bash threw a pretzel at him. "Talk to me in five years after you're married and have fucked the same chick hundreds of times. Tell me how much better it is then."

Ryder picked the pretzel off his lap and winged it back at Bash. "Why don't you ask Vicious? He's engaged now and has been fucking the same woman over and over again. Oh, wait? Isn't that your little sister he's fucking?"

Bash flipped Ryder the middle finger and then chugged down the remainder of his beer.

I'd probably regret it, but I asked anyway, "How did you know Talia was the one?"

He studied his beer bottle for a moment and then ran a hand through his hair. "I don't really know. We had sex before we even knew each other — you know the story — but it felt different. The chemistry was just off the charts. Right away, I knew I wanted to be around her and not just for sex. I was thinking about her all the time. Everything was more exciting when she was there."

Of course, I was thinking about Summer. It had been weeks since she left me at the airport and I still couldn't get her off my mind.

"Remember when she left me?" Ryder turned to face me. "I was all twisted up inside. It was the first time I'd ever felt like that. That was when I was living on your couch and you helped me win her back."

Bash snorted. "You sent her chocolate and shit. And she came running back."

"You don't have a romantic bone in your body, Bash." Ryder chuckled. "How are you ever going to get a woman to fall for you?"

Bash stood up to get a new beer. "I don't need a woman to fall for me, and I certainly don't need a wife. I've got all the women I need in my life — a nanny to help with Kody and more than enough groupies to meet my other needs."

My leg bounced up and down. "You don't have any doubts?"

Ryder grabbed a bowl of chips, set it on his lap, and began to dig in. "Nah. She stuck with me through the tour. I know she's the one. That just cemented it. When you find the right one, you just know."

It just wasn't that easy. "I was engaged once. And then I got burned by her."

Bash came back with his new beer. "I thought she died in a car accident?"

"Yeah, she did." My lips twisted with suppressed grief and anger. "I haven't felt even a tiny flicker of anything except lust for another lass until..."

Two pairs of interested eyes latched onto me.

"Until who?" Ryder asked.

"I met a girl." I picked at the label on my beer bottle. "She seemed different."

Bash raised an eyebrow. "Where have you been hiding her?"

"We spent a weekend together a few weeks ago. It was bloody amazing. I haven't clapped eyes on her since and I can't get her out of my head. 'Tis making me daft." The more agitated I became, the more my Scottish accent started to slip out.

Ryder laughed and then attempted to imitate my accent. "Scotty, yer aff yer heid for this lassie."

"Aye." I got up to get another beer. "I'm fucking wrecked."

"Did you try calling her?" he asked.

"Of course, ya numpty. She's not returning my texts. I know she's in Kentucky this week; I've been texting with her dad."

"You text with her dad?" Bash looked confused.

I grabbed a new beer from the fridge and returned to my spot on the couch. "Aye. Her parents love me. They think we're dating — it's a long story."

Ryder frowned. "Huh? Why do they think you're dating?"

I took a deep breath, not wanting to get caught up in the whole convoluted story. "That's not important. The important part is that she doesn't want to have anything to do with me."

"Why don't you invite her to the charity concert next week?" Bash rubbed his jaw. "Girls get all horny when they see us up on stage performing in front of thousands. Give her the VIP treatment. The after-party is going to be really classy, too. Kaylie said they are going all out to woo the donors. You'll impress the hell out of this girl. She won't turn that down."

It was a pretty good idea. "There's only one problem. She doesn't know I'm in the band. She thinks I'm a roadie."

"What the fuck, Knox. A roadie?" Ryder laughed. "Start over and tell us the story. It sounds good. We've got the time."

"It's not good. It's bloody radge," I muttered.

"Is it any crazier than our stories?" Bash was tapping a beat on the chair with his fingers. "I had a baby turn up at my door out of the blue. We thought he was Sidney's until the paternity test and I still don't even know who the mother is. That's pretty crazy."

Ryder added, "Talia crawled into bed with me, thinking I was her boyfriend. I woke up from a deep sleep with her sucking my cock and her pussy in my face. That's how I met my future wife. Your story can't be any crazier."

Sighing, I looked at my mates. I'd been keeping all this to myself for weeks. I was at my wit's end thinking about Summer and I needed their advice, even if I knew any advice the guys gave would probably be shite.

For the next twenty minutes, I told them the story, trying to stick to the facts, but I got sidetracked a few times talking about Summer. When I finished, Bash and Ryder looked at each other and smirked knowingly.

Ryder snickered. "He's got it bad."

"He's fucking toast." Bash shook his head.

I wiped a hand down my face. "Don't give me your rubbish. Tell me what to do."

Ryder scratched at the back of his neck. "You know how to lay on the romance. I couldn't believe all the cheesy shit you came up with when I was trying to get Talia back. You've got to do some of that. I think Bash's idea of inviting her to the concert is good. You need to come clean about being in Ghost Parker first, though. And maybe let her know your real name."

I looked away, staring off into space. Ryder was right. I had to tell her the truth about who I was. My being a rockstar might suddenly impress her, but I had wanted her to like me for me without all the fame and fortune. Instead, she had walked away, and it had become confusing. I was sure that she was attracted to me, but she was fighting her feelings.

She'd barely acknowledged my texts when I asked about her mother, and I couldn't think of a better plan. "Her birthday is a few days before the show. I could stop by her place and invite her to the show in person. I just need to find out her address."

Bash slouched in his chair. "That shouldn't be too hard to find out. Bring some flowers and romantic stuff. Girls love that. You'll probably get laid right on the spot."

"I'm not trying to get laid. Shite, mate. I'm just looking to see her again." Why did I even bother trying to explain? He had absolutely no concept.

"Sure," he replied with a roll of his eyes.

I ignored him and took another sip of beer. I finally had a plan. In a few days, I'd see Summer again. A surge of hope swelled within me.

# Chapter 22

---

**Summer**

IT WAS AN ORDINARY Thursday night, yet it wasn't, because today was my birthday. I'd purposefully didn't tell anyone at work, including my friend, Celia, so no one would make a fuss about it.

I'd gotten some well wishes on social media from some of my old friends from back home and a quick phone call from my best friend, Jade.

After I'd come home from work and heated up some leftover food for dinner, I got a video call from my parents. Since her surgery, I talked to my mother every day to see how she was feeling and check on her progress, but today's call focused on me and my birthday. Last month, when they visited me in L.A., they left a birthday gift hidden for me in a kitchen cabinet I never used — the one over my refrigerator.

At Mom's direction, I pulled out the small wrapped box and opened it. It was a gorgeous sterling silver infinity loop necklace and bolo bracelet set embedded with tiny, sparkling sapphires. It was a lovely gift; my mother had great taste in jewelry and fashion.

I was touched by the gesture of hiding the gift and surprising me. We talked for a while and when I was pressed; I told them that I was going out with some friends to celebrate. It was another white lie so that my mom didn't worry about me sitting home alone on my birthday. Lying to my mother had gotten to be a habit, but I'd protect her from worry and added stress any way I could, especially now as she was recovering from surgery and going through chemotherapy.

Now that all the phone calls and birthday wishes were over, I was a bit letdown. I was a young, single woman. I shouldn't be sitting alone in my apartment for my birthday, but that was what I had chosen. It almost felt like I was punishing myself — not allowing myself ever to have fun. Of course, my mind drifted to Scotty. I couldn't keep him off my mind. Doubts that I'd done the right thing had crept into my every waking moment.

I didn't have much time to further contemplate that thought because someone was buzzing my apartment. It was most likely someone buzzer bombing trying to be let in the building, but I got up anyway.

I pressed the microphone button. "Hello?"

The voice over the speaker was tinny and muffled. "I've got a delivery for Summer Meadows."

It was probably flowers from my parents. I buzzed him up and then went to my purse to dig for some cash for a tip. A few minutes later, there was a knock on my door.

I looked through the peephole in the door, and sure enough, I saw a giant bouquet filled with gorgeous flowers.

I opened the door and my mouth fell open. Holding the bouquet was the man that had been on my mind every single day since the spa weekend was at my doorstep. "Scotty?"

He gave me that sly, confident smile — the one that left my knees weak — that showed off his dimples. "Happy birthday, Sunshine."

"What are you doing here?" The words left my mouth before I could think, and I felt my face flush as soon as they escaped. His unexpected presence had thrown me completely off guard, and my heart pounded as I waited for his response.

He stood in the doorway, tall and strong, his smile radiating warmth. His brown eyes sparkled and his well-defined jawline was set with determination. His dark hair was styled neatly and just touched the top of his collar, and his clothes were perfectly tailored to fit his body. He looked even more handsome than I remembered.

"Can I come in?" He arched a brow.

I quickly stepped aside. "Yes. Please, come in."

He stepped inside and handed me the bouquet of spring flowers that contained a vibrant array of colors and blossoms in shades of pink, peach, and ivory. The scent of the flowers filled the room with a sweet, fragrant aroma.

"Thank you for the flowers. They're beautiful." I headed into my tiny kitchen to find a vase for them. "How did you know it was my birthday?"

Scotty was casually looking over my apartment as he followed me into the kitchen. "I asked your father when we first met."

My heart felt like it was about to burst out of my chest as I turned to face him. Butterflies fluttered in my stomach and my palms began to sweat. A thrill of anticipation surged through me; I couldn't deny that I was excited to see him.

Before I let myself get carried away, I needed to know why he'd come to see me. "When I was in Kentucky, my dad said that you were still texting with him. But you don't have to pretend anymore. I told my parents that we broke up. They were disappointed, but they got over it. So, you're off the hook. You don't have to fake date me any longer."

"I didn't come because of your parents, Summer; I came to see you." He shifted his weight from one foot to the other and cleared his throat nervously. "I've missed you," he said, with a pleading look on his face. "Please, give me another chance."

I wanted to jump into his arms and bury my face in his chest. I wanted him to crush me against him with his strong arms wrapping around me, but I had to be certain."A chance for what? I thought you didn't do relationships."

His brown eyes glistened with hope. "I was wrong. I want to see where this goes with us."

I felt myself caving. He was damn near irresistible. "You want to date? For real this time?"

"Yes." He nodded his head.

I needed time to think. I found the vase I was searching for, added some water to it, and then arranged the flowers prettily inside it. "I'm a little nervous about this, Scotty. You're a great guy, but I'm looking for a boyfriend who wants to spend time with me. Time that doesn't solely include between-the-sheets time."

He pressed his palms into the countertop separating us. "I want that, too. I mean, I want to fuck you, but that isn't all I want."

His deep, gravelly voice had my sex clenching with need. I'd gladly lead him to my bedroom right now and find out just how much he wanted to fuck me, but I needed to be cautious. "You have such a romantic way with words. It's a good thing you have that accent."

He stepped around the small island and pulled me into his arms. I'd finally gotten my hug. "Is that a yes, Summer? Will you go steady with me?"

"Go steady?" I couldn't help but chuckle at the old-fashioned phrase, even as I breathed in deeply, savoring the familiar scent of his cologne. His muscular arms tightened around me, and I felt a deep sense of comfort settling into my bones. "I'm agreeing to a few dates for now. I'd like to take things slow in case I'm making a big mistake."

"You're not making a mistake." He drew away from me and reached into his pocket, pulling out a long envelope. "I have a show on Saturday. I brought you a ticket so you could attend and watch the band. There's supposed to be this huge, fancy after-party that I thought we could go together afterward. It'll be a great time."

I swiveled away from him, not wanting him to see the panic in my eyes. "A show? Like a concert?"

"Yes, it's a charity concert. It's at The Shrine..."

He said something else, but I was too busy panicking. I didn't want to see him at work. He would be there with all the other crew. What would his friends think of me? Would there be other women hanging around?

It just wasn't my scene. The last concert I'd been to was when I was a teenager. I'd been particularly manic on a huge sugar high from drinking too much soda, and then I'd almost peed in my pants in the car when my friend's mom was driving us home.

Scotty wanted me to hang out at a concert alone while he worked and then go to an after-party? It sounded like absolute hell. I wasn't a wild party girl anymore, and I didn't do drugs. I wasn't even sure what Scotty was like. What if he was a drug user? He seemed perfectly normal during our weekend away, but who knew how he acted when he was around his friends? And what did he expect of me?

I needed to slow things down. We were still in the get-to-know-you stage. Without any finesse, I blurted out, "I can't go Saturday night. It's too much."

He put the envelope down on the counter and then gently grabbed my shoulders. "But you'll still go out with me? On dates or whatever?"

"Yes, I'd like to get to know you better." I still had major trust issues when it came to men, but I couldn't live my whole life in a man-free bubble.

He let out a sigh. "Can we hang out tonight, then? Or did you have plans for your birthday?"

"I have to work early tomorrow." That was true. "I was planning to celebrate with my friends this weekend." Celia and I were planning to hang out. Maybe I'd even tell her about my birthday.

He looked at me with an intensity that left me breathless. His dark eyes smoldering, his lips parted ever so slightly. I felt a wave of desire wash over me as I saw the corner of his mouth curl into a slight smile. "Can I stay for a while?"

I bit my lip. "Sure. I was just going to watch some TV. I can make some popcorn if you want."

Oh, God. What was I trying to do? Bore him to death?

♪♫♩♪

"Then what happened?" Celia's eyes were wide with interest as she listened to every single word.

I tapped a pen against my desk. "So then he stayed for a couple of hours. It was really nice. He kissed me before he left."

She leaned in closer to me, speaking low so that the people in the adjoining cubicles couldn't hear. "So, how was the kiss? On a scale of 1 to 10. One is a peck on the lips, five is an average, enjoyable kiss, and ten is a five-alarm fire."

I tapped my chin, pretending to think about it. "It started off as an eight, but then quickly morphed into a ten. I had to push him out the door before I started getting naked. He has this crazy, wonderful effect on me. I just want to jump his bones when I see him."

She snickered. "So, all it took was some flowers and you folded? What happened to Little Miss I Don't Need a Man?"

I slouched in my seat. "Yeah, I folded like a cheap suit. I've been missing him like crazy and I regretted the way I didn't even give him a chance. But he showed up out of the blue. After all this time, he showed up. That means he must feel something for me, right? And he agreed to the two of us dating, which he doesn't do. We hung out together and watched television for hours and we didn't even have sex. Those are all good signs."

She looked at me like I was insane. "Only you would think not having sex was a good thing."

"You know what I mean, right?"

Celia tucked a dark lock of loose hair behind her ear. "What was the thing on Saturday night that he ask you to do? And why did you turn him down again?"

I'd brushed over that part of the story quickly because I knew she'd give me grief about it. "It's a concert that he's working at and then he was talking about attending an after-party together." I shuddered. "There's no way I'm going. Who wants to go to a concert by themselves, anyway? There's only one ticket, so it's pretty useless, but you can have it if you want it."

"What concert is it?"

I didn't even know. "It's at the Shrine." I pulled my purse out of my desk drawer and took out the envelope. I broke open the seal and pulled out the ticket and a lanyard. "What is this?"

Celia pulled them out of my hands and looked at the lanyard. "Oh, my God. An all-access pass. He must have a lot of pull."

I was reaching for the lanyard to take a look when she shrieked like a stuck pig and then slapped a hand over her mouth.

"Quiet down," I urged. "You're going to get us in trouble!"

Her eyes were wide with shock. "Summer, these tickets are for the Ghost Parker concert. It's some special concert they're playing. The tickets were wickedly expensive, and it sold out within minutes."

I sat back in my chair. "Scotty said it was a charity concert."

"Ghost Parker, Sum!" She put her hand on my knee and squeezed. "Do you know who that is? They're so hot right now."

"Not really," I admitted. "They sound familiar."

"That song *Okay Babe*? You have to know that one. It's on the radio all the time. You'd recognize their songs if you heard them. God, Summer. The lead singer is so hot. They're all really hot." Celia fanned herself like she was overheating.

I shrugged. "You can have the ticket if you like them so much."

She held up the all-access pass in front of my face. "You could go backstage and meet the band."

I frowned. "I don't want to meet the band."

She threw up her hands in disgust. "I can't believe you turned this down. How could you pass this up? It's once in a lifetime. And the after-party? It's probably going to be filled with celebrities and rich people. I'm sure Scotty went through a lot of trouble to secure this ticket for you."

How could I make her understand? "What am I going to do at a rock concert?"

She clenched her jaw, furrowing her brow. Her lips drew down into a tight line as she sighed heavily. "I don't know, Summer." She forced a smile and shrugged her shoulders. "Have fun? Live a little. Why are you so scared of living life?"

"Am I really that lame?" I lowered my voice, almost whispering.

She placed her hand on my arm, the understanding in that gesture reaching far beyond words. "I get it," she said softly. "You've got a few battle scars—it's okay to be a little gun shy. But don't let a few assholes dictate your life. Get out of your own damn shadow and enjoy yourself."

"You think I should go?" I was hoping she'd say no, but she didn't.

"Let me put it this way: if you don't go, I'm going to kick your ass, girlfriend."

# Chapter 23

------------------------------------------

**Summer**

> **Me:** I am going to kill you.

I hit send on the text to Celia as I inched my way forward in the pack of humanity toward the general admission gates of the venue.

> **Celia:** I'm so jealous! You rock, girl. Go have some fun!!

Nerves churned in my stomach, making me feel mildly nauseous. My fingers flew over my phone screen.

> **Me:** Why couldn't I tell him I was coming? This seems like a very bad idea. How am I even going to find him after the show? What if I see him with another girl?

A girl bumped into me from behind, but I ignored her as I stared at my screen.

> **Celia:** If that happens, then you'll know he's an asshole. Then, just go meet the band and hook up with one of them.

I swallowed down a hint of rising bile. A few seconds later, I got another text.

> **Celia:** That's not going to happen. So don't freak out.

Fuck my life. I was so nervous. How had she talked me into this insane idea?

I still had time to back out. Hordes of people surrounded me, pushing me forward as we made our way slowly to the entrance. The air was filled with a sense of excitement and festivity, but I couldn't enjoy it.

Everywhere I turned, there were endless droves of people clamoring to get into the concert as quickly as they could. I kept my head down, gripping my VIP pass tightly in my hand. I could feel my heart racing as I continued forward.

When I reached the front of a huge bottleneck of people at the bag check, I placed my handbag on the table to be searched.

The lady noticed the ticket in my hand and then shook her head like she was disappointed in me. "You've got VIP tickets? What the hell are you doing in this line? Go around back to the VIP entrance. That's what you paid for."

She vaguely pointed around a line of fencing, impatiently waving me aside before checking the next bag as soon as the next person in line crowded in.

I circled around the fence, leaving the crowd of people, and began walking toward the back of the building. I hoped the entrance was clearly marked. Before I got too far, a security guard stepped in front of me.

"Where're you headed?" he asked gruffly.

Freezing in place, my words caught in my throat. I held out my VIP pass, sure that I must have looked so out of place, like an imposter trying to sneak inside.

"I-I'm looking for the VIP entrance," I eventually managed to stammer out.

The security guard gave me a hard look before pointing to the back of the building. "It's that way."

Nodding my thanks, I hurried away, not wanting to draw any more attention to myself. I made my way around the side of the building, trying to ignore the stares of the people on the other side of the fencing, who were heading to the entrance from distant parking lots. When I found the VIP entrance, I breathed a sigh of relief.

Venue staff ushered me past several security checkpoints, each waving me further inside to my destination. The energy of the crowd immediately swept me up in its enthusiasm. Everywhere I looked, people were dancing, laughing, and singing along to the music. A nervous anticipation bubbled up inside me as I made my way through the throngs of people.

After flashing my ticket to several more security people, I reached the VIP area where my seat was located. Only a few feet separated me from the front of the stage. My seat was definitely premium. Not many concertgoers had reached this section yet — there was still lots of time before the show started — but the ones who were already there were not dressed like the masses of people waiting to get into the show.

I was incredibly self-conscious. Everyone around me was dressed to the nines. While I had blended perfectly into the crowd before, I now stood out like a sore thumb. I was wearing what I thought was the perfect rock concert outfit: a black off-the-shoulder, midriff-baring T-shirt that was molded to my arms and chest and faded black jeans that were strategically ripped and torn with some shredding around the ankles. My cheeks flushed with embarrassment as I made my way to my seat and sunk down into it.

I pulled out my phone and rattled off a text to Celia.

> **ME:** I made it to my seat. It's right in front of the stage. All the VIPs around me are dressed up. What about the after-party? What if it's some fancy thing? You saw my outfit. I look like a try-hard poser. I think I'm going to sneak out of here.

My hands squeezed around my phone case as I waited for her reply. To my surprise, my phone rang. It was Celia. I picked it up and put it to my ear.

She didn't even give me a chance to say hello before she started talking. "You are not going anywhere. Take a deep breath and calm down. You made it to your seat already. At least watch the concert. You can always sneak off afterward. But I suggest you ask for Scotty after the show. He'll be very excited that you came, Summer. Remember, he wanted you there."

I looked behind me, watching the theater slowly filling up with people. "This place is so fancy. This is all so weird, Celia. I wish you were here."

A note of envy crept into her words as she responded over the phone. "Shit, so do I. Take lots of pictures and some videos, if you're allowed to. Especially of Ghost Parker. You are so lucky, Summer. Just relax and have fun. You're at a concert, for fuck's sake, not a gynecologist appointment. Unclench, girl."

I let out a chuckle. "You're right. Thank you. I'll call you tomorrow and let you know how it all went."

"You better!"

She said her goodbyes and then we hung up.

I took a deep breath and tried to calm my nerves. Scotty had invited me here, so I was determined to enjoy it. Activity bustled around me as I settled into my red velvet seat and played on my phone, waiting for the theatre to fill up and the concert to begin.

A few minutes later, a woman dressed in a black leather blazer with a white silk shirt underneath moved down the aisle in front of the stage and headed right for me. I could hear the clicking of the heeled boots she wore under her dress pants as she approached. I shrunk in my seat, wondering if she was coming to kick me out of the exclusive section.

Between her impeccable makeup, shiny red lips, and luscious blonde hair flowing down her back and her expensive, trendy outfit, I knew she must be someone important. The rows of delicate gold chains glinted around her neck as she stopped in front of my seat.

She thrust out her hand when I looked up from my phone. "Hello.

I'm Lacey Davenport, co-founder of Cyber Angels."

I had no choice but to acknowledge her. "Hi. I'm Summer Meadows," I said as I shook her hand.

Her forehead furrowed and her nose wrinkled, like she was trying to make sense of something. "I don't recall…" she trailed off, searching for the right words as she tilted her head slightly to one side. "You're one of our VIPs, but I don't recall your name. Are you one of our sponsors or donors?"

I swallowed nervously. This woman looked like an absolute barracuda. She could chew me up and spit me out in a second flat. "No, uh, Scotty invited me."

She cocked her head slightly to the side. "Scotty?"

Oh, jeez. Here was where I got escorted out by security while the crowd watched. "He's part of the crew."

"Oh!" She laughed. "You're a friend of the band. Thank God! I thought I had a rogue VIP donor that I hadn't wrangled properly. I don't know your friend Scotty, but there are a lot of different guys working tonight's show since it's a one-off."

A nervous giggle bubbled out of me. "I thought you were about to kick me out. Scotty didn't mention the dress code for the VIP section. I feel out of place."

She looked me up and down. "You look fine. Tonight's an exception because we're raising money for Cyber Angels and there's a party afterward with Ghost Parker."

"Scotty mentioned the party. Would I get tossed out if I tried to show up like this? He really didn't explain this event to me all that well and I'm new to … all this." Lacey seemed friendly enough, so I thought I'd ask and maybe relieve some of my anxiety.

"I'm hosting the after-party, so don't worry about it. Besides, the guys in the band and the crew won't be dressed up and none of them will care what you're wearing, either. In fact, I'm sure they'll appreciate it. You look great." She looked at her watch. "I've got to get back to Kaylie and schmoozing our donors, but Talia should be here soon. She's backstage with the guys right now. I'll text her and let her know about you. She'll take care of you until the crew finishes load out. I really have to run. I'll see you later, Summer."

"Bye. And thank you."

I watched as she walked away, turning the heads of everyone she passed. She was extremely beautiful and had such a commanding presence, but she'd been so nice to me. She'd accepted me without judgment, even knowing I was just friends with a crew member, that I felt much better. I didn't know who this Talia was, but I didn't even need her help. Lacey had given me the boost my confidence needed.

It was past 8 o'clock when the show was supposed to start, but the stage was still empty, even though the venue was at full capacity. I guess they were running behind.

A girl who looked like she could have just stepped off the stage herself pushed past the front row seats until she sat down in the empty seat next to me.

Her dark blonde hair was streaked with bold highlights of copper and purple and was woven together into an intricate braid. She was wearing leather pants that fit tightly against her curves, and her shiny, iridescent top gave her a rocker girl vibe. Her skin sparkled as if she'd rolled in glitter, and her piercing blue eyes looked like they held secrets no one else knew. She was the essence of feminine confidence and style.

She gave me a friendly smile. "Hey, I'm Talia. You must be Summer. Lacey told me all about you."

I checked the time on my phone. "The band must be running late."

"Oh, they'll be on any minute." Her eyes swept over the crowded section we were in. "I usually don't come out here to watch them, but with this venue set up and the VIP section for the charity people, I don't think we'll get crushed."

"Oh, that's good. There won't be any mosh pits?" I asked jokingly.

"Not today, at least. So, you are friends with one of the crew guys?"

I wiped my sweaty palms on my jeans. "Yeah. Scotty Stewart. He invited me here tonight."

Her eyes widened slightly. "Scotty Stewart?" she repeated slowly, as if not believing what she was hearing.

"Yeah," I confirmed. "Rock concerts aren't my thing, but we just started dating, so I decided to come. He doesn't even know I'm here. He gave me the tickets and I originally couldn't make it. But I decided to come and surprise him."

Her gaze shifted to the stage. "You said he's a member of the crew?"

"Yeah." Her weird reaction was making me uneasy.

"He doesn't happen to be from Scotland, does he?" Her hands were wringing in her lap.

I studied her face. "Yeah. Do you know him?"

She flinched, looking extremely uncomfortable. "Oh boy. I do."

"Why are you making that funny face? Is there something I should know?" My stomach sank. "Is he married? Does he have a girlfriend? Just tell me now. I've been burned by so many assholes in the past, I rather just know the truth before I get too invested."

Hearing my agitation, she put out her hand to soothe me. "No, he doesn't have a girlfriend or wife. But, he's not really a crew member, precisely. What did he tell you he does for the band?"

What did it matter? I tossed up my hands. "He said he goes on tour with them. He travels around the world and does roadie stuff, I guess. I didn't really grill him on all the ins and outs of it. He told my father that he was in 'music production', which was kind of funny."

She raised an eyebrow. "He met your father?"

I nodded. "Yes, both my parents. We went away on a weekend getaway with them."

She glanced up at the stage, but as far as I could tell, nothing was going on yet. "Very interesting," was her only comment.

I frowned. "I feel like you're not telling me something. Something important."

She cringed again. like she felt a lot of second-hand embarrassment. "I think you're about to find out."

I didn't have time to press her, because suddenly the crowd started going crazy. Even the rich VIPs in their designer clothes, dripping in their jewels and fancy watches, all stood up to cheer. The band was coming onto the stage.

I shook off my unease and let the crowd's enthusiasm sweep me up. I stood up and started clapping as the drummer took his place behind his drum kit and two other guys carrying guitars crossed right in front of me and positioned themselves on the other side of the stage.

A giant roar went up when the lead singer came out and stood center stage in front of a microphone stand. I had to bend my neck to look up at him. I was at eye level with his feet, but I could see why Celia had called him hot. He radiated intensity and, as I studied his handsome features, I definitely knew that I'd seen him before in the media. This was the famous Ghost Parker. There was only about a four-foot gap between the railing I was leaning against and the stage. He was so close that if he accidentally spit while he sang, I was sure to be showered with it. I turned on my camera app and snapped a few pictures for Celia.

There was another guy with a guitar on the stage to my right. He walked over and said something that got Ghost's attention. I pulled my gaze away from the enigmatic Ghost and glanced at the other guy.

My heart stopped as an electric jolt surged through my veins. I felt the hairs on my arms stand up and a wave of fire raced across my skin. My limbs felt like they had been encased in ice, yet I was drenched in sweat. I was paralyzed, unable to move or speak; I had never experienced such intensity before. It was like a searing bolt of lightning had hit me with a blast that shook me to my core.

Scotty was on the stage holding a guitar. I stared up at him, my mouth agape. He strummed a quick fiery lick on his guitar and then looked over at one of his bandmates and grinned.

Ghost began speaking into the microphone, addressing the audience, but I couldn't process anything he was saying. My eyes were glued to Scotty.

I realized that Talia had grabbed my hand. I looked at her desperately searching for answers. "What is going on? He's not a roadie?"

She squeezed my hand, wincing slightly. I couldn't hear her answer over the driving beat of the music, but I could lip-read quite well. "No. He's the guitarist for Ghost Parker."

Had he lied to me this whole time? The band launched into a song. Everyone was singing and dancing, screaming for the band, except for me. I was devastated.

I sunk down into my chair. My mind was numb. This must be some kind of cosmic joke. Time seemed to slow down, but I knew it was steadily marching on when the guy in the seat behind me bumped the back of my head for the fifth time. Ghost Parker had played several songs while I'd sat out the mayhem surrounding me in shock.

At some point, the shock must have worn off sufficiently to let a little humiliation in. And a touch of anger. I looked up at Scotty, watching him play his guitar for a few moments. He ruled the stage with confidence and swagger. There was no doubt he was in his element.

God, I was such a fool. My heart racing, I stood up. Somewhat rudely, I started pushing through the people standing in front of their seats, blocking my exit. I just needed to escape.

I made it to the end of the row before I felt a hand on my arm. It was Talia. She crooked her head for me to follow. She flashed our passes to several security personnel as she tugged me forward, and soon we were somewhere behind the scenes where the music was still loud but muffled. Maybe now I could think for a moment.

Talia kept leading me through the maze-like backstage. "Are you okay?"

"No." I clenched my jaw. "I'm upset, humiliated, angry, and ... probably some other things. Why would he do this to me?"

She led me through a door and then down another hall. "I don't know. It doesn't make sense."

My anger was burning off, and I suddenly felt exhausted and defeated. The last thing I wanted to do was to cry in front of these people. "I just want to go home. I didn't mean to ruin the show for you. Just point me to an exit and I'll call a cab to pick me up."

We came to an open space that looked like a lounge area. Tables lined the back of the wall and were covered with chafing dishes of catered food. A beat-up bar stood in the back corner with bottles of all shapes and sizes lined up behind it. A few catering personnel bustled in and out of the room carrying trays of food. The center of the room was mostly empty, but a few couches of dubious quality were scattered about.

Talia led me over to a couch and I sank down upon it.

A moment later, Lacey burst into the room. "I got your S.O.S. What's wrong?" She saw me sitting on the couch, and I must have looked like shit because she immediately turned her attention to me. "Summer! What's wrong?"

I dropped my head into my hands. I didn't want to face any of this.

Talia spoke up. "Summer is Knox's girlfriend. For some reason, he didn't tell her that he was in the band. She thought he was a roadie."

"Knox?" My voice croaked. I lifted my head. "Knox?" This time it came out loud and seething with fury. "What the fuck? Who the fuck is Knox?"

"Uh, Scotty is Knox," Talia said tentatively.

Lacey sat down next to me. "Talia, get her a shot of something!" She turned to me. "Shit, I didn't put it together earlier when you said Scotty. Yeah, the guys in the band call him Scotty sometimes. It's his nickname."

I groaned. "Fuck me. That's not his real name? Is he really from Scotland or was the accent bullshit, too?"

"No, he's really from Scotland."

I shook my head bitterly. "God, I even thought to myself that Scotty from Scotland was pretty odd when I was trying to find him on social media. How could I be so stupid? He and his stupid band must have been laughing at me the whole time."

Talia walked over with a shot glass full of clear liquid. I downed it without hesitating. It burned the back of my throat, but I hardly registered it.

Lacey rubbed my arm. "Look, I don't know why he did it, but he must have a reason. He's a very nice guy. I don't think he was trying to hurt you in any way."

"He's been lying to me this whole time," I muttered. Just like I'd been lying to my parents. We made a great team.

Talia sat down on the couch on my other side. "I don't know why he didn't tell you he was in the band, but he gave you the tickets to the show tonight. Maybe this was his way of telling you the truth?"

"It's a horrible way to find out." I leaned my head back and closed my eyes. "I spent hours with him Thursday night. He should have told me then."

"Right!" Lacey jumped in. "He wanted you to know. I wonder why he didn't tell you in person?"

I grunted. "Probably because I would have dumped him. I'm not looking for a guy like him. I seem to attract guys who are trouble and now that I know that Scotty is in a rock band, it's my cue to steer clear."

"Summer, I hate to keep running out on you, but I've got to get back to Kaylie. We're overseeing the entire fundraiser for Cyber Angels tonight." Lacey stood up. "But I don't think you should run off. The band will be busy after the show with a meet and greet, but then we're all heading to the after-party. You don't even have to see Knox until then. We'll take care of you. Then you can talk to him privately and hear his side of the story. He's not a bad guy."

"Sorry I disturbed your night." I gave her a little wave of goodbye.

She left, and then Talia turned to me. "Let's do another shot. Then you can decide what to do."

A couple of hours later, I was sitting in the back of a limousine with Talia, Lacey, and Kaylie. We were sipping champagne while they filled me in on the basics of Ghost Parker since I knew next to nothing about the band and how they tied into the band members. Kaylie was engaged to the bassist, but she was also the drummer's brother. Talia was about to marry Ryder, the other guitarist. Lacey was friends with everyone and was a bigwig at a rival record label.

We were startled when someone banged on the door window. The driver rolled down the partition. "Is this guy bothering you? Should I drive away ladies?"

Talia giggled. "Oh, it's Ryder. You can let him in."

The locks clicked and then Ryder was stepping into the limo and sliding into the seat next to Talia.

Kaylie frowned. "Hey, no boys allowed in this limo! Didn't you get the memo?"

"The other limo is too crowded." He stretched out his legs. "It's packed over there with the band and the security guys and some women that Ghost and Bash invited to the after-party."

The limo started moving. Ryder chuckled. "I snuck out. Sid is going to be pissed when he finds out that he's stuck over there."

Lacey topped off our glasses with more champagne. "Yeah, but now you ruined our girl talk. We were hatching plans."

Ryder snuggled next to Talia. "Oh yeah?" He glanced around, his gaze finally settling on me. "Well, hello."

Talia rolled her eyes. "Summer, this is Ryder, my fiancé."

"Nice to meet you." I took a big sip of champagne.

He sat up. "Summer? As in, Knox's Summer?"

Talia slapped him in the chest. "You know about her?"

"Uh, yeah." Ryder looked uncomfortable. "Knox said you weren't coming tonight, but that you two were back together. Um, I don't think he knows you're here."

"That's because she decided to come at the last minute and surprise him," Kaylie answered.

My eyes narrowed. The alcohol was giving me some liquid courage. "Imagine my surprise when I showed up and Scotty the roadie turned out to be Knox, a guitarist in a freaking rock band."

Ryder winced. "He was supposed to tell you first."

Talia turned to him. "How do you know all this?"

Ryder took Talia's glass and finished the rest of her champagne. "He told us after they broke up or whatever happened. She wasn't answering his texts, and he was trying to figure out how to win her back. We gave him advice."

"Oh, damn." Lacey snorted. "No wonder it all went to shit."

Kaylie held out her empty glass for Lacey to refill. "So, what was with the fake name and job? Why did he tell her that?"

"Shouldn't you be asking him all this?" He pulled out his phone and read a text. "Yep, Sid is pissed."

I was feeling tipsy and watching the girls grill him was proving insightful. "Tell me, Ryder. I want to know why."

Kaylie nodded her agreement. "We're asking you because you came into the girl limo. We analyze shit over here. So spill."

Ryder sighed. "I don't remember it all exactly. It started off just pretending they were dating. And then when things evolved, which Knox wasn't expecting, he had trouble coming clean about it. I think he liked being Scotty with Summer."

"Why?" I prodded.

"It was his way to weed out gold diggers and celebrity chasers." He paused for a moment. "He wanted to make sure that Summer liked him as a person and not for his fame or his money."

"When did he ever care about that?" Talia asked.

"The bigger we got as a band, that stuff started affecting us all. Did you ever notice that the bigger we got as a band, the smaller our circle of friends got?" Ryder looked around at all of us. The girls were nodding their heads.

"I see it a lot in the industry." Lacey turned to me. "I'm not saying that Knox misleading you was okay, but it makes more sense to me now."

My head was spinning. "I didn't know. I'm not a big follower of your band. Are you saying that you're famous? Like actual celebrities? When we were in Idaho, nobody recognized Scotty. I mean, Knox. Do people recognize you on the streets?"

"It depends." Ryder put his arm around Talia. "Ghost is recognized everywhere. Here in L.A., Ghost and Knox get recognized all the time.

They always travel with security. Hell, even Bash does on occasion. Outside of a tour and outside of L.A., it's hit and miss."

"That's so strange." I screwed up my face. "You're famous. Wait..." Something else hit me. "Are you saying he's rich, too? Oh my God!"

Ryder looked taken aback. "Why do you look so upset?"

"I didn't know about any of this." I pulled at the hole in my ripped jeans.

Ryder shrugged. "He's rich, but he lives like a pauper. No wonder you didn't know — his apartment is shit. We've been telling him to move to a better place for years now."

I rubbed my temples. "This is too much."

Ryder pulled Talia onto his lap. "Can we stop all this girl analyzing now? If I knew we'd be talking about all these girly feelings over here, I wouldn't have come. Let's pull over and make a swap. I'll ditch and send over Knox and Sidney."

"No!" I said a little too forcefully. "I'm not drunk enough to see him yet."

Lacey filled up my glass. "Then, let's get cracking."

# Chapter 24

**Knox**

It hadn't been long, but I'd missed being on stage. Nothing else came close to producing that intense adrenaline high that came from performing in front of a high-energy crowd.

On stage, with the lights shining brightly on me, the stare of thousands of eyes was palpable while I made my guitar sing for the audience. The experience was almost erotic as I coaxed sounds from my guitar that enhanced and blended seamlessly with the sounds being produced by my bandmates until the music pulsed like a living thing through the venue.

Even the meet and greet couldn't crush the high that was still coursing through my veins. I had to wiggle my fingers to relieve the bundle of excess energy that was building up in them.

Tonight's show had been the culmination of a few weeks of casual practice. On Monday, we would get back to a regular band schedule, working on new songs that we'd eventually take to the studio. I couldn't wait to get back to it.

I waited in the limo with my bandmates until the security guys waved us out. We were parked at the side entrance to the fancy hotel where the after-party was being held. We were told to be on our best behavior tonight since this party was for the mostly straight-laced donors and sponsors of Lacey and Kaylie's charity.

As we were led into the party, a woman in a slinky red dress stopped me and asked for an autograph. I chatted politely with her for a few minutes and then left to catch up with my friends, leaving the woman visibly disappointed.

Sex was a fun way to burn off the excess adrenaline from a concert, but I wasn't interested in any girl except for Summer and she was out celebrating her birthday with her friends. I'd love to ditch this party early and stop by her house tonight, but I'd promised Summer to take it slow. I didn't want to scare her off after she'd finally agreed to date me. Instead, I'd call her tomorrow and try to see if she'd do something with me, even if it was just watching TV with her like the other night.

And, as Ryder had said, I knew how to be romantic; I'd just turned that off somewhere along the way. I wasn't about to woo Summer half-heartedly. She wasn't going to slip away again. I was going to go all out until she knew how great we could be together. That thought left me more excited and hopeful about the future than I'd ever been.

I entered the large, open room, which held a flurry of activity — people milling about and waiters weaving through with trays laden with delicious appetizers. The guests in attendance were dressed in an eclectic mix of clothing, from elegant floor-length gowns to rock-star-chic outfits. People clustered around standup cocktail tables that were scattered throughout the room and at the two bars set on opposite sides from each other. The sound of conversation mixed with laughter filled the room as people mingled and conversed over the music playing in the background.

Ghost was always easy to pick out of a crowd. I spotted him right away, attracting a crowd of people near one of the bars. I headed his way.

Ryder intercepted me before I made it to the bar. He handed me a shot glass filled with clear liquid. "You're going to need this." He patted me on the shoulder. "Good luck."

I tossed the shot back. "What's going on?"

He didn't answer. He laughed under his breath like an arsehole, shook his head, and then walked away.

I accepted an appetizer from a passing waiter and then headed closer to the bar, where I saw Sid and Kaylie standing. Once again, I was stopped by a girl who looked way too young for a party like this; maybe she was the daughter of one of the donors. I took a selfie with her and was making polite conversation with her when Lacey put her hand on my arm.

She squeezed my arm rather forcefully to get my attention. "Knox, someone is here to see you."

I scanned the room, and then my eyes landed on her. She was standing next to Talia, not even ten feet from me.

Without looking away from Summer, I spoke to the young girl, "It was great talking to you. I've got to go."

I closed the distance between us in a few strides. The smile on my face felt like it stretched from ear to ear. I knew I should dial down my excitement, but it was uncontainable. She was here, and nothing else mattered.

I went straight to her and pulled her into my arms. "What are you doing here? I am so happy to see you, Sunshine."

"So, I was at your little show, Scotty. Or should I call you Knox?"

She cocked her head to the side with a half-amused smirk. "Your guitar licks are pretty decent ... for a roadie. Tell me, how precisely does one acquire such formidable music skills from pushing equipment around?"

My cover was blown. Not that I hadn't planned on telling her, but this wasn't how I wanted her to find out. I could feel my face flush and a wave of heat wash over me. My heart raced as I tried to think of what to say, sweat breaking out on my forehead.

"Summer..." I trailed off. I felt the eyes of my friends on us. They were all watching and listening and I wasn't about to make a spectacle of us. "Let's go somewhere and talk. I can explain all of this."

"Really?" She didn't look convinced.

Lacey handed her a full glass of champagne. "Go hear what he has to say. Talia, Kay, and I will be here if you need us. We can make sure you get back home safely."

I wanted to insist that I'd take care of her, but I bit my tongue. I held out my hand to her.

When she finally took it, I sighed with relief. Before she could change her mind, I led her through the room toward the exit. Hudson, my security guard, stepped forward before we could leave the room.

I glanced at the hulking man who'd become a friend. "We need a private place to talk."

He nodded and then led me and Summer down a hall and to a small room that looked like an employee break room. "I'll be right outside."

I was still clasping Summer's hand when she turned to me. "Who was that guy?"

"That's Hudson. He's my security."

I studied her face as she took in my words. "He didn't go to Idaho with you?"

"No. We decided it wasn't necessary. I only need him for high-profile events when we're off tour." I gestured to the olive green couch. "Let's sit down."

She pulled her hand away and then sat. I wanted to pull her into my arms, but instead, I gave her some room. The space between us felt unnatural, filling me with anxiety.

"I wanted to tell you, Summer. If I knew you were coming tonight, I would have." My excuse sounded lame.

She slumped against the couch cushions. "Your friends have been really nice to me. Plus, I've had lots of alcohol and I'm tired. I should be a lot angrier right now — like I was at the concert because I felt incredibly stupid, Knox. I was calling you Scotty like a total dork. No one knew who I was talking about."

"You're not a dork. My mates — only my best mates — call me Scotty sometimes." I could see why she was embarrassed, but none of my friends were going to judge her for this. Meanwhile, I'd most likely face relentless teasing about it for life.

She placed her untouched glass of champagne on the table in front of us. "They only call you Scotty because you're from Scotland. Ugh. And I told them you were a roadie. They must think I'm such a fool."

"I never meant for it to go this far, Summer. I was being selfish. I liked being with you as just plain Scotty. We were having fun together and your parents accepted me for who I was. I didn't realize I'd ... develop deeper feelings."

I was trying to open up to her and show a little vulnerability in the hopes that she'd realize this wasn't a game to me. It was hard to do. I hadn't exposed myself to rejection in a long time.

Her eyes shined with intensity. "You're in a rock band. I never would have given you the time of day if I knew."

My laugh had a bite to it. "I actually admire that. These days I only ever encounter women who use me. Even if I wasn't pursuing actual relationships with them, it starts to feel really twisted. It's only gotten worse the more popular Ghost Parker has gotten."

She rolled her eyes. "Rock star problems..."

"It's a tough life, baby," I joked. I slid closer to her as I turned the conversation more serious. "If we decide to pursue an actual relationship, you'll have the tough part. It can be hard to look past the groupies and the tabloids that print garbage to see the truth. You'll have to trust me, Summer, especially when I'm away and on tour. I've seen how hard that is on Talia and Kaylie, but it's working for them. And I've never seen Ryder or Sid happier than they are now. That's if you still want to give us a chance."

I held my breath as I waited for her answer.

"Everything is totally different now. These are all new waters for me to navigate, but I do want to try. I still want to take it slow." She broke eye contact with me and looked down at her hands as she explained, "My head is still spinning with all of this; I'm still calling you Scotty in my mind. It's just crazy. I need to make sure that I still like you in the morning when I remember that you're a big rock star. And you're rich, too. That's two strikes against you."

"Are you serious?" I laughed incredulously. "I'm still a normal bloke, Sunshine. Most of my money is just sitting in a bank account. I don't even know how to spend it."

She placed her hand on my chest. "I'm sure I can help you spend a little of it."

I captured her hand in mine before she could move it away. "What would you spend it on?"

She thought for a moment. "You could take me on a marvelous vacation. I'm talking white sand beaches. Crystal clear water. Frozen cocktails on the beach served out of pineapples. With those little mini umbrellas."

She was thinking about a future for us and I liked it. "And you in that tiny bikini? I love it. What else would you spend it on?"

She frowned. "I don't know. Oh, you should get a better place. Your friends said your apartment is a dump."

I laughed and then pulled her into my arms. I nuzzled into her neck. "Don't you want diamonds and jewelry? Or, I could buy you a new car. Or designer clothes. Stuff like that."

She wiggled on my lap. "I don't care about stuff like that."

"Me neither. I did buy a $60,000 guitar, though."

She sat up straight. "Oh, my God. You really are that rich?"

I looked right into her brilliant blue eyes. "It means nothing if I'm not happy. And you make me happy. We'll take it slow, but now that you know all my secrets, I'm not letting you run away again."

She scowled and looked away. "I guess we're both big liars"

I tipped her chin up with my fingers. "No more lying to each other. Okay?"

She nodded and bit her lip. "Let's call my mother tomorrow and tell her we're back together. Trying to work it out. And we'll tell them who you really are.

I groaned. "That should be fun."

"We can skip over the whole fake dating thing. One shock is enough for them.

I agreed. "What's important now is that we're really dating this time.

"Right."

"So, if we make this call tomorrow, does that mean I can stay with you tonight?" My eyes silently pleaded with her. "You already know I can be a perfect gentleman if we share a bed. Even if you crawl all over me."

"I did not!" She pulled back and crossed her arms over her chest.

"You must have pulled me on top of you."

I pulled her right back to me. "Your place or mine?"

She didn't hesitate. "Mine. It's old and tiny and charmless, but at least I wouldn't call it a total dump."

"Let's go, then."

She wrapped her arms around my neck. "Kiss me first."

I smiled, closed my eyes, and kissed her softly. The electricity ramped up quickly. I deepened the kiss, moving my lips with hers in a passionate embrace. Our tongues moved together in perfect harmony until we were both breathless, and I finally pulled away.

"That's all you get for now."

# Chapter 25

## Summer

It was a gorgeous day in early May for the Kentucky Derby. I glanced over at Knox as we strolled through Churchill Downs with my parents right behind us. He looked entirely at home among the sea of wide-brimmed hats and pastel dresses, sporting his own preppy outfit, while somehow still managing to look devastatingly sexy. I couldn't help but admire how he carried himself, his confidence as intoxicating as the mint julep I sipped.

"It's really crowded," I murmured, taking in the bustling scene before us. The racetrack was filled with excitement; people chatted animatedly, placing bets and laughing with friends. The women wore their best sundresses, accessorized with vibrant hats and sunglasses, while the men donned dapper suits or sport coats. The air was thick with anticipation — it practically crackled with energy.

"At least we're not in the infield. You said our seats were pretty fancy." Knox reminded me, raising an eyebrow as he adjusted his dress shirt, looking nothing like the rock star that I'd gotten to know over the past six weeks of dating for real.

I'd spent many Derby days of years past in the infield with eighty thousand other partiers. The party started early morning and by afternoon, the infield was like spring break gone wild. The last time I'd been in the infield on Derby day, it had poured down buckets of rain for hours, turning the atmosphere into drunken mud-wrestling debauchery. Even though some of my old friends still bought general admission tickets, I'd left those days far behind.

"My parents are in clubhouse box seats," I replied, "but their box was already filled. She was able to get us 300 Level seats through her friends, which are still really good. It's not Millionaire's Row or the Turf Club, but it'll be really fun."

"Let's go have some fun, then," he suggested with a wicked grin. I felt my pulse quicken. I still had to pinch myself sometimes when I remembered who he was and that millions of fans loved him and his music. How did I get so lucky to stumble into a relationship with him?

As we made our way through the crowd, I couldn't help but notice the scrutinizing glances Knox received from both men and women alike. Knox was careful not to react, but I was sure that people were trying to guess if he was a celebrity. And for a moment, I felt a surge of pride — the lead guitarist of Ghost Parker was my boyfriend.

"Summer," my mother called, breaking me out of my thoughts. "Your father and I are going to find our seats. Why don't you and Knox stay down here and enjoy the atmosphere?"

"Sure, Mom," I agreed, trying to sound casual. I knew the amount of walking we'd done was quickly tiring out my mother. "Go get off your feet. Hopefully, you're in the shade."

With a nod, my parents disappeared into the throng of people, leaving Knox and me alone to navigate the chaos together. As the next race approached, the excitement around us swelled, and I could feel it seeping into my bones.

Knox was a big fan of the mint juleps, but I didn't enjoy the bourbon as much. I gave him my commemorative glass half filled with the concoction and he downed it in one gulp. "Do you want another? Or something else?"

"A glass of wine would be great." I staked a spot against the railing while I waited for him to return. There was alcohol everywhere, so it didn't take long for him to return.

"Ready for this?" Knox asked, handing me my wine as we settled our backs against the railing, in position to watch the horses thunder past when the race began.

"Absolutely," I said, a grin spreading across my face. I couldn't deny the thrill that coursed through me at the thought of sharing these moments with him.

As we waited for the next race, I watched the ladies parading by showing off their Derby Day fashion. The key to a successful ladies' outfit was the hat. My mother was a master at finding outrageous hats and she didn't disappoint this year.

I was wearing a flirty, off-the-shoulder floral sundress that hugged my curves just right. The colors were in shades of vibrant pink with a green ribbon sash around the waist. My hat was the real showstopper, though — a wide-brimmed straw creation trimmed with pistachio-green ribbon and adorned with clusters of pink flowers that matched the dress. It was an unwieldy monstrosity that cast playful shadows on my face as the sunlight filtered through.

Not to be outdone, Knox wore equally eye-catching attire to complement mine that the band's stylist helped him pick out. He looked ever so dapper in a blue small-patterned floral print dress shirt, tucked into tailored beige pants and paired with a pastel green blazer. A matching pocket square added an air of sophistication, while his sunglasses kept him looking effortlessly cool. His light-colored fedora hat had a green chambray band that matched his blazer.

We made a stunning couple, and I was glad that my mother had insisted on taking dozens of pictures of us on her phone. I'd do my best to sneak in a few more before the day was over.

The only hint of sadness that hung over Derby Day was that my mother was still dealing with the side effects of chemotherapy. She still had many cycles of chemo to go through, but she was adamant that she wouldn't miss the Derby for anything. I wasn't sure how long she'd last, but I was glad that she could come.

Of course, my mother, ever the elegant lady, had dressed to the nines. She'd opted for a chic navy blue dress with a peplum waist, accentuated by her signature strand of pearls. She and Dad had dressed more conservatively, but Mom's hat was a piece of artwork. She wore it over a floral headscarf, with one side of the long scarf trailing over the side of her shoulder. Her navy hat towered high on her head, a concoction of feathers, flowers, and ribbon.

I pulled out the official program to check the race stats while we waited. We each had a horse we were rooting for — Knox had chosen based on statistics, while I had selected mine purely on the basis of its name. We clinked our glasses together in a toast — me with my wine, and Knox with his neat bourbon — and waited for the starting bell.

"May the best horse win," I said, trying to keep my voice steady despite the excitement coursing through me.

"Right," Knox replied, his eyes crinkling with amusement as he watched me practically vibrating with anticipation.

As the bell rang out and the horses burst forth from the starting gate, Knox and I couldn't help but get swept up in the fervor of the crowd. We cheered and hollered for our chosen horses, our voices lost amidst the cacophony of excitement around us.

My heart was pounding in time with the hooves thundering down the track.

"Come on, Lucky Lady!" I shouted.

Knox groaned as his horse fell behind. "Pick up the pace, Midnight Thunder!" His eyes never left the race.

I couldn't help but feel the thrill of excitement as we watched the horses gallop past, jockeying for position. Lucky Lady, an underdog, was pulling ahead.

The deafening cheers of the crowd momentarily drowned out my victory cry as Lucky Lady crossed the finish line. Knox and I shared a victorious grin, our exhilaration mirrored in each other's eyes. I couldn't help but think that maybe lady luck had taken our side, and maybe, life was finally taking a turn for the better.

Knox pulled me into an embrace, almost tipping my hat off as he kissed me. I grinned when he let me come up for air. He'd been pulled into the excitement of it all as much as I had. I'd placed a very small wager, so the amount of money I won wasn't even that substantial, but it felt momentous at that moment.

"Summer?" a voice called from behind me, cutting through the noise like a knife.

My blood ran cold as I recognized the familiar tone. It belonged to Brad, my ex-boyfriend — the one who had talked incessantly about us getting married until the day he dumped me and went off to college. Turning around, I found myself face-to-face with him, his brown eyes searching mine with the goofy grin on his face that I used to love.

"Brad," I acknowledged, my voice wavering slightly. I could feel Knox tense beside me, silently watching the exchange.

"Wow, it's been what? Two years since I ran into you?" Brad said, running his fingers through his styled hair. "You look amazing, Summer. I've missed you. We should hang out sometime."

His words might have sounded genuine to an outsider, but I knew better. I remembered the way he had convinced me that we were in love in high school, only to move on without looking back.

"Thanks, Brad," I replied curtly, forcing a smile. "I'm only in town for a few days visiting my parents. And I'm spending all that time with my boyfriend."

He moved closer to me. "Where are you partying tonight? Maybe we can meet up?"

I guess he didn't get the hint. "I'm not interested. I have a boyfriend."

"Really?" He looked skeptical, his gaze flickering over to Knox before returning to me. "That guy"—he gestured dismissively at Knox—"you're with him?"

"Damn right," I retorted, my voice steady and firm. I could feel the weight of Knox's hand on my waist, offering silent support. "He's a much better boyfriend than you ever were. He treats me with respect and love. Something you wouldn't know anything about."

"Come on, Summer," Brad insisted, his voice taking on a pleading quality. "I've changed since high school. Give me another chance."

"Oh, please," I said, my voice tinged with sarcasm. "You had your chance, and you blew it. And I'm not the same girl I was back then. I've grown up and I won't let anyone treat me that way ever again."

As I stood there, my heart pounding in my chest, I could see the hurt flicker across Brad's face. But it was quickly replaced by a familiar arrogance — the same arrogance that had wreaked havoc on our relationship.

"Fine," he spat out, his eyes never leaving mine as he turned to walk away. "You were always too damn needy, anyway."

I watched him go, feeling both relieved and vindicated. With Knox by my side, I knew I was strong enough to face my past and finally break free from its hold.

"Summer? Are you okay?" Knox's concerned voice broke through my thoughts as he wrapped a protective arm around my waist. His touch felt like an anchor, keeping me steady and grounded. I leaned into his embrace, grateful for his support.

"Thank you," I murmured, burying my face in his chest. "I'm fine now."

"Good," he said, pressing a soft kiss to the top of my head. "Because no one messes with my lass."

His declaration sent a warm glow throughout my body. I looked up at him, my heart swelling with gratitude. "You're amazing, Limpie Pie."

He groaned, his eyes crinkling at the corners. "Only for you, my wee Bouncy Bumpkin."

We spent the afternoon placing bets and cheering on the horses in the undercard races, giving back all my winnings and then some. We ate and drank, checked on my parents, and even ran into another old friend when we visited the paddock area. By the time "My Old Kentucky Home" was played, the crowd was worked up to a fever pitch. The horses entered the track to a giant cheer. Time seemed to stand still as we waited for what was called the most exciting 2 minutes in sports.

And then it was over. Instead of feeling the letdown of another fun Derby gone by, I was elated to have Knox at my side, experiencing it. I'd been to about a dozen Derby Days, but this was my all-time favorite.

With the Derby behind us, we made our way to an after-party hosted by one of my sorority sisters. where many of my old college friends were gathered. The atmosphere was lively, with people laughing and sharing stories of their time at the races. As we entered the room, I couldn't help but notice the admiring glances cast in Knox's direction. I felt a surge of pride that this gorgeous, talented man was here with me.

"Hey, aren't you the guitarist from Ghost Parker?" someone called out, causing a few heads to turn.

"Not tonight, mate," he replied with a charming smile. "I'm Summer's date."

"Wow, you really hit the jackpot, huh, Summer?" My friend Stephanie teased, giving me a knowing wink. I blushed, feeling incredibly lucky to have Knox by my side.

"Believe me, I know," I whispered back, the corners of my mouth lifting into a smile.

As the night wore on, we mingled and danced, losing ourselves in the music and each other's company. Knox was not a wallflower; he made a point to get to know my friends, and it was clear that they were just as awed by him as I was.

"Summer," he whispered in my ear as we leaned up against the wall together. "This has been an incredible day."

"I loved it too," I admitted, my voice barely audible above the hum of conversation around us. "Thank you for everything, Knox."

"Always, Sunshine," he promised, pulling me closer. "Always."

My heart fluttered in my chest as Knox took my hand and led me out of the living room, away from the laughter and clinking glasses. He looked back at me with a mischievous grin, his eyes filled with excitement and something deeper I couldn't quite put my finger on.

"Where are we going?" I asked, trying to keep my voice steady, but it betrayed me, coming out husky with anticipation.

"Somewhere more private," he replied softly.

As we slipped out the door into the backyard, we realized that there would be no privacy out there. Even more partygoers had arrived until the backyard was full of people.

I slipped my arms around his neck. "Are you ready to go home? It's been a long day and I'm ready for some alone time with you."

He gave me a soft kiss on the lips. He pulled out his phone. "That sounds perfect. I'll order a ride. What's your parent's address?"

I rested my head against his shoulder on the ride home. I must have dozed off because suddenly we were pulling up the driveway of my childhood home.

Reminding me of my teenage years, a small table lamp was left on for us in the foyer, but the rest of the house was dark. I clicked off the lamp and then felt Knox right behind me. I spun around and then pulled him closer. My hands slid over his chest and then I began unbuttoning his shirt.

He captured my hand and stilled it. "First, take me to your room, and then have your way with me, lass."

I grabbed his hand and as we slipped down the hallway, I felt a thrill run through me. It was like being a teenager again, sneaking around my parents' house late at night. An odd mixture of nostalgia and rebellion bubbled up inside me, and I couldn't help but giggle at the thought of what we were about to do.

"Shh," Knox whispered, smirking at me as he pressed a finger to his lips. "We don't want to get caught, do we?"

I shook my head, biting my lip to suppress any more laughter. The truth was, getting caught was the last thing on my mind.

My childhood bedroom looked almost exactly the same as it had when I'd left for college — the same pink walls, the same canopy bed with its ruffled curtains, and even the same posters of Justin Bieber and One Direction plastered on the walls. It seemed both strange and oddly fitting that I was about to have sex with a bonafide rock star while staring into the faces of my teen idols.

Knox closed the door behind us, and suddenly, the rest of the world ceased to exist. We were alone in our own little world, and all I wanted was to lose myself in him.

"Summer," he murmured, looking into my eyes as he pulled me close. "I've wanted you all day long. I've barely been able to keep my hands off you."

"We have to be quiet," I breathed, wrapping my arms around his neck.

He glanced over at my frilly bed. "You'll have to scream into that Barbie pillow, then."

My hands shook as they yanked his shirt from his pants with fervor. In an electrifying frenzy, our bodies were entwined in a flurry of fabric as we tore the clothes from each other as fast as we could.

Our breaths were labored and our movements frantic. I wanted to make this moment last forever, to savor every second that I could spend with him. As his mouth sought out mine, I could feel our connection deepening, my heart growing more entwined with his with each passing moment. It was as if all the puzzle pieces of our lives were finally falling into place, locking us together in a bond that could never be broken.

We moved together in perfect harmony as if our bodies were meant to be interlocked like this since the dawn of time.

"Knox," I gasped, feeling the heat building inside me with every thrust of his hips. "I—I can't keep quiet."

"Your parents need to build a guest yurt out in the back," he replied between grunts.

He sounded so serious that I broke out into laughter.

"You think that's funny, lass?" He slipped a finger between my legs to stroke my clit while he pumped in and out of me. I wasn't laughing any longer, because I felt on the edge of exploding.

A loud moan tore from my throat and then waves of pleasure began washing over me. Shockwaves of pleasure rippled throughout my body, radiating out from my center and down through my limbs until I was trembling beneath him. A few seconds later, Knox joined me with his own release.

Knox groaned as he let go of his passionate embrace and rolled onto his back beside me, both of us panting from the intensity of what we'd just experienced together. His arm gathered me close to him and suddenly I felt safe and secure for the first time in a long time — as if nothing bad could ever touch me when we held each other like this.

"I love you, Summer. You're my everything," Knox whispered, his voice shaking with emotion.

"I love you too, Knox," I replied, feeling tears prick at the corners of my eyes. "Always."

As we lay there afterward in the sweet silence, I couldn't help but wonder what would happen when Knox went on tour. Would he leave me behind and move on, just like Brad did all those years ago? Seeing Brad had stirred up some old wounds, that left me feeling slightly uneasy, until sleep eventually pulled me under.

The morning light filtered through the curtains, casting a warm glow across the room. As I stirred, memories of last night with Knox came flooding back, making me smile despite my best efforts to hide it. I could still feel the lingering heat of his touch on my skin, and it made my heart race.

"Summer," my mother called from downstairs. "Breakfast is ready!"

"Be right down!" I yelled back, quickly getting dressed and glancing over at Knox, who was still fast asleep. I blew him a quiet kiss before slipping out of the room, hoping my parents hadn't heard anything last night.

The smell of freshly brewed coffee and bacon greeted me as I entered the kitchen. My mother stood by the stove, flipping pancakes, while my father scrolled through his phone at the table.

"Good morning," I said, trying to sound casual.

"Morning, sweetheart," my mom replied, giving me a warm smile. "Did you and Knox have a good time at the party last night?"

"Uh, yeah, we did," I answered, feeling a flush creeping up my cheeks. "We had a great time."

"Sit down and eat," she instructed, placing a plate of steaming pancakes in front of me. "We need to talk."

My stomach tightened at her words. Was something wrong? Was she sick again?

"Okay, Mom," I said hesitantly, taking a seat at the table.

"Your father and I noticed how happy you've been lately," she began, her eyes softening. "And we wanted to tell you that we're so glad you've gotten back together with Knox. When you called to tell us who he really was, well, that made me worry. But it turns out our first impressions about him were right after all. He's a wonderful person and we can tell how much he cares about you."

"You've always liked him, Mom." I smiled, pleased by her words.

"True," she confirmed, sitting down across from me. "But he's lived up to all our expectations. You deserve all the happiness in the world, Summer. And if Knox is the one who brings that to you, then your father and I couldn't be more thrilled."

Dad put down his phone. "I agree, Jellybean. He's a keeper."

"Thank you, Mom and Dad," I said, my voice thick with emotion. "That means a lot to me."

"Of course, sweetheart," she replied, reaching across the table to squeeze my hand. "We just want you to be happy. And if Knox is what makes you happy, then we'll support you both every step of the way."

A feeling of warmth and love filled my chest as I looked into my mother's eyes. She had always been there for me, through the good times and the bad, and knowing that she approved of my relationship with Knox only made my heart swell even more.

"Also," she added with a sparkle in her eye, "grandchildren would be nice, sooner than later. I'm just saying."

# Chapter 26

**Knox**

THERE WERE MOMENTS IN life that settled around your shoulders like a heavy, draping weight. Those poignant moments weren't easy to shake off; they insisted that you stand up and take notice, a palpable force that made it hard to breathe. Their significance was felt deep in your bones. They were crossroads. They were moments that changed everything, whether we wanted them to or not.

Today was one such turning point. I was with my four best mates in the entire world and I knew we were all feeling the weight of this change. A wedding was such a happy occasion, but if I was feeling this reflective about Ryder getting married, I couldn't imagine what he was feeling right now.

Ryder had been with Talia for almost three years, and no one had a doubt that they were meant to be together. She, along with Kaylie and now Summer, and been incorporated into our inner circle, but marriage was something more permanent. There was no turning back from this. We'd never be the same five guys again. We'd never be able to recapture the craziness of those early days as a band.

It wasn't bad; it was just different. We were growing up and embracing life. It was scary and exciting at the same time. Ryder could still be a wild and impulsive guy. He could still be the life of the party, but Talia brought out an even better side of him.

As I stood there in the groom's dressing room, surrounded by my bandmates adjusting their tuxedos, I couldn't help but feel a mix of nostalgia and circumspection. Ghost, Ryder, Sid, Bash, and I had been through so much together. And now here we were, preparing for Ryder's wedding.

"Never thought I'd see the day when our very own Stroke would be tying the knot," Sid said with a grin, tugging at his tie as if it were trying to strangle him.

"Me neither," Bash chimed in, teasingly nudging me in the side with his elbow. "And Scotty, of all people, as the best man? What the hell?"

"Hey now," I retaliated playfully, trying to act offended despite the smile that tugged at my lips. "Ryder is a smart man. He owed me after living on my couch for months."

"True," Sid admitted with a chuckle, giving me a friendly pat on the back. "I guess you did earn your stripes there. And how about all the love advice? Who would've thought that Mr. Rock' n Roll over here had such a romantic side?"

"Romantic or not," Bash retorted, fixing his cufflinks with a smirk, "you still better watch your back, Knox. I fully expect to be the next best man, even though no one has officially asked me yet." He turned around and pinned Sid with a stare.

Bash and Sid had been best mates since they were lads, so there really was no doubt who'd be the best man at Sid's wedding.

Sid held up his hands. "Don't rush me. I've still got time before I have to get sucked into the wedding planning insanity."

Laughing, Ryder picked up a baseball cap laying on the table and threw it at Sid. "We're only scheduling our whole upcoming tour around your wedding, Sid, so you better not fuck it up."

"I've got it all under control." He walked over to Bash and laid his hands on Bash's shoulders. "Bash, will you be my best man?"

Ghost scoffed. "Don't you need to get down on one knee first?"

"At least give the man some flowers." Ryder shook his head with disappointment.

I couldn't help but pile on. "Seal it with a kiss."

Sid looked back at us. "Fuck off, you fuckers."

Bash nodded his agreement. "About time you asked me. I will be your best man. As long as you never joke again about fucking my sister."

Ghost knocked Bash on the arm. "It's not a joke, bro, if it's reality."

Everyone snickered. Poor Bash had to endure a lot of teasing that his best friend was marrying his little sister.

"All right, mates, it's almost time to leave." The good-natured teasing reminded me of how close we were, beyond just being members of the same band. We were brothers, and even though things were changing, that bond would always remain.

"Any last-minute advice from my best man?" Ryder asked.

I clapped him on the back. "Just remember to enjoy the day. You've overcome a lot of obstacles to get to this place. And look at you now, about to get married to the love of your life. You're going to become a father in November. Life is good, mate."

"Damn right," Ryder agreed with a grin, his nerves visibly eased.

Sid came to stand beside Ryder. "Our second band baby and our first band wife. Good job, man."

Ryder smiled. "Then it's your turn. Kaylie will be our second band wife. I wonder who is next?"

Everyone turned to look at me.

I laughed. "I've got a lot of work to do before I can convince Summer to tie the knot." Turning to Ghost, I asked, "What about you? Any thoughts on getting hitched someday?"

Ghost remained quiet for a moment, his eyes distant as if lost in thought. "I don't know," he finally answered, his voice soft. "Maybe one day, if the right person comes along."

"I'm going to remain single forever," Bash declared adamantly, shaking his head. "Why would you ever give up all your freedom? No ball and chain for me."

"Is that why Josie is your plus one tonight?" Sid teased, referring to Kody's nanny.

Bash scowled. "She is not my plus one. She's here to watch Kody so I can pick up one of the single ladies. The maid of honor is pretty hot, or there's always Ryder's step-sister, but she'll be too busy mooning over Knox."

I groaned. "Shite. I forgot to warn Summer about Arianna."

A knock sounded at the door. Ryder's father poked his head into the room. "Can I speak to my son for a few minutes?"

"Give us a few minutes, Dad," Ryder replied.

It had taken a lot of work, but Ryder and his dad had mostly repaired their once-troubled relationship over the past few years.

Bash grabbed some shot glasses and Sid began filling them with Jack Daniels Old No. 7 whiskey. Bash passed them out one by one. We stood in a circle, ready to toast Ryder.

Ghost turned to me. "Best man duties — you say the toast."

"Well, mates." I lifted my shot glass. "Since I'm going to be delivering the toast later, I'll give you a little preview of the uncensored version right now."

I looked around the circle at my mates and then began. "I'd like to say that Talia and Ryder fell in love at first sight, but we all know that's not true because it was pitch black in the room when they first met. Without even knowing each other's names or ever having laid eyes on each other, they got a taste of what was to come. Let's give 69 cheers to tongue in pussy and lips on cock at first sight."

I got the reaction I expected from the guys, lots of back-slapping, snickering, laughing, and fist-pumping.

Ryder had turned decidedly pale. "Please tell me that is not your toast."

"Easy, mate. Don't get your knickers all twisted. The censored version is PG-13, for sure." I raised my glass—" to Ryder and Talia,"—and then downed the shot.

Everyone followed suit and then Ghost clapped his hands together and flashed a smile. "Come on, we've got a wedding to attend. Everyone, huddle up."

We all huddled together, shoulder-to-shoulder, just like we did before we went on stage at every concert and tossed our hands into the circle.

Ghost looked around at all of us. "Let's go get our boy hitched. Ryder, we are behind you all the way. Ride or die."

"Ride or die," we cheered as we collectively raised our hands.

I patted Ryder on the shoulder as we started filing out of the room. "I'll send your father in. Take your time. I'll be waiting for you when you're ready, mate."

I only had to wait for a few minutes until Ryder's father exited the room and shook my hand before heading to the ceremony.

I looked inside the room. "Are you ready?"

"I'm ready," Ryder agreed, his voice filled with a mix of nerves and excitement as he took one last look in the mirror. "Let's do this."

As we made our way down to the picturesque beach where the ceremony would take place, I took in the breathtaking scene that lay before us. The sun was setting, casting a warm glow across the sand and painting the sky in hues of orange and pink. The waves crashed gently against the shore, providing a calming rhythm for the momentous occasion ahead.

We took our places at the front, with Ryder nervously fidgeting beside me. I patted his shoulder reassuringly, feeling honored to be standing beside him on his wedding day.

As the music began to play and the bridal party started their procession down the sandy aisle, I let my gaze wander over the gathered guests until they rested on her. Summer. She was sitting in the audience, looking absolutely stunning in her elegant dress, her hair cascading around her shoulders. Our eyes met for a brief moment, and I felt my heart skip a beat.

In that instant, I couldn't help but think about what it would be like to have Summer by my side forever, our lives completely intertwined. In my mind's eye, I saw her walking down the aisle towards me, her eyes shining with tears of joy; I saw us raising children together, their laughter filling our home with happiness; I saw us growing old together, our love only deepening as the years went by.

My heart raced with the possibilities, a fierce desire to make this dream a reality coursing through my veins. I knew that there would be challenges along the way, but I was willing to do whatever it took to make Summer mine and to prove to her that I was committed to our love.

I shook myself out of my daydream. Right now, I needed to focus on celebrating Ryder and Talia's love, and ensuring that their day went perfectly. Happily, the ceremony went off without a hitch. I really didn't have to do much except for handing over the wedding rings at the right time and escorting Talia's friend, Ellie, back down the aisle.

While the ceremony drew to a close, and the sun dipped lower on the horizon, it cast a warm golden glow over the picturesque beach setting. It was the perfect backdrop for Ryder and Talia. They looked so incredibly in love, their eyes locked together as if they were the only people on Earth.

The crowd of attendees moved back up to the hotel where the reception was set up. Before the festivities began, Ghost took to the stage at the reception to perform a song that he had written for the newlyweds.

My fingers itched as he strummed on the acoustic guitar. I couldn't help but want to be up there playing with him. Ghost effortlessly captured everyone's attention as he sang the lyrics that spoke of everlasting love, of standing by each other through thick and thin, and of finding solace in one another's embrace. His voice was mesmerizing as he belted out the words.

I weaved through the crowd, intent on finding Summer. I scanned the crowd, searching for her amidst the sea of faces. People cheered as Ghost finished his song and then the waiters and waitresses who'd been awed by his performance began circulating with their trays of hor d'oeuvres again.

As the DJ began playing music, I spotted Summer across the room. There she was, her laughter like music as she mingled with Kaylie, Lacey, and Greyson. She looked so beautiful, her blonde hair cascading in waves down her back, the setting sun casting a halo of light around her. Her smile was radiant, lighting up the room and filling my heart.

I crossed the room and took the spot by her side. She gazed up at me with a bright smile and I slid my arm around her. We socialized with our friends, and when the music changed to a slow dance, I offered her my hand. "Would you like to dance?"

Her eyes sparkled with enthusiasm as she took my hand, not hesitating for a moment. She answered with an exaggerated Southern accent. "Why, it would be my pleasure."

As we stepped onto the dance floor, our bodies moved together effortlessly. Our eyes locked, and we shared wide smiles, fully enjoying the romantic atmosphere of the wedding.

"You look beautiful tonight," I whispered in her ear.

She shuddered slightly. "Thank you."

"How about we ditch this party and head back to our room early?" I knew she wouldn't go for it out of respect for Talia and Ryder, but it would at least give her something to think about.

"There will be plenty of time for whatever is on your mind later," she said playfully.

I enjoyed holding her in my arms as we swayed to the gentle rhythm of the music. The world seemed to fade away, leaving only the two of us. When the song ended, I led her back to the table.

"Your best man's speech is coming up soon, isn't it?" Summer settled at our table, sitting next to Kaylie. "Are you nervous about it?"

I shrugged. "Let's just say I gave Ryder a little preview of it, and it didn't go over too well. I'll have to tone it down a bit, but I want to make sure it's a memorable toast."

"Knowing you, I'm sure it will be," she reassured me with a wink.

Later, after we ate dinner, the time came for me to deliver my best man's speech. I stood up and got everyone's attention. I began by recounting some humorous anecdotes from our years together as friends and in the band. Then, I focused on the love story between Ryder and Talia, sharing how it all began with a chance meeting that led to an unforgettable first kiss.

I was pretty sure that not many people knew the exact details about their first meeting when Talia crawled into bed with Ryder, thinking he was her boyfriend at the time. Talia was squirming in her seat, her cheeks pink, as she understood the double entendre behind my words.

"...and as they say, it was love at first lip-lock," I joked, eliciting laughter from the guests.

The guests cheered at the end of my toast, and then Ryder stood to thank me with a hug. I returned to my seat, where Summer's eyes shone with pride and amusement. "Good job," she praised.

After spending a lot of time drinking and dancing with our friends, Summer and I took a break to walk along the beach. The sand was cool beneath our feet, and the gentle breeze carried with it the salty scent of the ocean. As we walked hand in hand, our fingers intertwined, I couldn't help but feel a sense of peace and contentment wash over me.

"Sunshine," I began, my voice barely audible above the soothing sound of the waves crashing against the shore. "I've been thinking about us, about what comes next."

Her eyes met mine, curiosity and warmth reflecting back at me as she said, "What have you been thinking?"

"The band is going on tour in two months," I reminded her, feeling a touch of sadness at the thought of being away from her. "But I want you to know that I'm committed to making this work between us. I'd love for you to visit as much as you can while we're on the road if that's something you'd be willing to do."

Summer squeezed my hand gently, a soft smile playing on her lips. "I'd love that, Knox. I can't promise I'll be able to make every stop, but I'll do my best to be there for as many shows as possible. I've been a little nervous about what was going to happen."

"You know that I want to be with you, Summer. It won't be easy, but I've seen Talia and Ryder and Kaylie and Sid manage to make it work." I felt a swell of love for this woman who had captured my heart so completely. "I just want to do whatever it takes to prove to you that I'm committed to us, to our future together."

"Knox, I believe you," she whispered, her eyes shining with sincerity. "I trust you, and I trust in our love."

As the night drew to a close, we stood under the moonlight, our bodies pressed together as we shared a tender kiss. The connection between us deepened, and I knew without a doubt that I loved this woman with every fiber of my being. At that moment, I vowed to myself that I would do everything in my power to keep us together, no matter what challenges the future might bring. She was my forever girl.

# Chapter 27

----------------------------------------

## Summer

CELIA AND I SAT down for lunch on the patio, shielded from the hot August sun by overhead shade awnings. Strategically placed fans kept the air from stagnating and lots of greenery lent itself to a relaxing atmosphere. Our favorite outdoor restaurant buzzed with lively conversations, punctuated by the clink of glasses and laughter from other patrons. The scent of fresh herbs and spices wafted out from the kitchen, tantalizing our senses and making my stomach rumble in protest.

Celia picked up her menu. "We haven't had a chance to talk since Knox moved in with you last week." Her eyes twinkled with curiosity. "So, how's it going?"

Knox had decided not to renew his apartment lease since his place wasn't that nice and it'd be sitting empty while he was away on tour. I offered to let him move his belongings into my apartment and use it as his home base when he wasn't on tour.

He'd essentially moved in with me and it stirred up a whirlwind of emotions that had been consuming me ever since. It felt like two worlds colliding — mine, stable and safe, yet filled with angst from past heartbreak, and his, brimming with passion and enthusiasm until it drowned out my cautious nature.

"It's actually scary how easy it's been. My place is tiny, so living together has been ... intimate, to say the least," I admitted, feeling a blush creep up my cheeks. "I love playing house with him, Celia. A little too much."

A smile tugged at the corners of her lips as she took a sip of her iced tea. "Intimacy can be ... delightful. You two seem good for each other."

"Thanks." My gaze drifted down to my hands, and I rubbed them nervously on my thighs. "The last time I lived with a man, it turned into a total disaster. I told you about Jake. He was the jackass who stole money from me before he skipped town. It's hard not to feel a little apprehensive about sharing my life with someone again."

Celia reached across the table, placing her hand on mine in a gesture of comfort. She didn't speak, but her eyes conveyed understanding and sympathy.

"Knox is different, though," I continued, my voice barely audible above the clattering dishes and chattering diners. "He cares for me, and I know he wouldn't hurt me like that. Besides, he's loaded. He doesn't need my money. But still, old fears die hard."

As our food arrived, steaming and fragrant, we paused our conversation. But the weight of my concerns lingered, even as we began to eat. Would Knox prove to be different, or was I setting myself up for disaster?

"Summer, look at me," Celia said gently, waiting for me to meet her eyes. "Knox is not like Jake or any of those other jerks you've dated.

I know you've been hurt before, but you can't compare them. Knox loves you, and he's shown time and again that he's a good man."

"I know." I nodded, feeling a little reassured as I took a bite of my chicken entrée. She was right; it wasn't fair to hold my past against Knox. He deserved better than that.

"Speaking of Knox," Celia continued after a moment, "when does the tour start?"

My heart clenched at the mention, but I managed to keep my voice steady. "He's leaving next week. They'll be gone for months, playing shows all over the country, before they get a small break."

"Are you worried about him being away?" Celia asked, genuine concern reflecting in her eyes.

"Of course," I admitted, stabbing at a cherry tomato with my fork. "But we'll figure it out."

"Has he ever been on tour while dating someone?" Celia asked cautiously.

"No. Before me, he wasn't a relationship kind of guy, and from what Kaylie and Talia told me, the lifestyle on tour can be wild. Crazy groupies, casual sex, you know," I admitted, feeling a knot of unease in my stomach. "But I trust Knox. I have to, or this relationship won't work."

Celia dabbed at her mouth with a napkin. "But you said he wants you to go out and see him on the road, right? He wouldn't want you out there if he planned to get mixed up with that."

"I'm just worried that the distance and lifestyle might strain our relationship." I hesitated, biting my lip as I admitted my deepest fear. "I'll only be able to see him a couple of times each month due to our schedules. Honestly, Celia, I don't know if I can handle being apart from him for that long. It's going to be so hard... and what if he gets too used to life on the road without me?"

"Summer," Celia said softly, her blue eyes full of sympathy, "you're strong, and so is your love for each other. You guys will figure it out. Distance can be tough, but it doesn't have to break you."

"He'll be back in November for a long break for Sid's wedding and the birth of Ryder and Talia's baby," I shared, trying to sound upbeat but feeling the distance between Knox and me already. "It's just going to be tough to make do with only an occasional visit and knowing there are tons of girls throwing themselves at him."

Celia looked at me thoughtfully, her eyes searching mine for a moment before she spoke. "You know, Summer, relationships aren't always easy. But if you both truly love each other, you'll find a way to make it work. This will definitely be a test."

"True," I agreed. "If he passes this huge test, I just might be able to put my dating PTSD behind me for good."

She pointed her manicured finger at me. "If he passes the test, then you demand a ring and nail down his ass ASAP. He's a gorgeous, rich rock star with a sexy accent. What the hell else could you ask for?" She thought for a moment. "Maybe a hot brother for your best friend?"

I paused with the fork halfway to my mouth and raised an eyebrow. "He has two brothers, but they live in Scotland. I can inquire about their hotness."

She shook her head. "Scotland is a bit far. What about the other guys in the band? I still haven't been invited to any rock star parties. What's the deal with Ghost? He's reportedly single, and he's very hot."

I took a sip of water as I contemplated how much to tell Celia. "Ghost is a mystery. He's a great guy, but I don't know him all that well. I try to act normal when he's around, but I'm actually a bit star-struck by him."

She took a bite of her lunch and waved her fork at me. "I don't blame you, girlfriend. He's next level."

"Speaking of Ghost," I said, trying to change the subject, "Knox's 30th birthday is coming up, right before he leaves for the tour. I'm throwing him a surprise party this weekend. I've been secretly texting with Ghost to coordinate everything without Knox finding out."

"Oooh, that sounds amazing!" Celia exclaimed. "He's going to love it!"

"Thanks," I smiled, feeling a warm glow at the thought of making Knox happy. "I just want to show him how much I care before he leaves."

"Summer, you're doing something wonderful for him," Celia reassured me as she pushed her empty plate aside. "He's going to love it. Trust me. And more importantly, trust in your relationship with Knox. Don't let your fears overshadow the love you share. You can handle whatever challenges come your way."

"Thank you, Celia." I really appreciated having a friend who cared about me. "I needed to hear that."

"Anytime, girl," she responded with a warm smile. "That's what friends are for, right?"

"Right," I agreed, feeling more optimistic about my relationship with Knox.

As our lunch break came to an end, we stood up and embraced each other tightly, both feeling grateful for the support and friendship we provided one another.

"Come on, let's get back to work," Celia suggested, giving me one last reassuring squeeze before releasing me from her embrace.

"Sounds good," I agreed, my heart lighter and my resolve stronger than ever.

Not too long after I got home from work, I heard the familiar sound of keys jingling outside the door. Knox walked in, carrying his guitar, an exhausted yet satisfied grin on his handsome face.

"Hey Sunshine," he greeted me, leaning down to press a soft kiss on my lips. "How was your day?"

"Busy," I admitted, a small smile playing on my lips as I wrapped my arms around his waist. "But better now that you're here."

"Same here," he agreed, his eyes sparkling with genuine affection. "I missed you."

"Missed you too," I replied, my heart swelling with love for this man.

We decided to have a cozy dinner at home, just the two of us. The dimly lit room, the flickering candles, and the soft music playing in the background created a peaceful atmosphere that allowed us to focus on each other and forget about the outside world for a while.

Over plates of steaming pasta, we shared the details of our day, laughing at silly anecdotes and discussing what our friends were up to. Everything felt so perfect; I didn't even want to think about the challenges ahead.

As the evening progressed, I couldn't help but notice how Knox's presence had transformed my small apartment into a warm and welcoming haven. Even though our living space was cramped with his belongings now occupying every available nook and cranny, I found comfort in having him so close to me. The intimacy of sharing our lives like this only strengthened our bond and made me feel more connected to him than ever before.

"Hey," he murmured, pulling me out of my thoughts as we settled onto the couch after dinner. "You okay?"

I smiled at him, nodding in response. "Yeah, just thinking about how lucky I am to have you here with me."

Knox leaned over, planting a soft kiss on my lips. "The feeling is mutual, beautiful."

Our eyes locked, and the intensity between us became palpable. I could see the raw passion in Knox's eyes, the hunger for closeness and connection, and it ignited a fire inside me that demanded satisfaction.

"I need you inside me," I whispered, my voice barely audible as I reached for the hem of his shirt and lifted it over his head.

He didn't need any further encouragement. In one swift motion, he scooped me up into his arms and carried me to the bedroom, his strong grip making me feel safe and secure. With each step, our anticipation grew, our hearts pounding in unison as we prepared to surrender ourselves completely to one another.

Once we reached the bed, our lips met again in a searing, desperate kiss, our hands exploring every inch of each other's bodies as if trying to memorize the contours and textures. There was something almost primal about the way Knox touched me, his raw masculinity radiating from every pore as he claimed me as his own.

I reveled in the exquisite pleasure of our bodies joining, the way we fit together so perfectly as one. It was a dance of passion and desire, a symphony of sighs and moans that filled the room with an electric energy. Our intertwined bodies moved in a wild and wanton rhythm of pleasurable exploration. His hands passionately explored my most intimate places, as if he knew them better than I did myself until I was writhing underneath him.

Each exhalation flowed into the next as I climbed higher and higher on waves of pleasure. The ache built inside me until I was consumed by an explosive orgasm that left me trembling with ecstasy. I knew without a doubt that this man, this incredible, loving man, was my other half, my soulmate.

Afterward, exhausted but blissfully content, we lay entwined in each other's arms, our hearts still racing from the intensity of what we'd just shared. As sleep began to claim us both, I pressed a tender kiss to Knox's chest, whispering a quiet "I love you" before drifting off into a peaceful slumber.

The next morning, the sun peeked through the curtains, casting a warm glow over Knox's sleeping form. His chest rose and fell in a steady rhythm, his strong arms wrapped around me. I hated to leave, but work beckoned, and I knew I couldn't stay in bed all day, no matter how much I wanted to.

I carefully disentangled myself from Knox's embrace, trying not to wake him. He stirred slightly, grumbling something unintelligible, before turning over and burrowing deeper into the pillows. Smiling at the sight, I tiptoed across the room, gathering my clothes for the day.

I stepped into the bathroom, closing the door softly behind me. Turning on the shower, I let the water heat up as I thought about the road that lay ahead for Knox and me. The thought of the upcoming Ghost Parker tour sent a thrill of excitement through me, but also a pang of worry. Could I really trust Knox to remain faithful while he was surrounded by temptation? Would our love be strong enough to hold us together?

Shaking off my doubts, I reminded myself of Celia's advice: to trust in our love and the bond we shared. Knox had shown me time and time again that he was committed to us, and I needed to believe in him, in us.

With that resolve, I stepped into the shower, letting the warm water cascade over my body like a soothing balm. As the droplets washed away the remnants of our passionate night, I resolved to face whatever challenges came our way without cowering.

After all, if the past few months had taught me anything, it was that life was full of surprises, both good and bad. And together, Knox and I would navigate these uncharted waters, hand in hand, our love serving as a beacon to guide us through the storm.

# Chapter 28

**Knox**

Slowly, I opened my eyes, blinking against the morning light that filtered through the curtains. I was disappointed that Summer was not snug in my arms, but then I heard the sound of running water coming from the bathroom and realized that Summer was taking a shower to get ready for work.

It'd been less than a week that I'd been living at her place, but waking up with her by my side had become a necessary part of my life so quickly and effortlessly. I was leaving on tour soon, and the feeling was strangely bittersweet. Normally, I couldn't wait to get back on the road, but this time I was reluctant because I'd be leaving her behind. I knew she had reservations about me going, and I didn't blame her. I'd just have to work hard to prove my commitment.

As I lay there musing, I heard the distinct chime of a new text notification. I glanced over at Summer's phone charging on the nightstand.

A few more cheerful pings went off in rapid succession, making the messages somehow seem more urgent. Curious, I glanced at the phone and was momentarily stunned to see they were coming from Ghost.

Why would Ghost be texting Summer? I didn't even know that they ever talked at all, let alone texted with each other this early in the morning. It seemed odd.

I slid over to her side of the bed and the phone lit up again with a new text.

**Ghost:** He doesn't suspect a thing.

My blood ran cold. The words hit a nerve. They were secretive and suspicious. The screen went blank, but I couldn't tear my eyes away from it. What did it mean? Why would Ghost be texting my girlfriend?

The phone lit up again. I could only see a portion of the text from the preview window, but I saw enough.

**Ghost:** Meet me for lunch at

My thoughts spiraled. My mind raced with questions and doubts as I sat there, staring at Summer's phone. Was she really cheating on me with Ghost? I couldn't believe it. He was my best friend, someone I trusted with everything. He would never do that to me. And Summer was the love of my life. What we had was real. We were happy.

My eyes remained fixed on the lifeless screen, but I wasn't focused on it. I was remembering that day. The day Aila died.

I'd been living at my grandparent's cottage for four months. When Granda passed away, Nan decided to move closer to her daughter, my Aunt Mary, leaving the cottage empty for nearly three years. When Nan heard I was to be married, she offered the cottage to me and Aila, only expecting a pittance for rent.

Before the wedding, my friend, Hugh, moved in with me to help pay rent, since there were two bedrooms and I needed any extra cash I could get. I was working extra shifts at the sheet metal factory and playing some gigs at the local pubs at night to save as much money as I could. The wedding was proving to be more expensive than I bargained for, and I'd already blown a sizeable portion of my meager savings on Aila's engagement ring. I didn't want to start my new married life swimming in piles of debt. I even figured Hugh might stay on after Aila and I married, at least until a bairn was on the way and we needed the room.

Aila still lived with her parents while we were engaged, but she spent a lot of time at the cottage, even when I was at work. When I first moved in, she helped me clean it up and paint the inside. She set up a sewing machine on a small table in the corner and was constantly making things for the cottage: curtains, pillows, placemats, potholders, and table runners. It was beginning to look like a cozy home.

She also worked on her wedding binder at the cottage. After she'd leave, sometimes I'd leaf through it to get some idea of what she was planning for our wedding. She asked for my input occasionally, but I wasn't too picky with all the little details. As long as she was happy, I was satisfied.

It was a good thing that Aila and Hugh got along so well. Hugh didn't mind that Aila spent so much of her free time at the cottage. Of course, he was living there for cheap, but he was also my best mate, so he kept an eye out for her when I wasn't around. I played guitar for a local band and we worked a lot of late nights, especially on the weekend. Aila still had a midnight curfew, so she was always long gone before I got home on those nights, but at least I knew she wasn't at the cottage alone.

I don't remember what I was looking for when I went digging through her purse that day. It was nothing significant. The exact moment I found the note was seared into my brain, but everything that came before was fuzzy.

The note was on a small piece of paper, very innocuous-looking, except that it was ripped in half. If it hadn't been torn, it never would have gotten a second glance from me.

The rip didn't do much to disguise the hand-printed words:

```
You can't go through with it. We
need to talk.
If you don't tell him, I will.
```

Just three sentences. The handwriting was pretty distinct, so I was certain that it was Hugh's.

I interpreted the note quickly. 'You can't go through with it' referred to our wedding. 'If you don't tell him, I will' was obviously talking about telling me. Telling me what? The most logical guess was that Aila and Hugh were having an affair.

I didn't panic, because the thought was simply ludicrous. Aila loved me. We were getting married in mere days. Lately, she'd been so happy getting the cottage ready. We'd even talked about having wee'uns right away. No, I didn't doubt her love for a single second.

I was misinterpreting the note. There had to be a reasonable explanation for it. She'd laugh at me for even thinking that she'd been unfaithful. Maybe she'd give me a wallop for being such an eejit.

When she came into the room and saw me holding the paper, her face visibly paled.

My palms began to sweat and my heart started to race. "Aila, what is this?"

She didn't laugh or give me a wallop. Her eyes shifted nervously away from me. "It's nothing."

I stood my ground and demanded an answer. "Who wrote this?"

"No one! It's from work." Her voice cracked. "It's not mine."

I could tell she was lying. I knew her well enough to know when she was trying to hide something.

My face tightened in anger and I growled, "Are you cheating on me with Hugh?"

Aila denied it, but her words lacked conviction. She stammered, "I-It's not what it looks like! It's just a misunderstanding."

I crossed my arms and glared at her. "Explain yourself," I commanded.

Her hands were shaking and tears were flooding her eyes. "It's not what you think, Knox. I love you. Please don't do this."

"It's not what I think?" I roared. "Then tell me what it is. Tell me you did not sleep with Hugh while I was out busting my arse late at night to make some extra money to pay for this bloody wedding. Look me in the eye and swear it, Aila."

She was sobbing now. "I love you, Knox. You've got to believe that."

Rage boiled in my veins as she said nothing. Her silence spoke volumes and filled my mind with a million doubts. With blinding shock, I accepted the truth, even though it felt like a nightmare. The acidic burn of betrayal took root in my gut and blotted out all hope. My insides roiled, and my heart sank. My voice was deadly calm. "Tell me you didn't. Tell me you didn't fuck my best mate."

She covered her face with her hands and slumped to the ground on her knees. "Knox, please..."

I turned away, not able to look at her. I tasted bile in the back of my throat as I listened to her keening sobs. "Where is that bloody bastard? I'll kill him."

"Knox, no!" she cried. Aila scrambled to her feet and lunged for the door. With a loud slam of the door, she stormed outside. I wanted to chase her, to force her to deny everything, but I was nearly paralyzed with shock.

Stumbling back into our bedroom, I collapsed onto the bed. I didn't know then, but minutes later, she would be dead.

♫♪♩♪♪

I blinked my eyes, wiping away the memories, and slowly came back to the present. I'd spent years trying to figure out why Aila had thrown away our love and slept with Hugh. Did she stop loving me? Did she love him? Had they grown close all those nights I wasn't there? I'd eventually come to the bitter realization that I'd never learn the answers to those questions.

Aila was gone and Hugh and I never spoke more than a few words to each other after her death. Hugh moved out of the cottage the day after she died, cementing their betrayal of me in my mind. After the funeral, I began making arrangements and left for America as soon as I could. I had to get away from all of that hurt and anger.

The parallels to this situation didn't escape me. I was almost in the same exact position as I was that day when I was staring at the ripped note. I was faced with the evidence that the woman I loved was cheating on me. And, yet once again, I was in complete denial. I didn't believe it could be true. Our love was so real and so strong that it transcended that kind of thing. She wouldn't cheat on me. I just couldn't comprehend it.

Maybe Summer was like all the other girls, after all. Did she get a taste of the glamorous rock star life and decide she wanted more? Did she want a guy with the bigger celebrity, more status, more fame and fortune, with the paparazzi dogging his every move like crazed sycophants? A guy in the spotlight — the lead singer, not the guitarist. A charismatic man, mysterious and brooding, with a luxury apartment who knew how to spend his money. Not a cheapskate. Not a simple man, like me.

Fuck! Could it be true? Ghost had an enticingly seductive personality. No one could deny that. Could Summer have gotten swept up by that?

Doubts seeped into my bones and sliced through me like a sharp blade, cutting deep. My stomach muscles clenched as a wave of dizzying dread washed over me.

The shower water turned off, and I panicked. I was not going to yell at her. I was not going to confront her at all. There was no way I was going to relive that agony.

I needed to escape. As quickly as I could, I tossed on some clothes, grabbed my wallet, and searched around for my shoes. I bolted for the door, but at the last minute, I backtracked and grabbed my guitar. A few minutes later, I slapped on my ball cap, slid on some sunglasses, and made my way out of the building.

I had no idea where I was going, but I needed to be gone.

# Chapter 29

**Knox**

GOOD THING IT WAS five o'clock somewhere because I was smashed. My only plan was to numb myself as fast as possible, but it wasn't working. I wasn't numb enough.

I'd left Summer's apartment and wandered around the city aimlessly until I found a small park. For a few hours, I sat down on a bench and played my guitar, managing to hold my demons at bay for a short time. I'd even been tipped $5 by an old guy who shuffled over and chatted with me for a few minutes.

In my wanderings, I'd passed a hole-in-the-wall bar with a sign that said it opened at 11 a.m. When it was 11 o'clock, I grabbed my guitar, retraced my steps, and found that bar. The bartender was happy to open a tab and send alcohol my way. I sat at the bar with my guitar tucked safely between my legs and attempted to drink away my sorrow.

A few hours later, when I was closer to the numb I was searching for, I discovered that my wallet was missing. One of the friendly blokes who'd tried to strike up a conversation with me must have swiped it.

Fuck, I couldn't even care. I closed out my tab, took my credit card back from the bartender, and left. I had nowhere to go and not enough brain power left to figure out a solution.

My head was foggy, and I had no idea what to do. Going back to Summer's wasn't an option, and I couldn't turn to Ghost for help like I'd normally do. That option was cut off. Ryder and Bash lived too far away, so that left Sid. Suddenly, Sid's penthouse apartment seemed like the perfect place to hide from the world. Plus, Sid wouldn't give me too much grief. He was a good guy.

I found a cab and managed to get myself into Sid's building. I had a not-so-friendly exchange with the doorman, but eventually, Kaylie came down to the lobby, spoke quietly with the doorman, undoubtedly smoothing over any ruffled feathers I'd caused, and escorted me up to her apartment. She was literally escorting me — holding onto my elbow — so I guess I was staggering about like a drunk, even though I felt at least partially in control.

I'm fairly certain Kaylie and I talked for a while before I passed out on her couch. When I woke up next, Sid was home.

He handed me a bottle of water. "You missed band practice and didn't answer your phone. We were all worried. You've never blown off practice before."

I grunted and gulped at the water. What I needed more than water was more alcohol before the numbness wore off.

Sid looked down at me. "Kay said you showed up here wasted and said something about Aila? And Ghost fucked you over somehow? What's going on, man?"

When I sat up on the couch, my vision spun with dizziness. I was drunker than I thought. "I'm backing out of the tour."

The words were out even before I could scrutinize them. Where did that come from? Was that even what I wanted? Music was the only good thing in my life.

Sid laughed nervously. "Bro, you're shitfaced. And you're not making any sense. Whatever happened between you and Ghost can be worked out."

"Not this time, mate. I'm dropping out of the band and moving to Australia."

Sure, I was pure blootered, but I knew damn well my words would have a devastating effect on my mates. Why not pull everyone down to hell right along with me?

The room went silent as Sid stared at me in disbelief. Confusion and disappointment etched his face. I knew I was being irrational, but the pain was too much to bear.

Sid sat down next to me. "You need to sober up. You're not thinking straight. Why don't I call Summer? Maybe she can help you?"

"No!" I barked out, my voice echoing through the empty room. The mere mention of her name sent a wave of anger and pain coursing through my body. How could she do this to me? How could she betray me like this? I shook my head, trying to clear it of the toxic thoughts that threatened to consume me. "I don't want to talk to her."

Sid sighed and rubbed his face with his hands. "Look, Knox, I get that you're hurting. But you can't just shut everyone out like this. It's not healthy."

I knew he was right, but I couldn't bring myself to care. "If you want to help me, get me some more alcohol. The stronger, the better."

He stood up. "I'm going to get you some food to sober your stupid ass up. Then we'll talk."

"Right, mate." I laid back down on the couch and drifted off again.

When I woke up the second time, Ghost was sitting a few feet away from me on a chair he'd pulled up to the couch, fiddling with his phone.

I knew he'd come. Hell, there was a reason I'd pulled the fire alarm, so to speak, and said those things to Sid. I'd wanted him to come. I wasn't sure I was ready for this confrontation, especially with the effects of the alcohol wearing off, but it was too late to turn back.

I sat up and reached for the half-empty bottle of water I'd left earlier. Next to it was a bottle of pain medication. I shook a few pills out of the bottle and downed them with the remainder of the water.

"How much did you drink?" Ghost asked.

"No idea. I guess I'll know when I get the credit card bill." I rubbed at my aching temples. "Fuck, my wallet was stolen, too."

Ghost remained silent, and the silence was bothering me. I looked around. "Where are the others?"

Ghost put down his phone. "They're here. I told them to give us 15 minutes."

I knew they'd all come. That's what we did for each other. We were brothers. We were there for each other. That's why Ghost's betrayal hurt so fucking much. He was the man I trusted the most. Just like I had with Hugh.

Ghost leaned forward. "We all care about you, Knox. What the fuck is going on? Is it the anniversary of Aila's death? Sid thought it might be. You muttered something about her to Kaylie."

My stomach soured at the mention of her name. My voice was vibrating with anger. "You know what hurts the most about Aila's death? It's that she fucking betrayed me."

Ghost sat back. "You've never mentioned that before. You just said she died in a car accident a few days before your wedding. How did she betray you?"

I didn't want to dredge up all that old hurt and anguish again. I had plenty of new hurts to deal with. "It doesn't fucking matter anymore."

Ghost didn't let too many people get close to him. I was one of the few that got a peek behind the charismatic mask that he always wore to disguise his personal demons. He was a gifted musician with a larger-than-life personality and extraordinary physical beauty to match. Behind all that, was an incredibly smart and perceptive mind.

He wasn't going to let my remark drop. "You've been hauling around a lot of baggage since I met you. I'll tell you what my therapist told me: toss that baggage on the floor, zip it open, inspect the contents, and then unpack that shit. Put in the little drawers, close them up, and deal with them in pieces. But leave it behind. Don't haul the baggage around with you all the time." He tossed me a half smile. "It made a lot more sense when she said it, man. You need to do some unpacking."

I picked at the fringe on the decorative pillow near me. "None of that matters now. Did Sidney tell you that I'm leaving? I'm gonna go to Australia and start over. Leave this shit behind."

Ghost's eyes flickered with pain. "You're running again. You found something good here. Why would you leave that? Ghost Parker is your family. Don't run away."

"I hate this fucking town. It's dirty and filled with crime. The people are fake and plastic. It's time to move on. You'll be able to replace me easily. Actually, you wouldn't even need to. Ryder could take my spot. Me leaving wouldn't affect anything." The words were all true, but it hurt to spit out each and every one of them.

Ghost gripped the arms of the chair and took a deep breath. "We're all replaceable. We actually did replace Bash for a ton of shows. Davey was really good, but it wasn't the same without Bash. Everybody felt it. Ryder still struggles with the thought that he could drop out and Ghost Parker wouldn't miss a beat. He thinks he's expendable when you know that not fucking one of us thinks that. He's a part of us. You could replace me. Yeah, the look and sound might change, but it wouldn't mean the end of the band. It just wouldn't be our band. It wouldn't be the same without the five of us."

I scoffed. "Fuck, that's a dumb example. Ghost Parker is literally your name. You couldn't be replaced."

"Christ, Knox." He ran a hand through his hair. "So, this isn't a band thing? This existential crisis? I know you love playing and performing. Maybe the most out of all of us. And, a few days ago you were stoked to go on tour. So, what happened? Is it Summer?"

That's a bingo. I looked him in the eye. "Summer? Why would it be Summer?" I threw up some air quotes. "Fuck. I'm certainly not suspicious of a thing."

I shoved the same words he'd texted her this morning back in his face. The cold fucker didn't even flinch.

He leaned back and crossed his ankle over his knee. "You seem angry with me."

My jaw was decidedly set in anger. "You know why I'm angry."

"I think I'm starting to get an idea, but what the fuck does an idea do? I think you should tell me, Knox. Because you're way off base." His voice was steady and calm, but his eyes were burning fire.

The rage and hurt inside me were like a volcano that erupted after being bottle-up for too long. "Did you fuck Summer?"

The guy absorbed my harsh accusation with a poker face. My stomach twisted in agony as I waited for him to speak.

"You want to go ahead and tell me why you'd think so little of our friendship to believe that?" His voice was like granite.

"So, you're denying it? I saw the texts you sent Summer this morning about me not suspecting anything."

His eyes narrowed. "I'm not going to explain those texts, because you obviously only saw enough to jump to the wrong conclusion, but you'll find out soon enough what they were about. You better think long and hard before you throw away Summer's love for you with your jealous imaginings. And think about what kind of damage you're doing to our friendship. Why the fuck would you jump to that conclusion? It's a pretty big leap. I'm not just insulted, I'm wounded. Hurt that you would think that of me."

I growled at him. "What does that mean — you're not going to explain? You want me to just take your word for it? That there's nothing going on between the two of you?"

"That's exactly what I want you to do." He crossed his arms over his chest, his lip curling in contempt.

I either had to trust Ghost or walk away from it all. Was it possible that I'd just mixed everything up in my head? All the stuff with Aila. The texts from Ghost. Had I jumped to conclusions because of my past experience?

I didn't have a chance to decide when the other three guys, Sid, Bash, and Ryder, barged in. Their faces were pale with worry and their eyes darted around the room.

"It's been more than 15 minutes. What the fuck is going on? We're freaking out."

I glanced around at each of my brothers, each one here for me, and groaned. "I think I fucked up."

Ryder sat on the couch beside me and put his long legs up on the coffee table. "What's going on?"

"I, uh, I don't know. I saw something that triggered me. It was just like before — with Aila," I tried to explain.

Bash sat on the coffee table and Sid gave him a dirty look, trying to shoo him off. "Aila was your fiancée who died right before the wedding, right?"

"Fuck." My voice faltered. "There is so much more that I never shared with anyone. It's been trapped inside my head and slowly eating away at me. I've been a wreck for years. I thought I was getting over it, but I guess not."

Ghost spread his hands out. "Keeping it all inside is not working. Tell us. We're here for you, Knox. We're not going to judge you."

I hated thinking about that day. I avoided it at all costs. But as I told the guys what happened, the swirl of emotions — guilt, shame, grief, and the sting of betrayal — felt as fresh and as deep as they had that day.

Before today, I had never uttered to another soul my suspicion that Aila had been unfaithful to me. I could never be completely certain she was, but her reactions that day made me believe it was true.

Everyone was stricken by my story of how she died after our huge blowup.

"Fuck, that's so messed up," Sid said, his face twisted in pain.

My friends gathered around me and slapped me on the back or put their hands on my shoulders, telling me it wasn't my fault and that I shouldn't feel guilty.

I wasn't sure I'd ever believe them — I felt the guilt deep in my bones. But, I wasn't finished with my story.

"The day after Aila died, Hugh moved out of the cottage. He didn't say a word to me, just packed up his stuff and left. I saw him at the funeral, but he wouldn't even look at me, so I knew that what I suspected was probably true. We were best mates, and suddenly, he wouldn't talk to me."

"What an asshole," Ryder commented.

I continued the story and told them about the funeral. The day had been heavy and thick, and everything seemed to move in slow motion. My vision was blurry and my thoughts were muffled and distorted as if I were underwater.

After the service, I suppressed my guilt and accepted everyone's condolences when I was the one who had caused it all. I didn't tell anyone about our fight just prior to the accident, because I didn't want to besmirch Aila's reputation. I told myself it was to protect her memory — there was no need to upset her parents now that she was gone — but I worried it was really to protect myself. Because I'd caused the accident. I was the one that had yelled at her, had made her sob, and caused her to flee.

My bandmates began to repeat that the accident wasn't my fault, but I stopped them. I wasn't finished.

"This is probably the worst part. It took me months to make arrangements to get out of Scotland, but I knew I couldn't stay there with those memories haunting me. Right before I left, I stopped by Aila's parents' home to tell them I was leaving and say goodbye. It seemed like the right thing to do."

The guys closed in, ready to support me.

"Before I left, Aila's mum pulled me aside. She said they weren't going to tell me, but she thought I should know. They had gotten some test results back from the crash. No one was surprised when the test results for drugs or alcohol in her system came back clean. The big surprise, though, was that she was pregnant."

My mates exchanged nervous glances, their faces etched with worry. I heard the sharp intakes of breath, followed by mumbled curses from my friends.

My voice cracked as I echoed the shame and misery that had dogged me from that day. "Two innocent lives were lost that day. I may have caused the death of my own wee bairn."

The weight of my guilt felt crushing, like a boulder pressing on my chest. I couldn't bear to look at my friends, couldn't bear to see the judgment in their eyes. They had always teased me about my reckless behavior, but this was different. This was something that couldn't be laughed off or ignored.

"Aila and I had always talked about having a bairn right away," I continued, my voice barely above a whisper. "But I don't even know if that baby was mine. We were very careful about using protection. It doesn't matter. Either way, that bairn should still be alive."

My mates remained silent, unsure of what to say, until Ghost spoke up. "I know you feel responsible for the accident, but it really wasn't your fault. You're too close to the situation to see it clearly, but it's true. It was a tragic accident. You can't blame yourself. You need to talk to someone about this, Knox. The guilt is eating away at you like cancer. The only way to find peace from this is to let it go. I think a therapist can help you do that. I can give you Maggie's number. She's helped me a lot, and I've got a lot of shit to wade through."

Ryder agreed. "Ghost is right. The accident wasn't your fault."

Bash, usually the wiseass of the bunch, said, "I can't believe you've been holding all of that in. No wonder you're such a mess."

I wondered if I could ever truly let go of the guilt. It had become a part of me, a constant companion that I could never shake off.

Sid stood up. "So, what brought all this up so suddenly?"

"After all that happened, I never felt I could trust anyone again. Not a lass, not even my best mates. Anyone could stab me in the back at any time." I glanced at Ghost, but then quickly looked away. I was embarrassed by what I'd believed of him."I saw a text on Summer's phone this morning. It brought me back to the note I found in Aila's purse. I imagined the worst, but now I think I just overreacted."

Ryder gave me a friendly nudge. "Don't you see the way she looks at you, man? Like you light up her world. She's in love with you."

"Dude, did you confront her about the text?" Bash tapped his fingers restlessly on his thigh.

I rubbed at my temples. "No, not after what happened with Aila. I just took off."

"So, no worries, then." Sid paced back and forth in front of the coffee table. "She doesn't need to know how you freaked out. Sober up and shake this off, man. Don't even ask her about the text. Just trust in her love for you."

"I guess," I said hesitantly. "Luckily, I didn't do anything too stupid."

Ghost, who had remained fairly quiet, finally spoke. "Knox, if you're serious about your relationship with Summer, you need to tell her about Aila and what happened. And you need to find a way to let go of the guilt. Talk to a therapist if you can't work it out yourself."

I nodded stiffly at him. I was grateful that he was still there for me, even though I'd been a complete arsehole with my accusations. "Thank you." I looked around the room at everyone. "I'm sorry about before. Let's just forget about all that nonsense about leaving the band and taking off to Aussie, aye?"

Bash slapped me on the shoulder. "Fuck, yeah, we're forgetting it. You're not going anywhere."

The tension in the room seemed to dissipate as everyone chuckled. Everyone nodded in agreement and we all looked at each other knowingly, sharing a moment of brotherhood.

Ghost took the lead as we huddled up. "Ride or die."

"Ride or die!" We responded in unison.

# Chapter 30

## Summer

AS I GLANCED OVER at Knox, his strong hands gripping the steering wheel while he navigated the winding coastal road, I couldn't help but think about how much closer we had grown in such a short amount of time. His brown eyes focused on the road ahead, thick eyelashes casting shadows over his sun-kissed cheeks. After he had opened up to me last night, explaining his tragic past with his fiancée, Aila, who died in a car accident after some heartbreaking circumstances, I felt a deeper connection to him. He'd suffered a lot of guilt.

"Hey, what are you thinking about?" He asked, glancing my way with a small smile.

"Last night," I answered honestly, unable to hide the blush creeping up my cheeks. "And everything you shared with me about what happened in Scotland. I'm glad that you felt you could trust me with that."

"Ah," Knox nodded, taking one hand off the wheel to squeeze mine reassuringly. "I think talking about it helped. I've been keeping it all bottled up for so long."

I squeezed his hand back, knowing it was a big step for him to trust me with that part of his life. In return, I had shared my own heartbreaks — the ones that left me feeling raw and vulnerable. It was both terrifying and exhilarating to let someone in like that, but I knew our bond had only deepened because of it.

"Hey, remind me what we got for Talia again?" Knox asked, changing the subject as he pulled into Ryder's driveway.

"We got her that trendy diaper bag that all the new moms are getting. It was on her registry." I replied, picturing the hip bag that didn't scream 'diaper bag'. "And don't forget the sleep sheep. It's a fuzzy stuffed sheep that generates white noise like a heartbeat sound or rain showers. It supposedly helps keep the baby calm and relaxed."

"Aye, right. Good call on the sheep. I think she'll love it." His smile was genuine, and I felt a flutter in my chest. He was so handsome, especially when he flashed those dimples at me.

"Thanks, I hope so," I said as he parked the car and turned off the engine. He looked at me for a moment, his eyes softening with warmth and affection.

"Summer, I just want you to know that the way you listened to me and supported me last night ... meant a lot to me. And hearing about your experiences ... I want to be different from those guys who hurt you. I really care about you. I love you, Sunshine."

My heart swelled with emotion as I gazed back into his eyes. "I love you too, Knox. Thank you for trusting me." With that, we shared a tender kiss before stepping out of the car and joining the baby shower festivities, hand in hand, stronger together than ever before.

The baby shower was in full swing when we arrived, and the sound of laughter filled Ryder's backyard. Vibrant decorations adorned every surface, and a table laden with delicious treats stood in the center. I scanned the crowd and saw some familiar faces: Talia, looking radiant as ever; Ghost, charming everyone around him; Sid and Kaylie, laughing together at the buffet table; Bash, deep in conversation with Donovan, the band manager; and Lacey, working her social magic as she flitted from one group to another. Greyson Durant, a famous TV actor, was there. I'd never met him, but I'd heard he was good friends with Talia.

"Hey, you two," Ryder greeted us, a wide grin plastered on his face. "Glad you could make it."

"Wouldn't miss it for the world," Knox replied, clapping his friend on the back before handing over our gift — the diaper bag and sleep sheep. "Congrats again, man."

"Thanks, Knox. And thank you, Summer. Talia's gonna love this," Ryder said, nodding in appreciation. "I know she's not due until November, but we wanted to have the baby shower before the tour started when everyone was still available."

As the afternoon progressed, I participated in a lot of crazy shower games, imbibed a lot of the special punch, and heard a lot of funny stories about the band. It was an unusual baby shower, but apparently, the precedent had been set with the shower for baby Kody. I couldn't help but smile every time I caught Knox's eye, feeling for the first time like I truly belonged to this tight-knit family.

When the sun began to set, signaling the end of the baby shower, Knox pulled me aside. His brow furrowed slightly. "I think we should get going soon. Everyone else seems to be disappearing," he said, checking his watch. "It's getting late, and I'm sure everyone's tired."

"Actually," I said, biting my lip in anticipation, "there's something else I've planned for tonight. A little surprise."

"Really?" Knox looked puzzled but intrigued.

"Trust me, you'll love it," I assured him, taking his hand and leading him down towards the beach that lay just beyond Ryder's property. As we walked, the bonfire's glow became visible, illuminating the shoreline and casting a warm light on the faces of our friends who had gathered there.

"Surprise!" everyone shouted when we reached the beach, and I watched as Knox's eyes widened in disbelief.

"Happy birthday, Scotty!" Ghost yelled, raising a beer in salute to his friend.

"Summer, you planned all this?" Knox asked, clearly touched by the gesture.

"I did," I replied, feeling my cheeks flush with pride. "You deserve it. But I had some help from Ghost and Ryder."

The party was everything I'd hoped it would be — lively conversation, laughter, and dancing beneath the moonlit sky. Knox looked genuinely happy, and I reveled in the joy of making him feel special on his birthday. As we sat hand-in-hand around the fire, I couldn't shake the feeling that we had reached a new level of connection, one that could only grow stronger from here.

"Gather around," Ghost called out, grabbing his guitar and motioning for the rest of the band to join him. "In honor of our birthday boy, let's play a little something, yeah?"

"Sounds like a plan," Sid agreed, and Bash nodded along as he grabbed his drumsticks. They all settled down near the fire, their instruments in hand.

Knox glanced at me, a mixture of gratitude and amusement playing across his features. "You really thought of everything, didn't you?"

I shrugged, feigning nonchalance while my heart raced with excite-

# HOW TO DATE A ROCKSTAR 281

ment. "Well, it's not every day your boyfriend turns thirty."

"True," he grinned, leaning over to press a quick kiss to my lips before joining his bandmates by the fire.

As the boys of Ghost Parker began to strum their guitars and tap out rhythms on makeshift drums, I couldn't help but marvel at the scene before me. The firelight danced across the sand, casting shadows that seemed to sway in time with the music. The sound of waves crashing against the shore provided a natural accompaniment, creating an atmosphere that was both intimate and electrifying.

My eyes were drawn to Knox, who sat with his guitar cradled in his arms, fingers flying effortlessly across the strings. The flickering light bathed him in a warm glow, highlighting the angles of his handsome face and causing his eyes to sparkle like stars in the night sky. At that moment, he looked more beautiful than ever — a vision of raw talent and passion that left me breathless.

One song turned into two, and soon they were in a full-blown jam session. Knox couldn't look more content playing with his band in front of the small crowd of his closest friends.

As the music continued to fill the air, the rest of the partygoers joined in, singing along, and some of the more inebriated ones danced around the fire. The mood was infectious, and I found myself swept up in the laughter and shared memories that bound this group together.

I looked over at Knox, his eyes meeting mine as he strummed the last chord. The small crowd clapped, appreciating the impromptu concert.

"Let's drink to Knox," Ghost announced, raising his beer bottle in the air. "And to many more years of making music and memories together. And to another kick-ass tour."

"Cheers!" everyone chorused, and I felt my heart swell with happiness as we toasted to the man who had brought us all here, the one who held my hand and my heart, now and forevermore.

The laughter and music from the beach bonfire had long since faded, replaced by the gentle lull of crashing waves and the distant hooting of an owl. Well past midnight, Knox and I stumbled back to Ryder's house and found ourselves wrapped in each other's arms, lying on the plush guest bed at Ryder's house, our fingers intertwined and our breaths mingling as one.

"Summer," he whispered against my lips, his voice husky with desire. "I want you so much right now."

"Mmm," I breathed back, my heart racing with anticipation as I pressed my body closer to his. "I want you too."

He captured my lips in a searing kiss, our mouths melding together in a dance of passion and need. His hands roamed over my skin, igniting a fire within me that burned with every touch. I reciprocated, caressing his smooth skin and feeling the strength of his muscles beneath my fingertips.

As our kisses grew more urgent, Knox quickly removed our clothes, leaving us bared to each other in both body and soul. The warmth of his skin sent shivers down my spine, and I marveled at how perfectly we fit together. Our joining was passionate and tender, each movement infused with the profound connection that had grown between us.

"Summer," he groaned, his voice thick with emotion as he buried himself deep within me, our bodies moving in perfect unison. "I love you."

"I love you too, Knox," I gasped, overwhelmed by the intensity of our union. As we reached our peak together, I knew without a doubt that we had crossed a threshold in our relationship, entering a realm where love and trust reigned supreme.

The next morning, the sun streamed through the window, casting a golden glow across the bedroom floor. Knox's arm draped protectively over me, his steady breaths warming the nape of my neck. Reluctantly, I untangled myself from his embrace and slipped out of bed so that I could use the bathroom.

Knox greeted me with a grin when I returned. "Good morning. Did you sleep well?"

"Good morning," I replied, returning his smile. "I slept wonderfully, thank you. But, it's getting late. I feel like it's rude if we stay in bed all morning."

"Don't worry, I haven't heard anyone up and about yet, but let's take a quick shower and then head out," he said, his eyes twinkling with mischief. "Today, I have a surprise for you."

"A surprise?" I asked, my voice raising with excitement. "It's not even my birthday."

He chuckled and then led me back to the bathroom where we conserved water by sharing a shower, but probably used up most of the hot water. The shower had definitely left us both satisfied, though. After we got ready, when he led me outside to the car, Knox was whistling an upbeat melody.

I tried to interrogate him about my surprise during the car ride, but he wouldn't give even a hint.

His fingers tapped on the steering wheel. "I've missed driving, even if it's on the wrong side of the road."

"Me too. I miss my car, but driving in L.A. is a nightmare."

"Do you think I should buy a car? So we can do stuff that's further away on the weekends? Renting a car just to visit my friends is frustrating." He changed lanes smoothly and passed the car in front of us. "What kind of cars do you like? We can stop at a dealer and pick one up today."

I laughed. "Just like that? It can't be as easy as buying a gallon of milk at the grocery store."

"It's not that difficult if you have the cash."

Was he serious? "If you want to buy a car, you should just wait until the tour is over; otherwise, it'll just be sitting around idle."

He glanced over at me. "You could use it while I was gone."

"Is this my surprise? Because I really don't like driving in the city and then I'd have to deal with parking it somewhere." Having access to a car would be neat, but I didn't want him to think he needed to spend money on me.

"No, it's not your surprise. It was just something I was thinking about."

I thought we were heading home as we got closer to my apartment, but he pulled over and parked on the street about a block away from my apartment.

I was about to comment when I noticed the line of people on the sidewalk. "The Underground Coffee Bar! This is where we met."

He turned to me and winked. "So it is, Sunshine. I thought we could stop and get a coffee."

"Hmmm. And a few cannoli, too."

"Sure." He put on a pair of sunglasses and then slid a baseball cap over his head. "Just don't say my name out loud. Let's try to do this incognito."

"Sure thing, rock star," I teased, but I really didn't want any of the remaining time with him taken up by enthusiastic fans.

We headed to the back of the line, spilling out of the shop and onto the sidewalk. An eerie sense of déjà vu filled me. "I'm half expecting my mother to pop up out of nowhere."

Knox stood in line behind me, but after our next step forward, he wrapped his arms around me from behind and pulled me back against him, nuzzling into my neck.

"Scotty," I gasped softly. "Behave! We don't want Limpie Pie to come out to play."

He growled in my ear. "There's not a limp thing about me when I'm around you. Frankly, I wish we could just wipe away the memory of that particular nickname, my wee Bouncy Bumpkin."

I giggled. "I believe you denied it just as vehemently to my mother that day, too."

"Aye, I've got to defend my manhood," he whispered in my ear.

We moved up another step. "Remember when you made fun of me for dressing warmly? I mean, it was in the middle of winter!"

"I was just trying to get your attention, lass. It was the equivalent of pulling on your pigtails."

I turned my head to smile at him. "Well, I'm glad it worked."

"Me too."

We laughed about more memories of that encounter as they came flooding back, remembering the undeniable spark that had ignited between us that first meeting. After we ordered our coffee and cannoli, we stepped back from the line and waited for our order to be completed. A barista called out 'Summer', so I stepped forward to the counter and found my coffee. Next to the tall paper cup was a small wrapped gift that said 'Summer' in black ink on it.

"What's this?" I looked at Knox.

He shrugged. "Hmmm. I don't know. You'll have to open it and see."

We got lucky and managed to snag a small window table when the patrons stood up to leave just as we were passing by. As we settled into the booth seating, my gaze wandered over the familiar surroundings of the coffee shop. Despite the whirlwind of the past few months, it felt like time had stood still in this cozy little haven where Knox and I had first crossed paths.

I glanced down at the gift in the center of the table, eager to see what was inside. My fingers traced the delicate silver ribbon, curiosity piquing as I carefully unwrapped the tiny package. I opened the velvet pouch and slid out the necklace that was inside. It was an edgy-looking stainless steel chain with a beautiful pendant. I looked closer and realized the pendant was a guitar pick holder. I glanced up at Knox, my eyes misting up.

"Is this...?" I trailed off, unable to find the words.

"Yep," he confirmed, his chest puffing out with pride. "That's one of my old picks — from our last concert. I wanted you to have something to remember me by when I'm not around. The necklace came with a bunch of colorful picks, but that one is authentic."

"Knox," I breathed, genuinely touched by the sentiment behind the gift. "This is amazing. Thank you."

I pulled the other picks out of the pouch. "Ooh. These are so cute. Can you give me a private show using each of these picks, so I know you've used them all? Then they're all authentic."

I actually loved watching him play his guitar. Watching his fingers work the strings while he wrestled such amazing sounds from the instrument was a huge turn-on.

He smirked. "You know what happens when I give you a private show, woman."

I leaned forward and lowered my voice so only he could hear. "I get so wet that I have to jump your bones."

"Fuck, Sunshine. We can go back to your flat right now—"

I interrupted him. "Our flat."

"Right," he agreed. "But first, I have one more surprise for you."

"Another surprise?" I asked playfully as I slipped the necklace around my neck. "I don't need anything else, Knox. I love the necklace, and I'm going to wear it every day while you're gone."

"Ah, well," Knox began, reaching into his pocket and pulling out an envelope. "This surprise is for both of us, actually."

I took the envelope from him, my heart pounding in anticipation as I opened it to reveal airline tickets to Aruba. A glossy brochure displayed a luxurious resort on a tropical island overlooking a white sand beach and turquoise blue water. It looked like paradise. Stunned, I looked back up at Knox, my eyes wide.

"Knox... this is incredible," I whispered, my voice thick with emotion. "Is this for real?"

"Absolutely," he affirmed, his gaze steady and sincere. "I wanted to plan something special for us to look forward to during the band's break in November. It's a way for me to show you that I'm committed to our relationship, to our future. And I can't wait to go there with you."

"Knox, I don't know what to say," I murmured, tears prickling at the corners of my eyes. "You have no idea how much this means to me."

"Seeing you happy means everything to me," he replied softly, reaching across the table to squeeze my hand. "We've come a long way together, Summer. And I can't wait to see where life takes us next."

"Look at us now," I mused, while Knox's fingers traced circles on the back of my hand. "Who would've thought that bumping into each other like that day would lead us here? If my mother hadn't shown up and assumed you were my boyfriend, we'd still be strangers."

"Life is full of surprises," he agreed, grinning as he looked into my eyes. "And I wouldn't change a thing."

"Neither would I," I murmured.

Knox leaned across the table and captured my lips in a gentle kiss that spoke volumes about the depth of our love.

As we sat there, basking in the warmth of our shared history and the promise of a future together, I knew that whatever challenges came our way, Knox and I would face them together, hand in hand, and heart to heart.

As I held onto Knox's hand and gazed into his eyes, I felt an overwhelming sense of gratitude and love for the man who had shown me that true happiness was possible. Together, we would face whatever challenges life threw at us, our bond growing stronger with each passing day. And as I wore the guitar pick necklace close to my heart, I knew that Knox would always be with me, even when we were worlds apart.

Knox stood and pulled me into his strong embrace. "I love you, Summer."

"I love you, too," I breathed, burying my face in the crook of his neck and inhaling the familiar scent of him that had become my sanctuary.

I knew deep in my heart that our love was not fleeting or fragile. It was steadfast, unwavering — a force to be reckoned with. And together, Knox and I would weather any storm that came our way, forging an unbreakable bond that would only grow stronger with time.

# Chapter 31

**Summer**

THE SUN WAS HIGH in the afternoon sky, and its rays danced along the surface of the sea. It seemed like a thousand diamonds were scattered across its sparkling surface, each one reflecting little shards of light. The gentle breeze brought with it a salty scent of brine and carried with it the sound of lapping waves and the distant call of seagulls.

I lounged in the shade of a thatched tiki umbrella and took a sip of my fruity concoction, the Aruba Ariba. It was garnished with a cherry and an orange slice, and yes; they had added a miniature pink umbrella when I asked politely. The drink packed a punch, so I enjoyed it slowly as I watched Knox frolicking in the waves, kicking up spray and laughing as he attempted to boogie board.

I dug my toes into the warm, soft sand beneath my feet. The palm trees rustled in the breeze, swaying gently, while the tropical scents of hibiscus and plumeria scented the air.

Knox seemed to have given up his battle with the waves and began heading back to our lounge chairs. I flipped my sunglasses to the top of my head, so I could fully appreciate all the masculine goodness heading my way.

He had on a pair of perfectly fitted swim trunks, in a bright tropical print hinting at his adventurous spirit. His toned and suntanned body glistened with water droplets, and I couldn't help but admire the way his muscles flexed as he walked. His skin was tan and smooth, and his hair was rapidly acquiring sun-bleached highlights, giving him even more boyish charm.

As he approached me, I couldn't help but feel a rush of desire course through my veins. His deep brown eyes met mine, and I had to force myself to look away, not wanting to reveal the heat that was building inside me.

"Hey," he said, his voice low and rumbly. "How's the book?"

I glanced at the paperback book that I hadn't even cracked open. "I haven't got far into it. It can't really compete with paradise."

He threw his board down onto the sand and leaned over me to take a sip of my drink, dripping a few drops of ocean water onto my hot skin.

"Did you hear from Lara yet?" He asked as he settled onto the chaise lounge next to mine.

My mother had finished her course of chemotherapy and had just gone in for a follow-up appointment.

My smile was huge. "She's all clear. She doesn't have to go back for six months. The doctors were very optimistic."

"That's great news, Summer. Maybe we can visit them over the holidays and celebrate?"

"You'd do that for me? My mother would be so thrilled if I brought you home for Christmas." I chuckled, imagining her over-the-top reaction. "But wouldn't that be kind of boring for you?"

He ran his fingers through his wet hair. "Nah, your parents are great. Last year, Ghost and I spent the day together playing video games. We didn't even have a Christmas tree set up. It was kind of pathetic."

"Ghost doesn't have any family to spend the holidays with?" I didn't know much about Ghost's background, but he was a genuine and loyal friend to Knox and had graciously accepted me into his small circle. He was much different from what I'd initially expected based on his bad-boy rock star reputation.

"No," he confirmed. "He's not close to any family he has left."

"We can invite him to come to Kentucky with us," I offered.

He dug his sunglasses out of our beach bag. "I'm not sure he'd come, Sunshine, but it's sweet that you'd want to ask."

I was definitely going to ask. I wanted everyone I knew to be as happy as I was.

Later that evening, after we both showered, Knox had arranged a romantic, candlelit dinner for us on the sun terrace of our private beachside villa.

The table was decorated with white linen and adorned with a bouquet of exotic flowers in a vase. A bottle of sparkling champagne was chilling in an ice bucket nearby, and two glasses sat ready for us to enjoy.

The sky had turned a deep indigo blue, and the stars twinkled against the velvet backdrop. The waves lapped against the shore in a soothing, hypnotic rhythm, and the air was filled with the scent of exotic blooms.

Knox pulled out my chair for me, and I sat down, admiring his chivalrous gesture. He had changed into a casual linen shirt and linen trousers, and his hair was still damp from the shower. He looked so handsome and debonair that I couldn't help but blush as he gazed at me with his deep brown eyes.

He had chosen a delicious meal of grilled shrimp and mango salsa, served with a side of roasted vegetables and quinoa. We enjoyed our meal while being serenaded by the endless churn of the ocean waves.

We hadn't had much time to really talk since Knox got back from the tour. It had been a whirlwind of activity since he got home between attending all the festivities surrounding Sid and Kaylie's wedding to the birth of Ryder and Talia's daughter, Zoe.

We managed to talk on the phone every day while he was on tour and I'd been able to visit multiple times. I'd ended up seeing more of the behind-the-scenes part of being in a popular band, and it wasn't nearly as glamorous as I'd assumed. The concerts were fabulous, but the non-stop grind of touring was taxing. We didn't have a chance for a lot of in-depth conversations.

Tonight, we talked about everything: our friends, our families, funny things that happened on the tour, and the upcoming second half of the tour. Knox even told me about his video-therapy sessions with the therapist Ghost recommended, Maggie. Knox felt that he was learning things about himself and making steps toward healing some of the emotional damage caused by the tragedy of Aila's death.

When we'd finished our food, Knox reached over and took my hand, running his thumb over my knuckles. "Would you like to go out tonight and check out the nightlife?"

I leaned into him, feeling completely content and in love. "No, I'd rather stay in to do some other kind of exploring."

He stood up from his chair and took my hand, helping me to my feet. "I like the sound of that," he said with a wicked grin.

He scooped me up in his powerful arms and whisked me back

inside our villa and straight to the king-sized bed. My heart raced in anticipation as he put me down next to the bed and then knelt beside me. His eyes blazed with pent-up desire as he removed my heels, one by one, taking his time to caress my calves and linger over my ankles with his fingertips.

His fingers grazed lightly up my legs, sending a flush of warmth through me. He grabbed the hem of my dress and I felt it rising up along my body as it slowly exposed my body, inch by inch, until he swept it over my head in one swift motion. He made quick work of my bra and panties so that I was completely bared to him.

His eyes were dark and intense as his gaze traveled hungrily across my body. I felt a thrill of arousal course through me as he stood before me like a sentinel, his body radiating dominance and authority.

He didn't speak, but his gaze held mine and his presence filled the room. His expression was one of desire, mixed with a hint of danger. I felt my knees weaken, my breath coming quicker. I had never felt so aroused and drawn to someone before, and my body ached for him.

He took a step forward, and I felt his strong hands grip my hips. His touch was firm, yet gentle, and it sent sparks of pleasure through me. I gasped softly as he pulled me closer, his lips caressing mine. His kiss was passionate and demanding and sent my senses spinning. Waves of desire spread through my body and I clung to him, unable to get close enough.

He slowly released me from his embrace and his hands moved lower, gliding over my curves. His fingers were strong and confident, and my skin heated with pleasure. I explored his body with my hands, slipping inside his shirt, memorizing each inch, each contour. His muscles tensed as I touched him, and he groaned in pleasure.

He pulled away and looked into my eyes, and at that moment, I felt a connection between us that went deeper than anything I had ever felt before. I shivered in anticipation as he reached out and caught a handful of my hair. He pulled me closer, his breath hot in my ear as he whispered my name.

He moved his hands lower, and I felt bolder. My fingers fumbled as I impatiently unbuttoned his shirt and pulled it from his body. I wantonly explored him, my fingers tracing the muscles of his chest, my palms memorizing the feel of his skin. His groans of pleasure and the feel of his body beneath my touch drove me wild, and I felt the fire of my desire engulf me.

Not breaking our connection, he walked me to the bed and then pulled me down with him, capturing my lips in a frenzied kiss. Our kiss deepened as we explored each other's bodies, exploring new heights of pleasure. His hands moved lower, gripping my hips firmly as he pulled me closer to him. His lips devoured mine hungrily and his tongue thrust inside me passionately. I gasped with pleasure and arched my back in response to his touch, winding my arms around him tightly as our bodies moved together.

His hands moved across my skin like silk, teasing and tantalizing as he explored every inch of my body. My breathing grew faster as he kissed me harder, pushing us both further into this unknown abyss of desire. His fingers dipped between my legs and I gasped at the sudden shock of pleasure that coursed through me. His touch was gentle yet powerful, sending ripples of ecstasy throughout my body that left me trembling with a need for more.

I tugged at the buckle on his belt, and he must have sensed my urgency because he stood up and quickly shucked his pants before crawling back on top of me.

I could barely control myself as my hands explored his body, from his strong shoulders down to his firm chest and abs, and finally to his hot, throbbing cock. I gripped him tightly, feeling how hard he was for me, and slowly guided him inside of me. My soft gasp of pleasure joined with his feral groan of ecstasy when he thrust deep until he was fully seated.

An electric current raced through me, and I felt a warmth build deep within as we moved together, our bodies entwined in an intimate dance of pleasure. I felt consumed by him, my senses so overwhelmed with pleasure that I could barely breathe. His touch was firm and demanding, yet gentle and safe. I felt myself unravel in his arms, my body and soul merging with his in a way I had never experienced before.

A wave of pure euphoria washed over me as I let go, my mind and body dissolving into a million tiny fragments that were on the brink of complete extinction.

After we both found our release, we collapsed into each other's arms amidst a tangle of limbs and kisses, spent from the intensity of our passion but unwilling to part just yet. We stayed like that for what seemed like hours until finally, our breathing returned to normal once again and reality slowly began to creep back in.

He held me close against him until finally, I drifted off into a peaceful sleep, content and satisfied. My heart was full of joy and happiness, filled with a deep sense that I had found my soulmate.

# Epilogue

-------------------------------------

**5 years later...**

**Knox**

THE MOMENT WE ARRIVED at the local Christmas festival, I could feel the excitement building in my chest. It had been years since I'd spent the holidays in Scotland and I had forgotten just how enchanting it was. The air was crisp and cool, with the scent of mulled wine and roasted chestnuts drifting on the breeze. People milled about, bundled up in thick scarves and woolen coats, their cheeks rosy from the cold. Laughter filled the air as families gathered to celebrate the holiday season.

"Look at this place," Summer whispered into my ear, her breath warm against my skin. "It's like a Christmas postcard come to life."

I smiled, tugging her closer to me with one arm. She was right;

the entire town square had been transformed into a winter wonderland, complete with twinkling lights, festive wreaths, and a towering Christmas tree at its center. It was impossible not to get swept up in the magic of it all.

"Come on now, let's take the wee bairns to see the parade," my mum suggested, grabbing Grace and Carter's hands as they stared wide-eyed at the decorations surrounding them.

"Aye, sounds like a plan," I agreed, following close behind as Summer strolled alongside me, her arm linked with mine.

As we made our way through the bustling crowd, the sound of a brass band filled the air, signaling the start of the parade. We pushed our way to the front, securing a prime spot just as the first float came into view. Santa Claus himself sat atop a grand sleigh, surrounded by dancing elves and prancing reindeer.

"Santa!" Grace squealed, jumping up and down in delight as Carter's eyes grew even wider.

"Look at those reindeer, Knox," Summer said, her voice filled with childlike wonder. "They are so adorable!"

"Wait until you see the ones in the stable," I replied, grinning at the thought of her reaction to the actual live reindeer waiting just around the corner.

After the parade had passed, we led our little group towards the reindeer stable, the scent of hay and warm fur mingling with the festive smells from earlier. Summer gasped as she caught sight of the majestic animals, their antlers adorned with delicate ribbons and bells.

"Can we pet them?" Carter asked, his small face alight with curiosity.

"Aye o'course laddie," Da replied, gently guiding him toward the nearest reindeer. "Be canny now."

"Be careful," I translated for my wee 'uns.

As Grace and Carter reached out to touch the soft fur of the reindeer, I felt a surge of happiness watching my family enjoy this simple moment together. These were the memories that would last long after the music had faded and the lights had been taken down — the ones that truly mattered.

"Thank you for bringing us here," Summer whispered, her eyes shining with unshed tears as she leaned into me. "It's wonderful."

"Anything for you," I murmured, pressing a tender kiss to her forehead. "Merry Christmas, Sunshine."

A gentle flurry of snowflakes began to fall from the sky, dusting the ground and adding an extra layer of magic to the Christmas festival. The delicate crystals seemed to dance around us as we walked, turning the world into a winter wonderland. My parents led the way toward the mulled wine and hot chocolate stall, where a cheerful woman ladled out steaming mugs of the fragrant beverages.

"Here you go, luv," she said, handing me a cup of mulled wine that instantly warmed my fingers. "And for the weans, some hot chocolate."

"Thank you," I replied, passing the drinks to Summer and the kids. We all took sips, the comforting warmth spreading through our bodies, chasing away the chill of the December air. The children's faces lit up as they tasted the rich cocoa, while the rest of us savored the spicy blend of cinnamon and cloves in the wine.

"Let's away tae the town centre," my mum suggested, her eyes twinkling like the lights strung between the market stalls. "The Yule tree and carolers should be gettin' started soon."

We followed her lead, strolling past colorful booths offering handmade ornaments, knitted scarves, and freshly baked gingerbread cookies. The air was alive with laughter and excited chatter, filling me with a sense of contentment I hadn't experienced in years. It felt like everything was perfect.

The smile slipped from my face when I saw him. As we approached the town square, I caught sight of the familiar figure standing near the towering Christmas tree. Hugh. It had been years since our friendship had silently imploded in a mess of betrayal and heartache, but the sight of him still made my blood run cold. I could feel my jaw clench and my hands tightening around my cup of mulled wine.

"Knox?" Summer asked, concern lacing her voice as she noticed my change in demeanor. "Is everything alright?"

I hesitated, unsure whether to burden her with the ghosts of my past. But one look at her warm, caring eyes made me realize that I could trust her with anything. "See that guy over there?" I muttered, nodding subtly in Hugh's direction. "That's Hugh — my old friend. The one I think Aila had the affair with."

"Ah," she replied softly, clearly understanding the turmoil his presence had kicked up beneath my unaffected surface. "Do you want to leave? We can find another part of the festival to explore."

"No," I said, forcing myself to relax my grip on the cup and take a deep breath. "We came here to enjoy ourselves, and that's what we're going to do. Besides, I haven't spoken to him in years. I'll just ignore him."

"Alright," she agreed, squeezing my hand reassuringly. "But if you change your mind, just let me know. I'm here for you."

"Thanks, Summer," I whispered, grateful for her unwavering support as we continued toward the heart of the festivities.

The snow continued to fall around us, settling on our shoulders like delicate lace as the strains of "Mistletoe and Wine" drifted through the air. Somehow, despite the shadow cast by Hugh's presence, I knew that this Christmas would be one to remember — for all the right reasons.

A gust of frigid wind swept through the town square, lifting a whirlwind of snowflakes around us. The festive atmosphere was alive with laughter and the hum of cheerful conversations as I looked over at Summer, her cheeks rosy from the cold. Her eyes sparkled with excitement, and for a moment, my heart swelled with happiness — until my gaze drifted back to Hugh. He was staring directly at me, and then he started heading our way.

"Knox," Summer said gently, her fingers brushing against mine as she caught my lingering stare. "We can leave. You don't have to do this if you're not ready."

"I know," I admitted, my jaw tense as I watched Hugh hesitantly make his way toward us. "But if I don't face him now, I'll never be able to let go of the past."

Summer squeezed my hand reassuringly, her warmth seeping into me like a balm for my battered soul. As Hugh approached, I steeled myself for the confrontation I knew was coming.

"Knox," Hugh said, his voice strained with an emotion I couldn't quite place. "It's been a long time. Is this... is this your family?"

"Save it," I snapped, my anger flaring despite Summer's calming presence. "What do you want?"

"Knox," Summer murmured, her gentle touch a reminder that I shouldn't let my emotions get the better of me. It wasn't just about me anymore; our bairns were here, too, and they deserved a peaceful day.

"Ye weans, come awa' noo," my mother called out, sensing the tension in the air. "Let's away tae Santa's grotto while yer Da talks a wee crack with an auld pal." My parents whisked the kids away, leaving Summer, Hugh, and me standing awkwardly in the center of the bustling square.

Summer leaned in to speak with me privately. "Listen, Knox,"

Summer began, her voice firm but gentle. "You've been holding onto this for years. Maybe it's time to hear Hugh out and find out the truth — for your own sake."

I knew she was right. Closure would never come if I kept running from the truth. "Fine," I muttered, my gaze locked on the snow-covered cobblestones beneath my feet.

"Alright," I sighed, mentally bracing myself for the conversation. I turned to Hugh. "Hugh, this is my wife, Summer."

Hugh smiled at her. "It's a pleasure to make your acquaintance, Summer."

She nodded her head. "It's nice to meet you, too."

Not knowing about our falling out, my brothers had mentioned Hugh over the years. "I've heard you have a son?"

"Uh, yes, my lad, Alfie," he stammered, rubbing the back of his neck. "We've just had a new wee bairn, Finlay. My wife and I have two now."

"Congratulations," I said, forcing a smile.

"Thank you." Hugh shifted his stance nervously. "Congratulations to you, too, for your success with the band. I've been following you from the start and I even went to a concert a few years ago when you were in Edinburgh."

"Thanks." I nodded, feeling a small sense of pride in my band's success.

"Of course," Hugh replied, his voice softening. "I've always been a fan of Ghost Parker. You guys are amazing."

As we exchanged pleasantries, the snow continued to fall gently around us, casting a hushed blanket over the festive town square. The scent of mulled wine and roasted chestnuts drifted through the air, adding to the enchantment of the moment.

"Listen, Knox," Hugh began hesitantly, breaking the silence.

"There's something I need to tell you about Aila."

"Go on," I said, steeling myself for whatever revelation awaited.

"One night, while you were out playing a gig,"—he took a deep breath, looking painfully reluctant to continue—"Aila and I got together. I don't even know why it happened. It was only that one time. We both regretted it, and it never happened again."

I gritted my teeth. "I already knew that you fucked my fiancée, Hugh."

His wince turned to surprise. "You knew all along? Aila told you?"

"Nae, she didn't tell me," I glowered at him. "That day, I found out and confronted her. That's when she ran off crying and got into the accident."

I glanced at Summer, her face awash with concern and sympathy, and then back to Hugh. His eyes were filled with anguish, a far cry from the cocky demeanor I'd known so long ago.

"I want you to know how truly sorry I am for what happened with Aila," Hugh said, his voice cracking with remorse. "I hate that I so carelessly betrayed our friendship. I've regretted it every day since. Aila and I both regretted what we'd done. We agreed it was a rotten mistake and to never talk of it again."

"Then why did I find that note you wrote to her?" I accused in a tight voice. "The one telling her to not go through with the wedding? You were pressuring her to tell me."

"Aye." He looked down at his feet. "I thought you should know about it before you married her. There were other circumstances ... It was all such a long time ago. I made so many mistakes."

"Other circumstances?" A dawning realization began to bubble in my gut. "Did you know she was pregnant?"

"You knew?" Hugh gasped, his eyes glistening with unshed tears.

"Aye. Her parents told me. The bloodwork from the accident investigation came as a surprise to all of us." My words were bitter and sharp. "Including me."

"I found out only a few weeks before your wedding. She came to the cottage one evening and blurted it out. She was in a total panic." His voice trembled as he spoke. "She thought the baby was mine because we hadn't been careful that night."

The weight of Hugh's words hung heavily in the air, like the fog that blanketed the Scottish hillsides. Summer grabbed onto my hand, reminding me of her constant support.

"I told her that she had to tell you the truth." Hugh's face was etched with pain as he recalled that night. "If it was my bairn, I had to know. Aila begged me to drop it, but I threatened that I'd demand a paternity test after the bairn was born. She wanted to tell you after the wedding, but I didn't think that was right. She was hysterical, so I dropped it for the time being. She started avoiding me, so I left her that note. I knew I was putting her in a tough position, but ... I just never imagined what would happen."

"It was a horrible accident," I mumbled the words that the therapist had told me, finally starting to see a glimmer of truth in them.

"After the accident, I was too much of a coward to tell you. You were already grieving so much, and I thought it would be better for you if you never knew about the affair or the bairn."

The frigid air nipped at my cheeks as I stared at Hugh, his words slowly sinking in. I could understand his reasoning. I'd withheld Aila's affair and our fight before the accident from her parents for roughly the same reasons.

"But I couldn't face you after that," Hugh implored, his face begging me to believe him. "The whole damn thing was too shameful. I knew you would hate me if you knew what I'd done, so I moved out of the cottage."

I searched his face for any hint of deception but found only sincerity etched into his features. The hurt and anger that had drained me for so long began to ebb away, replaced by a quiet, uncertain sadness.

"Jesus Christ." I ran a hand through my hair, feeling the weight of the truth settle upon me like a crushing burden. "It all makes more sense now. I never understood all of it until now."

Hugh broke into my silence. "I'm not asking for forgiveness; I don't deserve it for what I did. I just couldn't keep it inside any longer. The guilt was eating me up whole."

One stupid mistake was like a domino that set in motion a chain of misfortune that had affected all our lives and led to tragedy all around, including the loss of two innocents. We were all victims in our own way and it all stemmed from one stupid mistake.

Perhaps talking through my issues with a therapist years ago had begun to heal my old wounds. Maybe having Summer by my side had blunted the pain of that loss. But. finally hearing the truth today left me feeling lighter. Less burdened down by the past. I was able to let go of the remaining guilt I'd held on to.

I'd always mourn the loss of Aila and her baby, but it wouldn't define me anymore. "Do you really think the baby was yours?"

Pain flickered in his eyes. "Aila was sure of it. The due date matched. I can't be sure, but I still grieve the wee babe. Every year on the due date of the bairn, I lay flowers on Aila's grave for them both." He swiped a tear from his eye.

I stared into the darkening sky as snowflakes danced down around us like tiny confetti, their icy touch both chilling and soothing.

"What happened was a tragedy all around," I said, clenching my fists, my breath fogging in the cold air, "you and Aila made choices that affected all of our lives. I can even understand how desperate and scared Aila must have felt to be in that situation."

I squeezed Summer's hand, grateful for her reassuring touch. Her unwavering support had given me the strength to face my demons, and now I could finally let them go. "I think we've both punished ourselves enough for that terrible day. It's taken me years to move on and find happiness again, but I did with Summer and my family. I hope you can move on from it, too."

A mixture of surprise and gratitude washed over Hugh's face as he thanked me, and then he disappeared into the crowd, leaving me alone with Summer.

"Good for you, Knox," she smiled, planting a tender kiss on my cheek. The warmth of her lips sent a shiver down my spine, reminding me just how much I loved this woman.

I looked into her gorgeous blue eyes and felt a surge of love and gratitude for the woman who'd become my rock. A sense of closure settled over me like a warm blanket. "I finally realized that holding onto grudges only causes more pain. It's time to let it go."

"Come on," Summer said softly, tugging me gently toward the grotto where our children awaited. "Let's go make some new memories."

As we walked away, my arm wrapped protectively around her, I realized that life was far too short to cling to old grudges. The past would always be a part of me, but it was time to embrace the present and cherish the love and happiness I'd found.

"Hey," I whispered to Summer as the snow continued to fall, "thanks for being my wee Bouncy Bumpkin."

She smiled, her eyes twinkling like the Christmas lights that adorned the town square. "Always, my wee Limpie Pie."

My face mirrored my displeasure at hearing the old nickname. "You know I hate that nickname. There is nothing wee or limp about my cock!"

Summer laughingly shushed my boisterous retort and then we turned our attention back to the Christmas festival, as we met up with my parents and our bairns. The snowflakes continued their graceful descent, dusting the cobblestone streets with a powdery white veil, and laughter and the sweet scent of spiced cider filled the air.

"Hey, there's the giant Christmas tree!" Grace exclaimed, pointing towards the towering fir adorned with twinkling lights.

"Let's go take a look," suggested Carter, his innocent eyes wide with excitement.

As we walked hand-in-hand towards the tree, the sound of carolers filled the air, their harmonious voices floating through the crisp night. I looked around at my family — Summer's radiant smile, the wonder in my children's eyes, and the love that surrounded us all.

At that moment, I realized just how lucky I truly was. I had two beautiful children who brought endless joy to my life, and Summer — the woman who had mended my broken heart and taught me to love again. They were everything I could have ever wanted.

"Knox," Summer whispered, leaning close so that her breath tickled my ear, "you did the right thing today. I'm proud of you."

"Thanks, Sunshine," I replied, my heart swelling with gratitude for this incredible woman by my side. "But you know what? I couldn't have done it without you."

As we stood beneath the twinkling lights of the giant Christmas tree, surrounded by the magic of the season, I knew that our future was bright. Together, hand in hand, we would face whatever challenges life threw at us and emerge stronger than ever before.

The End

# Next in Series

-------------------------------------------

**Bad Boys of Rock**

**Book 4:**

(Keep turning the pages for an excerpt!)

### How to Catch a Rockstar

**Catching a rockstar is never easy. Keeping one is even harder.**

*Shining brighter than a thousand suns...*
Ghost, the enigmatic lead singer of the rock band, Ghost Parker, captivates audiences night after night with his electrifying presence. On stage, his commanding performance is fueled by raw talent and an

oversized personality. Yet underneath it all, he is numb — a shadowy figure haunted by past traumas.

### *Caught between two irresistible and dynamic men...*

Remi joins Ghost Parker's tour for a work assignment and is quickly pulled into the glittering and scandalous world of rock and roll. She becomes tangled in the magnetic pull of Ghost's mysterious allure until their passion escalates into a fiery affair that threatens to consume them both. But Ghost is offering nothing more than a fling and her heart still belongs with another man. The last place she needs to be caught is between two dynamic men — a rock star and a mega-TV star.

### *Haunted by unrequited feelings...*

There is only one thing holding Greyson back from making a lifetime commitment to Remi — his confused feelings for another man. He's always harbored a secret desire for Ghost, but the feeling isn't mutual; Ghost can't stand him.

### *The three together...*

As lust and hatred intertwine, the three of them become entangled in a web of desire, jealousy, and deceit that threatens to destroy everything in its path. Caught in a whirlwind of a passionate love triangle, can they survive the fallout of their own dangerous games? Or will a shocking act of betrayal shatter their fragile connection forever? Some flames burn too hot to be tamed.

Grab your **backstage pass** to meet the boys of Ghost Parker and get ready for an electrifying tale of passion, betrayal, and the healing power of love. Turn up the volume as you indulge in this rockstar romance — a steamy tale of pulse-pounding beats, a tantalizing three-way relationship, and erotic encounters that will leave you breathless. Lose yourself in this glittering tale of deception, desire, and the redemptive power of love amidst the chaos of stardom.

Keep turning the pages to read an excerpt from
**HOW TO CATCH A ROCKSTAR**

# Arabella Quinn Newsletter

---

**Let's keep in touch!**

Sign up for my newsletter and be the first to know about new releases, sales, giveaways, and other exciting news. As an added bonus, you'll receive a FREE ebook as my thank-you for signing up!

Arabella Quinn newsletter
https://subscribepage.io/ArabellaQuinn

# Bad Boys of Rock Series

-------------------------------------------

Who doesn't love the tattooed bad boys of rockstar romance? **Get ready to toss your panties on stage — it's gonna get wild!**

**Book 1: How to Seduce a Rockstar** — A mind-boggling case of mistaken identity sets the stage for a scorching hot romance between Ryder, the sinfully sexy guitarist of a famous rock band, and Talia, the unsuspecting woman who stumbles into his life. After the erotic encounter with the mysterious and sexy stranger in his bed, Ryder's world is rocked.

**Book 2: How to Tempt a Rockstar** — Forbidden desires ignite in this sizzling romance between Sid, the tattooed bad-boy bass guitarist, and Kaylie, his best friend's little sister. When a tiny bundle shows up at Sid's door, Kaylie reaches out to help as his world turns upside-down. As the lines between love and lust lose focus, they must weather the tempest of forbidden desire and hidden truths to see if their love can survive the ultimate test.

**Book 3: HOW TO DATE A ROCKSTAR** — In this sizzling rockstar romance, enemies become lovers while secrets threaten to tear them apart. Knox, the lead guitarist with the irresistible Scottish accent, becomes entangled in a fake dating scheme with Summer to appease her meddlesome mother. When the lines between fake and real blur, Knox must confront his tragic past and face the truth that he's been battling. Can their budding relationship survive the harsh glare of the spotlight and the ghosts of the past that haunt them? Or will the truth shatter their hearts beyond repair?

**Book 4: HOW TO CATCH A ROCKSTAR** — Passions burn hot when Ghost, the enigmatic lead singer of a popular rock band, becomes ensnared in a tempestuous love triangle between Remi, a woman who ignites his dormant emotions, and her boyfriend, whom he despises. As lust and hatred collide with betrayal, can the three navigate the treacherous waters of a passionate love triangle and find redemption amidst the chaos of stardom, or will their dangerous games leave them shattered? The only question is—who will be left standing when the music stops?

**Book 5: HOW TO MARRY A ROCKSTAR** — Bash, the reckless and carefree drummer of a chart-topping rock band, is busy juggling fame, fortune, and fatherhood. Lacey, the sultry vixen, has been friends with Bash and his band for years. Their lives take an unexpected turn when one reckless night in Vegas changes everything, leaving them entwined in more ways than one. With their secret passions and insatiable cravings unleashed, they embark on a steamy friends-with-benefits arrangement with a side of untamed kinks.

# Also By Arabella Quinn

------------

**BAD BOYS OF ROCK SERIES**

How to Seduce a Rockstar
How to Tempt a Rockstar
How to Date a Rockstar
How to Catch a Rockstar
How to Marry a Rockstar

**ROCK ME SERIES**

Rock Me: Wicked
Rock Me: Naughty
Rock Me: Crazy
Rock Me:  Sexy

**ROMANCE NOVELS**

My Stepbrother the Dom
Impossible (to Resist) Boss
Being Jane


**THE WILDER BROTHERS SERIES**
(small town romance)

Fake Marriage to a Baller
Luke – coming soon

# Other Novels by Arabella Quinn

----

### MY STEPBROTHER THE DOM

A sizzling stepbrother romance with a twist:

For years, I had the worst crush on my stepbrother, Cole Hunter. We used to ride bikes, skateboard, and go fishing together — now I couldn't even be in the same room as him without my pulse racing. One cocky half-grin from Cole would have my face blushing while my panties melted. It was insane — and completely humiliating.

It was a painful secret that I guarded fiercely. Cole was off-limits. *Forbidden*. If he knew how I felt, I would die of embarrassment.

I avoided Cole for years, until one wild night, when my best friend took me to a club. I thought I was going to see a grunge band, but it turned out to be a much kinkier kind of club. A club where anything goes, and well, things got a little crazy. Make that a lot crazy.

No one would ever know what I'd done, right?

Then I discovered who the man behind the mask really was...

## Impossible (to Resist) Boss

A sexy billionaire CEO. His headstrong secretary. And a computer file that exposes her most secret and dirty fantasies about him.

**Lilliana**

*I hate my boss.*

He's an inconsiderate and demanding tyrant. I hate his juvenile rules, his micro-managing ways, and his selfish and unapologetic manner. But most of all, I hate how insanely sexy he is — how all the women around him can't help but fawn all over him.

He's a wealthy, ego-driven maniac that has a new bimbo at his beck and call with the mere snap of his fingers. Despite these irrepressible naughty fantasies I keep having about him, I wouldn't stroke his ego for all the money in the world.

**Jason Kaine**

*I may have found the one.*

After years of fruitless searching, I've found the perfect secretary. She's scarily efficient, not afraid of hard work, detail-oriented, and best of all, she doesn't complain about my important rules. She's a dream come true.

So why can't I keep the image of her, deliciously naked and spread out invitingly across my desk, from invading my head? I didn't get to where I am today by being stupid. I've got plenty of willing women to choose from who understand my absolute no-strings policy.

Lilliana is strictly off-limits, but I see the way her eyes devour me. I see how her pulse pounds whenever I get near. I know she's ripe for the taking, but that would be disastrous for both of us. It might be the worst mistake ever, but something's bound to give.

# About the Author

Arabella Quinn is a *New York Times* and *USA Today* bestselling author of contemporary romance. When she's not busy writing, you can often find her clutching her Kindle and staying up way past her bedtime reading romance novels. Besides contemporary romance, she loves regency, gothic, and erotic romance — the steamier the better. She also loves thrillers, especially psychological thrillers. She saves reading horror for when her husband is away on business but doesn't recommend that. She averages about five hours of sleep per night and does not drink coffee. Also, not recommended!

Arabella Quinn newsletter
https://subscribepage.io/ArabellaQuinn

# Excerpt

---

## How to Catch a Rockstar

## Two Years Ago...

**Ghost**

Everyone was entirely focused on Ryder. He captivated the audience with his newly dyed, blond punk hairstyle and his electric performance of *Rebel Yell*. It was impressive. Maybe I felt a twinge of ... what? Not jealousy. Not resentment. I don't know what. My band was up on stage and I was watching from the audience. It just felt wrong. I was the face of Ghost Parker, but I'd stepped aside so that Ryder could shine in the spotlight — so that he could impress Talia.

I used the moment while everyone was caught up in the show to slip out the back of the room through some sliding glass doors onto the patio. The sun had set, so it was cooler outside, but not yet chilly. The overhead patio lights were not on, but there was soft landscape lighting that highlighted the palm trees and greenery, and there were hidden fixtures that illuminated the paving stone pathways. I followed a path that passed by the pool and stopped in front of a railing looking out toward the blackness of the ocean in the distance.

In this hidden corner, I could hear the rhythmic sound of the relentless surf and only heard the faintest of notes from Ghost Parker jamming inside the house. It was a good place to escape the party.

I had only a few minutes of peace until I felt the weight of someone's eyes resting on me. My senses went on alert, but I didn't turn to see who it was. It was probably one of any number of girls who'd been watching me since I'd arrived at Tommy's house. The guest list was exclusive to friends; there were no random groupies here. It didn't matter though, guaranteed this person wanted only one thing — to get into my pants.

I rolled that thought around in my head. A good fuck might be a great distraction, but I'd have to ask the '15 minutes of questions' first. My therapist wanted me to stop having such utterly meaningless sex. She wanted me to get to know a girl, even if it was just for 15 minutes, before having sex. Baby steps, she called it. She was trying to teach me how to relate to people and how to build relationships.

The problem was that the more I got to know the girls, even after 15 minutes, the more I didn't want to sleep with them. Maybe that was the whole point my therapist was trying to make; I was making poor choices. But, sex was one of the few things in life that I enjoyed. The rush of being on stage in front of thousands was the only thing better than sex. And since they were the only two things in life that temporarily pushed me past the numbness, I wasn't about to give up either one.

With all the grappling in my head, it only took me an instant to make up my mind. I was going to let this chick blow me, whoever she was, and without the '15-minute getting to know her' bullshit. And I would enjoy it. Then I'd see if I wanted to stick around the party any longer or just disappear into the shadows of the night.

I turned, already flashing the smile that was guaranteed to make the ladies drop their panties but ended up raising an eyebrow in surprise. I could tell by the silhouette that this was no lady.

He took a step closer so that his face was out of the shadows. He held up a drink in each hand. "Jack and Coke or Whiskey Sour?"

I shrugged. "Either is fine."

He handed me the Jack and Coke and then took a healthy sip of his own drink.

I regarded him. "You're Talia's friend? We met on the party bus?"

"Grey," he confirmed.

I remembered watching him at the nightclub that night. The guy had really attracted the attention of the ladies. They had swarmed him so quickly, that our party had to leave the dance floor and head to the VIP section. He was almost too handsome and the skintight shirt he'd worn that night had shown off that he was in great shape, but guys like that were a dime a dozen in this town.

Maybe his popularity had intrigued me because that night I'd found myself watching him. I had a way of blending in with the crowd and avoiding notice when I wanted to, but several times I'd felt his scrutiny. It was as if he'd been aware of me all night. It'd made me slightly nervous, an emotion that almost never broke through the constant numbness. Still, I'd been curious about him. I'd even wondered what he was doing when I was busy getting a blowjob in the VIP restroom. When he left at the end of the night with a curvy redhead, it felt like the party fizzled. Everything seemed flat. No more weird nerves. I'd left the party, alone, right after.

I took a sip of the Jack and Coke and then leaned on the railing, gazing out toward the ocean. "I'm Johnny."

I surprised myself. I never introduced myself as Johnny. Maybe my therapist was finally getting through to me after all. She told me using my nickname, Ghost, was a way of hiding from intimacy. I wasn't looking for intimacy with this guy, so I immediately regretted saying it.

Grey rested his drink on the railing near my arm but remained facing me instead of looking out toward the ocean. "I've never seen you perform before tonight. You're ... just amazing. You mesmerize the audience. I was in awe."

His words weren't something that I hadn't heard a thousand times, but maybe because they came from a dude who was used to performing for an audience and weren't just tossed out by a woman that was trying to work her way into my bed, it felt like they meant something. Somehow, the words didn't feel so empty or calculating.

I took a hasty sip to stop myself from saying anything stupid. "Thanks, man. You didn't stay to watch Ryder?"

"No." He glanced down at his feet and suddenly he didn't look like the supremely self-confident guy that I'd observed all that night at Talia's goodbye party. His voice sounded gruff. "I saw you leaving. You looked lost. Like you could use a friend."

Something shifted inside me. I didn't know what I felt, but it wasn't something I was comfortable with. My heart beat faster. Maybe it was that he just got too close to my secrets. To my truths.

Surprisingly, my reaction was also physical. A flutter in my stomach. A tightness in my chest. A tightening of my cock inside my pants.

My jaw clenched as I snarled back at him. "Yeah? Well, you thought wrong."

♫♫♩♪♪

## Remi

I had nothing better going on, so after the end of the workday 'going on maternity leave' party for Celia, which consisted of cake in the break room, I accepted the invitation to go out with my coworkers to a local restaurant. Celia was a production assistant at Hollywood Exposé, the TV and online celebrity news conglomerate that I worked for as a feature story writer. She was one of those bubbly girls that everyone loved.

When I got to the restaurant twenty minutes later, Celia's table was full. I ended up at an ancillary table with other staff writers. Except for the two writers who wrote the script for Mindy Blakedale, the face of Hollywood Exposé, all the other writers and editors worked primarily alone. They were an observant and quiet bunch — not exactly the life of the party.

I'd asked a few of my colleagues what they were working on, but they all were a tight-lipped crew. No one wanted to give away their inside scoop, despite the fact we were all working for the same team.

I liked Celia and most of the people who worked behind the cameras at my job, but a majority of those friendly people were at the cool kid's table. I was stuck with the nerds. I probably could have barreled my way into that group, securing an empty chair from another table and shoehorning it in to be included with the fun group, but I was just too tired to make the effort. It had been a long and exhausting week.

I finished up my second drink and then started planning my exit strategy. I could just say goodbye and good luck to Celia and be on my way. There was no need for elaborate excuses even though it appeared that I would be the first to leave.

I said my goodbyes to the glum writer's table, then to Celia and several co-workers I was friendly with, and within a few minutes, I was slipping out the door into the fresh air.

It wasn't until I was in front of my apartment door digging through my purse and searching for my key that I found it.

It was a blue notecard with words scrawled in ugly black marker across it. The ink was badly smeared, but I could clearly make out what it said.

I know who you are
REMINGTON
watch your back

I couldn't help but hurriedly glance over my shoulder even though I was alone in the hallway. Fumbling with my keys, I nearly dropped them as I tried to unlock my door as quickly as I could. I didn't breathe until I got into my apartment and locked the door behind me.

My heart pounded as I stared at the card. *Remington*. Somebody knew. Who? And, what were they going to do about it? *Watch your back*. That sounded like a threat.

I let my purse drop to the floor. And then I slid down right next to it. I thought I'd left my past behind.

♫♪♩♪♩

# Greyson

I almost didn't go to the baby shower. *Because of him.*

But, in the end, I went. *Because of him.*

My friend, Talia, was hosting a baby shower for Sidney Anderson, the bassist for the rock band Ghost Parker. Out of the blue, less than a week ago, he found out he was a father. The mother had abandoned the baby on his doorstep claiming it was his. Now his friends were coming together to support him.

I was more of an acquaintance than a friend. I'd only met Sid a handful of times, but I was friends with Talia, and Talia was living in my beach house with her boyfriend, Ryder, who was a guitarist in Sid's band.

I liked Talia's friends. They partied a hell of a lot harder than me; they knew how to have a good time. Plus, with the whole rock star thing, they didn't make too much of my own fame. I was currently filming the 9th season of the primetime soap, *Devious*. I was the longest-running cast member, starring as bad boy titan, Colton Grimaldi, since episode 1 of the series. As my fame skyrocketed, it became nearly impossible to interact with people on a normal level, so having some friends outside of the acting world who knew me as Greyson and treated me like an ordinary person was refreshing.

So, here I was in my own house that I'd been avoiding since Talia moved in. I still wasn't too sure how Ryder felt about me. I usually stayed at my penthouse in Hollywood during filming anyway, so it was no big deal.

I carried my wrapped gifts, a baby monitor and a white-noise sound machine, up to the top floor where everyone was gathered waiting for Sid to arrive. Talia had done a great job decorating. There were balloons, ribbons, and streamers, all baby blue, everywhere. A huge banner draped across the wall exclaimed *It's a Boy!* And the tables were covered with *Oh, Baby!* printed tablecloths and piled with gifts. And, shit, there was blue confetti littering every surface of the house already.

I felt at home as soon as I stepped into the room. Right away, Talia hugged me, quickly followed by Kaylie. Ryder shook my hand and slapped me on the back. I was introduced to Ghost Parker's manager and his date and then greeted by a few others I'd met before.

The moment *he* walked into the room, I knew. *Johnny Parker*. He was the lead singer of Ghost Parker — known to almost everyone as Ghost. I kept my back to him, listening as his friends greeted him. My gut clenched when I heard his smooth baritone voice.

*Fuck. I was so attracted to this guy.*

It only took a second to disassociate myself from those feelings; I was a fucking good actor. I turned around, a neutral expression plastered on my face.

He was looking right at me. I didn't betray the riot of emotions that his gaze produced. Instead, my eyes swept right past him. I tried not to remember the last time I'd spoken to him — right after he performed live with his band at Talia's party. In just a few words, he'd left me shattered. Humiliated.

We never got close to each other during the baby shower, but I'd keenly felt his presence the entire time. He was amongst his best friends, in private, but he seemed so detached. It was so unlike when I'd seen him perform with his band, where his overwhelming magnetism touched the entire crowd. I briefly wondered if today he was under the influence of drugs.

Even though he was acting so low-key, I swore that he had an extra awareness of me. He was better at checking his emotions than most actors I knew, but he couldn't hide the fact that he had some kind of reaction to me. Not when I was watching him so closely. His eyes followed me. He noticed me. Quite possibly, it was nervous energy or even contempt; I didn't know. Maybe he was picking up on my attraction and it was disdain directed back at me. He wasn't unaffected, that I knew.

Of course, I was immediately aware when he went out on the deck. Marie followed thirty seconds behind him. I watched them through the slider door; I had to move so I had the right angle to see them. They stood talking to each other.

Talia stopped to chat with me for a minute and when I looked back up, they'd disappeared. There was no way off the deck except through the main slider into this room or the slider at the end of the deck into the master bedroom.

He hadn't come back inside here, so I knew he must be in my bedroom with Marie. I grew antsy waiting for them to come out. I paced back and forth, keeping my eyes on the bedroom door. I waited a few more minutes. Finally, I just couldn't stand it any longer. The party was still going strong. People were drinking and having a good time. Right now they were bobbing for baby bottle nipples. No one was paying any attention to me.

I slipped into my bedroom. It was quiet in there. I quickly scanned the room; it was empty, but the bathroom door was open. I moved further into the room and finally, I could see them. Marie was on her knees on my bath mat. She was kneeling in front of Ghost, her head bobbing up and down on his dick.

Ghost looked like a bored god. He stood casually leaning against the wall, his hand braced against the vanity countertop. His head was flung back slightly, and his eyes were narrowed into slits. His expression was completely passive, but he was breathing slightly heavier than normal.

I was instantly hard as a rock. I stepped closer, just outside the bathroom door, to watch. I couldn't drag my eyes away.

When I came into view, his eyes snapped to me. "What the fuck are you doing?"

I lifted a brow. "You realize this is my bedroom, right?"

Marie popped off his dick and, yeah, I was staring at it. "Oh, my God! Greyson! Do you remember me? We met on the party bus. I'm a big fan of *Devious*. I'm Marie."

I couldn't pull my eyes away from Ghost's dick. "I remember."

Marie shifted on her knees. "This is not what it looks like. We're just friends..."

Ghost made an impatient exhalation. "Did I say you should stop sucking my cock?"

Marie giggled and then wrapped her lips around his cock again and went to work. With each bob of her head, I thought I might blow my load right in my jeans. Fuck, my cock was throbbing.

I didn't move. I couldn't. I just watched. I alternated between watching Ghost's cock disappearing into Marie's mouth and watching his face. The exquisite ache that built uncomfortably in my balls was torture.

Ghost's breath came a little heavier and his knuckles turned white as he gripped the counter harder. I was amazed at how in control he was. While I was sweating with the effort to keep my own cock from exploding, not once did he thrust into her mouth.

He kept himself rigidly in check and his eyes never left mine.

It only took a couple more head bobs before he came. He threw back his head slightly and quietly groaned. I may have groaned with him. After milking him for a few seconds, Marie pulled off his cock looking pleased with herself.

She wiped her mouth while Ghost was tucking himself back into his pants. I was paralyzed with aching.

Marie turned on her knees and reached a hand for my pants.

Ghost blinked a few times. "What are you doing?"

Marie stopped, her hand resting on my jeans right over my painfully hard cock. She gazed up at me. "Tell me you want this? I want to do this so badly. This is so hot."

I just nodded. My dick was so hard; I desperately needed relief.

She quickly unbuckled my belt, unbuttoned and unzipped my pants, and had my cock out in seconds. It was thick and angry, the head glistening with pre-cum. Marie's mouth felt like heaven when she slid her tongue over my cock before taking me between her red swollen lips.

I was mesmerized by Ghost's face as he stared at my cock getting sucked off. It was no longer distant or vacant. His eyes were half-lidded with lust and tension coiled his lips. His cheeks were flushed and his nostrils flared. His intoxicating beauty hit me like a physical blow, ratcheting up the unbearable pressure in my balls, especially with his eyes zeroed in on my cock.

My hand wrapped around a hunk of Marie's hair, but it was Ghost's mouth I was imagining on me when Marie took me deep, the tip of my dick hitting the back of her throat.

A grunt escaped my lips and then a long hiss when she did it again.

The noise I made broke the spell surrounding us. Ghost tore his eyes from my cock and looked me right in the eyes. He suddenly looked pissed, a damaged immortal hell-bent on vengeance. I sucked in a breath, retreating from his wrath. I was about to come, but Ghost was already turning away from me. He stormed out of the room.

I closed my eyes and imagined his face. I imagined his mouth on me.

I spurted long and hard. Marie did a good job milking every last tremor from me, but she wasn't who I was thinking about.

**Chapter One**

## *Present Day*

# Ghost

*Whoop! Whoop! Whoop!*

The high-pitched blaring sound was splitting my head open. I grunted with disgust and rolled onto my side, burying my head under the pillow in the process.

*Whoop! Whoop! Whoop!*

It was loud. Deafening. And it wasn't letting up.

*Whoop! Whoop! Whoop!*

Somebody. Make. It. Stop.

It wasn't an alarm clock. It was so damn loud — way too loud to ignore. My foggy mind insisted it must be something more important. Was it a police siren? Fuck. Did I do something wrong?

*Whoop! Whoop! Whoop!*

I forced myself to think as I burrowed deeper under the pillow, trying to block out the shrillest part of the noise. I'd had my share of brushes with the law, so getting arrested wasn't a completely insane scenario to contemplate.

Where had I been last night? What did I do? I feebly tried to piece together the puzzle against the backdrop of the incessant noise.

*Whoop! Whoop! Whoop!*

Suddenly, the pillow was yanked roughly from my head. The frantic alarm blasted in my ears ten times louder without the pillow to muffle it. Fuck.

Someone was tugging on my arm. It was a girl. I heard a few of the words she was yelling at me, but the alarm drowned out most of what she said.

"Ghost, you—"

*Whoop! Whoop! Whoop!*

"Please!"

*Whoop! Whoop! Whoop!*

"We gotta—"

*Whoop! Whoop! Whoop!*

After a few thumps on my back and less than a minute of arm tugging, the girl gave up. Without opening my eyes, I felt around the bed fruitlessly searching for the pillow so I could block out the fucking noise.

*Whoop! Whoop! Whoop!*

Just when I realized I was going to have to actually open my eyes to locate the missing pillow, what felt like an entire bucket of ice-cold water was dumped on my head. Holy fuck!

*Whoop! Whoop! Whoop!*

My eyes jolted open from the shock of the water assaulting my face. The adrenaline that simultaneously surged through my veins had my body springing from the bed, my fists sailing through the air, ready to defend myself to the death.

*Whoop! Whoop! Whoop!*

I took in the girl who stood before me as I tried to steady my breathing. She was gesticulating wildly as she yelled at me, frenzy overtaking her face. A flash of memory from the night before came back to me. This girl. A sexy black dress. Lots of long leg showing.

Now she was wearing a baggy sweatshirt over leggings. No makeup. Messy hair. She was damn cute. I wanted to drag her back into bed with me.

*Whoop! Whoop! Whoop!*

I felt my cock jump as I remembered flashes from our night between the sheets. And. Oh shit. I was naked. I never slept naked with a girl overnight. What if she snapped a picture of my cock while I was sleeping? It'd be all over social media in a heartbeat. Ryder had learned that lesson early on for our band.

*Whoop! Whoop! Whoop!*

She had something in her hand, which was still flapping around wildly as she yelled. A cup. It looked like one of those plastic cups to rinse your mouth out after you brushed your teeth. A small cup. She'd dumped a small cup of water on my face. I grunted at the realization. Jesus, it'd felt like I'd been waterboarded, but it was probably only a few ounces of water at most.

*Whoop! Whoop! Whoop!*

Between the damn alarm endlessly clattering and the pounding of the pulse in my ears from my adrenaline rush, I couldn't really make out what this girl was screaming at me. There was one word that was coming through crystal clear, though.

"Fire!"

My brain was finally catching up. The fire alarm was going off. It was time to bounce.

*Whoop! Whoop! Whoop!*

As the realization sunk in, the girl turned from me, her arms still waving in the air above her head as she bolted out the bedroom door. I almost laughed out loud because she looked like a deranged muppet with crazy wiggling arms flapping around as she disappeared.

*Whoop! Whoop! Whoop!*

I looked around the room for my clothes. Her room wasn't clean, so it wasn't like my clothing rested in a pile on her pristine floor. There were clothes everywhere. And other junk girls tended to accumulate was littered everywhere — on dressers, on the floor, and absolutely overflowing a chair. Jesus, the more I looked, the more of a pig I realized this girl was. There were old plates with leftover moldy food on them scattered about. Soda cans everywhere. A few beer bottles. Papers, books, and notebooks strewn around the room. Lots of shoes. Just shit everywhere.

*Whoop! Whoop! Whoop!*

Near the foot of the bed, I saw what looked like a pair of men's jeans. I picked them up and recognized them at once. One of my favorite pairs. Well worn. Ripped in all the right places, not by a razor, but by years of use. They fit my body perfectly. I'd wear these jeans until they disintegrated. I poked around the clothes lying near where I found my jeans, searching for my boxer briefs.

I didn't find them, but fished my wallet from the bottom of the pile. Thank goodness. Luckily, my jeans were broken in and comfortable because I'd have to go commando. I didn't have time to dick around here.

*Whoop! Whoop! Whoop!*

I slipped on my jeans while scanning the ground for my T-shirt, but quickly realized that was hopeless. I'd never find it in this mess. As I moved toward the door, I glanced out the narrow window in the bedroom. I was up on about the fifth floor. I had been focused on other things when we'd stumbled in last night, so I was surprised to see that this must be a big apartment building. A ton of people had gathered on the lawn and road in front of the building. Some were wearing jackets. Some had blankets draped over their shoulders. This was Los Angeles, but November could be damn cold at times. Most of the crowd was looking up toward the apartment building. Some were even pointing. Two things hit me. I needed more clothes, and I needed to get the fuck out of here. Right now.

*Whoop! Whoop! Whoop!*

My eyes landed on a sweatshirt. I grabbed it and held it up, inspecting its size. It was probably huge on the girl — I still couldn't remember her name — but it wasn't quite my size. It would do in an emergency. I pulled it on as I stepped through the bedroom door into the rest of her apartment.

*Whoop! Whoop! Whoop!*

The apartment was clear. No smoke. No fire. No sign of the girl or any roommates. I crossed the front room toward the entry door and felt for heat before I cautiously opened it. Peeked into the hall. All clear.

*Whoop! Whoop! Whoop!*

I followed the exit signs toward the stairwell, pleased my brain was making the right choices — checking for fire and not using the elevator. I jogged down five flights of stairs, all while the blaring alarm spurred me on to move even faster.

Finally, I pushed out into the brisk fresh air, where the sound of the alarm was more muted. It no longer felt like it was boring into my brain. Outside, it was cold, and I was grateful I'd grabbed the sweatshirt. Unfortunately, it was a salmon-pink color. I glanced down at it. It was way too tight. The sleeves were too short. It had the word 'Princess' written across the chest in a shiny gold script.

I probably could have found something better to wear if I'd searched for a few more minutes, but the place was on fucking fire. So...

I took a step and felt the shocking cold of the concrete on my bare feet. Shit, I'd forgotten my shoes in the rush to get out. As I'd torn down the stairwell, I hadn't even realized I was barefoot. I grimaced as I looked up from staring at my feet and noticed the crowd.

I was used to being the center of attention. Used to thousands of eyes focused on me and every move that I made. I loved it. Made a living from it. Drew my energy from it. Performing was my lifeblood.

Yet, I felt a rumble of uneasiness as I saw a few phones lift up. Aimed at me. Some people had recognized me. It was only a matter of time before the entire crowd knew who I was. My head was pounding with renewed vigor. And I was wearing this awful, ill-fitting sweatshirt to boot.

It was time to disappear like a ghost into the mist. I took a few steps into the crowd. Blending in was better. Fuck, I didn't have my phone. I asked the nearest star-struck girl if I could borrow her phone to make a call. She nodded mutely and handed it over. I quickly punched in Bishop's number, which I had conveniently memorized for just such emergencies.

Bishop was my personal security guard. Last night, I'd purposefully left my cell phone in the men's bathroom and exited the club out the back door. It wasn't the first time I'd ditched Bishop. I was expecting an earful from him when he picked me up, but he was a consummate professional. He wouldn't take it personally, but he'd double down on his efforts to keep me under tabs. It was getting harder and harder to outmaneuver him. He was great at his job and I trusted him, but more importantly, he'd become more of a friend than an employee. Regardless, I vowed to keep him on his toes.

Bishop chuckled when I let him know it was me calling. I had to get the address from the phone's owner and then I told him I'd be waiting for him a block east. A few seconds later, Bishop promised to pick me up within 15 minutes.

Fifteen minutes was a huge wait, especially with half the damn cell phones in the vicinity recording my every move. While I'd been securing a ride, the crowd began to coalesce around me. Even more phones were aimed at me. A girl — my girl from last night with the unknown name — pushed through the crowd to reach me. She wrapped me in an enormous hug.

"Ghost! You made it out. I'm so sorry about the whole water thing. I didn't know what to do! You wouldn't wake up."

Fuck. That didn't sound good. I had to shut her up. Wrapping my arms around her to return her hug, I whispered into her ear, "Hey, babe. I gotta get out of here. Too many cameras on me. I'll see you around."

I pulled back. A sad look passed over her face, but then it brightened. "I had fun last night. Take my number and call me. Anytime."

"I had fun too." I pretended to enter her number into the phone, which wasn't actually my phone, as she dictated it.

She nodded at me. "And my last name is Buchanan. Dina Buchanan."

"Buchanan. Got it." I fake-entered her last name.

Other girls were watching our interaction. They got bolder. Soon, they were snapping selfies with me. This was turning into a meet-and-greet right before my eyes — the most hated part of my job. The atmosphere outside turned even more festive when the rumor circulated that the fire was a false alarm. Someone had supposedly burned some popcorn, which triggered the alarm.

My head was still throbbing as I chatted with yet another fan. At some point, the cell phone girl snatched back her phone and began snapping a million pictures of me.

I noticed a tall girl at the periphery of the crowd patiently waiting her turn to get a selfie with me, but other girls kept cutting in. After ten minutes of being mauled by girls and even a few guys, I caught her eye again. She finally stepped up.

"Can I get a picture with you?" she asked meekly.

I noticed her flip-flops right away. Some dick had stepped on my bare foot as soon as the crowd tightened around me and it had been throbbing in time with my head ever since. I'd been vigilant since then, trying to keep my bruised and freezing feet from any more abuse. I'd had one eye latched onto where everyone's feet were for self-preservation purposes.

She had pretty big feet for a girl. Her flip-flops had silver, sparkly straps.

"You can get a picture with me if you do me a favor."

Her eyes bugged out. "What do you mean?"

"I'll trade you." My eyebrows lifted. "A picture with me for your flip-flops."

"You want my flip-flops? You have a fetish or something?" She looked confused.

"Something."

She giggled, but then kicked off her flip-flops and handed them over to me. She handed over her phone to her friend and then we posed together. Her friend snapped a ton of shots. She thanked me and was about to leave when I grabbed her arm and pulled her back.

She had to be just under 6 feet tall. I didn't feel that much taller than her when I usually dwarfed other girls. Still, I was able to dip her and land a surprise kiss on her lips.

Her shock turned to glee as I righted her again. She squealed as her friend cried out that she'd gotten it all on camera.

Just then, some new siren sounds mixed with the unrelenting fire alarm from the building. Fire trucks were now coming down the street to join the melee. I glanced over my shoulder at the building but still couldn't see any blazing fire. All of this was for burnt popcorn. Who ate fucking popcorn for breakfast, anyway?

The noisy and chaotic arrival of the several fire engines momentarily distracted the crowd. Timing it just right, I made my escape and melted off toward the pickup spot.

The black Lincoln Navigator with the tinted windows pulled up to me. I hopped into the back seat and before my back even hit the black leather of the seat, the behemoth car smoothly pulled away.

Bishop had a crooked grin on his face. "Tell me you had nothing to do with the fire engines? Oh shit, what the hell are you wearing?"

Distracted, I ran a hand through my hair. "Don't even ask."

Bishop passed my cell phone back to me. "Keep ditching your phone like that, and I'm gonna have to chip you."

Tracking our phones was a safety measure that our security team employed. None of us liked it, but it had proved invaluable a few times.

I laid my head back against the butter-soft leather. "You can yell at me after I get a cup of coffee in me."

"You're cutting it close." Bishop glanced at me in the rear-view mirror. "Your appointment with the head shrinker is in 20 minutes."

My therapy session. Fuck. I closed my eyes. I forgot about that. We were in the middle of a 3-week break from the tour, and I always tried to see Maggie in person when I could. I briefly thought about canceling, but I knew she would bust my balls if I did.

I moaned with irritation. "Do I have time to make it home for a quick change of clothes?"

"Nope."

I glanced out the window when the car came to a stop. Bishop double-parked in front of a donut shop. "Don't get out of the damn car."

I snorted. I wasn't planning on going anywhere. "Pick up a donut for me. Lemon with lemon glaze."

Bishop muttered something while shaking his head before he headed into the shop. I took the time to send a quick text to Trudy, our PR rep, to warn her to keep an eye on social media.

Her reply came back quickly.

> **Trudy:** Really? What did you do? It's not even 10 a.m. yet.
> **Me:** I didn't do anything.
> **Me:** It may involve cross-dressing though.
> **Me:** Lots of photos and videos. **Trudy:** Fine. I'll check #ghostsightings and see how much damage you did.

Bishop had come back with my coffee and donut and we were on our way to Maggie's office when I got Trudy's next text.

> **Trudy:** Awww. You look so cute. You could have brushed your hair, though.

I took a sip of my coffee and watched the three dots as I waited for more from her.

> **Trudy:** My, weren't you busy! At least 12 girls from that apartment building claimed to have fucked you last night.
> **Trudy:** #GhostParker and #ghostsightings, and #ghostsmokeout LOL
> **Trudy:** You're trending, but everything looks fine. No biggie. Fans are eating it up. I'll monitor it.

I quickly typed a reply into my phone.

**Me:** Thanks, Tru.

Running my fingers through my hair, I tried to tamp down my bedhead but gave up a few seconds later. I looked like a crazy person, but therapists were used to crazy, so no biggie, as Trudy put it.

I couldn't help but add another text.

**Me:** And for the record, I only fucked 4 girls last night.

A few minutes later, we were pulling up to the nondescript building that housed Maggie's office. There were no signs announcing her practice; she had plenty of high-profile clients, so she was discreet.

After thoroughly scanning the area for paparazzi, Bishop deemed it safe for me to leave. He would be waiting at the rear exit when I was finished. Maggie's whole setup was designed to get clientele in and out without them ever being seen.

I grabbed the bag containing the donut, hopped out of the car, and waited at the door for Maggie to buzz me in.

**Chapter Two**

# Remi

What did my audience want? Gossip. Scandal. Juicy tidbits. A peek inside celebrity lives. An occasional sprinkling of feel-good stories where celebrities made a difference in the real world. Warmth and humanity could only be doled out in small doses.

Social media had preconditioned my audience to respond to entertainment delivered in neat 30-second sound bites. How did I keep them engaged enough to read an entire article that might take 5 minutes? Humor. Wit. Sensationalism. And, it needed to be written at a fifth-grade reading level, at least according to my boss.

I was writing a feature story about another reality TV family that just wouldn't go away. It was my third time writing about them. I'd rather poke my eye out with a rusty nail dripping with tetanus, but I had no choice.

So far, my article was more vapid than the family it was covering. I took a deep breath. Instead of getting frustrated, I needed to view this as a challenge. If I could take this story and spin it into gold, I'd prove what a talented writer I was. I needed to stop tormenting myself by recalling my degree in investigative journalism and ignore just how far I'd drifted from my dreams.

The article was technically finished. I'd hit my word count, but it contained nothing of value. It needed something more. Just like my mom used to finely chop up vegetables to hide in the meatloaf, I always tried to sneak into my pieces some tidbits of wisdom, some truths, or moral lessons that a tiny segment of my audience might pick up. This piece had nothing.

I had to attempt to redeem it. The problem was that this family didn't excite me one bit. I didn't watch their reality show. I didn't follow them on social media. My greatest wish was that they'd fade into obscurity, so I'd never have to write about them again. For now, I was stuck covering them — it was trying to craft sophisticated entertainment out of The Three Stooges.

I stared at my laptop screen. It was seemingly impossible. My brain screamed with defeat. It was like turning meatloaf into chateaubriand.

Speaking of meatloaf again, I was getting hungry. Maybe a Twix bar would kick-start my creativity. I leaned over to reach into my purse, which was shoehorned in the bottom right drawer of my desk, when my phone rang.

Darn, it was my boss. "Hi, Caroline."

"In my office." She wasn't one to mince words.

"Okay. I'll be right..." My voice trailed off. She'd already hung up.

It was fairly unusual to be summoned to her office, but I wasn't worried. My job here was secure. I produced quality pieces and my output was consistent. Maybe, fingers crossed, she had a new assignment for me.

I snatched a pad of paper and a pen from my desk and wound my way through the newsroom. The newsroom was a giant open space crammed with bumper-to-bumper desks, each containing at least two monitors. For as hectic as it all looked, it was a controlled chaos. Phones rang constantly, but most people wore headsets as they worked, so only a few one-sided conversations could be heard.

Caroline's office was only one floor up, so I took the stairs. She was on the phone when I arrived at her open door, so I knocked lightly on the door frame to get her attention. She looked up and waved me into the chair in front of her desk while she finished with her call.

My boss wasn't a stylish person. She looked like she spent a grand total of about five minutes on her appearance each morning. Her pin-straight, but thick blonde hair was cut in the shape of a helmet around her head. Her clothes were loose and boxy and always seemed randomly selected. She never wore a stitch of makeup or any jewelry.

Her appearance wasn't a priority; she channeled all her energy into her job. And she was absolutely amazing at it. She wasn't just my boss; I considered her a mentor as well. Plus, she'd taken a big chance on me. I owed her so much.

She hung up the phone and glanced up at me. "Would you close the door, please?"

I closed the office door and then returned to my chair, inhaling deeply to calm the skittering of nerves that had settled over me.

She looked me directly in the eye. "What I'm about to tell you doesn't leave this office."

I nodded my agreement.

She got straight to the point. "Mindy Blakedale is retiring. Losing her is a blow. She's been the beating heart of Hollywood Exposé for 12 years. Of course, we'll milk it for everything we can, but we have six months to transition to the new face of Hollywood Exposé."

I had met Mindy a few times but never worked directly with her. She was a minor celebrity in her own right and Hollywood Exposé treated her like a queen. She mingled with the peasants only when necessary. It helped that she was married to a famous movie producer who came from old Hollywood royalty. She was a true industry insider.

She folded her arms on top of her desk. "Jack Hoffman and I have been discussing her replacement."

Mr. Hoffman, as most of the staff called him, was the CEO and controlling shareholder of Hollywood Exposé.

Caroline tapped her thumb twice against the desktop. "As you know, Margot was being groomed as a successor to the position, but then she got snapped up by WCAU. The fool. She'd be sitting pretty right now if she wasn't so damn impatient."

My mind was racing. I didn't want to get ahead of myself, but why was Caroline telling me all this? Was it even possible that I was going to get the mother of all jobs at Hollywood Exposé? A silent squeal of amazement rippled through my brain, but I shut it down quickly. I needed to be on my game. Professional.

"Regardless,"—Caroline waved her hands to dismiss the subject of Margot—"I met with Jack last night and he wants Dawn Chambers to take Mindy's place. While she's an excellent choice, I did put in a word on your behalf."

The ecstatic thrill that had been buzzing in my body was quickly replaced by the sting of rejection. "That was really kind of you. Thanks."

Caroline smirked. "Dawn has seniority over you. She's got more time punched and more experience. She's a great field reporter with terrific instincts, and she's sat in for Mindy dozens of times over the years. Plus, she scores well behind the camera according to our focus groups."

Ah, it all made sense. If Dawn wasn't so damn short, she could be a runway model. She was gorgeous, petite, and stick thin. I had at least 15 pounds on her.

Caroline steepled her fingers. She vaguely looked like a supervillain. "You haven't had as much on-air work, but the field reports, red carpets, and on-air interviews you've done have gone well. And you think more quickly on your feet. Dawn has stumbled a few times in that respect."

My heart was thumping double time in my chest. I waited for Caroline to continue.

"You're very natural and composed behind the camera. We think you are very relatable to the audience. Warm and real."

I knew what her buzzwords meant. I wasn't a skinny twig, like Dawn, but maybe the audience would appreciate that. Ugh.

I'd watched my interview with Greyson Durant, who was now my boyfriend, at his penthouse when it aired. Grey scoffed when I groaned and said I looked fat. Let's just say, with the way I looked on screen, I hoped the camera really did add ten pounds. The wardrobe people made the unfortunate choice of putting me in a button-down sleeveless shell that made my upper arms look fat.

I needed to do some weight lifting to tone my arms, but who had the time? Maybe when days suddenly contained 25 hours, then I'd find some time to slip that into the schedule. God, I hated working out. I was more interested in shopping for cute workout clothes than working out in them.

"Jack has always valued my opinion, so he has agreed to consider you for the job."

She delivered the news in such an off-hand manner that I just sat open-mouthed and stunned.

One side of her mouth quirked upwards. "You've been working so hard, you deserve a shot at this."

"Is that wise?" I tried to hold back my doubts, but I couldn't. "Given my circumstances, I mean. I've been more behind the scenes here on purpose—"

She held up a hand to stop me. "Have there been any more threats?"

I shook my head. "Not since two years ago."

"See?" She raised her brows. "I did discuss that aspect of it with Jack. We've done some test runs, putting you on some high-profile pieces like the exclusive interview with Grayson Durant and we haven't received any blowback. Jack has his finger on the pulse of the industry; he'd know if this was going to be a problem. In fact, he thinks your—shall we call them 'detractors'—would be happier to see you in plain sight, reporting on entertainment news, rather than wondering what you were up to."

It made sense in a twisted sort of way. And there was no way Mr. Hoffman would take a chance on me if he thought I'd be a liability to the company. Maybe it was time to let my past go and put it all behind me.

Nearly ten years ago, I left Northwestern University a naïve young girl, ready to take on the world and make it a better place through investigative journalism. Only a few years into my job at a prestigious national newspaper, I attempted to break the biggest political scandal to hit in years.

Originally, I received an anonymous tip that pointed me to dig in a certain direction regarding a sitting U.S. Senator. It took me ten months to gather all the information I needed to take this despicable man down. Even after I was warned, not so gently, to back off over and over, I pursued leads until I had an airtight case against him.

The accusations were salacious. Charges of sexual assault, kinky sex, a secret child with an alleged Chinese spy, and liberal use of the so-called taxpayer-funded sexual assault hush fund being paid out to actual enemies of the state to keep it all quiet.

I had publicly available financial records, corroborating communication through FOIA requests, and unimpeachable witnesses. I had the receipts. It was there, almost right out in the open, but no one had the balls to go after this guy.

God, I look back in pity on my young, stupid self. Yes, even before the term 'fake news' was being bandied about, I knew that ideological partisanship ran rampant in the newsrooms. Hell, my journalism professors actually celebrated it, so seeing it out in the real world was not a shocking revelation to me.

In my naivety, I thought this particular politician had the correct letter next to his name so that I'd be championed as a hero for bringing him down. It was a hard lesson to learn, but some politicians were untouchable. At the top, there weren't two sides. They were all on the same team; it didn't matter if there was a D or R next to their name.

The prestigious newspaper I worked for would not touch the story with a ten-foot pole. Instead, I was demoted for my efforts. Same workload, lower rank, less pay.

In a fit of righteous ambition, I published all the material online exposing the Senator for all the world to see and judge.

The retribution that rained down on me was swift and severe. I was chewed up and spit out in a brutal fashion. Fired. Blacklisted everywhere, even from supposed independent papers and networks. No one would even talk to me. It was career suicide. I was told in no uncertain terms that no one bounced back from that.

What happened to the dirty Senator? Nothing. All the proof I'd collected was 'disappeared'. Destroyed. Wiped clean. My accusations hadn't even been a blip on his radar. He was still a member of the Senate to this day and was currently chairman of one of the most powerful Senate Committees. My work had absolutely no effect on the blatant corruption, but I'd destroyed my career.

It had been my red-pill moment — when my ideals were crushed and my eyes opened. I was forced to move back home with my mom, where I tried to start my own informational news site, reporting only on 'approved' stories under a pen name. I was constantly attacked by bots, shut down, canceled, and sent death threats.

So, I finally gave up. I worked menial jobs for almost a year until my mom remembered she had an old friend named Caroline who worked at Hollywood Exposé. Luckily, Caroline took a chance and hired me, knowing the whole sordid story. I packed up and moved to L.A. That was nearly five years ago.

It was no wonder I was a little hesitant to rock the boat now.

I swallowed nervously. "When is the decision going to be made? Can I do anything to convince Mr. Hoffman I'm the right choice?"

Caroline beamed at me. "Here's the exciting part: there's going to be a competition between you and Dawn. The winner will be taking over Mindy's position."

My nose crunched in confusion. "Competition?"

"You're each getting a long-term assignment with full creative control. You'll each have to develop a print piece and an online campaign dedicated to your subject to highlight a two-block slot during prime-time TV. It'll be a ton of exposure, so I hope you're ready."

"Wow." I was stunned. "That's huge. What are the timelines? What resources am I going to have?"

She pursed her lips in thought. "We haven't ironed out all the details yet. We're being very careful to make sure neither of you gets an unfair advantage. The budget, resources, and timelines will all be identical. Right now, we're thinking of four months to get the project completed. You'll only have the bare minimum of help, maybe a limited amount of hours with a camera operator, editor, and photographer each, because we want to see what you can do on your own."

Was I ready for this kind of pressure? This was a gigantic project. I'd done all of it in pieces for various projects, but never put it all together in one cohesive package. "What's the subject I'll be reporting on?"

Caroline grimaced. "Jack picked the subjects for each of you. He has a file of hundreds of story pitches that he's kept sitting on the back burner. He pulled out two that he felt were intriguing and topical."

"Why are you wincing like that?'

A puff of air escaped her lips. "Well, personally, I'm not a fan of either topic. And I think Dawn has a slight advantage with her material. But, I think it all depends on what story angle you choose. In my estimation, that will determine who wins."

"Okay." I nodded in agreement.

"I won't be giving out any advice, so don't ask. And, just so you're aware, Jack and I will be 100% neutral in choosing the winner. It will be based on the better story, the better presentation, the better reception by the audience, and the bigger buzz. Personal relationships will not come into play."

"Understood. So, what are the assignments?"

She rapped twice on her desk with her knuckles. "Jack assigned Dawn to 'black sheep royals'. You know how well royals always resonate with our audience."

My mind started creating hundreds of different creative story angles about royals. Shit, that was a good topic. "Hmm."

"You're doing a story about a haunted rock band." Her face was blank even after she dropped that dud on me.

I inhaled slowly. "What? Could you repeat that?"

She reached into her desk drawer, pulled out a file folder, and handed it to me. "It's all in there. The pitch that Jack's been holding onto. It's not much to work with, so you'll have to spin some magic. Have you heard of Ghost Parker?"

I thought for a moment. "Yeah. They sing that huge hit song 'Okay Babe'."

"Oh right," she replied. Then she started singing in a high-pitched voice, "Baby, baby, baby, oh, like, baby, baby, baby, oh…"

"No." I stopped her. "That's Justin Bieber. From a hundred years ago. When he was like 12 years old."

She shrugged. "Oh. I don't keep up with rock bands."

Clearly.

So, what did I know about Ghost Parker? I wracked my brain. They were pretty popular right now. They had that crazy hit song that had finally died down a bit. Thankfully. And they were the epitome of every rock band cliche: trashing hotel rooms, substance abuse, womanizing, and of course, egotistical, insensitive, and immature young male behavior. There was nothing special about them.

What a turd of an assignment.

"You're going to have to dig deep on this one. Dig up some skeletons in their closets and use them ruthlessly. The band isn't forthcoming about this haunting rumor, so you're going to have to be sly about it. Anything goes as long as you walk close to the line but stay on the legal side of it. We both know that Dawn is a complete pit bull, so you can't hold back, Remi. If you don't unearth something scandalous, you're toast in this competition."

We spent the next 20 minutes going over the particulars of my assignment. Even after I read through the preliminary research that had come with the original story pitch, I felt no better about it. Would this once-in-a-lifetime chance for major exposure in the entertainment journalism world turn into a giant flop in front of millions on national TV?

Ugh. I couldn't give up before I'd even begun. There had to be a way to turn this thing around. It was time to kick some ass.

### How to Catch a Rockstar

Printed in Great Britain
by Amazon